LOST WHISPERER OF THE SEAS

THE WINDBORNE SERIES

BOOKS BY LAUREL WANROW

The Windborne Series ~ for young adults

The Witch of the Meadows

Guardian of the Pines

Lost Whisperer of the Seas

Keepers of the Sea Cliffs

Solstice Gifts (Holiday Short Story)

The Luminated Threads Series ~ for ages 15 & up

The Unraveling, Volume One

The Twisting, Volume Two

The Binding, Volume Three

The Luminated Threads Volumes 1-3 Box Set

Science Fiction Romance ~ for adults

Passages

LOST WHISPERER OF THE SEAS

THE WINDBORNE SERIES

LAUREL WANROW

Sprouting Star Press

Copy Edit by Joyce Lamb
Cover Design by Deranged Doctor Design
Created with Vellum

Wanrow, Laurel

Lost Whisperer of the Seas / Laurel Wanrow. ~ 1st ed.
ISBN 978-1-943469-17-8

First Edition: July 2019

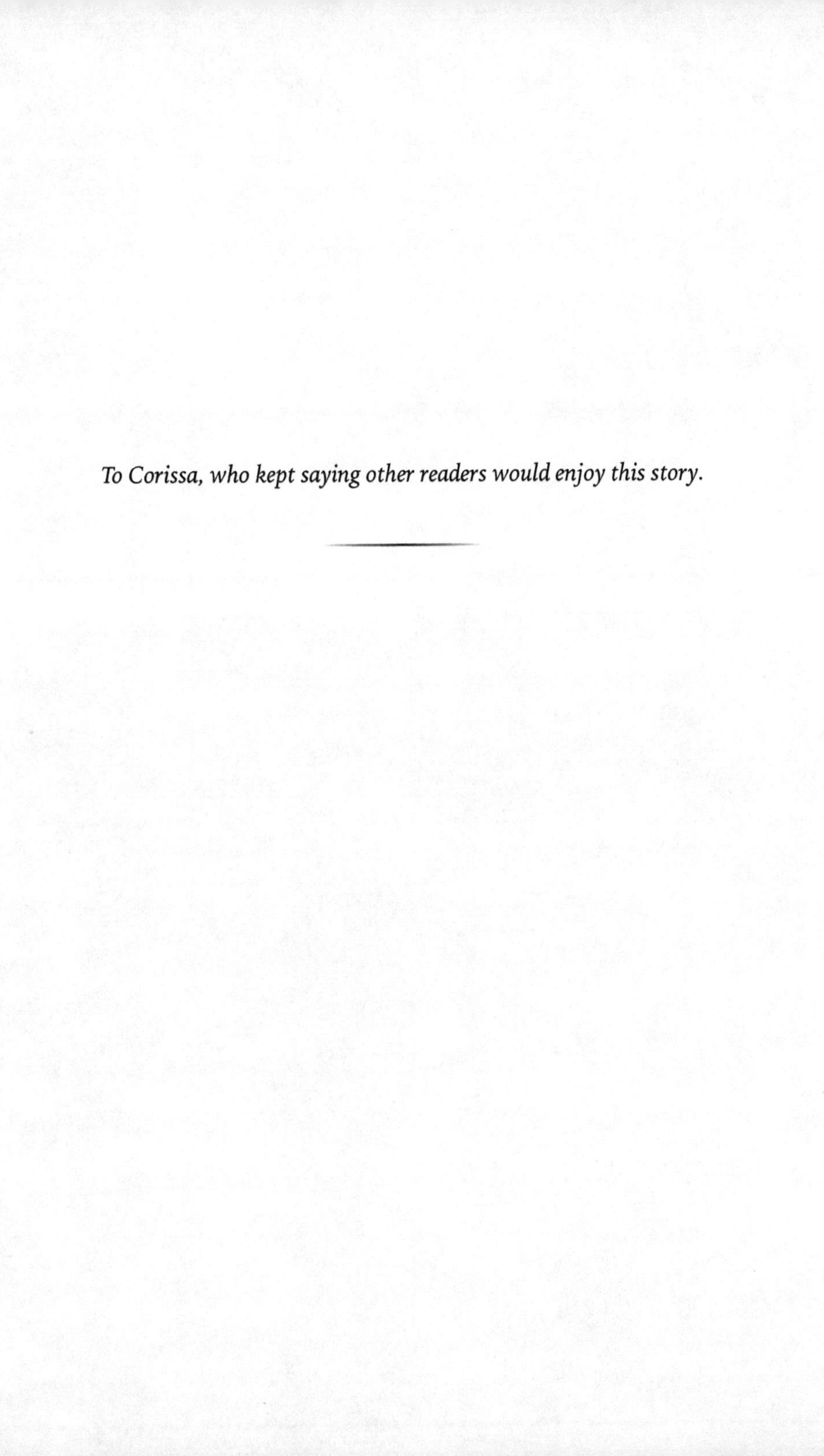

To Corissa, who kept saying other readers would enjoy this story.

MORE TROUBLE THAN BOYS ARE WORTH

Tern Bay enclave, in the Windborne Scotland District

Coral hovered, slowly flapping her feathered wings under the crisp September night sky. The last set of competitors had landed at the edge of the dueling arena below, its glowing borders the only light in the isolated valley. They withdrew the magic from their wings and shook hands. She was up next.

I have nae been so nervous about dueling since…

She'd never been nervous about throwing shockballs. Being the youngest of four ensured that, and improved her aim.

But across the arena, her ex-beau, Lemon, kept glaring at her. Earlier she'd had to tell him *again* that no, she didn't want to get back together. He'd been as nasty about it as a shark with a hook in his mouth.

And tonight, Lemon was a referee.

"He's not gonna give you fair calls," said the other referee, Pearl, coming to hover next to Coral. "Especially not with who you're up against. But I'll do my best for you." She knocked her light brown knuckles against Coral's leather-clad shoulder. The tall, brunette witch was always friendly and treated Coral like she lived here.

Few of the town teens did. Coral was in this port only once or twice a month, but that was more frequently than other ports on her family's rounds from the Isle of Giuthas. She'd claimed Tern Bay as her home dueling team three years ago, when she was thirteenth year and she'd followed her older brother to the secret matches.

"Thanks," Coral told Pearl and zipped up the insulated blue vest she wore over her black leather shirt and pants.

Next to Lemon, Spike, her opponent, was also adjusting his vest, a red one the color of his magic. Lemon wore a yellow vest, and the two best friends were whispering, their blond heads repeatedly turning toward her.

That friendship was one of the things that had come between her and Lemon. Spike hated Coral because she was an outsider to Tern Bay and because she was a witch and a better duelist. Spike was two years older and quick, both at maneuvering and with his forceful throws. Aye, her fiercest rival had better form, but neither his energy nor his aim was as strong as hers. Lately she'd been winning more, and this summer she'd gained the top position. She was proud to finally be the best at something, though outside of the duelists, she couldn't tell anyone— magical dueling was illegal.

Lemon held his arm up.

"Ready?" Pearl asked.

Coral's stomach felt like it was full of flying fish, and her fingers hummed with her magic, coating them in a messy blue glow. She siphoned it in. *Lemon's nasty attitude can't stop me.* She nodded.

"Good luck," Pearl said and held up her arm.

Coral and Spike flew toward their starting positions above the central circle, each on their side of a glowing dividing line, each holding one palm-sized shockball—hers neatly formed this time—as was allowed. The first one to force the other outside of the designated arena won the match.

"How about you and me, lass?" Spike called before they'd reached the center. "If you aren't with Lemon anymore, let's you and I give our magic a try."

"What?" She'd heard him, she just couldn't believe what he'd said.

"Spike," Lemon growled. "Back off."

Spike laughed, his red magic flickering around his fingers. "Coral can answer for her—"

"Nay," she said quickly, just as Pearl called, "Point taken for harassing your opponent."

Coral threw her a grateful glance. Spike shouldn't even consider that a possibility—she didn't. What trick was he up to here?

"That's right." Lemon flew up behind Spike. "Penalty. Spike sits this one out."

"In your dreams," Spike snapped. "She's not going to represent us at the title match. I am."

Hoy, that's what this was about? "You had your turn last year. Beating you the last five matches means I'm taking my turn as top duelist fair and square." Her braided hair bouncing, Coral darted into position. "Lemon, blow the start whistle so I can make it six."

Instead, Lemon flew forward and punched Spike. The fist to his jaw sent Spike off balance. He dropped backward.

With yelps, Coral and Pearl dove to catch him. So did Lemon. Spike regained his wings and heaved upward. He veered around Pearl and slammed into Lemon. Arms swinging, they rammed into Coral.

Grunting bodies shoved hers, then—

"Oof." The breath went out of her. The next thing she heard was Pearl screaming her name.

The ferocity made Coral blink.

Air was rushing past. Then magic tingled over her, bringing Coral alert. She arched her wings—what should have been an automatic reaction—but she'd already slowed, thanks to Pearl's energy net.

Pearl shot into view, shouting a warning to others darting skyward as she crushed Coral's hand in an iron grip. "Easy," Pearl said to her. "Let's get to the ground."

"Lemon? Spike?" she gasped.

"Gits! They're punching each other *upward*. The others will break it up. Luckily, I saw you fall."

Aye, she'd lost a dangerous amount of altitude for Pearl to have yelled like that. Pearl got her down, and Coral collapsed. The vest that guarded her energy cores from the charge of the shockballs had done nothing to pad the kick. Her shoulder throbbed. Sitting made it worse, so she leaned into Pearl while everyone got to the ground. The other older duelists gathered to confer, but much as Coral wanted to look tough, she couldn't even pretend to pay attention.

"Matches are over for the night," Pearl said, catching Coral's attention. "I propose that Coral retain her position for the title match during Fest. After this fight, other matches are up to her."

To Coral's surprise, everyone agreed. The rest of the fight that she'd missed must have been bad. The duelists began to leave.

Spike came toward her, and Coral's magic rose in defense. Pearl stepped forward and blocked him.

"I'm sorry you got injured," he said. "I was only after that idiot."

"Go home and sleep it off," Pearl said. "I'm sure you'll be best friends again tomorrow."

"Not much of an apology," muttered Shrimp, Pearl's younger brother.

Glaring, Spike started to leave, but hesitated when Lemon strode up.

"Don't court Spike," Lemon pleaded. "Say you'll give us another try. Your energy is as hot as it comes, even if you ain't much of a lass."

With her arm in agony, his typically thoughtless comment about her small bust sent Coral over the top. "I don't want to court you. Or you," she threw at Spike. "I'll decide who gets my hot energy."

He snorted. "Attitudes like that don't keep friends, lass. Watch your back."

The malice in Spike's tone sent a shiver through her. Others moved in to pull both boys away, but Spike shot out a shield and stomped off.

Pearl helped Coral magic on her sailor's breeches and a loose shirt over her dueling outfit—what she'd worn to sneak out—then a group of them left together.

The barest sliver of moonlight lit the rolling hills to the coast. Coral held her arm to her side and tried to breathe while Pearl and Shrimp slowed their wingbeats to match hers. The Scottish moor gave way to a rocky cliff at the edge of the sea. Below, white lines grew into waves that boiled and crashed against the shore. Coral spread her wings to glide on the wind with the others, but the first churning air current jostled her. New daggers of pain stabbed through her arm.

"Ouch!" Another gust blew her northward, and she had to careen along with it.

Gritting her teeth, Coral fought the airstream until she dropped out of it. They soared south toward the wizard town of Tern Bay, sweat coating Coral's brow. Shaking from the struggle, she let herself glide lower until the salt spray prickled her cheeks.

Pearl dropped to fly even with her. "You gonna be able to make it onto your ship?"

"Aye."

"That git," Shrimp fumed on her other side. "Lemon should have challenged Spike to a duel like any sane wizard, any *honorable* wizard. Who throws a real punch?"

Coral wanted to dissect their reasons, too, but flying was all she could manage. *The Peaceful Seas* was in sight, the only double-masted schooner docked among the fishing boats at the business end of town. At the breakwater, they split up. Coral skimmed across the fishy-smelling rocks and then the quiet harbor water, keeping level with *The Peaceful*'s hull. At midship—well away from the stern and her parents' stateroom—she popped over and landed lightly on the balls of her feet.

She'd made it. She waved to Pearl and Shrimp high above, then paused to listen while dissolving her wings. The magical matter rippled across her shoulder blades, the feel of a dozen little crabs scuttling across the sand. The energy ran into the channels beneath her skin and circulated to her storage cores. No sounds came from below, but a clattering of toenails raced across the deck. A furry black body hurtled into her calves and yipped in delight.

"Skipper, shush!" With her good arm, she petted the small Schipperke dog and listened again. She let out her breath. Not that her parents had ever caught her in the years she'd been sneaking off and back onto the ship.

Creak.

The sound meant little, but the subtle shift of weight on the schooner did. Had Lemon followed them? Coral magicked a protective shield over her body and whirled, her braids whipping about her face.

A figure loomed beside the nearest mast.

2

CAUGHT

Blue energy shot to her fingertips. It coalesced, and Coral threw the shockball. Her magic hit an answering flashshield with the same blue coloring. In the brief flare of light, she recognized the wizard.

"Salm!" she hissed at her brother and let the second shockball hum in her hand. Skipper's toenails clicked in a dance over to greet him and then back to her. She should have known it wasn't Lemon since her dog hadn't barked. Great Orb, what was with her? Clenching her hand into a fist, she absorbed the energy and tiptoed to meet him.

"Got you." Her older brother chuckled in his annoying way. "What has you on high alert?"

"You wouldn't believe it," she blurted and told him about the fistfight. "Have you ever seen wizards do that?"

"Never." Salm shook his head. "I thought those two were joined at the hip. I suppose when it comes to courting you, Lemon wants first dibs."

"Like that's going to happen. I don't need my magic hyped by Lemon's again, with all that sparking and sizzling. But he keeps going on about how, if we'd just learn to merge our magic, it'd be the best bonding ever."

Salm snorted. "It's your business, but I never did know what you saw in Lemon."

Neither did she, apart from a stellar first kiss, but she wasn't sharing *that* with Salm. She turned away even though he wouldn't be able to see her blushing in the dark. She'd thought splitting up with Lemon months ago would improve things in their group, but he—and now Spike—were acting all kinds of stupid.

"Does dueling have you so distracted that you're willing to test Spike's energy, too?" Salm asked.

Her head shot up. "Spells," she snapped. "You think I'd court the town bully? Especially not after he clobbered me good."

"I thought your stance was off when you shot that shockball." Salm nodded toward the arm crossing her belly. "Where did he hit you?"

"Shoulder."

Salm's mouth always ran at full tilt, but he had a gentle touch for injuries and animals. He lightly patted his fingers over her arm and shoulder.

She sucked a sharp breath.

"It's dislocated," he said. "Shall I pop it back, or will you have Ma see to it?"

"As if that's a choice," she muttered. "Go ahead." Coral pressed her lips tight, but when he straightened and lifted her arm, she cried out. For an agonizing moment, her vision blackened. Then with a *pop*, the pain disappeared.

"That better?"

"Aye, thanks." She swallowed and wiped her eyes.

"Come on, I know you can take a lot. Put ice on it and that herbal healing balm in the cabinet."

"Good idea, thanks." She'd gotten off light, thank the Orb. "Why are you topside?"

"Ma and Pop went to bed ages ago, if that's what you're getting at. Luna asked me to wait until midnight to come see her. She wanted to make sure her father had his tea and settled the lighthouse before we talked to him."

Salm never waited on anyone. He'd said he intended to court Luna this fall, but Coral hadn't taken her carefree brother seriously until now.

"It's nearly time." He nodded to the southern headland where Kittiwake Point Lighthouse blinked its regular rotations of passing light. "Since you're here to take the pup below without him making a ruckus, I'll go." He picked up Skipper and ruffled his fur in a friendly way before handing him over. "See you."

She cuddled Skipper close, threading her chilled fingers into the long fur at his neck. Salm ducked under the beam of the foremast and stepped onto the low edge of the bow. For a second, he perched with his boot tips hanging in midair. Then his wings unfurled through the slits in his shirt and he leaped. He gained height with a series of rapid downward strokes and flew off over the bay.

Coral heaved a sigh and rounded the deck cabin to the hatch leading to their living quarters. She carried Skipper down the companionway ladder and set him on the floor in the dark salon. He immediately scampered over to check his food dish.

"All right," she whispered. "I'll find you more." And some ice for her injury.

She'd just sealed the bag of cubes when the overhead lights snapped on.

"Coral?" Ma walked in from the stateroom, wrapping her robe closed, her long, sandy-brown hair loose about her shoulders. "Why are you up?"

Before turning, Coral snagged a towel to wipe her hands and dropped it over the ice. "Skipper was pestering me, so I—"

"My word, what happened to your cheek?" Ma tilted Coral's chin and peered at her face. "Is this a bruise?"

No. They must have hit her there, too. "It's nothing. Skipper knocked me one."

Ma's gaze fell to the counter where the corner of the ice bag showed. Then she reached up and flipped aside the collar of Salm's old work shirt, exposing the dueling shirt beneath. Her face froze for a moment, then she cleared her throat. "Coral of the Seas. Dueling."

"It wasn't a duel so much as a fight. And not my fight either. I just got caught in—"

"Don't think I'm clueless. This explains your assorted *accidents* whenever we dock in this port. Dueling is dangerous. Unsanctioned dueling is forbidden." Ma's voice rose with each word. "You get caught and you'll be explaining yourself in a Windborne courtroom."

"No one would report—"

Ma's hand flew up. "I don't want to hear it. I finally convinced your father that he and I could go on a holiday, and before we can even leave, you run off and jeopardize it. Plus, you've risked losing your magic by breaking Windborne law." Her eyes narrowed. "That settles it. You're staying with your sister."

Coral bit her lip. Staying at Manta's wasn't so bad. She'd be there anyway, what with working in her bakery this week. She could still sneak out and attend the title match on Saturday—

"And you're grounded. We'll be locking your magic in a quash."

3

ADRIFT ASHORE

"That's steep." Ty Sterling shifted on one of Dockside Diner's counter stools and eyed Octo, a ruddy-faced guy shoveling eggs into his mouth. Though bulkier than Ty, Octo wasn't much older—nineteen, maybe, to his seventeen—but the guy's confidence about his sailing skills clocked in decades higher. Forty? Enough that he'd jacked up the fee for his lessons to double what Ty had been told to expect.

"Ya want the sailing lessons or not? That's the price." Octo's voice blended into the din of Scottish accents spilling from the early breakfast crowd.

Yeah, this sailor's kid knew the ropes growing up here. *All* the ropes. Ty wanted to scoff and walk out the door. Yet he also wanted a job as a sailor, so he might need Octo's lessons. Ty swept off his red bandanna and wiped it over his face. After popping the last bite of doughnut into his mouth, he stood and brushed the crumbs from his white work shirt. A polite *I'll think about it* and he'd go.

"I watched yer test sail on my dad's boat." Octo waved a triangle of toast. "Ya might'a had some lessons back where ya came from, Yank, but ya ain't got a feel for the vessel on the ocean. No captain's gonna risk his boat in winter's rough waters with wha'cha got now."

The pit in Ty's stomach confirmed it—he was screwed. Not only was what Octo said true, but it wasn't the first time he'd heard it while running through every local sailor seeking a deckhand. Just not so bluntly.

He needed ocean practice. Being Windborne allowed him physical entrance into this enclave of winged wizards, but since he'd been born and raised in American enclaves, no one was willing to take him on. At least he hadn't told them about his wizard academy education. No—Ty shook his head—that would divide him further from these small-town wizards.

"That yer answer?" Octo asked.

"Er, no, it's not. That's me thinking how many people are gonna be on my case because their milk is late." Ty retied the bandanna—something only people back home in Colorado wore—over his shoulder-length brown hair. "Thanks, Octo. I'll get back to you."

"Righto. Jus' remember Fest is next weekend. All them other sailors comin' into town are lookin' sharp for the next lads to hire. Ya got *one week* to get yer act shipshape."

Ignoring Octo's smirk, Ty ducked through the swinging kitchen door. Surrounded by the heavy smell of bacon, he paused near the stove, well out of the way of the cook frying eggs. "Thanks for telling me Octo was out front, Keenan."

The lanky warlock dipped his head, shifting the ponytail trailing down his back. "Is it going to work out, some sailing time with him?"

"It might. He's got the boat and the time. Question is, do I have the exchange notes?"

"Same problem we all have." Keenan laughed and sidestepped to a prep counter. "Here's a carrot top for Pepper."

Ty caught it and waved as he left through the alley door he used every morning to deliver the diner's milk order. A sturdy black Highland pony waited feet away, harnessed to an antique delivery cart bearing the words *Dar's Dairy*. "Hey, Pepper. Your fans have remembered you. Look at this."

Pepper didn't waste time looking at the ferny leaves. He inhaled the expected treat.

Great guy, Keenan. He'd been friendly from the start, a reaction Ty didn't get from most of the wizards in this old-fashioned town. Mom had warned him Granddad's birthplace had little else besides the boating life he wanted, but Tern Bay was really off the map, way beyond the whole magically-living-under-the-radar-so-they-weren't-discovered thing.

Ty grabbed the handles of the cart and pivoted it from the wall. Pepper pulled the load of milk bottles, his leather tack creaking and hooves resonating along the boardwalk route the pony knew by heart.

Today's sunless beach echoed Ty's dreary mood. They passed the town's fishing sheds and businesses along North Dock—net repair, lumberyard and a general store carrying boating supplies. After only a month of these deliveries, boredom was setting in. He couldn't spend his days delivering milk with the sea tempting him only a few wing flaps away, the breeze coating his lips with tangy salt and the cries of the gulls reminding him he should be on a boat.

By this time of morning, most boats were out, the fishermen fishing or checking their traps, but the port held a larger vessel he hadn't seen before. The unfamiliar schooner was a beauty, with brightwork of polished wood above a blue-painted hull. Her name graced the bow in white letters.

"*The Peaceful Seas*." He whistled over the elegant ship. "What I wouldn't give to take a sail on you." Was she a classic or a replica of an older ship? And why was the schooner in Tern Bay?

The cart lurched from his grasp, and Ty jerked to catch the handles as Pepper strained in his harness toward an alley alongside a grass-green cottage.

"Okay, I get it. Time to be going." He'd make time to study that schooner later.

Ty guided the cart up the alley ramps that zigzagged behind the houses and shops painted every possible color—from robin's-egg blue to buttercup yellow and cotton candy pink. He'd made the majority of the dairy deliveries on the way down through the stair-step town. The last few stops on today's route would be quick before he emptied the cart at One Good Bun, the bakery.

At the town healer's cottage, he was bending to place a bottle into the porch cooler when the back door opened. He straightened and handed the quart of milk to a woman with gray hair winding through better than half the black curls framing her face. "Good morning, Lady Anemone."

"Good day to you, Tydell. Tell me again why an intelligent lad such as yourself is not at academy this fall." The older witch tucked the bottle into the crook of her elbow and crossed her brown arms. She settled her round body against the doorjamb. "Your parents let you quit your training and move here because…?"

Ty bit back a sigh. Lady Anemone was smarter than most in town—well, he hoped so, because if he needed a doctor, she was it. Besides Keenan, she was one of the few people who'd taken the time to talk to him. Unfortunately, his evasive answers never satisfied her. "Do you sail, ma'am?" he asked.

A sad smile crossed her face, and Lady Anemone turned toward the sea. Ty followed her gaze. Far beyond the crescent-shaped bay, the sun had broken through the clouds. The light glittered on the waves even brighter than on the snowfields back home.

"I did," she said softly. "I don't have the physical quickness to handle a craft on my own now, but I go out every chance I get."

"Me, too," he said. But he'd had precious few chances since

arriving in Tern Bay, and something wasn't clicking on the ocean. "It's never enough. I want to do it every single day, which is why I moved here."

"You can't waste a mind like yours on fishing. You need to go to academy." She punctuated this with a firm nod.

This time, Ty sighed aloud. "Can you keep a secret?"

"Of course I can," she scoffed. "A body who can't keep a secret can't keep a client."

Then this should get her off my back. "Believe me, my parents are totally behind education, being teachers themselves. I learned to read at three. I have been to academy. I've graduated."

"At seventeenth year?"

"I started at fourteen and finished by sixteen. Then my mom bribed me with apartment rent to stay another year, take extra classes and—"

"Grow up?"

By the Orb, do all adults think alike? "Yeah. I did that, too. By this summer, my parents were okay with me taking a break to pursue sailing. They even suggested I move to Scotland. Mom's grandparents were from here." It'd happened only after a lot of begging and because the Windborne agencies with the jobs he'd trained for at academy didn't hire anyone younger than eighteen. That gave him one year of freedom to live as he pleased with no pressure—or so he had thought. If some sailor didn't hire him, he'd be working for the dairy the entire winter.

Lady Anemone opened her mouth, but was cut off by a rapping sound from deep inside her home—someone knocking on the front door. She smiled and hefted her bottle of milk. "Glad to have more of the story. Talk to you tomorrow, Tydell." She closed the door behind her.

She wanted to talk more? Ty turned and left. He couldn't add details to what he'd already told her and still maintain his low profile in town. He'd have to steer the conversation away from himself. But to what?

His internal debate ended two houses later when Sir Porbeagle greeted him with, "Are you ready for Fest, lad?" The elderly owner of Shelter in a Storm bookstore sat on his back stoop, waiting, as usual, for his pint of cream.

"I guess so. I'm not sure what to expect, but Dar has promised me time off to talk to the sailors who'll be in town. I'm still trying for a shipboard job."

The wiry man jabbed his finger into the air between them, stopping just shy of Ty's chest. "Excellent. Excellent plan. Everyone will be here. From up and down the coast, from the islands, even from Ireland. Anyone who's got a boat comes when it's Tern Bay's turn for the Autumnal Equinox Festival."

Yeah, *different* boat owners who hadn't seen his inadequate skills. As Octo had said, he had one week to get his act shipshape. Somehow. "The equinox falls after next weekend, on the twenty-second, doesn't it?"

"Aye, Tuesday a week." Sir Porbeagle popped the cap on the pint bottle and tipped half its contents into his huge mug. Absently stirring the coffee into a pale brown, he peered up at Ty. "What is it you do over there in the New World for your equinoxes and solstices?"

"We have the ceremony for the holiday, of course. Every Windborne sticks with tradition, no matter what part of the world they're in. But mostly, my family picnics at the local park where everyone gathers. We American wizards don't travel and celebrate for days before holidays, like Dar said will happen with wizards at Tern Bay."

"Ach, you're in for a treat, then. 'Tis like a big party. For days." Sir Porbeagle patted his flat midsection. "I always put on a few pounds. The fried dough is quite tasty."

"That sounds good."

"'Tis. Of course, wizards don't come for the food so much as the company. There's the race as well."

"Race?"

"Aye, the youth sailing regatta. Always a treat to see how the young people have improved their skills over the years. The Tern Bay racers show well, but my favorite is that scamp from the isle yonder." He nodded in the direction of his shop.

Did he mean the one west of here? "The Isle of Giuthas?"

"That's the one. You watch for Salm of the Seas to get some pointers to help you out."

Yeah, well, great idea, but next week would be too late.

4

NOT A WIZARD'S WAY

After breakfast, Coral coiled ropes, rinsed out the dry bags and inventoried the frozen baitfish—tasks Pop had doled out while he and Ma packed for their holiday at Illusion Island.

"One slip and I'm marked prey," she muttered. "A ready target for every last chore needing doing." Pointing a finger, she shot blue energy to flip open the lid of their dock locker and threw in her armload of life jackets. A shower of blue sparks rained from her fingertips, one melting a spot in the orange nylon.

"Curses!" She swatted out the burning bits before anything else scorched. Controlling her jumpy energy was next to impossible when all she could think about was the upcoming quash and how her friends would laugh.

When Lemon found out, she'd be a beached whale, especially after she'd lashed out at him and Spike. *And Spike.* Spells, if he caught her alone...

She slammed the locker lid. A quash meant no matches. What top duelist couldn't take on matches? Would anyone suggest she step down from the title match?

Coral headed back to the schooner, her stomach twisting.

Her Tern Bay friends had the same limited-magic rules on the streets and would disappear onto the dueling moor in the evening. By the time the actual matches started, Ma and Pop would be back and return her magic. Her best strategy would be to avoid her rivals and keep the quash a secret.

But to do that, Salm would also have to keep quiet. She eyed her brother, completing his own task of setting up their dinghy-sized sailboat. His plans had changed. Luna had to help her family this week, so Salm would be staying in town, too. With both she and Salm here, Pop now wanted them to meet up with the dolphins and continue their training—

Hold on. *Without my magic, I can't speak with our dolphins.* If she couldn't give the young'uns their training directions, what was the point of sailing out to meet them? Come to think of it, she'd never sailed without magic as a backup either. She *could*, but why risk it? Perfect. She'd use their family's aquaculture work to avoid the quash.

Coral found Ma in the galley. Ma's flowered sundress swirled as she stowed the last of the breakfast dishes and, as quick as a cleaner wrasse, latched the windows in the ship's polished wooden walls. With a steadying breath, Coral wrapped a tighter control on the blue energy skittering through her.

"I'm ready to go to the bakery." She smiled oh-so-sweetly at her mother. "I'll have afternoons free to do the training with Salm, but I'm concerned about sailing with no magic. You know how vulnerable—"

"Ha! That's a good one." Salm clattered down the companionway ladder. "*You* worried about sailing? We won last year's Fest regatta with your bum skimming the waves to keep the craft upright. Tell another yarn, why don't you?" He batted her braids as he plowed past.

"Salm! Orb curse it, I swear I'll—"

"Coral!" Ma glared at her. "Watch your language."

She snapped her mouth closed while her grinning brother escaped down the fore passageway.

"Salm?" Ma called after him. "I'm shifting the power to charge our storage batteries." She crossed to the navigation desk and peered at the console controlling their wind turbines and solar panels, human technologies that ran the ship's instruments and household appliances. "Change it back when you need electricity."

Coral groaned inside. Ma knew the shutdown wouldn't matter to Salm—he wouldn't spend much time on the ship while in port. But no electricity to pump water would keep Coral off the schooner. "Ma? Pop wants the dolphin measurements done, and if I kept my magic, I could run the young'uns through their paces."

Ma sighed, which wasn't really a response.

"Just give me a warning for what happened last night." Coral kept her tone light, her desperation tamped down. "Salm comes and goes at all hours. Why not me? I'm sixteenth year, nearly seventeenth. It's but a two-year age difference."

"Age is not the issue." Ma glanced up from flipping switches. "Self-control is."

"I'm responsible." At her mother's cocked brow, Coral added, "For myself! I won't break the town rules and use excess magic on the streets."

Ma straightened, tucking stray hair into her French braid. "We've made our decision for your safety, and *I'm* thankful your sister has agreed to let you stay with her on top of her generous offer of the bakery job. You should be, too, when your other choice is staying with your grandparents on the isle."

"I *am*. I just want to stay on board instead of with Manta. And have my magic free to conduct the dolphin training, not locked in a quash. You don't know what you're asking—"

"Ha!" Salm ducked through the bulkhead and propped himself on the end of the built-in sofa while buttoning a leather waistcoat over a clean linen shirt. He'd even put on some fragrant aftershave, which only added to his better-than-you attitude. "How will a quash matter when you hold back your power when directing the dolphins? Last week, the animals slid in and out of a mere pretense of rounding up the schools—"

"They *did* gather the fish," she countered before he said more. "I *made* the counts. I'm *not* jeopardizing the balance of our fisheries, which a quash will." Leave it to Salm to notice that once or twice she'd had to preserve power because she was slated to duel Spike.

"Salmon." Their father, a tall, graying wizard, entered from the stateroom. "Don't bait your sister. You two will work together on the chores I've assigned." His bearded face looked uncharacteristically serious above a lime-green and fuchsia floral print shirt and coordinating green shorts, his vacation wear.

Spells! Coral crossed her arms and glared at her brother. How just like Salm to offer help last night and lord it over her today. At least he was the one netting trouble this time.

But Pop lifted her chin with a weathered hand. His blue eyes bored into hers. "Keep your nose out of trouble. I don't know what's happening, and I bet I don't want to. You must learn to control your temper and your inclination to use magic to solve your problems." He patted her cheek as Ma joined him.

Behind them, Salm leaned forward. "If you didn't *float* through your end of the work, I would've had time ashore before this week to pursue a partnership."

"Enough," Ma said. "Coral has nothing to do with your schedule. I'm sorry your plans have fallen through, but we've freed you up to see Luna." Then Ma fixed that same frown on Coral. The one that said *enough* better than any word. No more pleading, arguing or whining.

"Aye, ma'am." She sighed. "I'll do my work and keep myself out of trouble while you're gone."

"It's not much of a challenge, considering you're quashing her magic," Salm said.

Coral fisted her faintly glowing hands at her sides. "It's twice as hard to get along with wizards when you don't have magic."

"Then make it easy on yourself." He smirked. "Don't tell anyone."

Of course, now the know-it-all would think she was following *his*—

"She's showing her control, Salmon, when you aren't. No one should tell anyone, since illegal dueling is why we're doing it." Ma pointed to a pile of bags. "Please take our luggage topside and wait for us there."

Salm sauntered through the cabin's salon, purposefully angling his path closer to her. Orb curse it, she wanted to zap him.

Ach, that will only net me more trouble. Coral backed up. Another step and she bumped into her father. Salm hefted the bags through the companionway, then the sound of his footfalls on deck faded.

Pop rubbed his bearded chin, his gaze fixed intently upon Ma. They were thought-speaking, leaving her out.

"Coral," he finally said. "You've made clear your feelings about going to academy. We hoped you'd warm to the idea by visiting Windborne cities, by working for your sister here in town and getting a taste of independence. But this dueling matter begs *us* revisiting the academy decision."

"No!" Those busy cities they'd visited were confusing and full of strangers. Living in a building, spending her days cooped up indoors, far from the ocean, with no animals or her family… "I can't," she cried. "I'll do anything, please just don't make me go. I'll study harder with Ma. I'll—"

"What happened to that nice control I saw with Salm?" Ma's quiet voice broke through.

"I'll—" Coral sucked a breath, trying to find any kind of composure. "I'll be more help to the isle here."

"True. You have incredible power," Ma said. "You could be helping Giuthas seal the shielding rips, *if* you had your energy in hand."

Coral choked back a retort. No one knew she *had* mastered her energy—for dueling. It rose at a mere thought, collected the proper strength and clobbered her targets with eerie accuracy. Every single time she dueled.

Only when she dueled.

"I didn't mean enclave security," Coral ground out through clenched teeth. "I meant helping with our Seas habitat management."

"It's more than *helping*." Ma pursed her lips. "It's embracing the heritage of your magic. You've drifted from our family's mission, what we bring to the Seas and our natural world. You seem lost, Coral."

If she was lost, how had she become top duelist?

"Three academies accepted you after your interviews," her father said softly. "We think you should consider the winter session."

"But, Pop! You told me I didn't—"

"This fall." He shook his head. "I only said you need not go this fall."

Ma put a hand on her shoulder. "We're concerned for your future. You get reported to the wrong magistrate, and you'll lose your magic forever. This week, think on your choices and what we can do to help."

When Ma's hand lifted, Coral wanted to sag to the sofa. She still had a chance to decide for herself. Best to keep her mouth shut and simply nod.

With a last firm look, Ma smiled. "Are you ready? Where's your bag?"

Using her energy, Coral reached out and magicked a knotted

cord pouch to her hand. She slung its strap over her head and pulled her braids loose, the shells and glass pieces clinking together where they dangled from macramé strands she'd woven in. "All packed."

Her mother frowned at her with an often-used, tired expression.

Here it came. If just once Ma wouldn't bother her about her clothes. "What?" Coral blurted.

"Can't you, um… Well, I'm sure you have what you need. What about the bags for Manta?"

She stared at her mother. Ma wasn't going to ask her to put on a skirt? She was actually going to let her go ashore in Salm's outgrown clothes, her ship attire? Really, Ma must be feeling guilty. "I have the bags topside already," she answered cautiously.

"Very well." Ma turned to Pop. "Dolph?"

"Sorry, love," he said to Coral, "but the quash is the only way your mother and I can have easy minds while we're so far from you this week." He laid a hand on her shoulder to lock down her magic.

Biting her lip, she shifted her energy to its core positions, and her father's magic followed. One by one, it coated each core with an electrical wall that solidified with a snap, sealing it. Emptiness filled her gut as her eyes filled with tears. Curse it all. She would *not* cry.

The last core clicked shut, and the quash was complete. She could feel her magic inside her, but she couldn't use it.

Pop slid both arms around her and gave her a hug. "Bye, love."

"Bye, Pop." She turned and hugged her mother as well. "Bye, Ma. Have a good time in the Mediterranean."

With the tears burning again, she climbed the ladder into the warming fall day, picked up her bundle of knotted bags and descended their gangway. Squaring her shoulders, chin up, eyes ahead, Coral strode to the end of the dock and took the wooden walkway to the staircase up to the first level of town. Once on the balconylike wooden deckwalk that served as a street front, she avoided other pedestrians' eyes by running a finger along the smooth railing and gazing across the protective cove.

The Peaceful Seas looked sad and lonely moored with the sails down. She scanned the western horizon, where two mountain peaks rose into the cloudy sky, all she could see of her home enclave, the Isle of Giuthas.

Her magic quashed. Her family dispersed. Not staying on the ship. Not being able to go out with her friends. She felt…lost. But *not* like Ma had said.

At One Good Bun, the bakery Manta and Piper, her bonding partner, had opened six months ago, a "Sorry, We're Closed" sign hung on the door. Penciled on a scrap of paper below, another message read, "Will return by 8."

Huh? It was Saturday, one of their busiest days. They wouldn't just leave. Yet, sure enough, the door was locked. She scooted around the end of the buildings. In the delivery alley, she patted the dairy pony, then opened the screened door into Manta's fancy kitchen, gleaming with all the outside-world appliances her cooking-crazed sister could afford.

A movement beyond the bread-kneading table caught her eye. At the refrigerator, a fellow—definitely not Piper or the old dairy farmer—was bent over.

She paused. "What are you about?"

He jerked up, and his head slammed the shelf. It tilted. Bottles of cream slid forward, falling over butter and bowls of filling. The stranger swore and threw up his hands, flushing silver energy until the cascade hung suspended in a gel-like substance.

What under the Golden Orb is that?

5

THE STRANGER

Coral backed toward the door. The stranger, slender and muscular, straightened to stand only inches taller than her five feet. He wore the dairy's white work shirt and dungarees, but with a red bandanna capping his head like a pirate's headgear. Dark brown locks escaped beneath the edging.

"I am—or was—stocking the refrigerator. Do you mind?" He pressed the crown of his head, his long face scrunched half in a scowl, half in a grimace of pain.

Their gazes locked, and the sight of his eyes silenced her. They were silver. Dark, glinty, silver eyes fixed steadily on hers. *Oh, Orb curse it!* Silver eyes meant silver energy. She glanced at the glowing mass frozen in midslide, bottle tops poking out at awkward angles.

Silver.

She'd never met a wizard with this type of energy. Through stories, she'd heard silver magic was usually secondary to another color of magic the wizard used daily. He hadn't used another color for this emergency. Did that mean he didn't have one? From the tales, silver wizards who had only the one energy often preyed upon the energy of other wizards. Purportedly, they favored the quick-reacting blue.

Like hers.

"Just who are you?" she blurted, before remembering she was quashed. *No magic.* She had nothing at her fingertips to defend herself. Then again, she had no magic for him to steal either.

He turned back to the refrigerator. "The guy thanking the Golden Orb I caught this mess, because there's no more cream until tomorrow." He shoved the gelled bottles onto the righted shelf and reabsorbed the substance with wiggling fingers, like it took some urging to break it into pure energy again.

Ohh, interesting. Coral drew closer and bumped the kneading table. How would that work in a duel? It was likely something she couldn't combat, making this stranger dangerous. She backed up a few steps. She should leave...

He closed the refrigerator and resumed rubbing his head. "Who are you?" he asked, speaking more evenly this time.

Though not much older than she was, he appeared solemn and...confident. Those things set him apart from the local teen warlocks. When she didn't answer, he turned his head side to side, seemingly to ease a neck crick, but all the while scanning her body.

Curse him. Why did boys have to do that? Some days, Coral wished she'd been built like the warlocks in the family who were tall and broad. Not like her Ma and sisters, Wind and Manta, all small and delicately featured. Yet she didn't match her sisters in the chest department, so she didn't usually garner the same stares they did.

Crossing her arms over her slight figure, Coral tapped her foot. "I asked you first. It's proper you answer first."

His face reddened. "I'm Ty Sterling, the new dairyman. Your turn."

What kind of a name was that? "T-I, short for Tide?"

"No, T-Y, short for Tydell. My grandfather's name."

He talked differently. It wasn't his even tone, but his clear pronunciation of each syllable.

"You're from away," she said without thinking.

"I am. Will you tell me your name or not? Most people in town have introduced themselves, despite my lack of a local accent."

He certainly wasn't shy, but neither was his tone rude. Years of analyzing duelists in competition told her she could back off. A little. Coral stopped the tap of her foot and started to drop her arms, but didn't. His silver eyes were too intense. "Coral of the Seas."

"Ah, the sister Manta said was coming—"

The screen door banged. Coral jumped and swung around as Piper, a burly man with a brown goatee and ponytail, dropped a huge sack of flour onto the table.

"Ahoy!" Manta's partner grinned through the cloud of flour dust. "I saw the ship at the dock and knew you'd be here, Coral. Ty, I'm mighty happy for the cream. Double batches of the raspberry cream muffins planned with this." He slapped up another cloud of flour, hugged Coral and pulled her along with his energetic manner. "Come, I'll help you open the shop before I start on the afternoon orders."

She followed. Anything to escape the stare of the silver boy. While Piper retrieved the exchange-note box, Coral unlocked the door, removed the note and flipped the sign to indicate the bakery was open. Piper rattled off a few instructions, but she only half listened. She and Ma had helped in the bakery plenty since its spring opening.

How could she ask Piper about the silver boy—*warlock*—whom Coral had added to her list of people to avoid this week? Would he come to the dueling field? Every kid in town did at some point, and so far, her sense of this particular boy screamed *steer clear*. Bizarre and possibly dangerous magic. An outsider. Too different and too…good-looking.

They shuffled the breads and sweets on display, and Piper led the way to the pantry off the hall. "We still have half a rack of white and a rack of honey wheat. No extra muffins or pumpkin bread. Manta took them north to the Windborne inns and taverns along the coast as samples to see if we can attract some new customers. I'll have more out by ten."

"You're looking to expand already?"

"Manta is. In a few months, you may have a full-time job if you want it."

"Maybe. You know my compass says there's a ship in my future."

Piper laughed. "Aye, a ship I have the feeling we're helping to pay for. You'll be earning your exchange notes this time, lassie." His jovial manner sobered. "Manta plans to moor you with a new task, but I'm sure you're up to it."

She narrowed her eyes at his tone.

"For this week, to ready themselves for the Fest, two of the taverns have contracted with us to provide their dinner rolls. 'Twill be a fair exposure for us and a good bit of exchange notes on the business trade card, which I couldn't turn down. You're needed to make the deliveries."

But Coral's heart had sunk into her stomach at the word *taverns*. By his regretful expression, Fintail's was one of them. "No," she whispered. "Piper, I can't. Spike's family runs it, and Lemon works there. It's too dangerous for me. You don't know what Ma—"

"I do know what your parents decided." Piper patted her arm. "They wouldn't leave you in our care without telling us something that important. Give the deliveries a try. These boys, *Marlin* and *Barney*"—their real names—"won't attempt anything in town."

Coral crossed her arms and shook her head. Piper, who'd

gone by Hammerhead while growing up in this enclave, hadn't dueled in forever. "Ach, these *boys* are crazy. I bet you never approached your fiercest competitors this way."

Laughing, he took her by the shoulders and pivoted her out the door. "I didn't, but your worry is unnecessary. The rolls will be ready by two thirty. The deliveries need to be made by three. Just keep a civil tongue in your mouth."

"And you will bail me—oh!" Meters away, the dairyman slouched against the kitchen doorframe, his silver eyes appearing luminescent in the dim hall. Had he overheard? What exactly had they said? Judging by the number of bottles he'd saved from smashing to the floor, she wouldn't see him for a few days. Thank the Orb.

The bell on the front door jingled. Coral turned on her heel, pushed past Piper and greeted the customer with a smile.

Behind her, Piper said, "Ty, glad you stayed. I have an additional order for tomorrow."

Coral's smile froze as her stomach flipped. He'd be back so soon?

6

A GIRL DIFFERENT THAN OTHERS

Ty wrote down Piper's order, but all he could think about was how he wanted to talk to Coral again. The shells she'd tied into her hair were cool, but her clothes were the most interesting thing about her. People here dressed in a colonial or, he supposed more correctly, an old-world style. Dresses or skirts for the women, heavy trousers and linen, V-neck, stand-up collar shirts for the men. Coral wore one of those shirts with button-fly breeches and leather boots like those worn by boys straight from Williamsburg.

Outside, Ty loaded the empty bottles into the cart.

Clearly, she wasn't afraid of being different, and he liked different, especially on her. She was delicate and sweet looking, with a pointed chin and high cheekbones and the biggest clear blue eyes he'd ever seen. She'd given him an open stare, so full of interest that in the daze of smacking his head, he'd stared back, which had made her go all stern and frowning.

Ugh, she'd caught him checking her out. He shook his head at himself. What had gotten into him? She was a witch, so he had to be careful. If he hadn't learned that lesson last year, he was an idiot.

Still, he couldn't resist returning to the bakery—through the front door. An olive-skinned boy with freckles leaned on the end of the counter, talking to Coral between the comings and goings of customers. Judging by the boy's rounded cheeks and the trace of fuzz on his upper lip, the guy couldn't be older than fourteen.

More customers entered, giving Ty cover to hang back and watch. Yeah, Coral's confidence blew away any impression that she was too young to be here. Like his sister Juni, Coral was *petite*—the word his mom used in an attempt to pacify his sister, just as he got *wiry* when bullies had called him scrawny. Besides, for a Windborne, body size had nothing to do with the energy one could harness and wield. He knew that lesson well.

As he idled behind two witches deciding between the new choices of muffins, Ty magically enhanced his hearing to pick up Coral's conversation.

"—can't," she protested in a low voice. "Nowadays I work for Manta when we're at anchor."

"It'd only be an hour," the boy said. "She'll let you if you give her your sweet look."

"An hour today and an hour tomorrow, followed by another the next day, and what will happen? My sister will think I'm not serious and hire a local girl instead."

"So? Then you'll be free to sail, to fly, to do the things we did before they moved to town."

"Hold on, Shrimp."

Shrimp? No way, even in this coastal-centered enclave, no parent would stick a kid with that name. It had to be a nickname.

She helped a customer and then returned. "Aye, I could, but I wouldn't be building my fund. I have to think of my future."

"Pfft. You have plenty of time to save for your boat since you aren't going away. If you lie low about you-know-what, your parents won't bother you."

"I'm not sure. They're *thinking* about academies again. Hold on."

Her own boat. A "you-know-what" mystery. This small-town girl had more ingredients in her potion than most witches Ty had met at academy, which she might be leaving Tern Bay for—

"Your parents are pushing attending academy again?" Shrimp asked Ty's question.

"Not if I can help it. My talent is best put to use if I'm here, working with Pop to balance our fisheries. *And* I have to have my own boat to do it. Hold on."

Great, she wasn't disappearing soon. Hmm, that was a selfish thought. No wizard should pass up academy training. He *had* learned a lot during his three years there.

Coral finished with her customer, and Shrimp resumed the same whine. "You only think of your boring work. Let's go flying." His maturity wasn't much beyond Ty's twelve-year-old brother Dave's, and by the exasperated look Coral gave him, the guy certainly wasn't her boyfriend. *Thank the Orb for that.*

The door jangled—the last customer leaving. Silence fell in the shop, and Ty startled out of his revelry. Coral and her friend were staring at him.

"May I help you?" she asked coldly, her arms crossed.

Heat flooded his face. Ty pointed to a loaf of bread he and Dar didn't need and a stack of spicy-smelling molasses cookies. He was paying when the door jangled again.

Coral looked past him, and her face lit up. "Hoy, Oyster! And Cor. You've arrived early for Fest."

A handsome, sandy-haired guy strolled over. "A bit," he said. "Showing Cor around while we collect supplies. We've actually come to help my uncle clean up a mass of Styrofoam pellets that appeared in his estuary overnight."

"Spells! Up north?"

Oyster nodded. "I'm sure he'll be notifying Sir Dolph today and checking if you have some time to help."

"I, uh…" Her face reddened, and she glanced at Ty. "That river has been a continuing pollution problem for our habitat. Pop is gone. Let's talk to Salm."

Ty got that loud and clear—his signal to leave. He picked up his stuff and turned to go. The second fellow—a teen with red-brown skin and black hair falling in natural coils around his face—stepped back and got the door for him. "Thanks," Ty said.

He dipped a nod. "Good day," he answered in a clipped British accent, while back at the counter, Oyster and Coral were talking in hushed tones.

"Damn," Ty muttered to Pepper as he untied the pony's reins. "How did I blow it?" Had something gone awry during their meeting in the kitchen? She'd been plenty talkative to Piper in the pantry, although Ty had caught only fragments about deliveries and her not wanting to make them. She'd been upset. Maybe he could help…

No. What am I thinking? He had no time to think about witches, and she obviously had other friends to call upon. *Sailing lessons.* Ty looked over his shoulder while pushing the milk cart up the town ramps. He needed a crash course on ocean sailing if he wanted to snag a shipboard apprenticeship. Every ship he had to watch leave Tern Bay only added to his morning depression.

They topped the cliff, and the cart rolled onto the dirt road that led across the moor to the dairy farm. Ty called, "Whoa," though he hardly needed to bother. Pepper was already looking around, ears alert, waiting for his praise and a treat. "Hey, great job, old buddy. Bet you're glad that hill is over." He scratched the short, stiff hair under Pepper's black fetlock and laughed as the pony's soft lips snatched the sugar cube he offered. For his own treat, Ty dug out a cookie and took a bite.

"Should I try to see her again?" he asked Pepper. "Or let the whole thing alone?"

Blue eyes. She had to be a blue energy wizard, a pretty

blue... Okay, just thinking about her was fine. He didn't have to *do* anything. Not that she'd hinted that she'd be open to doing anything with him, even back in the kitchen. Had he sensed a rise in her magic? No, during their two meetings, nothing had been visible in her, only an odd feeling in him.

He shrugged and swept a hand over Pepper's flank as he walked back to take the cart handles. "I'll talk to her again and then decide."

At the farm, Ty unharnessed Pepper, wiped him down and released him into the pasture before unloading the cart and placing the returned milk bottles into the steam-spewing commercial dishwasher. Just as he finished sorting the receipts and payments into their proper boxes, the familiar stomp of work boots sounded on the wooden flooring, and Dar appeared, dressed in his usual overalls.

"Lad! 'Twas a quick trip. Ach, I would never venture *out there* by meself, but 'tis a wonder what a woman will get you to do." The farmer raked a hand through his thick gray hair, before waving it enthusiastically. "Come look at the stores."

Ty grabbed his bakery purchases and followed Dar to the house. Dar's widow witch friend, Ms. Scallop, must have convinced him to go into one of the human towns closer to her sheep farm north of here. Definitely, for there on the kitchen table sat a bunch of bags—plastic bags. Ty's eyes widened at the printing on them. "*You* went to ASDA?" It was the UK equivalent of a Walmart.

"Aye, smart you are, seeing that right off. I suppose shoppin' is what you do in the New World. For us country folk, 'tis an adventure."

"Well, it is for me, too." Ty grinned. "When we were kids, Mom wouldn't let us go into human towns and was all over me the last year when I shopped in human stores. You've got to be careful." Wizards used to their shielded Windborne enclaves wouldn't show magic in front of humans, but often forgot to watch their tongues.

Dar nodded. "Aye, but Scallop has learned to copy their ways. She sells her woolens to them for their coin, then uses it when she ventures out to exchange with them. 'Twas an amazing place, so full of *things*, things you can get for your home, for your table, your body and more, I suppose. 'Twas the limit of what I would allow her to drag me through." He dropped his voice to a whisper. "I felt meself goin' twitchy every time some human got too close. They be more like Scallop's sheep than my cows, racing around and bunching up."

Ty almost laughed at the image, picturing Dar trying to herd the other shoppers like he did his cows.

"But look at this, lad. I used some human coin Scallop held for me in exchange for repairs I made to her fencing this summer. She has this machine, and I know you will think highly of it, especially with Fest upon us." With a flourish, Dar gestured to a box on the counter.

"Hey, a microwave."

"Aye, you recognize it, but I bet I'm the first in Tern Bay to try the machine."

That didn't surprise Ty. Despite the solar panels gracing every roof, only a few of these insular people were making full use of the resources the wizard bureau HIT—Human Information Technology—brought to the Windborne world. Fortunately, Dar was one of them. A month ago, the Scottish farmer's stern interview had worried him. Ty had had no choice but to take the only job he'd been offered, or move on. Yet it'd worked out well. Dar was a good boss and a steadfast mentor in this tight-knit community.

"I set in a store of these special meals in boxes." Dar upturned one of the bags, and an assortment of microwavable dinners in colorful packages slid out. "They should come in handy for Fest, what with you trying to tail sailors and forward this plan of yours to work on a ship. We can tend the cows, have a bite and return to the festivities with no fuss."

Ty peered in the other bags and laughed. There had to be forty frozen entrées. "Wow, thanks. This'll be great with the time off you've promised me."

The farmer grinned. "Scallop assured me a teenager would be well-versed in modern machines. Do you think you can make it work?"

"Oh yeah, I can set up the microwave."

"There's a good lad. If you can see to cookin' up two of those box meals for our lunch, I'll finish in the office."

"Sure, I'll get started." Ty yanked loose the microwave box flaps.

Dar opened the door to go out, but stopped. "Thought of an idea for you while I was down on the dock putting in my order for grain. Good friend of my lads', Dolph of the Seas, has put his ship to anchor for the week. He and the missus are off on their own, but two of the Seas youngsters will be spending the time in town. Both teach sailing lessons. You should look them up. The lad is about your age, but the lass is nae much younger, and she's a bonny wee thing."

Was he talking about Coral? How ironic... No, how small town.

"See if Coral will teach you a thing or two. She's a feisty one, but you will nae get into more trouble than I would want to hear about." Dar winked.

What? Was Dar suggesting lessons, or going out with Coral? Ty's surprise must have shown, for the older man laughed and knocked him lightly on the shoulder.

"You take yourself too seriously, lad. Have some fun this week. The lass is helpin' her sister at the bakery, but they canna keep her there all day and night."

His gut knotted, warring between knowing this was a

terrible idea and hoping he had a chance. "Uh, sailing lessons, okay."

"That's nae my meaning, lad." Dar shook his head. "Coral is nae just some sailor, she's a witch. You do ken what to do with a witch, eh, lad?"

Ty knew. All too well. The things he'd learned had burned him before, but never again.

7

NEGOTIATIONS

oral had unloaded the dinner rolls onto the storage racks at Fintail's and waited while Spike's—er, *Marlin's*—mother counted them and handed her the tavern's signed receipt.

That's it. I'm out of here. She shoved her shoulder to the screened kitchen door and tugged the handcart through. *I can handle this to help Manta and Piper.*

"Ach, you're still about?"

Spike.

Coral froze. *Act normal, just act normal.* She threw a casual glance to where he perched on a pile of crates. The sight of her fiercest challenger chilled her, even with an apron slung over his shoulder. Spike would love to discover she had no magic this week.

With blond hair swinging about his shoulders, he leaped down, throwing his arms wide and flexing his biceps.

Pivoting, she wheeled the cart between them.

Spells, like a handcart would stop him. Yet it would keep the six-foot-tall warlock back a few paces, far enough so she wouldn't need to crane her neck to look up at him. "Sure. Who wouldn't want to stay in town for Fest?"

His hazel eyes brightened with his grin, making them redder than their normal orange-brown. "I'm ready to do this."

She knew he meant to *duel*, but they never said that word in town.

"What do you say to tonight?" He dusted imaginary dirt from his kitchen whites, flicking red sparks from his fingertips.

What a show-off—uh…oh. She'd flaunted more magic when challenging Octo last year. This, more than anything so far, made her loss of magic so poignant. Coral swallowed and forced a strong voice. "Can't. I'm staying at my sister's."

"Tomorrow, then?"

"No."

Spike squinted and sauntered closer. He pulled his hair into a band, but the motion didn't make the towering warlock look any less tough. "Are you avoiding me?"

I wish. But attitude was everything. He'd never know her guts were grinding *if* her face didn't give her away. She stepped around the cart to meet Spike halfway.

An odd rumbling made both of them turn.

A scooter sputtered down the ramp. Motorized vehicles of any kind were unusual in the settlements, especially one as small as Tern Bay. A fifteen-minute walk would get you from one end of town to the other, because flying—or other public displays of magic—wasn't allowed.

"A Vespa," Spike murmured. "Must be one of the Fest vendors."

The red paint shone without a scratch, and the chrome trims glinted. "No," she said, "it's new, too shiny to have been hauling stuff."

Its small tires easily swung around the tavern's delivery area, and the driver stopped. A fellow wearing a coal-colored shirt and black canvas pants stared at them. His thick brown hair settled like a cape over his ears.

Meeting his silver-eyed gaze, Coral blinked in confusion. The new dairyman she'd met at the bakery? He cut the motor and remained seated astride the Vespa, but nodded to her. Spells upon her, it was. Ty. Now that the bandanna and white clothes were gone, he looked completely different.

With a glance to Spike, she said, "Excuse me," and stepped over to the scooter.

Ty lifted his chin toward Spike and in a low voice asked, "Spike or Lemon?"

"Spi—I mean, Marlin. You shouldn't be knowing the other name," she hissed. Orb curse it, what else had he overheard when she and Piper were speaking at the bakery? Nothing she could afford to have repeated to Spike. She had to gain control. Her arms crossed automatically, but she managed not to frown. "What are you doing here?"

"I gathered from what you said earlier that you'd rather not make the deliveries," Ty said. "I have afternoons off and could make them for you if we can arrange a swap."

She cocked an eyebrow at him. "I may be interested, depending. I'll finish here and meet you at the shop."

Ty cast a look behind her to Spike. "I can take you back to the bakery."

She eyed the motor scooter. That would ensure he wasn't left here alone with Spike...and a trip on it might be fun. "Give me a minute." She strode back to her handcart and tilted it onto the wheels. "My lift is here. I'm going."

"Nay." Spike grabbed the handle and dropped his voice. "When can we...*you know*?"

"Not this week." Coral slid a sideways peek back at Ty. He was staring off to the ocean, but now she knew his ears were sharp. She leaned toward Spike. "I promised Manta a week of work. I cannot be put out of it."

A grin spread across Spike's face. "Are you admitting you might lose to me?"

Giving a snort, Coral ran her squinted gaze down his frame—

Curse it all! What was she doing? This act, her typical disdainful eyeing of an opponent, would certainly set the hook for Spike. "I'm admitting I won't take the chance when my sister is relying on me."

"Like that's ever stopped you before."

"Catch me next week." She tugged on the cart.

He tightened his grasp. "Next week you'll be gone."

"We're staying at anchor past Fest."

"Then you have time—"

"Look, Spike." Coral stepped closer and poked his chest. "I said not now. You'll just have to get over me representing us at Fest."

Red magic flickered in his eyes.

With a fierce glare, she yanked the handcart free and wheeled it over to the scooter. Ty handed her a piece of cord and gestured to the chrome rack at the back of the seat. She should be shaking, having bluffed Spike with no magic to back her up. But she wasn't. And if Ty's swap was good, she wouldn't see Spike again this week.

While she fastened the cart with a sailor's knot, Spike approached. "It's a fine machine."

"Thanks. Name's Ty. And yours?"

"Marlin," he answered, now all bravado.

She straightened, and Ty's gaze briefly met hers, a smile twitching his lips. "Marlin. Good to meet you. All set, Coral?" He slid forward on the black cushioned seat.

Right. She just had to get on the thing, and they'd be out of here. Balancing with her hand on the seat—careful not to touch Ty's rear—she swung her leg over the scooter as if climbing into the hull of a dinghy and settled down.

Ty started the engine.

The rounded fender had no handles, so she reached for the rear rack. The scooter rolled, and she swung sideways—the wrong way. She grabbed for Ty's waist. He stopped the Vespa, so she let go. It was too forward to touch a boy she had just met.

And a silver warlock. Her guts knotted. What had she done, accepting a lift just to steer Ty away from Spike? And now Spike was watching, grinning ear-to-ear in delight at her predicament.

Spells. Thank the Orb Ty hadn't flashed her. Lots of wizards couldn't or wouldn't control their energy and would let loose with a surge of energy over another's skin. If Ty hadn't controlled his, could his silver energy have gotten to hers despite the quash?

No. Breaching a quash would take more than a touch. The only way to secure herself was to hold on to Ty's body, like when she and her sisters had ridden a horse together. She'd chance it for the minute it'd take to ride out of Spike's sight. Gingerly, she clasped Ty's sides, her face heating.

A roar rushed through her. Coral's hands jerked, and she released him. Seconds passed before she realized Ty had only revved the engine, but the effect on her nerves was identical to being magically flashed by a wizard.

Spike leaned toward them. His lips moved, but she couldn't hear over the scooter.

Ty cut the engine.

"She beat you, also?" Spike asked.

She opened her mouth, then snapped it closed. She did duel in other ports, but Spike shouldn't assume that she and Ty knew each other from that. Spike hadn't spoken the forbidden word, yet her sinking stomach said if not today, then another time. *Please, no.* She didn't want anyone to bait her into challenging this *silver* wizard.

His thick hair swaying, Ty swung around to look at her, then Spike. "Hmm?"

Spike darted looks between them—he knew his mistake now. Watching him recover would be interesting. His gaze fixed on Ty. "What's she got over you that you're ferrying her around?" he asked, anger edging his tone.

"Not a thing," Ty said evenly. At Spike's doubting grunt, he asked, "It doesn't occur to you someone might want to ferry around a pretty girl for the fun of it?"

"Coral?" Spike burst out laughing. "You have a lot to learn, newbie."

She fisted her hands at Spike's insult. How dare he?

"Well, I'm going to have fun doing it, aren't I?" With a self-assured smile, Ty started up the engine and did the roaring bit again, cutting off the conversation.

Spike's gaze followed them as Ty circled to the ramp. He snapped his apron out and yelled, "You've no idea who you're with, ya fool." He turned on his heel and stomped into the kitchen.

Curses on that boy. Always had to get in the last word.

But Ty had called her pretty. His black shirt felt soft and warm against her palms, and his scent of cut hay filled her nostrils. Even a foot apart, a quiver pierced her stomach. Coral sighed. If he'd been any other warlock, she'd be scooting closer. She'd had magical interactions with plenty of warlocks over the last two years, enough to check out the whole boy-girl thing. None had made her feel like this. *Am I...reacting to his silver energy?*

Oh. This wasn't a *magical* feeling. Her face heated all over again. A smart witch would remember that this cute warlock was dangerous, maybe not this week, but certainly once Pop removed the quash. She had to give him a wide berth. Arrange a swap and be done.

Instead of going to the bakery, Ty steered the scooter to South Dock, a short distance from Fintail's. At the end, a pavilion provided a place for the older folks to sit and fish, or watch the sea. This afternoon, it was deserted. Ty drove into its shade and turned off the engine.

Coral dropped her arms, and he twisted around. Those silvery eyes bored into hers with curiosity.

"Who *am* I with?" he asked.

8

TRADING CONFIDENCES

Coral wished Ty's question was about something else, but he hadn't wasted time. Nice and open.

She climbed off the scooter, using the action to avoid his gaze and decide. Better to tell him herself, since he could find out from Spike anyway. "'Tis, uh, complicated." She glanced at him. "You canna tell anyone."

After a moment's thought, he said, "Okay."

Well, he hadn't answered carelessly. She put her hands on her hips, like she would at a meet. "Tern Bay's top duelist."

He frowned. "But magical confrontations are—"

"Against the rules, aye. We keep them quiet."

"You competed and won this duel?"

"Not just one. Multiple duels, three years running. Depends on how often we're in port."

Ty stared at her. "You must be powerful."

Thank the Orb the pavilion was empty. "Aye, that I am."

"Where did you train?"

Coral laughed. This wasn't going half bad. "It's against Windborne rules, remember?" She waved her hand to the sea. "Dueling is but a way to pass the time when you live on ship, after our lessons and work. Ma would send the four of us off flying to have a speck of peace. She didn't know what we were up to."

His brows shot up. "You and your sisters dueled each other?"

"Two sisters, a brother and myself. Does that make it more believable, that there was a boy involved?"

"No, I have sisters. I *know* girls can be rough." He swiped up the sleeve of his shirt. A four-inch-long scar crossed his shoulder. "It's dueling on your own, without a trainer, I can't understand. It's dangerous."

"Aye." Coral flashed a grin. "To be honest, it started as flying challenges. Skim the water, track a particular dolphin in a pod, hide-and-seek around the ship. Plus, some energy ball throwing practice that, well, sometimes fell into fights. Because the others were all older, and better skilled, I had to perfect my aim and flight maneuvers. I'd make mistakes. Often, one of them had to fish me out of the sea. If it was something we weren't supposed to be doing, they'd cover for me with Ma."

Ty's face creased in doubt. "She fell for it?"

"I got better at dodging them fairly quick. I didn't like the dunking."

"So, show me how good you are."

"Are you challenging me?" *Ah, spells!* What had she said? That flip response was…bad. A plain *no* would have been safer.

Ty answered in a toneless voice, his face now unreadable. "No, of course not. I was just curious. You're—you have no presence of power about you."

Had he been about to say she was too small to win a duel? Coral had heard that three years ago, but not since. What was this presence of power? It sounded like he could sense a Windborne's magic. Perhaps a silver talent? Thank the Orb, Pop had quashed her, though she couldn't believe she was thinking that.

She put on a nice smile. "I'm not a show-off. It's there. Your turn. You have sisters?"

"Yes, two older, one younger and a younger brother."

His answer was courteous, his expression solemn, maybe even guarded. Guess she could ask more. He had. "How many years have you?"

"How many… Oh, I'm seventeen. How about you?"

"I will reach my seventeenth year this winter. Why did you come to Tern Bay to work as a dairyman?"

"I didn't. That's the only job I could get," he said with resignation.

"I hear old Dar is picky about the sort he hires. You must know something about cows."

Ty grimaced and stopped just short of an eye roll. "More than I wish I did. When my family lived in Vermont, my mother decided we kids should have the opportunity to experience a working farm. Chores included milking three cows."

"Your family no longer lives in…Vermont?" Her parents had pointed out an academy there, or maybe close by?

"No, from there we moved to Florida, then to Colorado. My parents are defense trainers, pretty good ones, and every academy would like to have them. They chose Terraqua Academy in Colorado's Rocky Mountains."

Terraqua. She sucked in her breath. "Do *you* go to Terraqua Academy?"

"I, uh…I've graduated," he said in a rush. "I'm kind of ahead for my age. That's the reason we moved there—Terraqua Academy is willing to accept nontraditional students."

He didn't have to tell her that. So he was done at Terraqua. Too bad. She'd consider going there if he was there. "So why did you move here?"

Ty shrugged. "My mother's grandparents were from Tern Bay, and I wanted to live by the sea."

"Why not return to Florida or Vermont? Aren't they on the coast?"

"Florida's heat isn't for me, and Vermont"—he finally smiled —"isn't on the coast. You may be Tern Bay's top duelist, but your geography is atrocious."

Coral flipped a hand to zap him—as if he were Salm or any other local kid—before remembering nothing would happen. Spells, this quash was a pain. She strode away. At the edge of the pavilion, she realized she'd left the handcart. She turned, nearly bumping into Ty.

"Sorry, I shouldn't tease you. Why should you know the location of our states when you live in the British Isles?"

"When I'm Windborne, no need to," she scoffed. But inside she didn't feel so certain. He'd apologized? Usually, she was the one made to go apologize. That was, if Ma found out. He acted so differently from most warlocks. Maybe his magic wouldn't steal—*no, stop thinking about it.* She couldn't risk it.

"Ma is always after me about my studies. I'm a better duelist than student." She shrugged and began to untie the handcart. "I should get back."

"Don't you want a ride?"

Immediately, Coral heated. She whirled around, ready to tell him to bugger off with his slang suggestion of—

He was pointing to the scooter.

Great Golden Orb, someone had better explain to this American what *want a ride?* meant over here. But not her, not this time. "A *lift*, we call it." That would have to do. She halfheartedly tugged at the knot, then stopped… *I better not regret this.* She retightened the knot. "Sure."

Ty threw a leg over his scooter.

She climbed on behind him. Ah, the hands again.

"Hold on to me like you did before," he said over his shoulder. "It makes it easier to balance if you're moving with me."

She did, only then remembering they hadn't discussed the

swap. The scooter sputtered down the dock, up a ramp to the main level and crept along the boardwalk. They passed a few wizards, all who knew her and nodded in a friendly way. Or curious. But Ty didn't stay long on the main boardwalk before turning down the back alley. Then he ran the Vespa faster, and her heart thrilled at the sensation of flying along together. Oh, if only they could go up on the moor and ride the country lanes.

Maybe she could suggest that if they arranged a swap. He was cute. He didn't play games like these other fellows, or even duel. With her magic quashed, it'd be safe to have a little fun with someone nice. It could be a trial to learn if Ty was like Lemon and wanted only to play with her magic, or if he might be a boy she'd like to see again when they were in port.

At the bakery, he dismounted while she untied the handcart. "What kind of a swap did you have in mind for the deliveries?" she asked.

"Sailing lessons."

"What, you don't sail? Why do you want to live by the sea?"

"I do sail." Ty jerked his thumb seaward. "I rip at home, but oceans…"

At the word *rip*, Coral winced. But as he continued, it sounded like he meant going fast. On her home island, *rip* referred to only one thing: the dangerous energy rips their wizards were fighting to repair in their shielding. If they failed, they'd be exposed to the human world.

Ty was saying, "That's why I moved here, to become a better sailor." He kicked out a foot and dropped his head so his dark hair covered his eyes. "I, uh… Promise you won't laugh?"

Spells, the fellow was stuttering. "I promise."

"My goal is to live and work on the sea, but I can't get a job with any of the ships here to learn more, because I don't know enough about ocean sailing—how to deal with the changing winds and mysterious currents. I thought since you live on a schooner, you could teach me those techniques on a large boat."

"Oh, no." He really didn't know about larger vessels. "My parents would qu—" *Ach, that was too close to the truth.* "They'd anchor me forever on the isle if I tried to sail *The Peaceful* by myself. A schooner the size of ours requires two good sailors."

The movement was slight, but his jaw tightened. Upset, his body language said. Yet all he did was nod once.

"I understand. Thanks anyway." He climbed on the Vespa, started the motor and roared down the alley much faster than they'd arrived.

There went her chance to get to know him, er, to have *him* make the deliveries. Her shoulders sagged. Did she really want to spend time with a trainee sailor? One who made her stomach flip like she was seasick on land? No, it would be a pain in the rear…*but what a rear he has.* And shoulders, solid with muscles she'd love to check out. She huffed out a sigh and rubbed her forearms. Now she'd have to make those deliveries…unless she convinced Manta she should help Oyster clean up the estuary instead.

The screen door banged. She jumped and whirled. Her sister Manta stared down the alley, wiping her hands on her white apron that never seemed to get dirty. "Ty left?"

She'd seen? "Uh, aye." Coral pulled the handcart over to her sister, who after a full day of work still looked perfect, her long hair coiled in its netting, her neat white baker's smock pressed, the matching skirt trim and flattering. "You were spying on me."

"Who, me? Your favorite sister?" Manta slid an arm around her and squeezed tight. "It's nothing you didn't do to me."

"Aye, well…" Coral kept her gaze elsewhere.

"Shoe's on the other foot, eh? It's good to have you here."

"Uh, thanks. It's good to be here." Without meaning to, Coral glanced down the alley again.

Manta laughed and tugged her sideways. "He's a looker, as Granny would say. Come on upstairs. I have a surprise for you."

9

THE GAME

Ty gunned the Vespa harder than he should have and didn't stop until he rounded a corner. Out of the alley, he rolled at a snail's pace to the main boardwalk.

Curses, a swap hadn't worked. *And you better thank the Golden Orb it didn't, dude.*

She dueled. Illegally. Ty wiped a hand over his face. The very last thing *he* needed was to know of an illegal magical activity *and* not report it.

He'd promised her he wouldn't tell.

But when you earned the Master Wizard certification, you accepted its honor code.

He wouldn't technically be a Master Wizard until he turned eighteen. However, he carried a probationary license that identified him as certified to do the magic he'd trained for.

If I don't get to know her, then I can pretend I never heard her mention dueling.

Only problem with that was, after talking to Coral, he found her even more attractive than when he'd first met her. She was powerful, spunky, liked acrobatic flying, liked sailing and wasn't afraid to be herself.

But, to her, that meant dueling.

It's for the best we don't swap.

Now if only he could get his head to stop whirling…and his magic. His back was on fire, his silver energy still cavorting after trying to reach hers. What he'd seen in Coral—er, what *had* he seen? There had been *something* there, something in her magical essence. He couldn't define it, but it had a hold of him.

An urge that strong was a red flag.

He rumbled to the end of the boardwalk and stopped. He'd never admitted to his family that Juni's wasn't the only scar he'd gotten last year. He hadn't ducked fast enough to avoid a flying chair, but his sister had been right—although he was brainy, he still had things to learn.

Ah, Blessed Orb. Don't even go there. The right witch will come along. And sailing lessons. His gaze slid over the rhythmic waves flashing in the afternoon sun, the masts bobbing in time to the water and, below them, the colorful hulls of the ships. He'd find a position *on* the sea, hopefully before his year slipped away. Dar had assured him that fishing and hiring picked up in late winter.

Later that evening, after Ty'd completed the milking and chores, and Dar had gone to visit Ms. Scallop, Ty showered and put in his laundry. While scanning the freezer for a microwave meal, he realized he didn't want to eat alone. On a whim, he headed for town.

Sitting on a counter stool at Dockside, Ty toyed with the last of his chowder. He could order pie. He could make the most of the clear evening and go for a flight. He could keep trying to talk to the briny-smelling bloke at his side, but his monosyllabic answers weren't getting them far. He could walk over and see if the bakery might still be open.

The bell on the door jingled. With everyone else, Ty turned to see who it was.

It was her. Coral. Like she'd read his thoughts and appeared.

Coral didn't look his way. She headed behind the counter, toward the kitchen door and called, "Keenan?"

Everyone else returned to their food.

The owner's head popped up at the pass-through window. "I barely hung up the phone with Manta. Give me a minute." Keenan disappeared again, and Coral backed up a step and leaned against the counter.

Ty spooned up the last of his soup, trying not to look like he was watching her. She scanned the room, tapped her fingers on the bar's red laminate and looked over her shoulder out the window a couple of times. Geez, she was hot to get going. What to? Probably one of these duels she'd mentioned. It would be kind of stalkery, but he'd already thought of approaching her again, so why not tag along to see if he could keep her out of trouble?

Keenan burst through the door, three plates of steaming food lined up on his arm. "Be right back," he said to Coral before hurrying the dinners to a booth in the far corner. She slumped in place and checked the window again.

Ty extracted his wallet from his jeans and fingered his trade card. No, running the card with its magically inscripted exchange balance would take too long. Instead, he pulled out the last of his notes. He'd take out more when Dar paid him again.

Keenan barreled by, disappeared through the still-swinging door, then a half minute later emerged with a carton in his hand. Coral reached for it. "Thanks, Keenan. Manta says she'll replace it Monday when she goes to the wholesaler."

"Fine," the man said to Coral's disappearing back.

Ty was off his stool and striding the length of the counter before the door closed. "Gotta go, Keenan. This is for the chowder." He handed over the notes.

"No pie tonight?"

Coral was much more interesting than pie. Plus, he could always come back, perhaps with her. "Maybe later. See you."

Keenan glanced at the door. "Aye," he said with a knowing nod. "Watch yourself, lad."

Ty pushed his way out. Why did everyone say that? Power wasn't surging off of her. Not the way it did with some Windbornes. Like Marissa. He spotted Coral trotting half a block away already, her braids bouncing, her cream-colored pants a good target to follow in the dimming light.

Then suddenly he couldn't see them.

Picking up his pace, Ty nodded to an approaching couple, the only people between him and Coral when he'd lost her. Oh, right. They'd been near the green cottage where he and Pepper regularly took the back alley to the first level. Coral must have turned into it.

Ty reached the house and peered up the dim passage. No one in sight. Running, she could have reached the ramp behind this row of houses. He scanned the beach. Two guys were running—one hoofing it south, the other heading this way at a long-legged lope and looking right at Ty.

No, not at *him*. At the alley. Ty dropped to pretend to tie his shoe. The string bean of a boy with tousled blond hair swung into the alley. His feet pounded the boards.

This is interesting. And only partly because that was Elder Bentha's son. Ty didn't know his name, but he'd seen the guy during deliveries to the home of the head of Tern Bay's council. He either hated mornings or was perpetually grumpy.

A shortcut to the main level would let Ty see what went down. The perfect spying place would be the corner house. He followed the runner into the shadows and pictured the covered pink porch where he delivered a quart of milk on Mondays and Thursdays, the one decorated with a settee and a fern on a stand. The image was clear enough.

Hand in his pocket, he fingered the small glass float he'd

bought at the hardware store. It had been purely decorative before he'd infused it with his magic and strands of shielding energy he'd siphoned from this enclave's protective magic. The teleporting spell was one he'd mastered along with the techniques to swipe the energy, though casting a peregrinator wasn't allowed without a local permit. He could have applied, but he'd been bored, and the challenge to test one of his academy lessons in the field had been too tempting.

So, despite the town rule against public use of magic, Ty pictured where he wanted to go, flooded his channels with magic and dissolved his cells to pure energy. He combined with the stolen enclave magic and pereported to the space behind the fern, where he materialized and crouched against the wall.

He scanned the main boardwalk toward the bakery. No sign of her. Just a group of kids laughing and jostling each other as they sauntered, first forward, then back to the middle of the block. Clearly, they were hanging out near the bakery.

Crrrssshh! The faint sound filtered from behind him. Ty pivoted and peered over the alley-side railing in time to see a hand disappear into the narrow space between the house and a planter box of shrubs. The tips of the bay leaves swayed. It had to be Coral. Only her skinny body would fit in a space like that. Brilliant hiding spot. And just in time—pounding feet drew closer up the ramp at the end of the alley. Another set echoed on the boardwalk steps twenty-some feet off the front of the porch.

Ty sank into a squat behind the settee. "Whatcha doing?" he whispered into the fragrant branches.

Her sharp intake of breath resounded as if she'd yelled down the alley, and she jerked around, her wide eyes narrowing to slits when their gazes met.

"None of your business," she hissed. "Just scram!"

Shoot, she'd been more startled than he'd expected, but being told to *scram*... "It's a free town. I can stay here if I want to."

"Blast, I don't need you shadowing—"

Bam, bam, bam. Feet pounded the back ramp as the runner careened around the corner and stopped in the alley. An instant later, the head of the boy climbing the main steps emerged. It was Spike.

"Your friend *Marlin* just came up the steps," Ty whispered.

"Oh, thanks."

At least she was talking to him, even if it was sarcastically. Laughter rang out from the bakery kids. Spike rolled his eyes in disgust before he darted past Ty's hiding place and ran up the alley. He met the string bean runner, Elder Bentha's son. Their voices carried, but not the words.

"Who's the other guy?" Ty asked.

"Don't you have anything better to do?"

Ouch. Simple enough question, but it stung since he didn't. These scant minutes of chase and hide were the most excitement he'd had since leaving academy. His mind leaped, his adrenaline rose and his magic pumped, like it had during the mock espionage scenarios from his magical training. Ty sank onto his heels. "There's nothing going on more interesting than this," he admitted.

"Aye, there is. Go find it," she snapped.

"I won't give you away. Is this your form of dueling?"

It sounded like she'd snorted.

Man, if he were down there, he could read her face. But he wouldn't fit. The voices at the end of the alley trailed away, and the scraping of twigs replaced them—Coral sidling out from behind the planter. Quick as he could, Ty imagined the location and pereported into her path.

She startled back. "Out—"

"There are four others at the bakery door," he said.

"Oh—I—*Orb curse it.*" She melted behind the bushes again.

He followed into the shadowed opening, picking up the faint fruity scent he'd noticed when they were on the Vespa.

"Just leave me be," she whispered.

Even next to her he couldn't read her face—too dark—but this time her voice didn't come across so tough. He'd say she sounded scared—hard to believe if she really was the top duelist in town. Maybe she was skirting trouble? In the conversation he'd overheard earlier with Spike, she'd mentioned a promise to work for her sister, and just now she'd gotten that carton at the diner for Manta. If Coral kept her promises, perhaps he could soften her up into helping him?

Blessed Orb, what am I thinking? But he needed sailing lessons, and sailing lessons had nothing to do with dueling and everything to do with getting a job on a boat and…seeing her more.

Ty cleared his throat. "I'll distract them if you'll reconsider that swap I mentioned today."

She glanced his way. "You're a beginner. Teaching you would be more of a burden on me than hauling the buns."

Bombed again. "Then I may as well go." He stepped into the alley.

"I didn't say—"

"Hey! Spike!"

Ty froze. Someone's head came into sight through the railings, bobbing as he strode toward them, a slouching guy with short dark hair. He was one of the four from the bakery. "We're knackered with this mess. Find her quicklike if you want to…*see* her. Otherwise, the lot of us are done with this blarney."

Coral crept deeper behind the planter, and Ty shrank as far after her as he could.

Elder Bentha's son appeared at the back of the alley and trotted forward enough to half yell, "Eh, Tiger. Spike's off. Let's help him." Then he loped back, looked both ways and headed south. The guy from the bakery followed.

"What size boat were you using?" she asked.

Ah, interested now. "An International 420. On a bay when we lived in Florida and a lake in Colorado."

She groaned. "Pretty tame."

"Yeah, like Tern Bay on a calm day. I need practice with waves, currents and winds."

Three arguing voices echoed from the alley ramp, one louder. "I say she hid and you missed her. Go back and search while I get the others to do the same."

Light fingers touched his arm, and the scent of apricots wafted to him. "If we use our Sunfish," Coral whispered, "we could work on ocean skills for you, even though 'tis nae on a big boat."

Her accent was more pronounced now, soft and sweet—more Irish than Scottish. Yet her tone didn't sound like fake coaxing. Was the town's top duelist nervous?

"I'll show you the ropes on our schooner, even though we do nae go out. That would add to your learning. Would this plan suit you in exchange for a distraction?"

"Ach, if we have to," echoed one boy's deep voice from the alley. Grumbles of agreement signaled their movement.

Ty had to finish this deal. "Every day this week?"

"*Every*—ah. If you make the deliveries."

Footsteps drew closer.

"Agreed. You promise?"

"*Aye!*"

"Give me the box."

"Huh?"

"The box for your sister."

She shoved something at him. Ty pereported to the base of the stairs and charged up them, purposefully making a racket of his entrance. At the top, he casually glanced around and met Spike's gaze. He'd stopped right before the planter.

"Hey, it's Marlin, right?" Ty said. Ha, he never sounded this perky. If the guy knew him, this would never work. "Maybe you could help me out. That witch I want to get to know asked me to do her a favor. Coral needed to get this"—he hefted the carton...of baking powder—"to her sister, but had to meet her brother. Her sister is the one at the bakery, right?"

With a grin, Spike came forward, and Ty had to bite his inner lip to keep from laughing. "Aye, Coral's sister owns the bakery. Where'd you run into her?"

The remaining teens from the bakery watch shuffled closer, two witches in long skirts and the guy—Shrimp—that Coral had been talking to at the counter this morning.

Ty pointed over his shoulder. "Up at North Dock. Mad at her brother for not showing up. Thought I'd give her a hand."

"Good plan, mate. Say, I must go." Spike gestured to the bakery teens and jerked his chin for them to follow. Without waiting, he bolted down the stairs, his blond ponytail streaming behind him.

Watching was too obvious, so Ty headed for the bakery, approaching Shrimp and the witches. Closer now, he recognized one of them, too. Weeks ago, he'd met the black girl with her long braids tied back at Lady Anemone's—her niece, Olive.

Her gaze skittered off him. She leaned toward the others and said, "I need to get home."

"Aye, so do I." A tall, brunette girl pressed her lips tight as they passed by, and Shrimp eyed him.

"Look, there's naught for it." The boy's whisper just reached Ty's keen ears. "I'd rather be in trouble with Spike than with Mum and certainly not with Coral." Murmurs of agreement sounded. Their footfalls thudded faster and louder, and before Ty reached the bakery, they hustled past him.

He waited until they turned a corner, grinning like Spike had as he walked back to the pink house. So much for gang alliances. And now he had his sailing lessons secured.

"*Psst*, Coral. The coast is clear."

She poked her head out, looked skyward and fixed him with a patronizing look. "There was no chance of rain today. Has everyone left?"

This wasn't the first time his clichés had been misunderstood. "Yeah. You can go home now." Flights, she was cute. So self-assured and worldly acting when she'd never lived anywhere but on her family boat. Though maybe they traveled to far-off places on it. He wanted to ask, but when Coral edged from behind the bay bushes and took the carton he held out, he rechecked the main boardwalk.

Gesturing her forward, they fell into step and strode to the bakery door. She opened it and entered before turning, her face poker-blank. "I'm finished for the day once I, or *you* make the deliveries. Could we sail then?"

"Afternoons. Fine."

"Good." She swung the door forward.

They had a deal. That's what he'd wanted. He guessed... though more time with her would have been... He turned away.

"Uh, Ty?"

He flipped his gaze back to her. "Yeah?"

"Thanks." She nodded once with a slight smile at her lips and then closed the door.

Yes! Magic surged through him, and Ty's body lightened, his shoulder blades warmed—

Spells. He'd nearly magicked out his wings right on the boardwalk, definitely a town no-no. Ty stumbled forward, quickening his strides, heading south—the *opposite* direction of Spike. He passed the last lit windows and dashed onto the dark beach, finally unfurling his brown wings.

Flapping hard, he rose as he ran and flew over the wet sand to the crashing waves. He swooped down and then arched his wings into a glide low enough to let the salt spray cool his face.

We have a deal. I'll see her tomorrow. We have a deal.

The words flowed to the rhythm of the rolling waves, and his beating wings carried him to the rocky headland. High above the water, Kittiwake Point Lighthouse flashed its warning beams, a signature sequence of two shorts and one long.

In the beam of light, two figures darted in and out. A guy and a girl, her long skirt swirling as she spun. Yet not all the females here wore them, as he had just... Ty's grin faded as their chase ended in an embrace within the revolving beam's path. When the shaft of light moved off, the couple remained lit.

Aw, man, they were merging their magic. Doing a good job of it, too, judging by the intensity of the glow. They must have been bonded for some time to have gotten their energies to cooperate and combine like that.

Ty whirled away to give the kissing couple some distance before he rose to the moor. He wished he were with a witch. *With Coral.* He put more effort into flapping upward. Coral had been more aloof than most witches he'd befriended, but she interested him more because she didn't flirt with him using her energy. Some academy students had done it playfully, but his previous girlfriend, Marissa, had done it seriously. At twenty, she *had been* worldly when she'd snared him a year ago at sixteen. That alone should have clued him in to her real intention.

A gust of warm air buffeted him. Ty set his wings into a relaxed glide and let the thermal rising over a pile of broken basalt carry him upward while he puzzled out the time with Coral.

If she truly was the town's top duelist, why had she been hiding? He couldn't sense magic within her, so *maybe* she wasn't as proficient as she professed to be? Was she afraid to confront Spike because she *couldn't* take him out? Many of this old-fashioned Windborne town's ways were strange to Ty, but that hadn't been a game or illegal dueling.

I need sailing lessons, so as long as I have no contact with dueling, I'm in the clear.

And if Coral didn't actually *duel*, getting to know her would be fine.

You only met her today.

Yeah, good to remember. He was almost certain Coral was nothing like Marissa, but it wouldn't hurt to get to know her better before he got *too* interested. Not long ago, he hadn't been so cautious. In October, it would be a year since he'd snubbed his sister to prove he could handle anything life threw his way. A year since Marissa had duped him.

The swirl of warm air slowed the farther he rose. Vultures would have left this thermal by now. With a few strokes, he topped the cliff edge and spied the dairy's whitewashed farmhouse a quarter mile away. Home, until he made another move.

What color would Coral's energy be? A fiery orange? Or a bright yellow? Either suited her personality. He couldn't tell yet, just that being close to her piqued his energy. How long before her energy showed an interest in him? What if it didn't?

One step at a time.

Was he ready to try? Ty rubbed his chest. He hadn't thought he could stand another heartbreak, but the mysterious thrill this sailing sprite gave him was quickly outshining the risk of having his heart torn apart again.

CLEAR TO SAIL

Coral bit her tongue and gave Ty the extra minute to adjust their dinghy-sized sailboat into another turn around Tern Bay. After all, he'd rescued her, though he had no idea how much trouble he'd saved her.

Between working for Manta and giving Ty lessons, she had every excuse to steer clear of the town duelists and dueling. *As long as I keep out of trouble this week in town, Ma and Pop have no reason to send me away.*

And Ty wasn't the raw beginner she'd expected. Not once had he called a line a rope. He'd even properly referred to the line controlling the mainsail as the mainsheet. He'd handled the Sunfish's sail and tiller with no mistakes—or instruction—in his helmsman position opposite her.

"You're doing well," she said.

"Thanks, but even I know that's not saying much in this light breeze. Sad, 'cause I'd like to do some planing in these lower waves."

She cocked a brow. "In your—" She slapped a hand to her mouth, stopping the rest: *dreams, sailor boy.*

Now he was peering at her. "Pardon me?"

How could he possibly think they could balance the boat and a full sail on their first time out? One slip while skimming the waves that fast and...*nice, be nice, he saved you!* "In your, er, steps for planing, uh, tell me what you'd do."

"On a reach like this, I hold the tiller steady and wait for a gust to sustain. Then I catch it with the sail."

"You understand the starting point. Go on."

"When the boat accelerates, I trim the sail to keep it full, hike out and ride it."

Well...exactly. He might be ready for planing after all. "Where do I have to be, as your crewman?"

"Same side and leaning out with me." At her gesture to continue, Ty added, "While moving aft to balance us."

"Good, but not too far, or we'll drag the stern. But none of this will happen in these variable gusts. You're too much of an optimist."

"What can I say? It's my first time out in a week. I want to do it all."

She couldn't help smiling at his frankness. "You like going fast, I see."

"You bet." He grinned back. "In the boat, on the Vespa and flying. You must, too, since you like dueling."

"I, er..." Why was he looking at her like that? Like he was poking for information? In the small space of the Sunfish, she could only turn away. "Do you want to take her around again?"

"I do, if it's not too boring for you."

She shrugged. "Let's do it." This wasn't the first time she'd sailed with a beginner. Back home on the isle, where they were the only sailing family, someone wanted lessons every summer. The last few months, it'd been Ash and Lady Mimosa's middle two boys in this boat, but they were younger and needed more showing and telling, keeping her head occupied.

Ty didn't. He was her oldest student ever and, as Manta had said, definitely a looker. Looking helped time pass...looking at his thick hair, his curious eyes, his biceps. Too bad he wore another smooth shirt under his life vest. If only these clouds would blow off, it'd be warm enough for her to shed Salm's old shirt covering her bathing suit. Maybe Ty would do the same. She'd love to check out his chest and how much chest hair he had.

He luffed up the sail to turn them into the wind dancing over the bay. He knew what to do, so Coral tilted her face to a beam of sun between clouds while they tacked along the length of North Dock.

All morning at work, she'd weathered her motherly sister's jet stream of worrying. Manta had fussed about the rip in the magical shielding that Pop was trying to locate along their ocean boundary. But that was miles out, not close to where Coral was holding Ty's first lesson. She didn't dare tell Manta that Pop now suspected *two* rips had formed, because Manta had already sent Piper to keep watch on the lesson. He was washing windows, his ladder propped against the golden wall of the bakery.

Coral didn't need Manta's help. Ty's eyes were enough of a reminder to be careful. She stole another look at him as they neared the end of the dock. He met her gaze, and her cheeks heated.

"Ready about," he said.

Coral checked the water before them, though at this time of the day no boats were entering or leaving the bay. "Ready."

Once more, he completed the tacks without talking, focusing on checking and rechecking the sail, the tiller and their course, steps that were child's play to her and her brother. Salm wouldn't have the patience to sit through this level of sailing.

She had more to think about than sailing.

Ty finished the turn, and they glided across the mouth of Tern Bay with a wind that seemed to be picking up. It plucked strands of Ty's brown hair and gave him a carefree look. His dark brows and golden tan made those silver eyes seem even lighter, mystical and oh-so-irresistible.

Stop it, already. Think of something else. "Ty, we were in such a rush to get on the water I didn't ask about the deliveries. Everything went fine for you?"

"For me, yes." He ducked and shot her a grin under the sail. "Marlin was surprised to see me walk into Fintail's with the trays, then grumbled about not being able to find you last night."

"Aye? What did ye tell him?"

"You know your accent gets stronger the more nervous you are?"

What? No one had ever told her that before. She slowed her words. "Please, what did you tell him?"

"Nothing. He and Elder Bentha's son followed me out, I think to make sure you weren't just waiting. Then we talked about my Vespa. Lemon is a very interesting nickname."

He was poking for information again. Worse, neither duelist was letting up the pressure on her to duel with Spike again. "That's all?"

"There. At the other tavern, the same two girls and a guy from last night at the bakery were hanging around. Olive, I've met. The other two look like siblings, the brother younger by a few years?"

Great. Olive, Pearl and Shrimp all knew she was supposed to be making deliveries, and even Ty had realized they'd come looking for her. "He is younger, but don't underestimate him."

"What's that supposed to mean?"

"At fourteen, he doesn't look like he could do much in a duel, but he can."

Ty nudged her foot with his under the hiking strap in the bottom of the cockpit. "I told you yesterday, I have no intention of dueling."

Her stomach lurched like the boat had dipped. What was

with the toe touch? Flirting? Or an attempt to win her to his opinion? Either way, nothing sensible about her reasons for dueling was coming out of her now. "You never know," she said as neutrally as possible.

"Coral. *I* know. I won't get drawn into magical competition."

Chicken. Probably steered clear because that gel energy of his took too much power to keep up...a reason he could be looking for blue energy to steal. Or was he intimidated because she'd told him she'd won all those duels?

Coral sighed. Too bad. He was so fine, and she longed to run her fingers through that hair, the thickest, prettiest hair she'd seen on a boy. Last night, she'd worked Ty into her favorite fantasy—the one where she prebonded to a warlock to see if they got along, he had his own boat, and in her nineteenth year, they made a permanent bonding application, and she moved onto it with him.

She glanced at him. *Spells, too forward.* She had to know him better first. If he was as perfect as Manta thought, maybe he didn't want to *steal* her energy. If they continued to get on, and once Pop released her power, she and Ty could check out each other's magic. If the energy exchange was exciting, they could prebond to explore whether they'd like to spend more time together. If he lived here and they were docking every few weeks so Salm could see Luna, then she'd see Ty often.

A snappy autumn breeze blew through her shirt-sleeves. A shiver ran down her spine, making Coral tighten her grip on the hull. Who was she fooling? Too many *ifs* plagued this plan—the greatest being this boy. Likely, a beginner sailor would give up when the seas became rough this winter. Then Ty would go home to Colorado. They were too different. It wouldn't work.

Spells. Stop thinking about him until you know him better.

She turned around to check on Piper. He had their new sign, shaped like a giant loaf of bread flanked by muffins, propped against the front of the store and was installing the oversized bracket to hang it. Sir Porbeagle was helping, at least with advice.

"Ready about?"

Hastily, she checked their position. On the last trip around, she'd warned him not to get so close to South Dock because the prevailing winds could blow them into the posts. But he'd done fine.

"Ready," she answered.

Ty stared at the dock, focusing on his tacks.

Why'd he have to go and touch her? It had been just a toe touch, but what did it mean when he touched her like that and no flirt of energy passed? Even without magic, that touch messed up her insides and set them fluttering. It was a good thing they were sailing and she had to stay on her side of the boat, with the tiller between them.

The Sunfish sailed parallel to South Dock. A number of townsfolk hung over the railing, watching their progress, the sole craft on the water, including Pearl and Shrimp, and—

She groaned. "How did they get off near the dinner hour?"

"Who?"

She jerked her gaze from the two blonds draped over the railing. "Spi—Marlin and Lemon are watching us. At the end of the dock near the tavern. Kitchen whites, blond hair?"

Ty squinted at the figures, Spike now leaning his head close to Lemon's tousled yellow mop.

"Will they give you a hard time about being out with a landlubber?"

"No." Because she wouldn't be around for Spike to pick on her. And if Lemon knew what was good for him, he'd say naught to her for weeks to come. Yet, just then, their gazes met. She didn't look away, and neither did he. Huh. She couldn't read him. Long seconds passed as they sailed closer, and then he gave her a nod and turned to Spike. The two straightened from the rail.

There'd been no smirk. Lemon had yielded. Left, even, his break probably over. Her breath released.

"You don't have to lie to me," Ty said. "Take satisfaction that you've ridden on my scooter. The guys are dying to and won't ask."

Really? This was too good, especially on top of Lemon backing off. She grinned in spite of promises. "Aye, and where would he be putting his hands?"

"Not on my body. It's reserved. Ready about?"

Reserved? Could he mean...no, for *her*? Flights, that would be—

Ready about? She jerked around.

Spells, they were close enough to shore. What was she doing with her head in the clouds with a beginner at the helm? Suppose she couldn't call him that anymore. Ty hadn't been daydreaming like she had, and during this second round his skills shone through.

"Ready," she answered.

Ty shifted the tiller.

Just who *was* his body reserved for? He probably meant he had a partner, darn—

Whoosh! A gust hit them from the leeward side, the shore, and the sail ballooned with wind.

"What the—" Ty let loose of the sail and tiller. Still, the boat tilted. His weight—on what *had* been the correct side of the Sunfish—added to the boat's list.

Coral stretched her slight frame as far off the deck as she could, but the boat pitched farther. Too late, Ty scrambled to join her.

The deck rose to vertical. Ty plunged into the water. The sail followed. As she plummeted, Coral automatically tried to hover herself. Without her magic, it didn't work.

"Eeeeeeeeeeee!" she screamed and, for the first time in years, fell in.

LESSONS LEARNED

own, down, down Coral sank into the murky water. She
kicked. Her limbs dragged in her sodden clothes, but her
life vest popped her to the surface. At least the sea was still
warm from summer.

"Coral? Coral!" Ty shouted.

Rolling with the waves, she sucked in a breath. "Here." Salt
tainted her mouth. She spit and grabbed hold of the mast.

"You okay?" Ty asked across the half-submerged sail.

She swiped away her dripping hair. "Aye. Are you?"

"Yep. You're lighter. Can you get over here and roll up with
the boat while I right it?"

She blinked in surprise. Obviously, he'd done this before.
"Coming." Steadying the mast so it wouldn't knock her on the
head, Coral ducked under it and joined Ty at the rudder.

He handed her the line for the sail and, with a light grip,
crab-walked around the end of the boat. "Guess we're fortunate
it didn't totally turtle."

She sighed. He didn't know about floats, but in other things
he acted incredibly like an old hand—such as this, moving about

the capsized craft without tipping it further. "Pop put floats in the top of the sail, so it won't roll completely over."

"Ah, good idea." On the other side, Ty's soles *thunked* on the daggerboard. When he called, she loosened the mainsail so it wouldn't catch the wind when righted and then flattened herself into the partially submerged cockpit, clung to the hiking strap in the bottom and yelled, "Ready."

His weight levered up the boat. The mast and sail rose, then the hull scooped Coral up. Relieved, she scrambled to her knees, automatically shoved aside the boom and grasped Ty's wrists to secure him at the side.

Flights! He had long, strong fingers, and his forearm tendons flexed in thick cords. How would those arms feel around her shoulders? Or middle? Or with her back snugged up to him? *Ah, stop it.* Her stomach and chest went all funny and hot again.

She shouldn't have touched him, but she couldn't let go now without him noticing. Curses on Manta's errand for putting her in debt to him. Curses on her body's reaction to a wizard who probably wasn't even available. "You're a regular hand at this," she gasped, the first thing she could think of.

"I am." He grinned up at her as he bobbed with the waves. "Although I should be embarrassed to say so, I've done it a lot."

"Um...practice makes perfect, as Ma always says."

"But now you have to help me out—which side is windward? I thought the prevailing winds here came from seaward, until that gust overtook us."

Thank the Orb for his question—sailing instructions didn't require thinking. "Prevailing is your key word. Along the coast, winds can come from any direction, so don't feel bad. One errant gust can be anyone's undoing." She squeezed his wrists in shared sympathy, then realizing what she'd done, looked around for the wind—which, with her hair and clothes plastered to her, she knew was out of the southwest. Folks on the dock were watching—all but Spike and Lemon. They'd left, probably laughing.

"Hoy, Coral!" Piper waved from the water's edge. She waved back and gave him a thumbs-up. He returned it and pointed skyward.

With his brown feathered wings spread, Salm glided into a hover off their bow. Skipper wriggled into a frenzy upon seeing her, yipping and scrambling to be set down. Salm hefted her dog and pointed a finger at his nose. The yipping stopped. "Impressive recovery, you two."

"Thanks, but it's not complete until I'm back in," Ty said.

Why had a compliment been the first thing out of Salm's mouth? She should have thought to tell *her* student this before her brother had. She glared at him, but kept her voice even when saying, "Right, but so far it's been good. Windward is southwest from the sea, just as we thought." Ty clung to the hull and continued to crab-walk around the boat. "Salm, this is Ty. Ty, my brother, Salm."

Ty nodded. "Pleased to meet you. And the little guy?"

"Skipper," Coral told him. "How's he doing, Salm?"

"The pup's fine. We were taking off to help clean for tours at the lighthouse when I saw you flip the sail upright. Nice to meet you, Ty. We can put our fears to rest about your ability on the water."

We. Blast. Hopefully, Ty missed the reference that her family had been discussing him. Coral joined Ty at the other side of the boat, shifted her weight back and reached out a hand.

He started to meet her grasp, then hesitated.

"Magically lighten yourself to get in," Salm said. "We do it all the time."

"Thanks, but I better finish this without. I took human-led lessons, so if I have to go back to them, I don't want to slip up." He shook his head at Coral and pointed to the far stern corner of the cockpit space.

She shook her head in return. The bay water was warm, but the late afternoon air wasn't. "Take my hand so we can get going."

He raised a brow. "You think you can give me a hand *and* counterbalance my weight?"

Salm laughed. "What's the worst that could happen? You take another dunking?"

Coral rolled her eyes. "Which you *won't* see. Take my hand."

Ty did.

"Ready? Go."

As he kicked hard and rose, she yanked and lurched back to grip the opposite side of the hull. The boat tilted, but Coral hauled him over the edge and then shifted balance to right them. Ty rolled into the bottom of the cabin. He stared up at her as she lowered onto the hull ledge.

Laughter burst out above them, and Salm fluttered his wings to rise. "See you two onshore."

Ty came to life and scrambled up to sit opposite her. "Geez," he muttered. "I never would have thought you could do it, as skin—petite as you are." He grabbed the mainsheet and tiller and steered them toward the dock.

She sniffed. "Leverage. Same way you flipped the boat. You just have to know what you're doing."

"Apparently, you do. Thanks for being such a sport about the dunking. I appreciate you taking it all human-style. I was afraid you'd started doing some sort of magic sailing shortcuts on me. Since that's not the way I learned, it would have thrown me off."

From her seat, Coral searched Ty's face. Was he really ignoring the obvious—she didn't use magic because she couldn't? She was all about magic, as everyone who kept telling her to limit it knew.

Everyone, meaning the adults. Other wizard teens didn't care. Especially the boys. Wouldn't Ty be like them once he saw her energy? If the tales about silver wizards were true, that made him an odd one to speak up for avoiding magic. Especially after he'd done all that pereporting around last night. What was with him?

At least she had a reasonable excuse to not use magic. "Pop insists we sail like the rest of the world."

"Your brother suggested I magic in."

A growing breeze cut through her soaked clothes, turning her shrug into a shiver. "Right. Pop's not always with us, but we sail correctly, or can. It's required for competition, since wizards have varying degrees of power. It wouldn't do to have magic be the determining factor in a sailing race."

"Sir Porbeagle mentioned a regatta during Autumnal Fest, but I didn't see a time on the schedule."

Wrapping her arms around her middle, she huddled into her life vest. "They wait to decide the day based on the best weather."

"That doesn't give the competitors much time to prepare, much less hear about it."

"Word gets around fast in a small community. You're either ready, or you're not. It's better to have a decent wind than none." She waved a hand at their half-filled sail.

His lips twitched. "What do you suggest?"

"You're at the helm."

A laugh burst from Ty, and her heart leaped. *Flights!* He positively sparkled. A twinkling silver energy twittered around him, and Coral found herself grinning despite her earlier intention. *This is what it's supposed to feel like. With this boy, I could do...the things Lemon wanted to do.*

Maybe.

Ty's outburst subsided into a chuckle. "Ah, Coral, spoken like a—"

"Sailor," she inserted and with an impish grin added, "Now show me your stuff, sailor boy."

He grinned back.

Spells! Had she meant to flirt? *Calm, calm, just ride it out.* She ducked behind the mainsail to hide her smile, and Ty turned his attention to sailing.

They glided across the bay and docked in her family's visitor space—none too soon with the wind chilling their soaked clothes. She straightened her stiff knees and stepped shakily to the dock. Barely able to hold the mooring line, she tried to tie it off with numb fingers.

Footsteps sounded behind her. "Here, Coral." Piper grabbed the line and shoved a large warm towel at her. "Manta knew you'd be cold from that dunking, having no way to—"

Her frantic hand to his lips halted him. Piper looked stricken, and they both shot glances to Ty, but he didn't seem to be paying any attention. He turned from lifting the rudder and tugged the daggerboard out of place, exactly what needed to be done to store the boat.

"Sorry," mouthed Piper, before he leaned toward Ty. "She sent a towel for you, too."

Coral stepped to the center of the dock, dropped the towel and stripped off the life vest and wet clothes down to her bright blue bikini. No sense wasting the towel Manta had magically warmed for her.

Skipper dashed up just as she finished. He bumped his warm nose over her calves and pranced in place to tease her into lifting him. "I must be cold, if your nose is warm." She crouched to scratch his ears.

"Leave the pup, you're covered in goose bumps." With a flick of his hand, Salm levitated the towel and magically threw it at her. "Tomorrow, you better wear your wetsuit. Ty can borrow my old one, the green one from before I shot up a foot."

With jerky movements of her stiff arms, Coral swung the towel around her. Shuddering and closing her eyes, she snuggled into softness and apricots—Manta used the same soap Ma did. If only Ma were here to serve her a bowl of soup to finish warming her on the inside. Sometimes, having no body fat wasn't fun.

"Hoy, lad," Salm snapped. "Just remember that's my sister you're gawking at."

Her eyes flew open as both Salm and Piper laughed. Towel around his shoulders, Ty bent over their dock locker, but his reddening neck confirmed her brother's implication.

Coral stalked toward Salm and, in the middle of him taking the sheets from Piper, punched him in the arm. "Stow it," she growled.

He laughed. "Try telling me again when you're not holding a towel over yourself." He jumped back as she aimed a kick. "And when you're wearing boots. Come now, Coral, I wouldn't be much of a brother if I said naught. Now I've said it, and you can do with him as you please."

"Oh, lovely." She recrossed her slipping towel and anchored it under her folded arms. "Just announce it to everyone." Her gaze skimmed to Ty, who was leaning against the locker and once again watching her, his silver eyes shining and his mouth curled at the corners.

Spells! She'd wondered if he was interested. He might be blushing, but there was nothing shy about the way he looked at her.

Heat flushed across her neck to cover her face. It had happened again, this funny sensation. Magical or not, this wasn't the place to sort it, or the smile twitching at her lips.

Ty returned the smile, stood and extended a hand to Salm.

"Thanks," he said as they shook. "Having three sisters myself, I understand the role. Please let me know if I overstep any boundaries again."

"Ach, we don't want you looking to Salm for that," said Piper. "Manta will tell you."

"Excuse me." Coral inserted herself between her brother and Piper, both a head taller than she and Ty. "This is my business, and as usual you all don't need to be butting into it like cleaner wrasses. Salm and Piper, would you be so kind as to finish for us? I'm going to see if Manta has something warm to eat. Ty, would you like to come, too?"

His gaze darted to Piper and Salm, but he said, "Sure."

"Let's go." She pushed past Salm, scooped up her wet clothes and briskly led the way off the dock. Truth be told, she wasn't very cold anymore.

TOO MUCH DOESN'T DO IT

Under the pretense of magicking his clothes dry, Ty delayed to calm himself before he followed Coral's towel-clad form up the ramp. She'd invited him home. Well, not exactly home, but to her sister's place. Marissa had never included him with her family, so maybe this was a good sign. Plus, Coral had asked despite her damn brother outing him for ogling her.

His neck and face heated again. This family didn't hide much. Coral was as *feisty* as Dar had said she was.

When they arrived, Coral ran upstairs to change, leaving him to help Manta take hot biscuits from the oven. The scent of buttery flour made him realize he was hungry, but worse, that he missed eating with his family. Piper returned and so did Coral, and Manta served fish stew and honey with the biscuits.

It was as comfortable as being at home. The four of them laughed about the dunking and how Piper's new sign was left magically suspended, but no one caught his use of magic. Because Salm had gone to Luna's, the conversation took no wild turns, and Ty's body spared him more bouts of blushing. Yet his thoughts kept circling back to Coral's magic—or rather, the lack of it. Why couldn't he feel her energy? Hers *had* to be triggering his urge to touch her.

Unfortunately, his job at Dar's couldn't wait. "I have to go milk some cows," he told them. "Thanks, Manta, for the wonderful dinner."

She smiled. "A hearty snack, really, to stave off the water's chill. You're welcome."

Coral rose when he did. "I'll walk you out."

His heart skipped a beat.

But once through the front door, she drifted to the railing overlooking the smooth surface of Tern Bay at low tide. He had a few minutes, so he joined her to watch the sun making its way down and the shadows lengthening across the beach below.

Coral sighed. "It's so pretty here. The sunset tonight should be a good one."

"You must see plenty of sunsets living on a ship."

"Aye, but rarely over still water. It'll be a double one with the reflection."

"If I hurry, can I make it back in time to watch? Milking takes about an hour and a half."

She shook her head. "It'll set faster than that, and I'll only have time for a glance myself, what with helping Manta prepare the bakery for tomorrow's business. Afterwards, I'm free to go on board to fetch my wetsuit and one for you as well for tomorrow's lessons, if you'd like to borrow one."

"I would. Could you wait and take me onto your ship?"

She didn't answer. Was that too intimate a request since her family lived on board? Just when he was about to apologize, she said, "Aye, that would be fine."

Still, it was awkward, and both of them averted their eyes. Then something touched him from behind.

His energy rose before he confirmed it was only her fingertips brushing his sleeve. Too late, he was shifting to a guarded stance with his hand outstretched, a honed reaction to years of magical defense training.

Coral snatched her hand back, her eyes wide with alarm.

Argh, how could he? Here, and with her? Mind reeling, he dropped his glowing hand and straightened to a position not so…adversarial. But his energy refused to back down. It hummed through his channels, fighting to shimmer through his skin. No way he wanted that to happen. It'd be worse than blushing.

"Uh, sorry," he said. "You startled me." And confounded him. No energy had emitted from her…so, was something wrong? With her? With him? Had he been reading her wrong and she *didn't* like him?

She waved her hands, palms out. "I didn't mean to," she mumbled, her gaze flitting over his chest and avoiding meeting his. "I wanted a closer look at your shirt. What do you call this material?"

"My T-shirt?" Was that all she was interested in, the difference in their clothes? "It's knit cotton. I noticed no one wears it here."

"We get all our clothes local, made from linen. Is cotton comfortable?"

Okay, his energy was still zinging uncontrollably, but he could handle talking about clothes. After all, he had three sisters. "Yes, it is. Would you like to try it on?" *Hell!* Where had that come from?

Coral frowned. "Why would you offer that?"

"I, uh, maybe when you're wearing that itty-bitty bi—I mean, your swimsuit—we can switch shirts." He wanted to see her in the bikini, but did he have to tell her? "Or not. Just wear your suit." Damn. He'd spent too much time with Marissa and her innuendos. How could he recover from his energy carrying away his mouth? "I suppose you made it also?"

Coral blinked. "No, my mother brought them back for us

from Greece last year. She said they were quite popular at Illusion Island. But..."

He prepared for a smart rebuff from this girl, tamping his silver as best he could. Then she didn't say anything, and his energy wouldn't let it go. "But what?"

"Why would you care if I wear the bikini again? I have naught to show off, compared to some witches."

Ty burst out laughing. Indeed, the Seas were an outspoken family, so unlike his. She looked annoyed, but he couldn't help himself. "Same as not showing off this power you supposedly wield? The one you're cleverly keeping from me. Why is that?"

She bit her lip. "You don't use magic much yourself."

"No? I used it last night more than I have since moving here. Dar told me I'd be on the street if I blew off Tern Bay's rules. He and the cows don't have time to deal with the hired help being in trouble."

"I don't understand the 'blew off' part, but old Dar has hired many a local wizard, only to let them go."

"It means not sticking to the rules. I try to, except..." He grinned. "When I need to help out a friend. But I can't risk being let go. I won't slink back home to Colorado. If I don't earn an income, it's beans for dinner."

Coral nodded. "The same position Salm will be in soon, but we say 'kelp for dinner.'"

The conversation had gotten sidetracked. "Why are you hiding your magic from me?"

Her smile faded. She turned and gripped the railing, her gaze fixed on the horizon.

He'd made a mistake. They might be becoming friends, but she must not share his excitement to perform an energy check. Or even confide in him. He was pushing things, like Marissa had.

Oh hell. This had too many similarities to that relationship, but on his side this time. He was the older of the two of them.

The more magically trained and skilled. And very likely, the more experienced in other areas, thanks also to Marissa. He grimaced at what was now a bad memory.

Coral was nothing like Marissa. She was sweet and honest and, from what he saw, worked to earn what she had. He shouldn't push her, and he certainly shouldn't push himself. Until he'd met Coral, he hadn't missed having a girlfriend. He had to be sure on every level this time. He glanced at her.

A frown marred her pixie face.

He needed to leave, to give her space, to get his head back, using any excuse. Cows were a good one. Tapping the railing with his fingertips, he leaned closer. "Sorry to make you mad. Your magic is your business. I better get to the milking."

She rubbed her hands together. "Are we still on for later?"

"The ship visit? If you want to."

"Aye, sure. Why not?"

"Well..." He waited for her to say, *Don't bother*.

"I'm not mad. I just don't...feel like myself."

"From the cold water? Maybe tonight's not great to get the suits, then," he said, trying to keep the regret from his voice.

"Nay," she blurted. "I mean, aye, it is. You want to see the ship. Tomorrow, I have to work all day. Then you have the deliveries. Getting them then would cut into our sailing time, so tonight's the best time." She took a breath and smiled. "Really."

That was a lot of words to say yes, especially when she hadn't been talking much before. Maybe she did want to spend more time with him? *Just stow it already, dude. Witches like to talk.* "Okay, I'll be back." He nodded goodbye and walked away.

At the pink house, he checked to see if the alley was empty and sidled into the shadow of the planter box. "Get a grip," he muttered. He flexed his fingers and released his quelled silver. It flashed, loose and sparkling for a moment, and then sank back into his skin. Everything in his channels calmed to a near-normal flow.

Curses on his reactions, and on Marissa and her blue energy. Except, he could blame only himself for developing a fondness for blue merging. For merge they had, over and over, until he was willing to say yes to whatever she asked of him, because combining their blue and silver energies had worked better than any of his merges with yellow, orange or green energies.

Coral had to carry blue energy, as much as her presence cranked up his energy. But clearly, the witch wasn't going to tell until she was ready. And that wasn't today.

Groaning, Ty checked left and right and defied the town rules again by using his peregrinator. He landed at the gate leading to Dar's farm outside of town and began jogging down the lane. What he really needed to do—go off to the moor and throw out energy balls—he couldn't. Not with the cows waiting.

One of those brown and white cows spotted him. It called out a long deep *mooooo*, which set the others to lowing.

"Hold on, I'm coming." He ran to open the barn. A piece of paper fluttered on the smaller door recessed in the larger one. The note read:

I have gone to help Scallop ready her wares for the Fest. I trust you can handle the beasts on your own. See you in the morning. Dar.

Ty stared at the cows crowding the fence in the adjacent pasture. This presented possibilities. Heck, Dar wouldn't care. He used magical touches to move the cows from the field to the milking room and out again.

Giving a little smirk, Ty flung his arms wide. Shots of silver streamed out in quick succession. The barn doors flew open, the solar-powered lights surged on, and deep inside, the engine powering the milking machines rumbled. The pasture gate unlatched and yawned open, letting the cows shove through. He counted off ten and pointed his finger. Another silver stream coalesced into a bar of glowing light to block the rest.

Flicking energy blobs from his fingertips, he directed the first group inside. He might see some sunset color after all.

13

SHOWING OFF THE SCHOONER

Donning a robe, Coral stepped from the tiny bathroom into the rest of Manta's big surprise—a new guest bedroom in the attic with the most luscious four-poster bed tucked into an added dormer. A *double* bed, huge to a girl who slept in the smallest cabin on *The Peaceful*, with only a bunk, clothes storage and enough space to turn around.

Salm was sure to squeak when he found out about the attic room. Already, the bilge rat had asked to live at Manta's to be closer to Luna. The answer had been a firm nay. Manta and Piper didn't want a permanent roomer. But for this week, the guest retreat—with built-in cabinets sporting Manta's pretty touches of seaside paintings, starfish and candles, and the glorious bed with shell-patterned sheets and a yellow comforter —was hers.

Coral grabbed her brush from the counter and rushed to recheck the view over the window seat. The bay had indeed remained still, and like a dark mirror, it reflected the lit clouds. The boardwalk below was busy with folks, but not—

"You goose," she told herself. "'Tis too early for him to have finished the milking." She'd hesitated when Ty had first asked to go onto the ship alone with her. His weird energy had looked so risky yesterday, but after a few hours of sailing and having him at the table with her family, he seemed normal. Fun. Charming. Er, too charming. Sighing, she sank onto the seat to brush out her hair. Manta had known him a month and trusted him, so she'd give him a chance.

He lived alone—or pretty much alone, as everyone knew Dar's arrangement with Ms. Scallop. Shrimp had said Ty had naught to do with the Tern Bay kids or the moor. How did Ty spend his time? On the farm? Did he do stuff with anyone… with a prebond? He was old enough, seventeenth year…

Spells. Her imagination was soaring with the gulls, as Ma would say. *He'd* made no reference to a prebond. And while he hadn't *directly* suggested an energy check, what else could all those questions about her magic mean? Was he determining if her energy was worth stealing?

Manta trusts him.

Coral threw down her brush. Did she even want to check a silver wizard's weird energy? Everything else about Ty Sterling was so intriguing. If his energy was any other color. Or if she didn't have a quash! Giving a boy a show of her magical interest had always worked… Hoy, it hadn't *worked*, just started things off. She still hadn't prebonded with anyone.

She split off a section of hair, and her fingers flew into braiding, working in one, then another of the macramé twists she'd left on the seat. Ty was as smooth as his shirts. He always knew what to say and presented a blank face when she most wanted to detect his feelings. Without her magic, she couldn't act her usual self, or speak without thinking. Thank the Orb her work at the bakery was limiting contact with the other duelists.

"Coral?" Manta called from the door down on the second floor.

"Come on up."

Her sister ran lightly up the stairs. "Ach, would you look at these bits o' broken color? I don't get up here often enough to enjoy the effort we put into it."

Coral glanced to the lights dancing about the ceiling from the fancy half circle of stained glass at the top of the window. "Looks like when we chase escaping energy at the isle's rips. We could use an extra hand when you're out next. It's taking all of us." Coral lifted her chin to the clothes Manta carried. "What are those for?"

"Blouses and my nicer shorts that I thought you might want to borrow to wear around town."

Coral caught her lip while finishing her last braid. "Maybe."

Manta's violet eyes lit up. "Try them, please? Ma would love to see you out of Salm's old dungarees."

And she'd love for Ty to see... "Not a word to Salm. Or Piper. If they embarrass me in front of Ty, I'll—" *Spells*. What would she do?

Manta patted her knee. "Naught will be said about your attempt to catch Ty's eye. Leave that to me. Try the blue one. It'll bring out your eyes better than it does for me."

Rising, Coral turned and shed her robe. She flipped the blouse around her back and slid in an arm.

"Coral!" Manta gasped. "Don't you have a bra?"

"Why?" She rolled her eyes. "The little I have stands up all by itself." She began buttoning under her sister's disapproving gaze.

"That's not the point. Have you no modesty? People can tell if your—"

"Nothing sticks out, Manta. Not a thing." Coral sagged down onto the seat, folded her arms over her flat chest and stared out the window. "Not my chest or my hips or my bum. Nothing sticks out on me to say I've become a woman. If I didn't have long hair, most people would think I'm a boy."

Manta sighed. "Many people would be happy with a body like yours."

"Ha, they should try it, then. It gets cold too easily and over-looked too often." She frowned at her sister—Manta had changed from her loose bakery uniform to a fitted floral dress. "I would be happy to have one like yours, a little more rounded in all the right places."

"You're a very pretty girl, and Ty is not overlooking you."

"I'm not sure Ty wants more than sailing lessons."

"But you said—"

"I know I did." Coral swiped a finger over her watery eye. "Maybe it's all wishful thinking. I want to find the right partner so bad, I sometimes—" She jumped up and grabbed the breeches she'd worn earlier. As she bent to step into them, the trousers flew out of her hands and into Manta's. Instead, her sister held out a pair of white shorts.

She took them. "Do you really think it will help?"

Manta rolled her eyes. "I'm with Ma on this—you shouldn't be in a hurry to prebond. But I remember how tough it is to be on the move on *The Peaceful*, so aye, I believe different clothes will help." Manta folded Salm's old breeches. "Where does your wishful thinking lead you?" she asked.

Manta understood how lonely it was. Coral stepped into the shorts. "Imagining the boys are saying things they are not," she muttered. *And doing things they are not.*

"Daydreaming doesn't hurt. But you must be careful to not run away with dreams. Like last year." Manta nodded. "You went too far trying to convince Beri—"

"Drop it," snapped Coral.

"Fine, but I hope you take this week without mag—er, take this week to change your patterns. Listen to this fellow and really hear what he has to say."

Coral zipped the shorts and fixed her sister with a frown.

Manta laughed. "Sounding like Ma, right? Got it. Let's get on with your new look. Sandals?"

"In my bag." Coral picked up the small rope pouch she'd

brought from the ship. Digging through the magicked interior, she removed three shirts and a pair of breeches before she found one sandal and then the other.

When she held them up, Manta had on her disapproving look again. "You sneaked a spelled bag out after Ma forbade your use—"

"She knew. It's the only one I brought, so she had to know."

"Did you work that into the shopping bags you made for me?"

"No, they're plain rope bags."

"Well, not so plain. I really like their wave patterns, as do others. Today, two women asked where I'd gotten my bag and then wanted to know if you had more to sell. I said I'd find out."

"Really? Do you think I could? Then I'd have more exchange notes to put toward my ship."

"You could. Think about the time it takes you and materials and come up with a price. I can help, if you want. Talk them up, too."

"Thanks." This could be really exciting, to go into business for herself. She slipped on the sandals and smoothed the hem of the blouse over the shorts.

"These are nice. Much smaller than Salm's breeches." A thought occurred to her. "Hey, what are you doing with shorts? I didn't see you wear them all summer."

"I wear them to the beach, when we manage to get there." Manta cast a critical eye and signaled Coral to turn. "This is what I was talking about, clothes that reveal your figure... Still a little large." She flicked a stream of violet magic, and the shorts tightened. Manta gave a satisfied nod. "They look good on you. I'll take you to this shop up the coast when Fest is over."

"Thanks. But..."

"But what now? He's going to be back soon."

"I like the blouse, but I'm going to be cold. I'll have to wear a sweater or cape and ruin its slender look."

Manta looked at her speculatively. "I have an idea, if you'll do one thing."

Coral groaned. "A bra. You're going to talk me into wearing a bra, I can tell."

Waiting in front of the bakery, Coral had to agree this was a look Ty couldn't ignore. Instead of the blouse, Manta had let her wear one of the fancy angora sweaters she'd bought from Ms. Scallop. Coral fingered the edge of the soft fuchsia neckline and stopped herself from adjusting it again. Manta said doing so would just draw more attention to it. Ach, she never wore tops with dipping necklines or ones so clingy they showed her figure.

Her figure. Ha. Her current curves came from the cinch gathers of the sweater and Manta's padded bra, magically sized down to fit her. Manta wouldn't make it any flatter, even after Coral had told her Ty had seen her in the Grecian bikini and would know this wasn't real.

"You've got imagination, *he's* got imagination. Give the fellow something to work with, Coral," Manta had said and pushed her out the door.

The milking must be finished. The sun had set, but the clouds still held their colors. Townsfolk strolled the boardwalks in the balmy evening. Others prepared for Autumnal Fest by stringing golden lights on rooflines. A family was outlining their boat rigging, the two kids flying with loops of light, while their dad bellowed directions from the deck.

In the quiet, another set of footsteps approached, and someone cleared their throat. Ty.

Coral steeled her stomach that churned in an unladylike fashion and turned from the railing. "Hi."

His combed hair was wet, and he'd changed into blue canvas trousers, this time with a dark red shirt tucked into them. More of the same soft knit material she longed to run her fingers over.

"Hi." He passed a look over her before transferring his gaze to the sky beyond. "Pretty...uh, the sunset must have been pretty tonight. Sorry I'm late."

Huh? He wasn't going to say anything about the way she looked? Spells, it wasn't worth the trouble to get boys to notice these things. "Are you ready to go to *The Peaceful?*"

"I am. Lead on."

With Ty's soapy scent filling her nostrils, she walked beside him through town and then onto North Dock. Coral's brain whisked through all kinds of reasons he hadn't noticed or commented on her appearance, while keeping her gaze straight ahead. Her racing mind slowed, and a thought popped in: *We aren't courting.* She had some stuff to get from the ship, and he wanted to see it. Although he'd showered, he probably did that after work.

If only she and Ty had already prebonded. They could be walking along the beach, or flying out over the ocean, hand in hand, searching for a dolphin to play with. But they weren't. Maybe he was mad—oh, maybe he'd jumped to the same conclusion when she hadn't talked? "You're not saying much. It's getting late, I suppose, for a dairyman."

"I got caught up in my thoughts." A smile twitched at his mouth. "I'm not mad, just not feeling myself. Whereas you look like you're feeling much better."

"Er, good. I mean, I am." So, was that a compliment on her outfit?

"It's beautiful," he said, raising her hopes. "The schooner."

Sheesh, it wasn't about her.

"How big is she? Seventy-four feet?"

"Her length is ninety feet." They had arrived at *The Peaceful Seas'* gangway. "Ma and Pop bought her when they bonded, so they've owned this schooner nearly thirty years."

"Was it new then?"

"Used, like one Salm has his eye on. A local builder crafted her in the 1960s based on a classic '30s design, but modernized the keel for speed and stability in rough seas. A double-masted is sailable by two, but easier with a crew of three to four."

"They must have known what they were doing. How old were they?"

"Twenty, but both had come from sailing families. Pop's older brother Ray and his partner stayed alongside them for a month or so. That's what we did with Wind and Bass—my oldest sister and her partner—when they first got their sailboat a few years ago. Come aboard."

Instead of turning on the power, Coral lit kerosene lanterns for them with the box of matches they kept in a cabinet near the helm. As she thought he might, Ty liked the old-time accessories that went with the original schooners, though they certainly didn't use whale oil.

She took him from stern to bow. It soon became clear he knew the name of every part, through book learning and the tour ships he'd been on in Florida. Of course, he'd been restricted by the rules on those tours. Tonight, he was free to open every hatch, ease along the polelike bowsprit, inspect their wind turbines mounted off the railing and sort how the lines and pulleys raised the sails. She laughed, finding herself strangely drawn by his enthusiasm.

He peered upward, swinging his lantern aloft. "Do you mind if we hover up to take a closer look at the ratlines and boom?"

Orb curse it! It hadn't occurred to her he'd request *that*. "Nay. I mean, aye, I mind. Another day? 'Tis getting late. Manta is expecting me back, d'ye ken? We have work in the morn'. You have work in the morn', so 'twould be best to fetch the wetsuits and go."

He was watching her intently. Coral lowered her lantern, and their faces fell into shadows.

He shrugged. "Okay. The thick accent is telling me something's bothering you. I'll come back another day, as long as you're happy. Where do we get the wetsuits?"

He wanted her happy. What did he mean by that? "There'll be plenty of time after Fest for all the lookin' you need," she threw out and darted toward the companionway at the back of the deckhouse.

Down in the main cabin, Ty dawdled in the salon, looking around the living area and galley while she darted into the fore passageway and opened a storage locker. By the time he caught up—carefully stepping through the ship's bulkheads with their raised thresholds—she had the wetsuits. She handed Ty a green one.

"This is Salm's, but there's another here." She pulled a black one off a hanger. "You may as well try them on and pick the best. Use Salm's cabin."

She showed him the hook to hang his lantern. As he closed the door, she shuddered. That was close. She'd nearly had to tell him about her punishment-related quash. That'd be embarrassing. She couldn't imagine Ty ever being in trouble. He always seemed so diplomatic and confident.

With a shake of her head, she scurried into her cabin and hung her lantern. She didn't want to tell until she was sure of what he thought of her. Following Manta's advice, she collected the few feminine pieces of clothing she owned. She needed her cape, too. The autumn weather had turned chilly.

"Hey, Coral? This green one fits me. You want me to rehang the black one?"

"Aye, thank you," she yelled before dropping to her knees to get the box of cord stashed in her closet. If she took it to Manta's, she could start on another rope bag. She shoved aside the boots and stuff and lifted the box.

"Here," Ty said behind her, "let me help."

She whirled as his foot swung over the magicked bulkhead. "Stop!"

He froze as she scrambled up. How long had he been there? "Go! Quick!" She threw herself against his chest.

"But, I—sorry—ahhhhh!"

They stumbled through the doorway, and he tripped over the wooden edging. Down he went, grabbing her arms and carrying her over with him. They fell together, her on top. She pushed up to sit, then pivoted and checked his feet. Out. "We made it. We're safe—no flash."

"No flash?"

"We didn't trigger the alarm." At his confused look, she added, "The *magic* alarm on my cabin. I'm not allowed to have boys in there."

Ty burst out laughing. "Your parents worry about you having boys in your cabin, but this is okay in the passageway?"

She frowned at him. "Ye dinnae ken my parents. 'Twould net me serious punishment."

That made him laugh harder.

If he were Salm, she'd cuff him. Since he was nearly a stranger, she held back, barely. She placed her hand down to brace herself to stand and, for the first time, looked at where she sat.

No wonder he was laughing. She straddled his legs.

Ty levered up on his elbows, his face within a foot of hers. "No alarm will sound out here?"

Her heart pounding in her ears, Coral stared into those liquid silver eyes before dropping her gaze to his lips. They were thin, stretched in a grin over his straight white teeth. The whole sweet parcel came closer, his lips pursing.

He was going to kiss her. *Kiss her!* Coral's lips parted, her breath caught.

"Coral?" someone bellowed from a distance.

They startled apart. Her ears picked out the footsteps on the gangway. On *their* gangway.

"Your father?" Ty whispered.

"He'd be safer," she muttered and rolled off him. It was Spike. And likely Lemon, too. Leaning against the wall, she covered her eyes with one hand. Why did these things happen to her? She should report them to the town elders for trespassing. Or get Salm, Manta or Piper to. But she couldn't, because Spike and whoever else was with him were also duelists, and if they got in trouble with the authorities, they'd find a way to drag her down with them.

Her parents would then…the feeling of walls closing in set her heart racing.

"We know you're there," called another fellow. Tiger.

"Who is it?" said Ty.

She took a breath. "Spike and Tiger."

"Are they why you're not allowed to have boys in your room?"

"No!" She lowered her hand to glare at him. "Watch what you're implying. It's Manta's fault I'm stuck with an alarm. Later, I'll tell you why, but now we need to get out of here." She eyed his hand resting on his knee and, drawing a breath, covered his fingers with hers. His skin was warm, and he smelled as sweet—*not now.* "Can you use your peregrinator and take us back to the bakery?"

Tilting his head, Ty listened to the tromping of feet on the gangway—probably Pearl and Olive were along—and gave her a speculative look. His fingers twitched, but he didn't draw back his hand.

Her stomach knew that type of calculating look. He was trying to figure out what she wanted so he could ask for something in return. Pretty quick, he'd think to ask, *Why is Tern Bay's top duelist afraid to meet her competition?* She should just tell him. Just tell him right now. "I-I want to report people trespassing."

He took the globe from his pocket and offered it to her. "First, shouldn't we get a look at who's here?"

"No!" The cry burst out louder than she'd intended.

The feet stopped, and a laugh carried to them. "Aye, you must be in there."

Spike. Coral's stomach lurched.

Ty shifted and folded up his knees, pulling his hand away. She grabbed his long fingers and clutched them with both of her hands.

Oh Blessed Orb, this was pitiful. She swallowed as he stared. "I can't work it."

"Then come with me to check them out."

"No—I—" *Spells*, there was nothing for it but the truth. He'd probably laugh and leave her here. Well, she could shimmy out the window, drop into the bay and swim ashore. She shivered. *Spells*, she didn't want to think about the state she'd be in once she got there, but she'd prefer hypothermia to her trapped energy getting fried by Spike.

She raised her gaze to tell Ty, but his open mouth stopped her. He shook his head and pressed his lips together, clearing his throat.

Thump! Someone hopped onto the deck. The walls vibrated as another person dropped overhead. *Plop! Plop!* She counted. Five…six…seven. Orb curse it. With this many, Octo and Shrimp had to be in the group, too. She let go of Ty's hand and got her feet under her. So did he.

"Coral, come on up," Spike called. "All we want to do is talk to you."

Their shuffling feet sounded like scraping amidships, still near the gangway. No one headed around the deckhouse to the companionway. Going below on someone else's boat was an even more serious violation of privacy than coming aboard without permission. In case they did, the windows were larger and easier to jump out of in her parents' stateroom. She stood up, feeling like an octopus was squeezing her lungs.

"We're waiting." Spike's taunt sailed clearly through the hatch.

Ty had risen beside her. "Do they really want to talk? It's not an excuse that we should check out before we pereport?" he asked at her ear.

"I'm afraid to." She steeled herself and whispered, "M-my magic is q-q-quashed. So, um..." She shrugged and stumbled down the passageway, through the salon and into the stern. Almost to her parents' stateroom, Ty caught her elbow and stopped her.

His body radiated warmth at her back as she recurled her arms around her belly and studied her feet. He wasn't laughing, but she couldn't face him.

"That's why I can't sense its presence in you. I'd wondered why you had no response to me when I checked—" He didn't finish, but he didn't drop her arm either.

The octopus released her lungs, leaving Coral floating. He'd checked to see if she was interested in him. Here she'd been thinking he was switched off when it came to her. Face carefully blank, Ty waited for her to speak. My, this fellow was proper. Flashing a smile, she said, "Oh, I'm havin' plenty of response to you."

"Magical, silly." His fingers tapped lightly on her upper arm in a teasing way, and somehow they moved together, her chilled shoulder securely against his solid chest. The scent of cut hay wafted between them.

Suddenly, her breathing didn't seem quite right, and her whole body went strangely quivery. By the Golden Orb, her magic must be trying to break its bindings.

Nay, it couldn't. This was...other feelings.

"What are we going to do?" Ty's breath was warm against her braided hair.

"Hide?"

As another call came from overhead, he said, "I don't think that'll work."

"Could you pereport me out of here?"

"I could. Not sure it's the best solution. What if next time I'm not with you?" His other hand rose to her shoulder and squeezed, causing her knees to melt.

"I-I dinnae know."

"Do you always rely on your magic to get you out of sticky situations?"

She shrugged. It was getting hard to think.

"I saw a pretty spunky witch handling herself verbally yesterday at Fintail's. It impressed the hell out of me."

It did? "But there, Spike wouldn't dare do anything. Here, he might. I have no fallback plan."

Octo yelled, "Coral! Get yer bum out here, or we'll have to come lookin' for ya."

The scariness of the situation returned like a cold dunking. Swimming ashore still wasn't such a bad idea.

Ty turned her by the shoulders and arched his brows. "I can be your fallback plan."

She eyed him. "No offense, Ty, but there could be seven of them up there. You said you don't duel."

"Not the way you do, but I think I can hold my own and get us out of here, energy unfried."

Unfried. How did he know—

"Coral! Last chance." Spike this time.

Despite how inexperienced he might be, Ty offered to back her. Manta had said to listen to him, but the feelings he gave her were just as important. Turning toward the companionway, she shouted, "I'll be there in a minute."

"Attagirl." He squeezed her shoulders.

Right. "Could I, um, would you mind showing me this energy of yours we're relying on?"

"Looking for a little courage?"

She nodded.

Ty brought up his hand. Over his fingers, a miniature vortex of silver energy spun. He bounced the mass, and it settled into a lazy swirl within his palm, glowing brightly in the dark corridor.

It certainly appeared powerful, but did he know how to wield it? Coral flexed her fingers and stared into its depths. "It's a beautiful color and…strong looking."

"Touch it, if you like."

She started. An energy check? He looked dead serious, not teasing about her quash. She couldn't… Besides, wizards offered an energy check only if they intended to seek bonding with another, prebonding in their case. She didn't really know him that well. Those stories could be true that he was after her energy. "Nay, you aren't familiar with our ways, and we don't have time to be talking about it now."

"True." His energy snapped out. "We should head topside."

Coral wiped her sweaty palms on her shorts and nodded.

14

TAKING ON THE CHALLENGE

Ty drew his energy back into his hand as soon as Coral ascended the companionway. *Why did I open my big mouth?* Every time he thought he could relax, he screwed up. These wizards were not Terraqua wizards. Their Tern Bay rules were too particular, their people too cautious.

Or sometimes not cautious enough. Would they toss magic about on deck? He wouldn't think so, not in the middle of the populated harbor. He pulled his illegal peregrinator from his pocket. At least she hadn't asked where he'd gotten one. *Won't mention this again.*

It activated in his palmful of energy, and he visualized a spot off the hull. Cold air snapped at his ankles from the water below, and he shuddered at the thought of her swimming to shore. Now he knew why she'd considered it. No magic. Curses, that had to be scary around this crew. Later, he'd solve the mystery of how that image of her squeezing through a porthole and swimming had transferred to him.

Over the edge of the hull, he counted seven teens on the deck. When three of the boys swarmed into a hissed argument, Ty moved to the boom behind the mainmast's intersection, a spot thickened by the folded sail. The night had become shadowy enough to hide him, and the breeze had picked up, but not enough that he couldn't hear the debate about *matches* between Marlin-Spike, Lemon and a big guy Ty recognized: Octo, the expensive sailing instructor he'd turned down.

The others—the same ones who'd been outside the bakery last night—watched with halfhearted interest: Olive, Shrimp and his sister and the slouchy, dark-haired boy he'd heard called Tiger.

Coral appeared around the side of the deckhouse. She looked bored, which Ty knew was a bluff. Only the witches noticed her. They elbowed each other. With a glance at the boys' argument, the brunette sidled up to Coral, her long skirt swinging. After a moment's hesitation, Shrimp followed her.

"I kept telling them this idea smelt of rotten fish," she whispered with a crooked smile.

"Aye, Pearl was voted the one to fetch you from below," the boy added. "I decided to follow along to fetch *her* back up again. Mum would quash me if I let anything happen to her."

Pearl rolled her eyes. "They say they want to talk. Tiger and I will back you up on that." She smirked. "If Shrimp gives us a chance."

Oh man, the kid didn't deserve this name.

"Thanks." Coral smiled and wiggled her fingers as if she actually was running magic through them.

Pearl knocked Coral's shoulder. "I've missed you around."

"You look very pretty tonight, Coral." Shrimp gazed at her like an adoring puppy as they sauntered to midship. "Is that a new sweater?"

"Aye, it is. Thanks."

Ty pressed his palm to his forehead. She did look great, and he'd had plenty of time to compliment her. Instead, he'd analyzed her energy and tried to get a rise from her. Now he just wanted to stupidly shout, *She's with me.*

Okay, these guys weren't *against* Coral. Still, as she'd answered, Coral had casually scanned the deck. She was looking for him.

Pearl moved off to link an arm through Tiger's. Only the Golden Orb knew what they saw in each other. The pretty, tall brunette towered over Tiger's slouchy, shapeless form. Probably had an energy thing going.

These three were allies, so Ty could ignore them. That left four others: Olive. Spike. Lemon. Octo. Olive had come across as smart and shy the time Ty had met her, but that didn't mean anything away from her formidable aunt, Lady Anemone. Spike was boastful and pushy. As usual, Lemon looked majorly grumpy, and it wasn't early morning this time. He seemed the most volatile, with Spike coming in second. At the diner, Octo had come across as laid-back, a younger copy of Piper in his burly physique and same brown hair. Hopefully as reasonable.

His assessment done, Ty pereported to the shadows of the deckhouse—as if he'd also come from below—and walked up behind Coral. He lightly touched the small of her back, catching another whiff of apricots. He kept the peregrinator in his other hand, just in case.

Coral leaned into his fingers with a slight adjustment of her shoulders. Pride rippled through Ty. They were a team, and that made a silly grin—

"Hey, the fellow with the scooter," Shrimp said, snapping Ty's focus back. A welcoming expression crossed Shrimp's face an instant before he frowned, his gaze darting between Coral and Ty. Surprise, then anger flashed over his face.

They had everyone's attention now. Expressions shifted— some satisfied, some wary. The witches leaned together and whispered. The three boys resumed arguing.

Ty kept one eye on them, as well as the battle of emotions waging over Shrimp's face. Touching Coral might have been a mistake. Now as unhappy as Lemon, Shrimp might ditch his alliance with Coral, and if Shrimp was as strong as they all inferred... *Aw, come on.* Surely Shrimp was mature enough to know that Coral was too old for him. Yesterday couldn't have been the first time she'd turned him down.

Ty let his attention slip from the kid to the hostile males shoving past the others. Lemon turned to growl something at Tiger, who dropped his arm from Pearl and shook his head. He spouted something back, but Lemon had already moved even with Spike, who glared at Ty despite Lemon ranting into his ear.

They are about to erupt.

During his training, situations of open confrontation like these sometimes held more surprises than chase-and-hide ones —because you expected surprises when people were hidden. For the first time, someone was relying on Ty's training in a situation other than a practice exercise. His energy hummed, but remained controlled within his channels. He was only the fall-back plan. This was Coral's jurisdiction.

She held her ground, shifting into a disgruntled stance of fists on her hips and one foot forward.

The warlocks stopped a few feet off, putting Shrimp in the middle. He didn't step in either direction. Several looked from him to the burly Octo. Okay, more proof that no one wanted to mess with Shrimp, but why Octo when Spike had established himself as leader by demanding Coral come talk?

Spells, I don't know these duelists at all. He had to be careful, for Coral's safety.

She flicked her gaze over them. "Must be pretty important if you're seeking me out aboard our boat."

"Aye, we see ya are busy and will make this short." Octo nodded to Ty. "Yank. Gettin' yer act shipshape, I see." He peered down at Coral. "Spike and I had it out last night. It's now me ya will be meetin'."

"Fine," Coral said. "You may take his place."

"Aye, but he has no place. I wish to set one."

Leaving the touch of Ty's hand, Coral stepped past Shrimp and up to Octo.

Shrimp pivoted in his watch, expressionless. *Good competitor.*

"I'll explain it to you as well," she said. "I've promised my sister I'll be there to help her every day before dawn through Fest. I don't break promises. After Fest, I'll meet you."

Even though no one had said so directly, she was still agreeing to duel. Something in Ty couldn't let that go. "You've promised to help me after Fest," he said. *Please play along.* It was a vague suggestion; she could insert anything remotely appropriate.

Coral turned to stare at him. Ty leaned against a mast, forcing his body to relax and propping his elbows so his hands dangled, his energy ready. More important, he could see all of them at once and directed his slight smile at the taller and much bigger wizard over Coral's shoulder.

Octo eyed him, his chin lifted, eyes not blinking. Fine, that was fair. However, the look Ty garnered from Lemon was something else, narrow and intense. Hold it. Perhaps Lemon—who was older than Shrimp—actually did have a history with Coral. The instant the idea occurred to Ty, he knew that if this guy had any rank in their group, he'd have already challenged Ty. And blasted.

What *was* he getting into with this witch?

Coral pivoted back to Octo. "That's right, I did," she said nonchalantly.

"Could we complete our arrangements first?" Ty asked.

Octo opened his mouth, but Lemon pushed past him and stepped around Coral, knocking her shoulder. "What she does with us is no business of yours," he hissed down at Ty.

Ty didn't move a muscle under the towering blond wizard's stare. His energy shifted to the tips of his fingers, still concealed. Great, one of the crew was hyped, and neither of the leading duelists was calling for a stop. Octo huffed in irritation.

Spike stepped back, grinning broadly. The others jostled to the sides for better views, and Ty mentally ordered his blasts.

"It is now," he said. "She and I have a deal, and I'm not backing out. Besides, he said *he* was the contender." Ty lifted his chin toward Octo. He needed to appear to be unversed in this type of dueling. He wanted to keep this nonmagical as much as Coral did. "You his agent? Or his second, is it called?"

The grin fell from Spike's face at the same time a frown crossed Octo's.

"Nay." Octo shoved Lemon aside before the reddening guy could get out a word. "I handle my own business, as ya well know. Here's the plan. If I win, ya release her to settle with me first."

Ty considered it a moment, still watching Lemon from the corner of his eye. The guy stared at him, breaking off only when Spike nudged him. It might have been a trick of the few town lights, but he thought there'd been a yellow glow at Lemon's fist.

He'd have to watch his back—from two sides. Shrimp was standing at the group's fringe, with his arms crossed. Not at all the position of someone ready to leap to another's defense.

"What kind of a...competition do you have in mind?" Ty asked Octo.

"The only kind that counts, milkman. Or is yer magic as weak as yer drink?"

Trash talk. The big guy had an edge.

"Now hold on here!" Coral pushed herself between the two and shoved each back, keeping her hand on Ty's chest as she faced Octo.

Probably worried he'd gone further than he could handle. She really had no idea what he could do, or, he thought with a grimace, what he should and should not do. Blast it. He was letting himself get too caught up in this. And as Coral's sweet pixie face turned to him again, he knew why.

Ty pressed his lips together. He could not risk his Master Wizard status by getting involved in an illegal duel, tempting as it was.

"I am not a piece to be bargained for," she stated firmly. "I decide with whom I make deals and when."

"Aye?" Octo growled. "That's the danger of playin' with a wizard who does nae ken our ways. This lad seems to think ya are nae yer own *agent* anymore, and frankly, I'm happy to get in another practice while ya educate him."

Spike snorted. "Aye, Coral, perhaps you'll have more luck teaching him to duel than to sail."

Her eyes narrowed at the taunt. "Surely more luck than we've had teaching you to keep your mouth shut about...things."

Desperate to stop this from escalating, Ty grasped her at the waist. "I think our sailing lessons are going quite well. Perhaps that's the competition you'd like to take on?"

Everyone laughed—ridiculously hard—but the distraction broke them apart, and Coral flashed him a frown as Shrimp sidled up.

"Lad, I haven't seen you duel, but I have seen you sail. Take on the duel."

Curses, he wasn't that bad. Ty brushed by, pulling Coral along to square off with Octo. "Do you always handle these things through"—they'd now said it—"dueling? Seems to take the adventure out of the challenge."

Still laughing, Octo shook his head. "Ya are on, Yank. When?"

"How about this Fest regatta? I understand it's a straight sailing race, no magic allowed. That should put us on even terms."

"Aye, it *should*. The winner of the regatta, then, is entitled to Coral's time first."

"Agreed." Ty stuck out his hand, though the guy seemed too happy for this to be smart.

Eyes wide, Coral batted it down. "I am *not* the prize."

"A place in line with ya is the prize," Octo said.

"What if someone else wins?" Ty asked.

Octo had a quick answer. "Whichever of us fares better. Ya never know who'll come to regatta at Fest, so that's the only way to handle it."

"And what if I win?" Spike said. "She'll be back to dueling me."

Octo frowned. "Nay, make yer own deal. This one's mine." He stuck out his hand, and deftly avoiding Coral, Ty met it.

15

QUESTIONING THE STORIES

"I cannot believe you chose sailing," Coral whispered the moment her fellow duelists stepped off *The Peaceful Seas'* gangway.

"Neither can I." Salm's unusually quiet voice preceded him as he stepped out from behind the fore deckhouse, followed by Luna. "You have guts, mate." He clapped Ty on the shoulder, and Ty shrugged.

Salm grinned. "I like you. Clever way to keep Coral out of—" He shot her a questioning look.

She threw up her hands. "He knows. I was stuck and needed his help." She tried to glare at Salm, to show him and Ty and Luna that the trespassing duelists hadn't rattled her. But they had.

This could have been bad. Although Octo had done the talking, Lemon's scorching looks were burned in her memory. He'd almost blasted Ty, too. She knew the signs. Thank the Golden Orb for the jostling of boys. They'd distracted Lemon. Too many hormones in the lot of them.

"I wouldn't have had to tell Ty," she said to Salm, "if I'd known you were on board."

He held his hands aloft in surrender. "We weren't on board until you tripped the alarm. Why didn't you choose another spot, then you wouldn't have interrupted our—ouch!"

A flash of magic smacked Salm's shoulder. "Salm!" Luna hissed.

Ty stepped back and leaned against the mast again, arms crossed. Smart. He had a lot of siblings, too. He knew how to navigate rough waters.

Luna whispered in Salm's ear, and Salm listened in a way that he never would to Coral. She'd always liked Luna. Luna had sisters. She knew Coral was at her rope's end. And she took charge where Salm was concerned. She *looked* like she fit in with the enclave's folks, wearing skirts and such like Ma and Manta. But then there were times like now, when she released her white-blond curls from their usual tight band and they fell in a huge puff around her head.

"It was my fault," Ty said.

"Of course, it—" Salm choked off with a glance toward Luna.

Ty grinned. "Not what you think. I went in to help her lift a box. I had no idea being in her room was off-limits."

"Hoy," Coral said. "You think I'm stupid enough to invite him in and have Ma and Pop—say, they transferred the alarm to you?"

"Aye. An alarm for the entire ship. After you left, we figured it'd be a good idea, with Fest and all and me gone most nights. Sorry. Forgot to tell you."

"I bet," Coral snapped. That's right, she hadn't seen her doorway flash. Still…

"Should have been Manta," Salm was saying, "but she needs her sleep with the bakery. I should tell the council they trespassed. What do you think, since they're friends of yours?"

"Not all of them," Coral said. "Not anymore. But you can't. They'll drag me into it. Spike."

Salm side-eyed Luna and nodded. He understood with no more than that. Which brought them back to the alarm.

"You're nae nineteenth year yet. This is a stupid double standard that I can't be on the ship."

Salm pointed. "I didn't get in trouble for dueling."

"As if you never did it!" The blasted know-it-all. She swung her arm, fingers flung out, magic—

"*Argh!*"

He reflexively danced aside, chuckling when he realized no magic was loosed, but his hand had also risen, and Luna had caught it, silver energy flaring around her fingers.

Silver. Luna? Coral shrank back as Luna turned toward her—

But she sweetly asked, "Can I help you bring up this box?"

She stared into Luna's sympathetic gray eyes that she'd never given a thought to. With her nearly white hair and white wings, it all fit. "Uh, thanks," Coral mumbled and forced her feet to move toward the companionway.

She'd never considered what type of magic Luna wielded. Salm had never mentioned it—not that she was her brother's confidant—but he'd never allow his power to be stolen. He'd kept his interest in Luna secret until recently, and Coral didn't even know how they'd met. Luna and her sisters had never participated in Tern Bay's dueling. It probably wasn't easy to sneak off at night from a lighthouse keeper's family.

Below, Coral led the way down the fore passageway. Now that she knew Luna's energy color, did it change anything? Luna was serious and quiet, but nice. She'd told Coral she couldn't fathom the idea of living on a boat, but she'd said it politely.

Once in her cabin, Coral tossed the shoes and boots back into the closet and spotted another blouse to add to her pile. Luna took it, fingering the blue waves Granny had embroidered on the long sleeves and hem.

"Pretty. I haven't seen you in this. Will you wear it for Fest?"

"I could."

"Or to dress nice for this boy?"

Coral half hoped Ty wouldn't figure it out and half hoped he would. Since he'd mentioned her magical interest, he must be curious about getting involved with her. Could she confide in Luna? Coral slid her cape off the hanger. "Aye."

Luna smiled. "Splendid. Salm filled me in. I wish I knew more about him so I could help you, but we pick up our milk in town. These are all very pretty. You'll look delightful when he sees you."

"Maybe. Mostly, we're getting together to sail, so I'll wear a wetsuit."

"Just continue to wear the bikini under it for when you strip down."

Spells! Blabbermouth Salm always brought trouble.

Luna gathered up the clothes, her gray eyes quietly questioning. Coral bundled her cape in her arms. She should take a chance and trust Luna. After all, she couldn't ask the boy she was interested in if he would be safe. That seemed like sending a tuna to befriend a dolphin.

"There's another thing," Coral said. "I, um, noticed you have silver magic. Ty does, too."

Luna's eyes grew round. Coral felt sick, until a broad smile spread across Luna's face. "No wonder," she said mostly to herself and sank to the edge of Coral's bunk.

Coral sat, too, unsure what to make of this. "What do you mean?"

"Do you feel anything within your quashed energy?"

"I feel all kinds of *things*. Tonight, Ty admitted he's been looking for a magical response in me. But I've heard..." What was the nicest way to say this?

"Spill it," Luna said.

"That a silver wizard can take you over and steal your magic."

"Bullsharks. Old sailors' tales. I can no more easily control anyone than you can. Any wizard can steal another's power. That's why you must always know the person so you aren't left in a vulnerable position. I don't think you'll be placing yourself in such a position with Ty just yet." She tugged one of Coral's braids. "Will you?"

She grinned at the older girl. "I did plan to wait until I had my power back to check him out."

"Good. I recommend you keep your interactions magical at this point. Blue energy is very attractive to a silver wizard. I'm not surprised to hear he's approached you."

"What will happen to me when I touch his energy"

Luna grinned. "I noticed you said *when* you touch it, not *if*. You want to touch it?"

That warm feeling spread over Coral again. She rubbed her arms. "I do," she whispered. "I *really* do."

Luna nodded back. "That's the way I feel about your brother. I want to be with him, even though I'm so unsettled by the idea of living on a boat."

"Could you two put some wind behind your sails?" Salm called down the companionway. "The men in your lives are anxious to see you again."

Coral sprang up, ready to shout, but Luna caught her wrist.

"The short version is this," she said quickly. "If Ty is an honorable warlock, you have nothing to fear. You have checked out other wizards' magic?"

Coral nodded. "Manta taught me how to do it and guard myself."

"Then you know what it feels like regularly."

"Not what's *usual*. My energy is too jumpy to merge. We've only ended up with swirling, never even the start of combining to one hue. You've done this with Salm?"

Luna side-glanced at her. "Aye."

Well, Coral hadn't really thought her brother was off with

Luna just holding hands. Were they also, um... "Is it...is it like having sex?"

Luna rolled her eyes. "Now, how would I know, seeing as how we're not bonded and it's not allowed? Your Giuthas rules are much stricter than ours." She stood.

"You follow them rather than yours from the Tern Bay enclave?"

"My father is..." Luna turned to the doorway. "I don't wish to offend your mother. According to Salm, magical interactions can be tested before prebonding. Once your energy is unlocked, check out Ty. Merging isn't the intimate thing you're thinking. It's a different type of power to use for fun or whatever. Do you have all you need?"

Luna's firm change of topic, added to Salm calling down again, ended the conversation. They carried everything to the ladder, and her brother hauled stuff onto the deck. Once topside, Luna decided she and Salm would take Coral's things to the bakery, leaving Coral to put away the lanterns with Ty.

"Thanks," Coral whispered to Luna, hoping that relayed her undying gratitude for being left alone with Ty again.

"See you at Manta's." Salm smirked, as only her brother could. "Don't keep me waiting."

16

SETTING OUT THE RULES

After Coral put out the lanterns, she and Ty headed for the bakery. They didn't touch. They didn't talk.

The silence was driving her crazy. This wasn't at all where she'd seen things going when they'd been below, in the dark, hiding from Spike, and nearly—*Blessed Orb*. She had to say something before they went inside. If only her insides would unknot.

The bakery door opened, and Piper leaned out. Spotting them, he grinned and threw the door wide, gesturing them inside. "We're heating up some haggis for a late dinner. That soup's long gone."

She glanced at Ty and caught him looking at her before he hurriedly looked away. Hoy, she'd blown her chance to talk to him.

Piper led the way through the darkened shop and upstairs to their living space, where Manta held a fistful of silverware.

"Coral, would you set the table, and Ty, can you carry things from the kitchen?" She disappeared through the door without waiting for an answer.

Piper filled the water glasses, but as Coral finished the place settings, she realized Salm was nowhere around. He had to be in the kitchen with Manta—and Ty.

Her pulse jumped. *Flights, were they telling him off?*

Coral burst through the swinging door. Three heads swung toward her from around the island. Aye, a lowdown. And what else had Salm said to Ty on the ship when she and Luna had been in her cabin? She turned on her brother. "What are you saying to him?"

He lifted his hands, a serving dish in each. "How good Manta's cooking is."

She crossed her arms and fixed him with a look. "As if."

Her use of the city phrase they'd picked up last year broke her brother's poker face. Salm grinned in his annoyingly superior way. "Just the rules, babe, just the rules."

"I can do that myself!" It came out louder than she'd wanted.

"Aye, you *can*." He waggled a finger at the side of the applesauce bowl, and a wave of his energy pushed her aside so he could exit.

Coral clenched her jaw. It would be safer if she didn't respond. Her gaze shifted to Ty, who followed after Salm with the leftover biscuits.

He winked.

That flustered her more.

"We'll talk later," he whispered.

When the door closed behind him, Coral turned on Manta. "Did you have to?"

"Aye. He needs to know the isle's rules, Ma and Pop's rules. I don't want him to get in trouble with them because you get too excited and forget them." She opened the refrigerator.

Coral clenched and unclenched her fists before she asked, "What did he think?"

Manta put the butter and jam into her hands. "I don't know. He only had time to nod before you burst in. But my duty to Ma is done."

That her sister wouldn't continue to nose into her business with Ty was unusual for their family. Manta donned oven mitts and moved a pan from the hot oven to the counter. The heat and spicy scent of the meat pastry filled the kitchen, so like Ma's galley. "Uh, thanks."

"I'm still here if you need me, but you're nearly seventeenth year. I do remember handling my pre-prebond checks at that age." Manta smiled.

"And being oh-so-annoyed with Wind and Salm for tattling on you."

Manta picked up the haggis. "Exactly. Let's eat."

As soon as the meal ended, Ty excused himself. "I hate to be rude, but if I'm not to bed by nine, I won't be in the barn by four, and the cows will start calling. Dar hates that."

"No excuse necessary," Piper said. "'Tis nice to have company who keeps the same schedule."

"I'll see you out," Coral said.

Salm rose and shook Ty's hand. "See you tomorrow at noon, then."

"Noon?" she asked as they descended the stairs.

"Salm's going to show me your ship in the daylight. I hope you don't mind?"

"No, I'm surprised, though. He likes his sleep."

"He mentioned that, but he also wants me to win the regatta. He said he'd help with the lessons as well."

"Ah, you're lucky. He's a better racer than I am, and you do show promise. I'll ask what he has in mind."

"He'll wait until you get back?" Ty jerked his chin upward.

"Aye. He never misses a chance to poke at me."

Once she closed the bakery door, Coral didn't waste her new chance. "Tell me about being a silver wizard."

"My whole family is silver, except my dad, who's double— silver and blue. I don't know any different." Ty shrugged. "My energy has a strong defensive quality. It's calm and plays well with others."

"What?"

"Sorry. It's a phrase the humans use to mean getting along. Silver energy merges easily with most other types."

"I suppose you've tried merging with others?"

Ty nodded and stopped walking, looking toward the sea.

Coral folded her arms around herself. She didn't want to ask if those merges had been successful. In fact, she wished she hadn't asked. Time to get to her real question and see if there was any point to standing out here in the cold any longer. "Are you prebonded to anyone?"

Ty met her gaze. "No. I wouldn't have left Terraqua if I was."

Her body lightened at his answer. But again, Ty's face gave her no clue to his feelings, and something didn't feel right. "What did they tell you? My siblings."

"Holding hands and an initial energy exchange are fine. Beyond that, I better wait to talk to your parents and plan to make a trip to Magemoor with you. That's in Ireland?"

"Aye. The Isle of Giuthas enclave is part of the Ireland District. Until eighteenth year, Giuthas only allows prebonding, so that's what the application at Magemoor would be. If, uh, you would be wanting to do that with me."

"I'm…interested in talking about it more. I think two days of knowing each other is short to decide. Manta said the prebonding trial is four months?"

He is interested. Excitement thrummed through her. "Aye, that's the minimum before you can end it and prebond with another. The whole trial is a year, or until both are eighteenth year. But, um, did Manta and Salm tell you the rest?" Blast, she hated this. A shake of his head confirmed they'd left the awkward details to her. Or—Coral chastised herself—she'd interrupted before they'd had time to finish. This would drown his interest in her for sure.

"My family makes us wait until nineteenth year to go on to bonding. Life on the sea is not for the faint of heart, Pop says. His parents and his grandparents kept this tradition. He says before that, they lost too many youths who set out on their own too early and weren't skilled at decision-making to save themselves when their ships ran into trouble." Coral reeled off the story she'd heard all her life, the one she'd discovered that many hot and bothered boys did not want to hear, especially after they'd shared a few energy exchanges while pressing together more than their hands.

Instead of looking discouraged, Ty leaned against the rail as if settling in for more talking. What happened to getting home for the cows? He must not understand. Ty looked around, and she did, too. No one else was on the deckwalk right now.

"I wanted to believe that hide-and-seek game was what you call dueling," he said quietly. "It wasn't, was it?"

She shook her head. "I was hiding from them because of the quash. It's real dueling, in an arena, with referees."

He slowly nodded. "I have rules, too. About dueling. I can't."

The pieces came together. "That weird gel. Your peregrinator. And"—she shivered as she remembered the sight of it—"your powerful magic. You've finished academy. Your parents, didn't you say they're defense trainers?"

"They are. I'm trained, too. I know you asked me not to tell anyone about the dueling, and your group tries to keep it hushed, but maybe you aren't keeping it hushed enough? If the wrong person found out, you could be in serious trouble. Like, beyond Tern Bay's council."

"I know," she whispered. "Spike and Lemon... I've never seen any duelist act as crazy as they've been these last few months. Now that you point it out, aye, it makes sense someone could slip."

"I can't afford to get in that kind of trouble. Since we're

talking about prebonding, then you need to know that I can't if you continue illegally dueling."

No dueling? Not do the thing she was the best at, what made her magic soar?

"Sorry. I don't mean to make it sound like an ultimatum." He shrugged. "But you shared your restrictions, and that's mine. I can't be involved in dueling in any way. You should consider that before we discuss prebonding."

Aye, she would. "As long as we're making things clear," she said, "with prebonding, kissing and touching are permitted. Nothing more—no, um, sex."

"I get it. Like at Terraqua, you have to be bonded. But what about more magical stuff?"

"You mean a merge?"

"Yeah."

He still looked interested, but now she didn't understand. "That's allowed. You've merged your energy with others, so you've been prebonded."

"Er, no. In Terraqua, they're much looser with the rules. It's a huge wizard settlement, one of the largest. Meeting and merging with someone is easy without formally applying and all that."

It sounded so casual, even more so than Tern Bay's rules. "Your parents...?"

"They didn't know. I lived on my own in an apartment the last year. They let me move here alone. My family isn't like yours."

Her *interfering* family! She stamped her foot. "Blast it. If they had just kept—" *Quiet.* Face hot, she turned, feeling like running back to the bakery, but she made it only two steps. She didn't really want to leave, so she dropped her elbows to the rail and held her face in her palms.

A hand brushed her shoulder. "No, no, you misunderstood

me. I like it. They're keeping you safe." He laughed suddenly, a strange, awkward sound breaking from his throat.

She looked up. Was he being sarcastic?

Ty leaned beside her, elbow to elbow, not quite touching. His face—now a foot from hers—was eager and earnest. "You're a minor. Your parents and family should be involved. Then no one gets hurt."

A minor? Coral straightened and crossed her arms. "I'm not totally inexperienced."

They stared at each other for a long minute before he said, "I'm not going there. Sailing lessons at three when I finish the delivery?"

Of course he still wanted lessons. But did he see her strictly as an instructor, or also as a witch he wanted to know better? Or had all the rules and restrictions changed his mind? She started to ask, but she didn't want to head to bed with the wrong answer. "Aye, three."

His mouth crooked into a smile. "Good night," he said and walked off down the deckwalk.

Hugging herself, Coral walked back to the bakery. Had her family's attitude that she was the precious kid sister who needed protecting gotten a hold of Ty, too? Well, just wait until she got her magic back and showed sailor wannabe Ty Sterling exactly how safe she could keep *herself*.

17

A BREAK FROM THE USUAL

Hoist the mainsail! Batten down the hatches! Kiss the gunner's daughter!

From the moment Ty climbed aboard *The Peaceful Seas*, Salm had peppered his instructions with common nautical terms, weird sea references, pirate jargon and…bilge?

Salm greeted him with "Ahoy, matey," but was the rest of this bilge—Salm's term for foolish talk—really used by the Seas family? Everything with Salm was carefree and wild, and Ty's head swam until Salm finally admitted he was a drivelswigger— a reader of nautical adventures—which took his jests to another level.

Time raced by, and Ty thought he was catching on until Salm squinted at the sun and proclaimed, "Yer wench will be setting a school of piranha on your aft."

Ty checked the old brass compass they'd been using for the lesson, certain he must have mistaken the direction of the prevailing wind and would have some sort of sailor bad luck.

"Mate, 'tis time." Salm pointed to town. "Get to the bakery before Coral has a major hissy fit."

With a start, Ty's gaze jerked to his wristwatch. Two forty-five! Was she really the kind to pitch a fit? He bolted across the deck.

"Be there in a few minutes meself," Salm called. "We'll make short work of Manta's buns and continue your education on the *Midnight Marauder*. I bet my dear sister has forgotten we're to measure fat levels on the young'uns today."

Ty didn't wait to figure that one out. He sidled down the narrow gangway and took off running.

The handcart stood loaded and waiting at the back door, and as Ty charged up the alley ramp, Coral's voice came through the screen. "I do *not* know why I trusted him. Boys are all alike when it comes to being reliable. One minute, they promise faithfully, and the next, they have found someone better to do things with, leaving you hanging!"

Ty hesitated. Should he just take the cart and go?

"Shush, love," Manta said. "Plenty of time. We're done here now. Why don't you run down to the dock and fetch him? Salm probably has him anchored on *The Peaceful*, playing sailor, that's all."

"Fine. That'll give me a chance to give Salm a piece of my mind, stealing away *my* fellow just because he's free this week and I'm not."

Ty smiled. *Her fellow—wow.* But much more eavesdropping and he'd be demoted to Salm's level. He banged on the door. "Coral? You there? I'm sorry to be"—she appeared in the door-way, arms crossed and her nose wrinkled up—"late."

She sure was cute, covered in flour and wearing an apron several sizes too big...except for the irritated look she fixed on him.

"I'm not—" Shoot, he couldn't say *leaving you hanging* without her knowing he'd overheard. "I'm here. And Salm is coming. Can we split the two orders so each of us can take one? He said you're supposed to help him today, and I could continue my lessons on a different boat, the *Midnight* something."

Her hand flew to her mouth, and all trace of anger dissolved. "I forgot. We're to do the checks today." She whirled around. "Manta! Where is the other cart?"

Ty reviewed the order papers. Just as he and Coral had the trays split between the two carts, Salm came strolling up, and they left.

A half hour later, they climbed onto a larger sailboat than the Sunfish he and Coral had taken out yesterday. Luna joined them and took the helm of her family's boat, the *Midnight Marauder*. It had a mainsail and a jib, like he'd used on the 420 sailboat at home, but was several feet longer, so nicely sized for four.

"Ty, would you prepare for our departure?" Luna asked, as if he sailed with her all the time.

He glanced at Coral to get her reaction. She was his sailing tutor, and he did *not* want to mess that up—things had been going too well. They hadn't talked today, and her manner was still standoffish. Only because he'd been late? He couldn't be certain he hadn't missed something last night. Perhaps his dueling rules had changed her mind about him.

With an eye roll, she pointed to the lee side—where he *knew* he was to sit—and reached down to take a line, the jib sheet, and pass it to him.

Spells, he did *not* look that incompetent. Seconds later, Coral sat beside him—their life jackets almost touching—clearly planning to back him up. He followed Luna's directions without help, regaining his pride. Out on the open ocean, appearing stupid rewarded him: The hull bounced with the waves, and Coral slid against him.

Whoa! His energy jumped. Ty let it surge as they raced forward. The wind cooled his flushed face quickly with their growing speed, though his thigh against hers was plenty warm.

She didn't move away. He kept his gaze on the horizon, his fingers clenching the jib sheet and his ear tuned to Luna's directions. This promised to be an exciting ride.

Salm draped himself along the wide bow, binoculars trained on the horizon. "A little to port," he said, waving an arm. "I scouted them earlier and asked them to remain between the first headland and the end of the Isle of Giuthas. They were herding a school of tuna they didn't want to lose, with the young'uns and all."

Someone was netting fish, then? He'd thought this trip had something to do with marine life, but perhaps another boat was waiting? He couldn't see it from here.

"Affirmative." Luna made the adjustment. "Ty? You can take the helm and the mainsheet now that we're clear of the bay."

Well, here went nothing. While Luna shuffled closer to Salm, Ty performed the first zigzag tack maneuvers to sail upwind. He issued direction calls to Coral as she handled the jib and he manned the mainsail and tiller. She responded promptly, giving the appropriate calls back, and they sped out to sea.

The *Marauder* was a dream to sail, graceful and responsive. Of course, it helped that the wind blew at a steady seven knots, unwavering in its direction. Before long, he hit his rhythm. Only toward the end of his lessons in Colorado had he ever felt so one with the craft and his co-sailor, working as a team to harness the wind's energy. He kept his gaze fixed on the island on the horizon and floated in his success, his enthusiasm and body energy riding on high like the boat as it skimmed the water's surface.

Without warning, a spark shot off of him.

"Ow!" Coral snatched her hand back with a cross-eyed squint. "You don't have much control of that."

What had happened? Usually, he had perfect control. "Uh, sorry. I guess I was too wrapped up in sailing. Did I hurt you?"

Coral dropped her hand to her side. "Salm signaled to slow because we're approaching them."

Them? No boat was in sight, but Ty slackened the sail. Salm still peered through his binoculars, flicking a finger ahead, but not moving otherwise. Luna had stopped paying attention after she'd joined Salm on the hull, seemingly oblivious—or asleep—alongside him, her arm draped over him. Ty glanced at Coral for a clue. She was looking at him, but quickly turned away, her gaze falling to her hand again before darting to the horizon. Her thumb was circling over the tips of her fingers.

Had he burned her? On an impulse, he braced the tiller with his knee and drew her arm to him. She gasped, her eyes flitting everywhere but to him.

"Slow the boat more," she whispered, as if telling him a secret. She blushed a bright red.

He eased off on the mainsheet.

"I didn't mean to. You can have it back." She rolled her hand palm up. Pinched between her fingers and thumb was a ball of silver energy.

He stared at the swirling magic, a small amount, just bigger than a marble and definitely his. "How?"

She shrugged. "It leaped. I didn't mean… I don't want you to think I *took* it. I have no power to do that, so, um, here." She pushed the miniature energy ball at him.

He made no move to take it. "No, of course not. I know you don't. I—"

"Stop!" Salm barked.

They jerked upright. But Salm wasn't looking at them. Ty's gaze darted to Coral, and they both sagged in relief. Geez, he was nervous.

"This is far enough," Salm called back. "The wind will carry us the rest of the way." He glanced over his shoulder, did a double take and grinned broadly. With a wink, he turned away and whispered to Luna.

Ty let the mainsheet go, and Coral did the same with her line. The sails swung around until they hung limp, and behind them, Coral shoved the little ball of magic forward again. "It's yours, and I haven't a right to be having it. I thought about what you said last night. Days ago, I was upset not to be able to duel. I love it." She licked her lips. "I *loved* it. Now, I'm not sure it's so important."

Time to take another chance. His energy obviously felt he'd waited long enough. Drawing her hand into his, Ty folded her fingers over his energy. "Keep it, would you? I didn't send it over. My energy chose to check you out. I, um…it, um—" Shoot. The warmth of a flush crawled up his neck. If he didn't hurry, he'd chicken out. "I like you. A lot."

Coral looked at him blankly. A gull cried in the distance. Salm and Luna's whispered conversation reached them as if from another room. The boat bobbed, and Ty hung waiting, like a sail with no wind. A roaring grew in his ears, and he realized the sound came from his energy coursing through his channels. Why wasn't she saying anything? *Please don't let me have broken some mysterious rule.* Or worse, she didn't want to check out his energy. He should drop her hand.

She licked her lips again, but didn't say anything.

Ty felt ill. He'd really messed this one up and hadn't a clue how to get out—

Something hit the boat. The hull rocked up and tumbled the two of them into the cabin. The thing hit them again. And a third time.

Salm yelled, and Coral scrambled to her knees, laughing, and hung over the hull. "No. Stop. You can't do that today. Stop, stop!"

The battering stopped, but the rocking didn't. Ty's head whirled. His energy wouldn't calm down. Suddenly, he knew it was more than racing energy. *Oh no.* He pushed himself up to the side, where he promptly threw up.

"Eeewww!" Coral squealed. "Salm, make them stop. Ty's sick."

He heaved again and again. Someone knelt at his side, put an arm around him and held a hand to his forehead as he pressed against it. The pressure of the hand helped. He settled into a gasping rock with the boat. His eyes swam with tears. Finally, he wiped at them and spit. Yuck.

A cool towel appeared on his neck. "Thanks, Luna," Coral said. "Here, Ty, have some water, but don't drink it, only rinse."

He took the bottle and swished, wiping his eyes in time to see several fish racing through the rolling waves to the spot where he'd spit. "What are they doing?" he choked out.

"Looking for more." Chuckling, Salm hovered off the side, his wings arched and fluttering. "You've been chumming the fish, mate, and got them into a feeding frenzy." He pointed to the churning water off the stern. "Wanna have another go at it?"

Ty groaned. Puking in front of Coral was embarrassing enough without Salm making it into a joke. He chugged another mouthful of water and shot a stream at Salm.

He darted away. "I'll take pity on you today and not return it," he said over his shoulder. "Get your bearings. We have to wait for the excitement to die down."

At his side, Coral grimaced, holding back none of her disdain. "Boys. You are both disgusting."

"Sorry. I usually don't get seasick." The taste was nasty. He closed his eyes and magicked a swig of mouthwash into his mouth, swished and spit. Let the fish *chum* on that. He shifted to sink into the cabin.

"No way, mister." She grabbed him under the arm and pointed to the seat at the stern. "Keep your eyes on the horizon, your face in the breeze and your mouth near the side. I don't wish to swab the decks after you. Salm's made it clear you're my student and my responsibility."

The look she gave him was so pained he couldn't help asking, "Is that so bad?"

She sat beside him, avoiding his gaze. "I don't know. You were doing so well handling the boat, I was thinking you had a chance to win the regatta. Then you lost it."

He had, big-time. He'd also lost the chance to hear her answer to his declaration. Okay, saying *I like you* wasn't quite a life-changing statement, but the way his body had gummed it up, it might as well have been. What was with him and his energy? He'd never felt so thrown off-balance near a girl before.

Now he didn't know how she felt, or if she'd even accepted his energy. It could have gone flying over the side. He should ask if she wasn't interested anymore, but wasn't sure his stomach could work its way up to getting the words out. But if he didn't…

Ty cleared his throat. "I don't think my throwing up was entirely due to the waves."

"You don't usually have a pod of dolphin playing football with your boat?"

Was she trying to distract him to avoid discussing them… it…what he'd said? "What?" he finally asked, but she started to laugh, leaned over the side and banged the hull. Three raps.

From the bow, Salm said, "Coral, do you think that was wise, given he's been ill—"

Wham! The boat rocked wildly back and forth, and a dolphin rose out of the water, squeaked and propelled itself backward. Then it dove. Seconds later, a tail flipped up within feet of them and slammed down. Water hurled into the boat, Ty smashed into Coral and they crashed to the cabin bottom.

She burst into laughter as loud as Salm's yell of, "Stop!"

"Spells, it is dolphins," Ty blurted.

"Uh-huh," she whispered, her face inches away. Her gaze dropped to his lips and stayed there as she leaned into him.

Whoa. She cuddled closer, small and warm, his arm around

her and tightening, one of her legs thrown over his. Bright, silver energy flashed out of him, surely setting his body aglow.

Coral froze, eyes widening, then half closing as his magic washed over her.

"Oh no," he gasped.

She sighed. "Oh no, indeed."

18

BROKEN BOUNDARIES

Ty reined in his magic, and the glow around him receded. What to do now? Had Salm and Luna seen? Before he could move, Coral gently pushed away, her gaze fixed on him. His energy threatened to break out again, so he remained still and held it tightly.

She rose to all fours, her head hanging above his and braids swaying with the roll of the boat. "I'll accept the excuse that dolphins battering the boat is what made you ill." She flashed a wide grin. "But now they're back, and we need to start with them." She ducked under the boom and scampered forward, where she and Salm exchanged a few words, punctuated by Coral's retorted, "Stow it."

Yeah, Salm and Luna had seen. Boy, they were sure loose about chaperoning. Piper had indicated Salm wasn't one for enforcing boundaries, so Ty had no idea if he'd gone too far.

Though it wasn't like he had *allowed* the energy to burst out.

He sat up. How had it escaped him? First, the little piece, and now a whole wash. He peeked below the mainsail. Salm and Luna hovered some distance away, leaving only Coral perched on the hull. Even seeing her clad in an old wetsuit, he still wanted to put his arms around her, so this went beyond noticing she was pretty.

Flights. Ty rubbed his eyes. Her energy must be calling his. He'd never felt such an attraction, except for blue wizards. Like Marissa. But even with Marissa, it'd been a few weeks of dating before he'd felt so out of control. Then, she'd stepped in to *help him* control it.

The *help* had been a trick. Months later, when he'd been more removed from the trauma of the relationship, he'd learned in a defense class how she'd done it. Long before making the offer, she'd put an energy exciter in him. According to his defense instructor, that pea-sized bit of energy could disable a wizard if the perpetrator was skilled enough in directing the exciter to rev up the target's energy to the point of noncontrol. A prudent wizard conducted a self-check frequently, especially if his reactions near another wizard seemed unusual or erratic.

His instructor had laughed and added that, unfortunately, *unusual* or *erratic* also described energy's reaction to extreme attraction—otherwise known as love.

Ty eyed Coral. Love. Was it possible? She hadn't put an exciter in him—he'd checked. Besides, she seemed too innocent for that type of trickery, though she was certainly comfortable with their exchange. Well, not *exchange*. None of her energy had passed back to him. But...*spells*. In the bottom of the cockpit, Coral had looked like she knew what she wanted. She wanted him.

Ty grinned.

Coral was comfortable being close to someone. Maybe more than he was.

As if reading his thoughts, she turned and smiled. "Feeling better?"

He returned the smile, feeling goofy through and through. "I am."

"It's time to join the party, then, don't you think?"

"Aye," he said, mimicking her accent. "That's exactly what I think." He crawled around the mast and shoved the sail out of the way so he could kneel beside her and watch.

Flying over the waves, Salm and Luna made a rough triangle with Coral in the boat, the waters between them roiling with dolphins. But not in a haphazard manner. While the three wizards gestured with hand signals, the dolphins skimmed the water's surface in two circles traveling in opposite directions.

Coral threw him a quick glance. "We're running them through practice paces, the training exercises that don't use magic. We're nearly done." She twirled a finger in the air.

Across the water, Salm nodded and did the same, and Luna copied them. The dolphins stopped, and ten heads popped out of the water.

"Whoa," Ty breathed. "I've never seen this many bottlenose dolphins in one place."

Coral laughed. "And you still haven't. See the light belly? They're common dolphins."

With his brown wings arched, Salm swooped over the watchful animals, tapped one of the smaller ones on the head and led it with a dangling fish. The others dropped and milled around.

Salm brought the dolphin up beside Coral and flipped his hand. The dolphin rolled to its back.

Coral gestured to the animal. "Pet him, will you?"

Ty leaned over and stroked the pale belly, pushing a film of water off the rubbery skin. "I'm impressed, but why are you training dolphins? I thought your family did something with fishing."

"We do." She unlatched a dry bag from a tether in the cabin. "The dolphins tell Pop how the fish populations are faring, where the schools hide and herd them for us." She handed off a scanner and small clipboard to Luna, who then ran the device behind the left flipper.

"Microchip identification," Coral told him and extended one end of a measuring tape to Salm.

"A couple of times a week, we come out and play with them, teaching them the tricks we need them to do so we can perform the procedures," Salm explained as they maneuvered the tape over the animal's belly, calling the numbers to Luna. "With plenty of rewards." He stroked a persistent nose away from a pouch at his hip, slid his hand into it and then waggled a fish teasingly. "Lift tail."

The dolphin did, and Coral grabbed the appendage and measured it, too. "Done."

"There you go, big boy." Salm slid a final fish into the dolphin's mouth and pushed it away. He followed it, tapped another head. That dolphin swam into place, and they started again.

"Is this the same way humans train captive dolphins for shows?" Ty asked.

"Magic improves our ability to communicate with them in ways humans can't," Salm said, "but Luna says it's very similar."

"My family went to the humans' Sea World when we vacationed in Florida," she said.

Coral frowned. "Why would you go to a dolphin show when you can just come out here and see them?"

Luna laughed. "My father thought it'd be a fun comparison to human lives where most people never get this close to sea life. That was before I knew your family and saw your work in person."

"Aye," Salm said. "Imagine how much fun your future life could be, talking and playing with dolphins while sailing a lovely classic wooden schooner?"

Luna's light manner fell away, and Salm immediately added, "Or a modern ship of your choosing?"

It was clear from her frown that didn't suit her either.

Salm began apologizing, and under her breath, Coral said to Ty, "Pop taught all of us how to communicate with sea mammals. Wind and Manta never caught on the way Salm and I have, but Luna has an ability that Pop wishes to encourage. So does Salm, but for other reasons." She tilted her head toward her brother, now whispering in Luna's ear. "Do wizards work with wildlife in Colorado?"

"Elk herds pass through Terraqua, and we have plenty of ground squirrels and foxes, so the wizards who take care of the shielding must allow wildlife through it. But I've never heard anything about training."

"Then what do the people in your settlement do?" she asked curiously.

Sheesh, Coral's parents hadn't done her any favors with this isolated way of life. No wonder she feared leaving for academy. "The wizards there are farmers, shopkeepers, security officers, chefs, teachers, uh, whatever it takes to run a city. It's human-like, because Terraqua is so large. The academy is one of the largest in North America, and the headquarters of HIT is located there." As well as one of the primary Department of Magical Regulation offices.

"HIT, aye, Human Information Technology." Salm had returned to the hull with another small dolphin, Luna somberly wielding the scanner. "They've visited us, and Pop keeps in touch with their staff to learn new aquaculture techniques the humans are using." They began another set of measurements.

"I've heard that term aquaculture several times," Ty said.

Salm glanced up from his tape measure. "In the Seas' case, 'tis multi-trophic aquaculture."

Ty frowned. "That's a mouthful."

"Aye." Coral rolled her eyes. "One he likes throwing around since he's close to having his own boat to conduct the habitat management." She darted a wide-eyed look toward Luna, but she kept her gaze on her clipboard. "It means we're balancing all parts of the marine ecosystem, not just focusing on raising fish."

"When all of them balance, folks from the isle can harvest from a variety of seafood so we don't overfish," Salm said. "Pop determines the various limits within our waters."

"Your waters?" Ty raised a brow. "You've commandeered them from Scotland?"

Coral shot Salm a look, a question without words.

"And Ireland," Salm said slowly. "Cooperatively, the Isle of Giuthas and Tern Bay enclaves have magically zoned off a portion of the Irish Sea with some rather tricky boundary magic. The humans find it unnavigable. Their boats seem to"—his hand swam to and fro—"slip through the area. Over the years, 'tis become a refuge for wildlife. Pop's brother, our uncle Ray, manages a similar area to the south, and their cousins manage others off Ireland's coast."

Man, this was different, even in the Windborne world.

"The seaside enclaves hold treaties with the nearby inland ones that set out exchanges for their land products. Our efforts pay back the humans by boosting the fish populations. Lift tail," Salm said to the dolphin and showed him another fish.

"I had no idea Tern Bay engaged in this type of agreement."

"You're an outsider. No one would be telling you."

That explained why—ah, spells. He pressed a palm to his forehead. "That's why I can't get work on a boat."

"Probably. They're waiting to see what kind of a lad you are."

"But, uh, now you've told me."

"Aye." Salm shrugged and gave the dolphin his fish. "I can tell already."

Oh. That meant—yeah, they were friends now. "Thanks, Salm. This has been very educational."

"Too educational," Coral said. "Salm, get another young'un to come over. I want to finish. I'm starving."

"You're always starving. Ty, I'm warning you, you'll need to stash more than a morsel about you to keep this witch happy."

Coral threw him a haughty look and retrieved a waterproof bag she'd brought on board. "Don't worry, I have cookies to tide me over till dinner, though now I'm not sure I'll share."

"I am." Grinning, Salm gestured with a bit of a blue sparkle and whisked the bag from her hands. Cursing him, she lunged as he fluttered out of reach.

Ty looked from one to the other of the siblings. He could easily snatch back her snack, but Luna had backed away, arms crossed and disdain clear, so he took that as a sign to stay out of it. He glanced at his watch. "I should head back soon for milking."

Salm stopped unrolling the bag. "Righto. You said you'd fly from here."

"Will you come back?" Coral asked, then called to Salm, "Will we still be out in an hour and a half?"

He shook his head. "We're nearly finished, and I haven't found the other pod."

"Pop won't like hearing that."

"Lost 'em. Even here." He touched his temple. "Without you and Pop also magically keeping touch, they've slipped off."

She frowned. "Have you tried around the north end of Giuthas?"

He nodded. "All the usual places. It's like they're gone from the habitat."

"In a few days, Pop will be back, and we'll find them." Still, Coral looked concerned.

Luna glided closer on her white wings. "Salm?" she said in a cajoling tone. "Could we have the picnic we discussed? With a bonfire? I left work early to join you this afternoon, and you said you'd make it worth my while." She hovered before him, putting her hands on his shoulders.

Salm encircled her waist, his face taking on a serene look.

"Ah, woman. It's not what I had in mind for your treat, but if that's what you want?" Luna nodded. "Then I am yours to command."

"I wish he was mine to command," Coral muttered. "I'd have lots of fun with that."

"Not as much fun as they're having," Ty whispered.

"Aye," she whispered back. "Do you suppose they've merged but without showing it?"

"I know they have." And Coral was wrong about them not showing any magic. The waves were sparkling below them…no, beyond them. "They're good at it. Fast," he said, while studying the odd pinpricks of magic. It wasn't anything he'd seen or heard of in his training. Below the sparkles, a swirling stream of dark water looped the crests and dips of the rolling waves.

Coral slid her small hand down the inside of his forearm and interlaced her fingers with his.

Soft, warm. Nice. But then Luna and Salm found each other's mouths and kissed as if they hovered alone over a moonlit midnight sea. Their frank exchange made him nervous. Would Coral behave like Salm? Other than the handhold, she hadn't moved, and the smooching pair certainly wasn't about to interrupt anything he and Coral did. Ty glanced to her. Her tongue ran over her lower lip before her teeth caught it.

He looked away. The looping stream of water was gone. He flexed his fingers, holding tighter to his silver, controlling it while he searched the water. When he found stream again, one black loop portion had enlarged.

That wasn't right. Warning bells cut through everything else. He snapped alert, grabbed Coral's shoulder and pointed. "What *is* that?"

"Flights, no!" she cried. "Salm! A rip is right behind you."

19

SWEET MOVES

Coral dove for the tiller, snatching up the mainsheet line before she fell into the seat. "Ty," she snapped. "Help me turn the boat away."

He bounced into the seat beside her. Salm and Luna were already herding the pod to safety with hand signals and probably thought-speaking calls she couldn't hear without her magic.

Angle into the wind, Salm sent into her head. At the same time, Ty asked, "Into the wind?"

"Aye," she barked to both and wrenched back on the line. Ty grabbed it from her as the mainsail filled. She dropped both hands to the tiller and held fast. The *Marauder* careened around and tilted. She was sure they'd capsize. Then Ty leaned, and Luna landed on the upturned bow, crouching with her fingers spread and wings flattened, her eye on the boom. The boat rebalanced and lurched forward.

Coral blew out a breath and looked over her shoulder. The rip was receding. The colorful magic strands blinked out as if they'd never been there.

Ty clapped her on the shoulder, letting his hand linger. "Good moves."

"Quick thinking," Luna added. "I'm thankful none of us slipped into it. Or the boat."

Coral's heartbeats slowed as the urgency died. This was the rip Pop had been looking for since the Giuthas wizards had closed another three weeks ago. "Pop's guess of this one's location was off. This is the boundary between the isle's property and Tern Bay's. That shouldn't be weak, not with their enclave's energy."

"But now we've found it," Salm called down. "I bet it's the cause of our missing dolphin pod."

Coral's hand flew to her mouth. "You think they fell into the ether?"

"Nay." Salm still looked grim. "If the rip had grown to a rift, there'd be a whirlpool leading to the void." To Ty, he said, "Every *rip* connects two entrances—or exits—in the isle's shielding. If this one's outlet is hidden in the forest, our dolphins may be stranded on land and...dead. Head back to the harbor while we mark the area. Luna?"

Luna straightened and leaped from the boat, wings beating to catch up to Salm, this time with no lovey-dovey stuff. Coral sighed. If she had her magic, she'd also be marking the rip. Instead, she and Ty sat, knees touching, heads craned to watch as the boat sailed on and Salm and Luna grew tinier, circling the spot. Then, shimmering curtains of magic billowed from their hands, and they formed a magical column around the danger zone, half in blue, half in silver.

"Bet your huge Terraqua enclave isn't suffering from energy rips," she said.

He shook his head and returned his gaze forward and adjusted the sail.

"The Isle of Giuthas is an even smaller community than Tern Bay, and our older folks are having a hard time magically keeping up. Two years ago, the council realized that our land wasn't producing the energy needed to support all of us, but by then our shielding had thinned and rips formed."

"Bring in more wizards, then."

"It's nae that simple. A fair number of wizards apply, but then they discover how isolated it is and how old-fashioned a lot of the isle's policies are. Those that continue must test if their magic will work with habitats that have been magically cultivated in specific traditional ways for hundreds of years." She shook out a clenched hand. "Would you consider restrictions that take a year to comply with, to live in the middle of nowhere?"

"I'd need to know more," he murmured, not enthusiastically.

"A few new folks passed their trials this summer. Another wizard started a month ago and is almost for sure in because he's won over one of our prickliest elders."

"Is that enough additional magic?"

She shrugged. "All the rips haven't been sealed, but the elders don't seem as desperate. They say the shield took years to weaken, so it will take several years to rebuild."

"But you haven't even found all the rips?"

"The ocean ones are tricky, and since we're an island…" She rolled her eyes. He'd probably figure out soon enough that the Seas couldn't keep up with their regular work and the searches. Once Pop was back from holiday, they'd assign more zones to volunteer fishing boats.

Salm and Luna landed on the bow, and Salm tossed Coral the bag of cookies. "Let's get the *Marauder* back so I can report this to Tern Bay. I've sent the message to Granpop. He'll start a search on Giuthas."

"But they won't repair the rip without Pop, will they?"

He shook his head. "No one would summon him back from a holiday when five more days won't matter. By then, Uncle Ray and Wind will have their schooners positioned to lend a hand."

Good. Her magic would be back to help, too. She'd focus this time and prove to Ma she didn't need academy training for control. "What about the picnic?" Coral asked.

Her brother looked at Luna, who looked at Ty and asked, "Want to come for a picnic after you're done with your work?"

"I'd like to. Where will it be?"

After the milking and chores were done, Ty flew offshore to find the northern cove Salm had pointed out earlier. The *Midnight Marauder* bobbed in the waves off the beach. Four figures circled a fire—Luna with her white curls, Manta with her light brown hair blowing freely and Piper and Salm with their dark heads. Where was Coral?

Yipping caught his attention, and Ty automatically adjusted his wing angle to turn northward. A black ball of fur streaked across the wet sand, scattering a flock of sanderlings. They landed a dozen feet away. Skipper barked and ran through them again. Far behind was something better to watch—a lithe figure alternately walking and trotting at the surf's edge.

Coral wore a long, tie-dyed dress in swirling blue and purple. Her braids swung as she twisted to scan the skies, first above the cliffs and then out to sea. She spotted him and waved.

Clutching the plastic bag carrying his contribution to the dinner, Ty arched his wings and dove. Stooped in a forty-five-degree angle, he gained speed and focused on her growing size. Silly, really, playing chicken with a witch who had no power, but he did it anyway. She responded in kind—crossed arms, spread feet and lifted jaw. Her challenging posture urged him on. Closer and closer, he zoomed until he made out her grin.

She didn't duck, or even flinch, as he skimmed the air a foot above her head. Ty banked sharply and whirled to spin corkscrews around her. She twirled, following his path until he dropped lightly a few feet away and drew in his dark wings.

She skipped up, as if to hug him, but at the last moment, she tucked her hands behind her.

Disappointment flooded him—*nope, dude, no going back.* He'd promised himself he'd ask her if *she* liked him.

"Hi," she said. "I'm glad you came."

He clasped the bag. "I wasn't sure if you would be."

"I asked you to join us."

"But you never responded after I told you…" *Okay, do it.* "How I feel about you."

Grinning, Coral placed her hand on his chest. She drummed a beat with her fingers, but he wasn't going to be distracted this time. He kept his gaze on her face, though her crystal-blue eyes and her apricot scent only muddled his head more.

"I appreciate a wizard who speaks his mind," she said. "I was afraid we'd be beating around this bush for a week. I like you, Ty. I like your silver energy, too." She giggled and glanced at her hand.

His gaze followed.

Whoa. The bit of silver he'd given her wound in and out of her waving fingers. She had no magic. How was she doing it?

She laughed and patted him. "It's so easy, your silver. It flows and follows."

Spells, no merge, but she was still channeling it?

"It gives me a feeling of kinship with you, warming my heart." Her voice dropped, barely audible above the crashing waves. "It warms my body, too." She smiled in a very self-assured way.

Great Golden Orb. What was she saying? His magic flickered wildly, and Ty squelched it. "Uh, good for…um—" He couldn't look her in the eye. "I'm glad you like it."

"Sorry!" Coral's smile faded, and her hands dropped from him. "I thought that'd make you feel better while we waited for my energy to be released."

Her energy. He didn't even know the color of hers, and she

had him hypnotized, unable to function. What would it be like when she had it free? He both dreaded and looked forward to it.

"Sorry to make you unhappy," she said. "It'll be worth your wait, from what Luna says."

"Huh? What does *Luna* know about...me?" Ugh, nervousness had made that sound...sharp.

Coral hugged herself, her hands half disappearing in her long sleeves, and she turned from him. The wind wrapped her skirt around her legs, and the loose hair around her face whipped about. "I, uh, have blue energy. She said you would like it."

It took a moment to register. She had blue. He knew that. Well, no, he hadn't *known* that for sure. She had blue. And she was stepping away.

Ty caught her arm. "Blue. Blue is good." The last word came out a squeak as he wrestled back a surge of magic.

Slowly, she turned, very close to him. "Only good?"

"Uh, excellent, actually. I've had very good merges with blue." Oops—he shouldn't have mentioned other merges.

She shifted closer, putting her body a hair's breadth from his. "Have you now?" she asked, a challenge in her voice.

"I have," he admitted, and everything began to blur. He'd intended only to brush back a wisp of her loose hair, but somehow they tilted together. He'd thought it would be a quick kiss.

She apparently had other plans. Her arms slid around his neck, and then his arms were around her.

Coral tasted of the sea, fresh and salty. That much sank in. Between her fingers in his hair, the crashing of the waves and the inner roar of his energy, Ty lost control. It rushed over her, back to him, then repeated. Something was there. His energy couldn't reach it, but that was okay. Her magic left him flat-out mesmerized.

For a time, Coral didn't make a sound. Then her lips stopped moving. Her hands tightened on his shoulders and pushed.

He cut the flow of his energy. It wasn't as difficult as before, as if his curiosity had been satisfied. Maybe hers, too, since she stepped back. His arms felt empty. She'd been firm and bony against him. In the rush of energy, he hadn't noticed until she'd left. Ty rolled his lip between his teeth, tasting her again. Mmm. Why hadn't he been paying attention to *that*?

Her gaze traveled up from her study of their feet, and she laughed nervously. "We best stop. I don't want you mad that I'm getting all of the fun. It's not fair, but when my parents return, I can show—"

Ty burst out laughing. *Fun.* He didn't have to worry. He swept aside her hair and kissed her nose. "Thanks for your concern, but I'll be fine. I wouldn't mind keeping things physical for a while." Oh Great Orb. He'd said that out loud?

Her eyes widened, and Ty wanted to flee. He'd pereport back to Dar's and, starting tomorrow, make all of his bakery deliveries before their lights went on, never giving himself the opportunity to say the wrong thing again. Or…should he explain?

Her lips parted, and she whispered, "Physical? You mean… *physical?*"

No, explanations about his history were not happening. Nothing he said now about Marissa would be good, especially the way Coral was looking at him, obviously thinking he meant hooking up. "No, I mean, uh, just not magical, or…*too* magical."

She frowned. "There is nae *too magical* for me."

"Whatever. Your choice." Aaahhh! What was wrong with him? Time to move his feet, not his mouth. "Hungry?" He scooped up the bag he'd dropped in the sand, then linking their arms, he propelled her down the beach toward the fire.

She eyed him, but didn't shove him away. "Aye, I am."

"Good. I brought the burgers, remember? Better put them on to cook."

"Indeed," she said a few paces later. "Dar's meat is always

the best. We don't get it at home on the isle, only fish, seafood and game birds, you understand?"

No, he didn't understand why they were limited, but thank the Golden Orb she switched topics. She couldn't feel this casual about what they'd just done. He sure didn't, his pounding heart reminded him. But on the flip side, his energy had calmed and settled in a warm puddle at his lower core.

"Skipper will be so excited. Oh, Skipper!" Coral pulled free and spun around. The dot that was her dog ran a football field's distance down the beach. "Ty, will you help me catch him, please? Without magic, it can be very difficult."

"Okay." He thrust the bag into her hands. "What do I do?"

Coral told him how to net the dog with magic strands, but when Ty swooped down the beach to head Skipper off, the dog turned tail. Coral set the bag down and bent to encourage Skipper. He ran and leaped into her arms. When Ty landed beside them, she was crooning, petting and making over the little beast in the sappiest manner.

Geez, she had a lot of love to share—with her dog, her family... Ty wanted to be the recipient of those finger caresses and sweet words. When he straightened from collecting the bag of burgers, a smile played on her lips.

"Thanks, Ty."

"You're welcome."

She shifted the dog to one arm and reached her free hand to him.

This fit the rules Manta had told him. "Just holding hands?"

She smiled. "Just holding hands. It's a good start."

"I..." *Less said, the better.* Ty smiled back. "Right."

20

FAMILY INTERVENTION

Coral laughed when Salm approached Ty and her, wielding a stick like a sword and barking orders that Ty give up his treasure. With a wink to Coral, Ty refused, and it became a game of keep-away.

Spouting pirate language, Ty and Salm darted around her, Luna and Manta, using them as shields to fend off each other. Piper continued feeding a roaring fire to build a bed of coals until Manta shrieked—in fun. He leaped to defend his lady's honor by challenging Salm to a duel. Instantly, each held a rapier and parried their way across the sand in a continuation of the fencing lessons Piper had been giving Salm. They insisted Ty join in, until Manta announced that, after baking all day, she wouldn't be cooking.

It'd been lively and comfortable with Ty fitting well into her family's escapades. But they were never left alone for more than half a minute, something she had to tackle with Manta.

Ty noticed—how could he not?—and during dinner, he'd kept close. Oh, so nicely close. Not always hand-holding, but near enough. If he wasn't at her side, his gaze was already on her when she looked around, watchful while he laughed and joked with the others.

Back at her sister's, a light shone in the living room when Coral made her way upstairs just after nine o'clock. Manta had tried to wait up, of course, to hear what had happened after she'd left the picnic—but she'd fallen asleep on the sofa, only her face visible above the compass rose quilt Ma had made.

Coral couldn't go to bed without talking to someone. She sank into the upholstered chair opposite Manta and, with a sigh, closed her eyes. The best part of the evening had been Ty's jacket. After the sun had set, they'd eaten, and as the fire died, she'd gotten chilled and asked Manta to magic out her cape. However, she couldn't remember where she'd left it, so instead, Ty magicked his jacket from his house. He helped her into the soft material that cut the wind. Fleece, he called it. It wasn't sheepskin, but it was made from recycled plastic bottles. Piper plied him with questions about this technology, already being researched by HIT, and they debated whether it'd ever reach their small settlement, and if it did, would the old-timers accept it. Plastic packaging, after all, wasn't used here.

Coral shivered now, as she had then. Ty knew so much about the mysterious human world. Would a country girl with no worldly experience and limited education interest him for long? She should have done as Ma asked and taken her studies more seriously. Her small figure she could do nothing about, but her mind was open for growth. And her magic. It would be fun to have some magical tutoring from a fellow who'd trained at that huge academy.

She shivered again. Piper hadn't started the furnace yet, and now that she'd finally stopped moving, she felt the house's nip. She reached to call the throw on the opposite chair...nothing happened. She groaned.

Manta's eyes fluttered open. "Coral. Not too late, is it?" Her gaze flitted to the clock on the mantel. "Hmm, reasonable for

Salm. He's keeping to the agreeable side of life in my book." She yawned.

"Yours and Ma's as well, but not necessarily mine." Coral hoisted herself from the deep chair, leaned across to grab the throw and fell back again, spreading it over her.

"Come now. Salm spent more time with us than he has in months. He's been so focused on Luna. He behaved civilly, didn't tease and included Ty in his game and lessons. It's so nice to see that serious young warlock change course—"

"Spells, Manta. *Serious young warlock?* Twenty-second year, and you sound like Ma. Look out."

"Humph. Looking out *is* what I'm doing."

"Aye, I suspected you were behind it. Salm didn't disappear among the rocks with Luna, as he usually does. He kept Ty talking the whole time and insisted we leave soon after you did, before it was totally dark, so Ty could pilot back the *Marauder*."

Manta rolled her eyes. "Did you expect he'd leave you alone on the beach to make out? Besides, you shouldn't forget Ty needs the practice. He's in the regatta now, thanks to you."

"I know," she said with a groan. "And it's helping. His confidence was up on this trip home. Quick and sure, even maneuvering in the busy bay at high tide. It's just I would have liked a minute alone with him."

"He walked you back, didn't he?"

"I wanted that minute around the fire. Not on the street, at the house or where anyone could see. It's not the same romantic feel as the beach at night, snuggled together next to a fire, *alone*."

Manta snorted. "Plenty of time for *that* next week." She waved Coral's dream evening away and shrugged off her covers to sit up. "When Ma returns and you're not my responsibility. When she sees what's going on and can get you to Magemoor."

Coral's eyes narrowed. "What do you mean?"

Manta shook a finger at her. "Don't think Salm has missed

one interchange between the two of you. Nor the telling of it. The speed of it, even with your magic locked, has even him nervous. That's saying something, lassie."

"Nervous?" Coral laughed. "Not Salm. More like he wants to tease me about his status of being eighteenth year. He can freely prebond—as soon as Luna agrees—and do all I want to be doing."

Manta rose and gathered her quilt around her. "He's not teasing this time. Please be careful around Ty until Ma and Pop return."

Why were they telling her what to do? She'd been taking care of herself alone at night and certainly around warlocks. Warlocks she'd touched, a lot, and more than their hands. Coral huffed.

With a shrug, Manta headed for the stairs.

It was quite unlike Manta not to lecture. She was busy, with Fest and all, but she wouldn't shirk her duty to Ma, especially if they'd decided Coral needed watching. They? Salm...

Shoving off her wrap, Coral jumped to her feet and followed Manta to the hall. "You don't mean Salm intends to watch me like an osprey until they return?"

Manta nodded without changing course.

"That's not fair! I need some time alone with Ty to decide if we should try a prebond—" She clamped her jaw tight on the words she hadn't intended to let Manta hear.

"And you want him to?"

"Terribly. He's like no warlock I've met." She rubbed her hand over her belly. "He makes me feel..." Oh. That good feeling was in her energy core. Coral dropped her hand before Manta could see.

They trod up the stairs. At her closed bedroom door, Manta turned. "He makes you feel what?"

With her sister eyeing her that way, she could not say, *All warm and thrilled inside.* "Er, happy. He's fun to be with. I just want to spend more time with him."

"Then spend *time* with Ty. But refuse the energy he's spreading on you—"

In spite of herself, Coral drew her breath.

Manta raised a brow in return. "Aye, Salm watched you with his spyglass. We're worried where that's going so quick and without you having your magic."

"Right," snorted Coral. She walked the few paces to the attic door. "Like Salm and I used to *worry* about you and Piper. Salm is looking for something he can use to pick on me. Good night, Manta." She closed the door behind her before Manta could make her promise anything. Like keeping Ty's energy at bay, something she surely didn't want.

He seemed to, though. The hug goodbye he'd given her had been the briefest a potential beau had ever bestowed after a declaration of mutual like. Even more surprising, he'd managed the hug without releasing anything magical.

Still, she smiled as she started up the stairs. Ty's magic was so lovely. With Lemon, she'd liked the excitement—at first. Then, his yellow energy had spurred hers into crazy surges and sparks that muddled her head and never allowed their energies to blend. Somehow, each time they'd broken apart, she hadn't been able to hold her power, and he'd always gotten a portion of it, making Lemon fired-up and her out of sorts.

Other wizards before Lemon had been downright turned off by her energy's sparking, banishing any hope of a relationship. Best to take things slowly with Ty and not ruin their nice start.

She was halfway up the stairs when a low murmur caught her attention. She inched up to peer through the railing spindles. Stretched along the window seat, Salm and Luna kissed, her fingers entwined in his hair.

Spells. This was her room. They shouldn't be using it for a tryst.

21

<hr>

NOT SO BAD ADVICE

Coral tiptoed up the last of the stairs. Salm and Luna were fully clothed, but fully engrossed in each other. She sneaked across the room and poked Salm's backside. "Are you merging?"

"*Fireballs!*" Salm flailed, lost his balance and slammed into Luna.

Coral crossed her arms and glared. Salm didn't notice, though Luna was rubbing her forehead and doing her share of glaring back.

"What has taken you so long?" Salm asked. "I want to talk to you and do nae wish to spend my night waiting."

"From what I see, you haven't been bored. Why didn't you walk back with Ty and me? Then you could have talked to me when he left."

"Precisely *my* suggestion," Luna snapped. She rose and crossed the room to lean against a bedpost.

"And have your eye on the horizon every time I try to flag you down? Nay. I left you to say goodbye to your wizard, and you didn't get into any trouble doing it, so we came up to wait."

He'd spied on them here, too? The urge to zap her overbearing brother washed through Coral—until she noticed Luna frowning. She didn't need to make Luna any angrier, not if she wanted future help. She forced her fingers to relax, only then remembering nothing would come out of them anyway.

Spells, she'd just ignore Salm's interference. His gaze did seem earnest. Perhaps what he had to say was important. She moved her hands to her hips and added an eye roll to show she still didn't approve.

"Ty washed you with his energy," Salm said, "while you have no defenses. That's not right—"

"I invited it." She had to fix this so Ty didn't look bad. "He stopped when I asked."

"Are you comfortable with him?" Luna asked.

"Aye," she answered quickly. Salm and Luna were too involved in this for her liking. "I know it's early for you, but I have to get up at five and would like to go to bed now. Is there anything else?"

"Nay," Salm said, while Luna answered, "Aye," at the same time.

They stared at each other for a moment, until Luna shrugged.

What else had Luna wanted to say? Coral was curious, but she was tired of explaining herself.

Salm cleared his throat as he stood. "Ty seems like a good fellow. He's a mite older than you are, lass, and worldlier, coming as he does from the city. I wanted to assure myself you had things in hand with your magic being stowed."

Coral nodded. Salm was actually being nice, without being a know-it-all.

"Righto." He gestured to Luna with a tilt of his head. Then, unfurling his wings, he stepped onto the window seat, pushed open the window and leaped into flight.

Luna hesitated. "Your own sister is here, but if you need anything at all, please let me know." She left as Salm had.

Coral closed the window. For wanting to talk, Salm hadn't said anything important. She changed into her pajamas, brushed her teeth and climbed into bed. A reflection off the bay cast a faint light about the room as she waited for the cool sheets to warm. She brought out her hand and formed up the marble of silver Ty had given her. Rolling it between her thumb and forefinger, she felt a pleasant warmth spread through her again. The memory of Ty's wash? Or something else? Too drowsy to tell, she simply gazed at the swirling clouds lazily moving through the little sphere.

"Coral?" came a call from the window.

She bolted upright, palming the energy as Salm's shadowed figure hesitated on the sill. "Can I come in again?"

"Luna changed your mind?"

He scrambled inside and leaned against the same bedpost Luna had ten minutes ago. "Aye, there's no being with that woman when she wants you to do something. And now that I see you have a piece of him, 'tis a good thing she persisted."

Coral flopped back. "Spells! The minute I get my magic back, I swear I will have yours. Fried, snarled, drained, *something*."

He cocked his head. "That's it? You're not going to leap on me like an octopus and get in a few good punches and kicks so Manta will come running to see who has attacked you?"

She drew her brows as tight as they'd go and crossed her arms. "Let's just say I'm too tired to bother."

Salm shook his head in his annoying I-know-better-than-you way. "I think you're sedated." He came around the side of the bed and put out a hand, gesturing with his fingers. "Give it over. How much do you have?"

"First, you tell me what you came to say."

Her brother turned and walked away.

She tracked him, unsure what to think. Salm rarely walked away from confrontation. Neither did she, for that matter. Yet, with her magic locked away, she felt less inclined to argue. She formed the ball of silver into her palm again and brought it from under the covers. She didn't feel sedated. Only having warm feelings about Ty. She placed his magic on the far side of her pillow as a test to see if it called to her.

His back still to her, Salm propped one boot on the window seat. "You know I never tarried when it came to checking out a witch's energy."

"Aye, even when you should have been working."

He threw a quick grin her way and turned to sit. "That's not the point here. I did it enough that my energy relaxed and could do it, a sort of training, really. You and I are alike in that respect. We both harbor strong but nervous energy. I expect you've discovered 'tis difficult to make it meet another wizard's energy?"

At her nod, he continued. "Merging is another major effort in control." She nodded again. "You've succeeded at it?"

Coral's mouth twisted, and her eyes rose.

"I thought not. However"—Salm paused dramatically—"you will with Ty's silver."

She snorted at his theatrical spin.

"Laugh, but it's true." He shook his head. "Luna put me off for weeks. When she finally agreed to the idea, we merged on the first try. No effort on her part or mine, and neither of us thinking it possible that night. Thank the Orb the lass is a goddess, for she carried me to nirvana and back."

Coral groaned. "I don't need to be hearing about your out-of-bounds sexual exploits."

"Your mind is where it shouldn't be, lassie. I said naught about sex. I'm talking about the intensity of a merge with silver magic, a blue magic's merge with a silver, at any rate. I'm trying to explain that, when you are free to do it, your merge will carry you off."

"Good," she said. "I wish Ma and Pop would hurry home so I can get to it sooner."

He pretend-swatted at her. "That may be your attitude now, but once you trip into a deep merge, you better know who you're with on the journey. He looks to be a fine lad, but I'm warning you, do all your checking out with your guards in place. The wrong kind of wizard can gain control of your power, like that old warlock up the coast who was tricked into giving over his house by some vagrant wizard. That'd put you in far more trouble than even *you've* been in."

She remembered the creepy story of a fisherman finding the man near-to-dead on the beach because he'd been spelled to walk in circles. Salm had a good point. "Fine, I will," she conceded.

"So, how much of Ty's energy do you have about?"

She picked up the small glow and extended it on her flat palm.

He took it and eyed her for a response. She didn't give him the satisfaction of one.

"You don't have a problem letting go of it?"

She shook her head.

"And this is all? Hardly enough to affect you." He dropped it into her hand again. "Yet you're pleasant to be around now. Wait, don't tell me you're in love?"

Coral sent him a stony stare and folded her fingers around the magic.

Grinning, Salm stood. "Righto. I promised Luna I wouldn't fight with you. Otherwise, she promised she *would* have more words with you than me, if you get my drift. See you tomorrow."

After his departure, Coral fluffed her pillows and adjusted the comforter, trying to get comfortable. Now she had too much to think about. A merge with Ty should work. She didn't understand how energy color made a difference, but if Salm said *his* magic had mixed immediately with silver energy, then she wanted to try. Imagine finally being able to completely merge.

Oh. Repeated merges were against Windborne rules when the couple wasn't prebonded. No wonder Salm had this conversation with her privately, since he and Luna hadn't made an application. Why not, if they were that close? Maybe Luna's complaints about living on a boat were the problem. Poor Salm. He could be such a bilge rat, but he was her brother and she wanted to see him happy.

Which brought up something she hadn't considered: Ty wanted to sail, but did he want to *live* aboard a ship?

2 2

VERY HONEST, VERY FAST

As familiar as Coral now was with Ty's energy, she knew the instant he came up behind her in the bakery hall. She threw a smile over her shoulder and said, "Give me a second," before finishing with her customer.

The moment the person left, emptying the shop, she turned to Ty. "Good morning!"

He glanced around.

No *hi* or kiss or...anything? She swallowed her disappointment. His behavior was off from yesterday. If he'd been one of the dolphins, she'd be taking a closer look.

"I hope you'll understand..." he started in a solemn undertone.

No! Those were familiar words—relationship-ending words. They hadn't even started anything, for spells sake!

"Salm offered to take me out again at noon today. Coral, I need every opportunity I can get to practice sailing. I'm sorry, it seems kind of rude to get lessons from him when we had our arrangement."

She sagged against the doorframe. Her breathing started

again. He wasn't dumping her...so why wouldn't her stomach settle?

"You look upset. Please pretend I'm your brother and tell me off. Then promise we can go out at three to continue our lessons."

Blessed Orb, he'd only been worried about her reaction. A giggle broke from her throat. "I will *not* pretend you're my brother." She leaned over and brushed her lips against his. "'Tis the last thing I wish to do with you," she whispered.

His face reddened and flashed silver, and she giggled again. She reached to caress his neck at the same time the door jingled its customer warning. Ty stumbled back.

"See you this afternoon," she said before turning and singing out, "Good morning."

At two thirty, both Ty and Salm showed up. Coral had thought they might and already had the bread deliveries split between the two carts. They ran off in different directions.

She'd changed into her bathing suit with the wetsuit overtop and was packing a snack when Salm came back. He leaned across the empty kneading table and grabbed one of her cookies. "We've knocked out his ocean problems, and he's gotten a knack for the tide and winds. Ty's good. He could win."

"Oh, that would be so nice for him," Manta said from her desk alcove. "It'll get Ty noticed by those stuffy old fishermen. They put too much stock in who wins."

"Aye. I had several offers of apprenticeship upon winning the Southport regatta last year." Salm stuffed the last of the cookie in his mouth.

"Why didn't you accept one?" Coral retorted as he picked up another cookie. To avoid a fight, she went to the storeroom for more.

She returned in time to hear Manta say, "Leave me out of it."

Salm spun to her. "Do you mind if I join his lesson with you?"

Coral wrapped the molasses cookies in a cloth napkin, put them into her dry bag and rolled the top down. Salm seemed sincere about Ty's chances. She clicked the bag clasp shut to form a loop handle. "You're really taking him on as a student?"

"Aye."

Manta pivoted on her stool, opened her mouth, then turned back to her paperwork. The unsaid words were there as plain as though she'd spoken, ones they'd all heard from Ma: *You two should work together.*

The screen door creaked, and Ty walked in, closing the door with his fingertips and looking from one to the other of them. He knew he'd interrupted something, and she appreciated that he hadn't loitered outside. That was the type of fellow he was, a good one. One she wanted to hold on to. "Fine, I admit you have a mite more experience than I do."

Salm flashed a grin past her to Ty. "Told you I wasn't bragging."

Coral grimaced. "No, he's not. You're lucky to have Salm as an instructor. I'll bow out." She set her dry bag on the counter as Manta pivoted once more, smiling broadly.

"Oh, no. You're still coming." Salm looped the bag over his arm and scooped Coral around the back. "You're his designated crew. Wish us luck, Manta," he tossed over his shoulder.

"Fair winds," she called.

Right, the *designated crew*. Typical that her older brother was slotting her into that usual role. It grated that Ty might be going along with him.

Ty said goodbye to Manta and smiled while he held the door for Salm to hustle Coral out. He stuck close as the three walked along the back alley ramp *southward*. Before Salm had even gotten her agreement, he must have made plans to use Luna's family's boat again. He'd assumed he could take over.

"I had our mate here," Salm said, "go into the town clerk's office today to register for the regatta."

Aye, and he'd even signed up with Ty.

"We ran into...I forget his name."

"That was Octo," Ty said.

"Aye, Octo. He had a fit seeing me with Ty. Said no way was this a legitimate challenge if I was in the craft. We put down your name for his crew."

She side-glanced at Ty for his reaction, but Salm had increased his pace—and hers—on a down-sloping ramp, leaving Ty behind. True, the lessons were about winning a race, not spending time together, but her part seemed all but dismissed. She pulled against Salm's tugging. "So, you need me"—her voice broke—"in name only?"

Salm—who didn't notice with his mission in mind—snickered. "Babe, he needs you in ways you two have not even begun to explore. But this week he'll settle for crewing."

Ty jogged up, his face sliding into a frown as their gazes met. "Whoa. Stop right here." He jostled between her and Salm.

She ducked from his puppy-dog eyes, which would undo her further. He caught her arm, a light touch of his thumb circling on her arm. *Spells.* With dueling all these years, one would think she'd had enough practice concealing her feelings, but that wasn't something she did around her brother, not when they lived so closely on a ship. They let it come out and moved on.

"Please?" Ty said. "Doing well in the regatta is only part of what interests me. I'm enjoying our lessons, being with you and...I want to do this with Salm *and* you."

Again, this boy had the smooth words, exactly what she needed to hear. How could she say no with those beautiful eyes pleading and his thumb stroking? Aye, his touch brought an odd feeling to her. Coral looked at her arm. Nothing showed under her wetsuit sleeve—of course nothing showed. Nothing could escape from Pop's quash.

Seeing her pointed look, Ty dropped his hand. "Sorry."

"Just what are you trying to do with that..." *Magic.*

A hearty chuckle came from behind her.

Curse it all. "Salm, leave us alone for a minute."

"Aye, just keep walking." He gave her a little shove before he jogged down the ramp and disappeared around the corner.

Stopping to spite him, Coral turned to Ty and bobbed up her arm. "Are you coaxing me with your energy?"

He flinched back, a fleeting wave of hurt passing over his face. "No!" He stepped off a pace, shaking his head. "No," he repeated. "That's the last thing I'd do to anyone, you especially. I don't play those tricks. They're dishonorable. I'd lose my status. If I go back, I'd be..." He pressed his lips closed.

"You mean your status from that training?"

Ty looked around as if he expected eavesdroppers to be hiding nearby. Linking arms, he turned them to follow Salm and spoke into her ear. "Like dueling, dishonorable behavior would limit my ability to return to...a position. I didn't mean for anything to happen, but my energy seems pulled by yours. I'm sorry. I'm having a hard time not touching you after yesterday."

How could he say this—and lines like wanting to see her in her bikini and keeping things physical—but then claim he liked the safety of their rules? He'd also pulled his magic off her quickly. Why was he so open, yet so careful? Who was the real Ty?

Her magic would have told her. She'd never had to have a completely verbal conversation with any other warlock she'd been interested in. Why hadn't she asked Manta for advice? Surely she and Piper must blab about all this stuff after their years together.

At the end of the alley, she steeled herself for a stab at talking. "Aye, yesterday was different. I haven't had such a feeling from a wizard." His touch had sent a thrill through her, something she wasn't sure she wanted to share with him yet. She shifted her shoulders in a dismissive gesture. "Probably the quash. I'm not feeling myself without my energy."

"But what about this feeling now?" Lines creased Ty's brow. "Is it bad?"

His look told her everything. He had no idea. No magic meant no message, and no message bothered Ty. In a rush of understanding, she knew—he felt just as insecure about where they stood as she did.

Weaving her fingers with his, she said, "It's good, Ty."

They stepped onto the main boardwalk, holding hands and having the most private conversation she'd ever had, on the most public thoroughfare in town. The few people passing gave them little smiles. She dropped his hand as they sauntered on, not looking at each other.

"Will you give me another chance to try to control my sneaky energy?" he asked in a low voice. "I'm trying, but...I seem to be losing to it."

"This ever happen to you before?"

"Once."

"And?"

"It didn't end well."

"You think it'll be the same with me?"

His silence lasted long enough that she stopped. South Dock stood ahead, with Salm waving them forward to three sailboats rigged and ready to go. Ignoring him, she studied Ty's tense face.

She sighed. The only thing to try was more talking. "I want a chance to test our magic together. If you do, too, then I promise in four days you can see my magic. But to do that, you need to stick around, sailor boy, and keep showing me your stuff."

There, that ought to be clear enough where *she* wanted the winds to carry them on this trip. She spun on her heel and walked down the pier.

23

A CLOSE RUN

Ty grabbed Coral's arm just yards from the boats. He had to tell her. He had to tell her *now* and gauge how she responded. "I do. I want to see your magic. I'm in for the checkout." The words poured out, and he realized he meant them.

A week ago, he hadn't been ready. He'd still been agonizing over falling for Marissa's ploy and guarding his heart from more hurt. But Coral didn't care about his academy status. She wasn't fawning over his skills or the reputation of his magic. He'd done what he'd promised himself and kept those hidden. She liked him for him. And like any wizard, Coral wanted to make sure they were magically compatible. So did he, and that magical check would be his next step in shaking off his bad history with Marissa.

The smile he was trying for pained his taut face. He gave up, only to see Coral's brow furrow.

"That was not an ultimatum," she said. "We can talk more." Her eyes flicked to their audience—Salm, Luna, another girl who had to be Luna's sister and a guy. "Later."

But she needed more information—now. Ty ducked closer

and said, "I'm nervous. So here's an idea: Maybe you ought to ask before you touch me."

Her brow smoothed, but her eyes narrowed.

He gave a little shrug. "My control is questionable, especially when I'm surprised. Warnings would help."

Wrinkled brow again. "Touchin' is a problem?"

"It's *your* rules that specify hand-holding only."

Her face twisted.

"You said yourself it's until prebonding." He shrugged helplessly. "Then other touching is allowed."

She bit her lip, and he realized what he'd said: *prebonding*. Which meant *no dueling*. They weren't there. Best to keep the mood light. "Whoa, sailor witch. I'm not promising anything until I see your stuff. Your *blue* stuff."

It worked. She smiled as her very words came back at her. "It's just... It's not like anyone here, in Tern Bay, *sticks* to the rules. You're so sweet."

Sweet? It had nothing to do with that and everything to do with being safe.

"So we'll nickname him the Candyman," Salm interrupted from behind them. "Get your kiss an' shake a leg, lass. The wind's a-blowin' good now."

With a funny twist to her mouth that caught at Ty's heartstrings, she folded her arms and leaned in. "You heard the captain. May I?"

Kiss him? What had happened to the Isle of Giuthas rules? Oh well. Ty swept his energy into its cores and locked them. He gave a nod and steeled himself for a repeat of yesterday.

When her forehead bumped his, she was laughing. "My brother is..."

"A bloody scoundrel? I know."

"Aye. But worse, a carbon copy of Pop. I hope you can handle it. Ma despairs of their behavior in public."

"And you?"

She shrugged, dipped forward and brushed his lips. "I get a kiss out of it."

He did, too—with wildly swirling magic that no one knew about but him.

The wind had picked up—a front coming in, Salm said—making the sailing good with steady currents. Salm's assembled racers paired off, a helmsman and a crewman: Ty with Coral, Luna with Salm, and Luna's sister Nebula with her friend Kelly. The appearance of their boats sailing out to the starting point attracted attention in quiet Tern Bay. Old folks lined the railing under the pavilion, and a group collected along the dock near the entrance to Fintail's.

This practice of Salm's ran the same course as the Fest regatta and used the same-size boats the race required—4.2 meters long with two sails and crewing two people. Seemed that most Tern Bay families had one brand or another of the 420 class, and Salm had secured Dar's son's for Ty to practice with and use for the regatta.

The run to the outer edge of the bay let Ty familiarize himself with this 420, a pretty yellow craft named *Perfect Day*. Without super-sailor Salm in the boat, Ty felt totally in charge. He liked that about sailing with Coral. Even though she was more experienced, she didn't flaunt it. But he hoped she wouldn't let him flounder just because she'd turned the instruction over to Salm. He side-glanced at her. Their gazes met, and they flashed simultaneous grins. *This is going to be great.*

The three sailboats jockeyed into a rough line near a permanent buoy, and Salm flew over to explain the course. On race day, two anchored boats would designate this starting line. They faced south for the first leg across the predominant wind out of the southwest. A buoy a hundred yards off the end of South Dock marked the first leg's turn, and another off the end of

North Dock marked the second. The third leg returned them to the starting buoy.

"Got it?" Salm asked, and Ty nodded. "When all of the boats are stopped and sails luffing behind the line, the regatta official calls the start. The racers have a three-minute window to cross the line, and their time is noted. At the finish, the time is again noted and the difference calculated to determine the winner. Since there are only three of us and we'll start roughly the same, we'll leave off the timing for now. Concentrate on getting your fastest start when I blow the whistle." Salm returned to his boat, leaving Ty's hands white-knuckled on the line in anticipation.

The whistle blasted immediately.

"Bilge rat," Coral snapped.

Each boat's crew sprang into action, pulling the jib sheets tight, while the helmsmen luffed the sails and adjusted the tiller. The sails caught the wind, and the race began. Beside Ty, Coral sat silent but alert as she waited for his directions. He made the tacks. Things looked straightforward, so he needed no help. Their racing atmosphere differed so much from his earlier lesson with Salm, who'd kept up a running commentary on life and everything it involved—at least from Salm's viewpoint.

Ty looked around to compare the positions of the others to their boat.

"Eyes ahead," Coral said. "Salm says you need only look to your first turn at this stage."

Squinting against the glare coming off the water, Ty saw she was right. Rubbernecking at the others had altered his course, slight for now, but another half minute of inattention would have cost him precious feet in drifting. Adjusting the prow to line up with his destination, he searched for his next move. Nothing came to mind.

The wind blew in a steady northeasterly direction, perfect for reaching South Dock, and the craft skimmed the water at a reasonable clip. The three boats rounded the buoy and began the run to North Dock almost together. With the wind directly behind them—and it harder to catch wind in the sails to go straight north—this middle leg would be very slow. They could expect the same during the real regatta.

Then Luna's craft pulled ahead. The two were the same model—how had she done it? Now Nebula's moved forward of theirs. Ty frowned as Salm grinned and waved.

"He says you're holding the tiller too true to the buoy and missing the full power of the gust," Coral said. "Ease off and tell me to tighten up."

Ty did just that, and seconds later their craft surged to catch the others. "Salm is thought-speaking instructions?"

"Aye. It's a race in name only. He wants you to notice the points that'll gain you the yards that could make a difference in a close run."

"Whoa."

She looked around, a frown creasing her brow. "You don't want his advice? It's good. You should really—"

"No, I do. The racing tips are helpful. I'm surprised your brother is thought-speaking with you."

"*To* me," she corrected. "I have no magic to respond." She rolled her eyes. "Normally, it would be annoying, but it's to help you, so I'm saying naught."

"Thanks."

"You didn't thought-speak with your siblings at home?"

"No." Not that they couldn't, but because they'd been home-schooled, he'd seen too much of them to want to have them in his head any more than they were.

"Hmm. We always have, our whole family. It's much easier on board to be able to communicate, especially with the chores we do in the sailboats or kayaks with the animals. Pop isn't always in earshot when you need his help."

The three boats had sailed halfway across the mouth of Tern

Bay. Ty kept his gaze on their destination, yet he couldn't stop thinking about the Seas family. "When we were hiding from Spike and company on board your ship, I received your thoughts about escaping through a porthole and swimming to shore."

Coral whipped her head around. "What?"

"It was an image, not thought-speaking, but… I've never had that happen before."

Nebula's boat skimmed a few feet forward—

"Watch out," Coral cried.

Argh. Both of the others were pulling ahead. "Does Salm have any more instructions?"

"Instructions, no. Comments, yes, all aimed at teasing me, so I won't repeat them." Coral groaned. "Now he says you're not paying attention to your preparations for the turn. What has your attention instead?"

Damn. The older wizard rocked with laughter and shook his finger.

"If you cannot attend to business, he says he'll replace me with Luna."

With focus, Ty found the strength of the breeze and caught up at the turn. On the last leg, he gained. Then Ty's and Salm's boats were neck and neck—proof that Salm had his skills down to the point of being able to talk and joke at the same time as sail. Ty couldn't. Not if he wanted a chance against Octo.

24

PRACTICE MAKES...MORE PRACTICE

The prow of Ty and Coral's boat shot past the buoy, trailing Salm's by a foot. A *mere* foot. *That means I have a chance.*

He had to work at his focus. His thoughts were proof of this, because even after Salm flew over and repeated that he'd been talking too much, Ty wanted to finish the conversation with Coral.

As soon as Salm left, Coral said, "The dolphins and I send images back and forth. It's often easier than words. I suppose that's what happened."

Then this was normal for her and her energy. Except... "Your magic was quashed."

She shrugged. "I can't explain it, other than I really wanted to tell you, but I was afraid."

They circled to return to the starting line for another run. "How do your sisters' partners, and Luna," he added, "feel about being left out of your thought-speaking?"

"We don't do it in person. We talk when someone is near enough to hear. Luna hasn't caught on well because she won't spend the time it takes on board to develop the skill. Piper and

Bass spent lots of time living on *The Peaceful*, so they're as versed on our frequency as if they were born into it."

Their closeness was fascinating, but the fact that her sisters' future bonding partners had lived on their boat intrigued him even more. Luna had been invited as well, but chose not to.

If he and Coral prebonded, would he be invited to live with them? That wouldn't be right, having his dream offered to him through a relationship. When he received a shipboard job, it had to be because of *his* merits, or it wouldn't be fair to her or him.

"You're bothered by our skill at this."

This girl didn't miss a thing. "It's not like we weren't close when everyone lived at home, but our family is more reserved, I guess. Probably because my parents both worked outside of home. They weren't around all the time like yours are."

"Humph," she grumbled. "You see family ties as a good thing, and they are in some ways. I've always had companionship, someone to teach me things, toughen me up. But in other ways, I've been watched out for, shuffled from one to the other's care, rescued when I didn't want to be and, these days, too smothered by what they think is best for me. I yearn to be free to be myself, but..."

She shrugged and waved toward Tern Bay. "I see you as so brave. You came halfway around the world to a settlement where you knew no one, to do something you have only the barest knowledge of. Not the cows—sailing. If I had half your bravery, I would be at academy learning all kinds of new things, instead of biding my time in a quash because my parents have decided I need help controlling my magic."

"You're only sixteen," he said before thinking.

Her gaze narrowed. "What were you doing at sixteenth year?"

"Attending classes at academy."

"Most of the day on your own? Getting there on your own, deciding what you would wear, what you would eat, who you would talk to, what work you would attend to when you arrived home?"

"Uh, yeah. So how is that so different than your life?"

Coral threw up a hand. "The confines of the ship. We live and travel together. Someone sees and comments on everything I do. My daily activities are Ma overseeing my education and Pop my work. Often, we must drop everything to see to some problem in our habitat. My days are dictated by fish."

"You said you like the work, and my parents taught me as well at home, remember? I had my work doled out, chores, too."

"Not after sixteenth."

"You said they *want* you to go to academy? So go. Being scared won't last. It'll change your life, and if you don't like those changes, come back and figure out something else." And it'd get her away from dueling.

She gave him a stony stare.

He'd overstepped—they weren't close enough for this level of advice. "Don't listen to me. I don't exactly have a stellar track record in decision-making." Another thought occurred to him. "Did any of your siblings attend academy?"

At first, she stared off, and he thought she wasn't going to answer. "No. Nor do many from the Isle of Giuthas go. If I do, I'll be the first to leave in fifteen years. The witch who did, Lady Heather, returned unexpectedly this summer. Well, sort of returned. It's a long story. My parents set up lessons with her in order for me to learn more modern ways to ease my mind."

The sentences were short and clipped, like a bad secret she only half wanted to divulge.

They were nearly to the other boats. Ty shook it off. He had to. He wouldn't get another practice like this. As soon as their sails were luffing, Salm blew the whistle.

This time, they won. Coral clapped him in the shoulder, and Ty lifted a fist as Salm flew over.

"Blimey, me hearties! Did someone threaten ye with a cat o'

nine tails?"

Whatever this pirate jargon meant didn't matter. Salm was pleased, and Ty was thrilled.

"Now that you have the wind properly in your sails, we will run you up to the crow's nest for another look."

Ty glanced at Coral. "What's he saying?"

"Racing tricks," Salm answered, and with a nod, he flew back to his boat.

"Stuff you have to look out for." Coral sighed. "Nothing that is *exactly* cheating, but can kill your chances."

The next run, Ty lost. Sorely.

As they circled to return to the start, Coral said, "Salm's not keelhauling you. This is real racing."

No, Salm wasn't doing this to be mean—his gleeful manner had dropped. Ty gave a curt nod. "I get it. I might be too new at this to win, but I'll tell him to bring it all on. I'll give it my best shot." Run after run, the other boats caught him in typical tricks —being run alongside, cut off, nosing the tiller.

Salm and Coral coached him in how to avoid the tricks, but his awkward efforts cost him time. If he lost to Octo… Ty closed his eyes. At least he wasn't racing Spike.

At the dock, Coral bent to pull the daggerboard, right where he was wrapping a line, and their gazes met.

"It'll be harder than I thought," he said quietly. He'd have to come up with something else to protect her. He leaned closer. "Thanks for crewing. And…everything."

She tipped up her chin, inches from him.

Salm shoved between them. "Coral, help Luna stow the gear while I walk this scallywag out to Dar's and review a few points."

Behind Salm, Coral had her hands fisted. Ty shot her a grimace. "See you later?"

"Aye, that'd be nice," she said through clenched teeth.

Hopefully, she meant it.

TERN BAY NIGHT LIFE

The afternoon rushed into evening for Coral, with a quick dinner so she and Manta could get in extra baking. Her organized sister kept things moving, so they had the last of the cookie dough on the trays while the boardwalks were still busy with passersby. Manta took over cashier duty to sell warm cookies and let Coral resume work on her rope bags while waiting for Ty. Manta joined her on the bench out front between waiting on customers and getting cookies out of the oven.

Wooden booths with colorful awnings, tables and folding chairs had cropped up throughout the day along the beach boardwalk. The vendors were carrying boxes down the ramps and tying canvas tarps over them to guard against the night's dew. More booths, more people, more activity. Fest would officially start in a day, although the equinox wasn't until Tuesday.

Coral kept an eye out in case any of the duelists came by. It was too early to be up on the moor, but none did. When she spotted Ty weaving through folks, her heart leaped. It soared when he greeted her with, "You look nice," and slid onto the bench beside her.

Pausing in her knotting, she leaned toward him for that kiss she'd missed earlier—just as Manta emerged from the bakery again.

Her sister frowned and shook her head, and when a neighbor greeted Manta and also looked her way, Coral straightened.

"Ugh," Coral muttered. "Sorry, but the family chaperones are circling." She took out her irritation on the bag, poking, twisting and pulling different colors of cord in an ever-growing line of looped netting. In ten minutes, her opportunity would come to escape with Ty.

"What's this project you're tied up with?" he asked.

She groaned. "Ha-ha. They're knotted bags, for which I have two orders. Manta's town friends don't have this sailor's skill to make their own. I'm hoping if I deliver their bags in time for shopping at Fest, they'll spread the word and bring me more business."

"Ah, this would be popular in a community where plastic is shunned. Did you make these, too?" He gestured to the macramé she'd tied into her hair at her temple when she'd left it loose tonight.

Hoy, *now* he was taking note of her appearance. "Aye." She touched the spiraled cord threaded with shells on her neck. "The necklace, too."

He brushed aside her hair to peer at it. But Manta's gaze kept cutting to them.

Will she not let up? Coral had to admit the situation was a smidge uncomfortable, here on the deckwalk where anyone could see. Gossip would have her prebonded to him before she even had a chance to know her own mind—and her energy's reaction. "What happened to asking about touching? Don't the same rules apply to you?"

His hand fell away, but Ty didn't move back. "May I?"

She eyed Manta, who was saying goodbye to the neighbor. If Coral wanted to learn which was the real Ty—the open or closed one—she'd have to push a little, despite Salm's warning. "Not here," she said quietly. "Be ready to leave." She tilted her head toward her sister.

Understanding, Ty nodded. "Could you make me a necklace with a shark's tooth I found?"

"You are full of it. You don't have a shark's tooth, nor would you wear a necklace."

"I do." He magicked the fossil into his palm and held it out just as Manta dropped onto the bench with them.

"That's one of the largest mako shark teeth I've seen," Coral said. They passed the two-inch stone tooth around, admiring the shiny gray enamel and finely serrated edges. "Still sharp. It didn't spend much time rolling in the waves."

"Where'd you find it?" Manta asked.

"Three coves north, a beach that Dar said to try after that big storm a few weeks ago. He used to take his kids there and has jars of shells and teeth."

"Ah, that is a good spot. Some of the other teens from Giuthas are there at the estuary cleaning up a Styrofoam spill. Maybe we could help them next week and do more hunting." Coral peered at him. "You really want it on a macramé?"

"I'd wear it. That twisted pattern is in style with surfers, and I can't show it off very well in my dresser drawer."

Coral took out a spare piece of cord. "Long enough to hang to your collarbone?" She dragged the measuring cord along with her fingertips around his neck, suppressing a grin when Manta rolled her eyes.

Then Manta's cookie timer rang, and she jumped up. "I'll be right back," she said pointedly and hurried inside.

In a second, Coral had everything stuffed into a bag. "Hold on," she told Ty and darted after Manta. Her sister was already disappearing into the back. Coral sneaked to the counter and shoved her bag safely onto the shelf beneath. Outside again, she snatched up her cape, swung it around her shoulders and waved Ty along. They briskly walked toward the south end of town.

Thank the Orb she'd dressed warmly in long sleeves and a long skirt. She wouldn't be tempted to go back anytime soon.

Just beyond Fintail's, running feet pounded on the boards behind them. She cringed, expecting Piper, but the shout of, "Coral!" wasn't from him.

Ty grabbed her elbow and activated his shield as they turned. It bubbled them inside a thin silver barrier that flared and faded from sight as Tiger ran closer.

She frowned at Ty. "There you go again with the touching. And more," she muttered. Honestly, he presumed too much—both that the boys were stupid enough to do anything in town and that she needed his help.

But when Lemon appeared behind Tiger, she wasn't so sure. He glowered, looking far more threatening than an ex-beau should. Aye, these boys were acting crazy, as she'd told Piper.

"Thanks for waiting," Tiger said. He must have gotten enough sleep, or was in good favor with Pearl today. He stood straight and had his dark hair brushed back. "Spike saw you, but cannot get away from his mother, so he sent me to ask if you're coming up tomorrow. You can bring him, if you like." He nodded toward Ty.

Her eyes narrowed. She stepped out of Ty's grasp, breaking through the shield. She smiled her dueling smile, the one that told opponents she planned to win.

Tiger backed up.

From the corner of her eye, she saw Ty's jaw tighten. He hadn't followed her forward. *Just as well.*

Lemon was hanging far enough back that it appeared he was giving this conversation some privacy. But she knew that scowl and hunched shoulders meant different. Spike had him on a tight leash, giving this job to Tiger and probably ordering Lemon to let Tiger do it alone. Lemon's hands cast no energy glow—both a surprise and a relief.

So Spike had taken over in her absence? It should have been

Octo, the runner-up duelist. He kept an even keel and stayed out of the petty bickering that Spike and Lemon had been jumping into with other duelists.

"Tiger," she practically purred, "I am well aware of what I can and cannot do. Why does Spike want me there tomorrow?"

He glanced around, making sure no one was in earshot. "To welcome the out-of-towners for Fest, as is your place. You don't need to *participate*. We've seen you every morning at your sister's and understand that wasn't a story. I told Spike it's just like me needing to be on my brother's boat, or him at the tavern, or Lemon delivering council messages for his mother. You have a job now."

She nodded slowly, letting the smile ratchet down a notch. They were acquiescing to her position. But...why was she holding on to it? Pride? She'd proven herself over and over. And what was it getting her? Nothing she could brag about in public and certainly no leverage with her parents. Or Ty.

Tiger ran a hand around the back of his neck. "Spike said, uh, we'll allow only limited numbers of challengers to spar on the first nights, mainly to determine levels for the beginners' tournaments. Other teams have submitted their top duelists for the intergroup title match on Sunday."

She should quit. She could do it now. Simply tell Tiger she wouldn't be there tomorrow or at all during Fest.

"You'll be there to compete, right?" Tiger asked. "Or you forfeit to Spike."

"Octo, you mean."

"Nay, it's Spike after last night."

Did this mean Octo wouldn't care about the sailing regatta? She glanced at Ty.

He shifted a step closer, and Lemon did the same, his scowl deepening.

Tiger, however, looked at Ty in an almost friendly way. "Don't concern yourself about the regatta, lad. Spike is aware you only have an agreement with Octo. He'll be asking you to meet up separately."

"Why?" Coral snapped. Blast, she'd shown her anger. Instantly, she plastered on the bold smile again. "Be a mate," she said firmly, "and remind Spike for me that any new person starts at the bottom, not the top. See you later, Tiger."

Spells, she was so tired of these dueling problems and not having her magic to solve them. She spun on her heel, furious and not able to keep it from showing for another second. She walked off the boardwalk and into the darkness.

26

WEIRD WARNINGS

Instead of following Coral, Ty kept his gaze on Tiger, though he knew Lemon was the one to worry about. But looking at that guy would trigger him, as sure as Ty was standing here.

Tiger shrugged and walked away, not acknowledging Lemon as he passed him. Then Ty had no choice but to glance at Lemon. He glared, his mouth working as if he was about to say something, but instead he followed Tiger to Fintail's.

Damned confusing. Especially not being a part of their group nor having seen their unauthorized duels. Ty chewed his lower lip as the guys disappeared into the tavern. He wouldn't duel, but on the other hand, he didn't want things settled for him. He could take care of his own battles, thanks.

And apparently, so could Coral. She'd ignored his shield.

I'm such an idiot. Asking, he should be *asking*, not assuming. Just because she'd sought his help the night on the ship didn't mean she'd need rescuing or decisions made for her, as she'd told him her family did. He did *not* want to fall into a brotherly role with her.

Heaving a sigh, Ty jogged down the beach to catch up. He walked beside Coral to the headland, clambered over the drier rocks at the cliff side and then continued along the breaking surf out of sight of town, all the while waiting for her to speak. The wind had picked up, stronger than it'd been this afternoon. Plus, the tide was coming in. The waves crashed higher and louder than they had during the beach picnic, their roar making it easier to hold his tongue.

Coral stopped and tapped her foot, arms crossed and brow furrowed. She faced the sea, not him, which Ty took as a sign in his favor.

"I get it," he said. "You're the top duelist, they follow your lead and do as you say."

"Most of them do."

"You don't need me protecting you."

"Not normally."

"I wasn't implying anything by it. I had no intention of insulting you. I'm just worried about you, because I haven't seen what you can do. Sorry. Forgive me?"

She squinted into the distance. "Aye. You don't know our ways."

He released his breath. "I know enough to realize you don't know how to handle me since I'm not one of the duelists. I don't have a second, secret society name."

"Not everyone has one. Periodically, you get called something that sticks. Mostly, it's the regulars, and I'm still not *a regular*." She blew out a breath.

"Like Shrimp because he's short?"

"Actually, that's a nickname Pearl gave him as a baby." She toed the sand, looking anything but the tough magical wielder she purportedly was. Under the faint light rotating from the lighthouse above them, she simply looked like a sweet girl—and a very pretty one. "You've said you won't duel, so I suppose I shouldn't worry."

"You shouldn't. Do you have a name?"

She looked up, wrinkling her nose. "Spike has tried to get them to call me Angler."

The name sounded shady. But she held his gaze, frank and steady. Still, his stomach clenched. Should he—Ty tightened his hold on his energy and extended his hand. "Can we talk?"

She withdrew a hand from under her cape, and her fingers clasping his were warm in his clammy palm. As they walked to the end of the cove, Ty gleaned from her reluctant answers that the names weren't chosen, but adopted as each duelist's style became apparent. The Angler name came about because Spike claimed she used trickery, like the deep-sea fishes.

Ty's stomach curled at her admission. He *had* become involved with a girl who played games with others. He tried to get more information to settle his nerves. He learned that Spike blasted only one shockball at a time, but usually one forceful shot was all it took. Shrimp's dueling name was Puffer, because with magic he became much larger. Pearl's fancy flight maneuvers won her the epithet Graceful. Tiger liked to get close and pounce, and Lemon had yellow energy.

"Yellow? I thought his name came from his constant sour look. He never talks, always hangs back and glowers. Except for that once on your schooner when he looked like he was going to deck me."

She hesitated. "I've seen him resort to physical violence only once."

Yeah, well, the alternative for an angry wizard wasn't great. It did seem she'd been involved with the guy. If she admitted it, it'd be easier to reveal his troubles with Marissa.

"Listen, don't pay attention to him. Focus on your sailing and the regatta. Though, er, it might be a good idea not to talk to him either."

"Why's that?"

"Uh..." She collected up her hair and dropped it over her shoulders. "Just don't. Look, I've tried to turn the conversation twice, and you're not taking the hint. I don't want to talk about dueling anymore. I ken you don't approve."

"Could you answer a last question that's more personal?" He rushed on before she could say no. "What tricks do you use to beat a competitor?"

"Bluffing, as you saw tonight, but I don't do that outside of the dueling arena. I've been nothing but honest with you, and I intend to keep it that way." She squeezed his hand. "I'm thinking of stopping. The changing attitudes have made dueling less fun and more, um…" She sighed while holding his gaze. "Out for blood."

Ugh. It was as bad as he'd feared. He chose his words carefully. "It's hard when things fall apart. Isn't there anything else fun in these ports to replace it?"

"Aye." She cocked her head, twisting her lips. "Kissing."

What? Not that he didn't want to kiss, but her answer was so honest, and she sounded so confident saying it. Then she jerked her chin for him to follow. She spread her cape on dry sand up the beach, shed her shoes and settled cross-legged upon it while he was still removing his shoes.

"May I hold your hands?" she asked when he lowered to face her.

He offered his hands, palms up.

She laced their fingers. "Our arrangements have been good for you? The asking to touch. And kissing?"

"It's been good." He wanted to just leave it at that, but her warm fingers stroking his begged for more. "Better than good."

"For me, too," she said, so low that he barely heard her over the waves. She ducked her head in a conspiratorial manner. "Never has it been like this with someone. And if you can't duel to prebond—" She shrugged. "I'm considering giving up my overglorified rank to spend time with a nonduelist."

How could she be so sure when he wasn't? He hadn't seen enough of Coral, especially her magical side. The memory of his ex-girlfriend and the way she'd left him still haunted him. Finding the words to explain that nightmare was hard, though he wanted to...

He was still debating how when Coral asked, "Why are you so nervous when you say things are good between us? I think we can be good together if you give it a chance."

He found himself nodding, maybe agreeing, maybe acknowledging she had a point. Why spoil this with a rehash of a bad relationship? Not after a fun day together, sailing, kissing...this evening on the beach. A gush of good feelings came over him. Aw, shoot. Guys weren't supposed to have these romantic sentiments that his sisters mooned over. Yet here, with the starry night, the beach, Coral's candor and their closeness without physical or magical intimacy, he relaxed and let himself smile. It'd be fun to discover what they might have together.

Again, Coral read him. "Come on over," she said sagely, clearly meaning his energy. "Let go."

Ty swallowed hard and let magic seep into his channels. Then hers.

They sat chastely, bodies a foot from touching, hands meeting midway, his energy free to explore her channels, following the call of her magic. Her cores were sealed, so his magic wheeled away to circle her magical system, then wend its way back, over and over again.

Heady, that's what it was. And...was something happening? He closed his eyes. The whole feel of his energy had changed. He looked Coral over, but couldn't see any difference in her. "What are you doing?"

"Naught. I just allowed you access. Your energy is..." She sounded perplexed. "Happy? It's yours. Tell me what you're doing."

"Letting go, like you suggested. Yeah, happy. Are you happy?"

"Aye, but differently than usual. I, uh—" A nervous giggle

broke from her. "I typically have very jumpy energy. You may not like it."

"Don't assume that," he said. "Everyone says I need more liveliness. That may be what my energy finds so attractive in you. How's this different for you?"

"It's a feeling close to peace. There's not a jumpy strand in your system, so it's calming. But I'm missing something, you ken, by not having my energy free."

Whoa, right. He started to pull in.

"Don't stop. Let's do it for a few minutes." She looked around. "Uninterrupted. It's an interesting experience." Her eyes glistened above their flexing fingers. "I should do it to you —have you quash your energy and run you full of mine. 'Twould liven up your life."

No other wizard he'd met had ever suggested such a thing, nor had he heard about that in any academy classes. With her, it sounded like fun. "You're a bizarre wizard, plotting more weirdness for us."

"Am I?"

"Uh-huh, but I mean that in a good way."

Coral leaned closer. Soft puffs of breath warmed his lips. "Ty, can I..." Instead of finishing, her mouth moved against his in the sweetest kiss.

Whoa—this was—wow. Soft, sweet, salty. Coral's sea flavor reminded him she was a girl, and he was a boy, not just a wizard analyzing an interesting piece of different energy. His need for magical connectedness faded, replaced by a surge to his gut and a tightening in his jeans.

Flights above—no! One thought in that direction, and his mind put on the brakes, though his mouth kept kissing. Curse Marissa—and that he was even thinking of her with this great girl kissing him. Before Marissa, he'd been into freely kissing... like...this. But since Marissa, completely letting go had been impossible to consider.

Ty gripped Coral's laced fingers. *She's different. She won't hurt me...* He didn't want to stop her sweet kisses. An onslaught of sensations muddled his brain—the strangely charged energy, his overheating body and his ears aching with a high-pitched squeak. Ringing ears? Not bells, definitely a squeak. Ty nibbled her lower lip, and the warning squeaked again.

Warning? Stop? They should stop? Yeah, maybe...

When he paused, Coral lolled her head sideways and peered at him through half-open eyelids. "Mmmm...holding hands... kissing's oh-so-right with you."

Couldn't argue with that. Ty dipped his lips to hers.

Squeak!

He froze, and so did she. "Yes," he murmured. "It's perfect." He kissed her again.

Squeak!

"'Tis," Coral whispered, "'cept that weird squeak your energy keeps giving. Like it's signaling..." She bolted upright, pushing him into the sand as she sprang to her feet.

"What the..." Ty stared after her as she ran into the surf.

Her skirt dragged with the waves, wrapping tight to her legs. Wrenching it loose, she waded farther out, hopping with each roll of water, propelling herself waist-deep into the breaking whitecaps and shadows.

He stumbled to his feet and trotted down onto the hard, wet sand. "Coral!"

Squeak! The previously distant call sounded clearly, despite the water crashing over his feet. Shadows rose and lowered, independent of the waves.

Dolphins!

More squeaks rang out. One animal rose near her, and Coral patted the sleek back. It dropped with a splash. Drenched, she spun with the roll of the next wave, and another nuzzled her shoulder.

Ty walked ankle-deep into the chilly water. Ugh, but if she

could handle the cold, so could he. Hopefully, the dolphins would allow him to approach. Coral had stopped petting them and was searching frantically toward the south where the next cove was just visible. She swayed with the waves and the pushing of the dolphins. Faltering, she took a few steps, stumbled and balanced with a hand on a dolphin's back. Ty was almost to her when another dolphin came up behind and shoved so hard, she went face-forward into the sea.

Ty dove and grabbed her. They came up sputtering, clinging together. "Coral! This is crazy. Let's go back to the beach. They can play with you in the daytime."

Shivering and fighting the shove of the waves, she squeezed his arm. "I canna c-communicate properly, but th-they say a whale is b-b-beaching. I need to st-stop it."

27

TO THE RESCUE

Coral stumbled through the waves. Only Ty's arm kept her upright. "You go b-back." She yanked the drenched skirt, got it off her legs and hitched the heavy fabric over one arm. "Tell M-M-Manta to get Salm. That it's Annie." Likely, that made no sense to Ty, but Salm would understand. She had to run to the next cove, had to find the baby whale they'd nursed back—

Ty caught her around her waist. "I can't let you catch your death." He fumbled beneath his shirt, and she saw the glass bobber only when the pereport began.

They landed in the bakery's kitchen. Manta shrieked, nearly dropping a tray of cookies. "Coral! What have you been doing?"

Coral followed her sister's gaze down. Her clothes were plastered skintight, while a puddle of sandy water grew on the tiles. Her ragged breaths left her stammering as Manta bore down on her.

Ty's arm tightened in support. "A whale is beaching itself," he said. "The dolphins told her. I made her come back, but it's urgent."

"It's Annie," Coral managed. "Taylor's baby." After they'd

nursed her back from a propeller scrape last year, she couldn't die!

Manta tutted, like Ma would. "Those minkes, always in trouble." She pulled Coral close to the open oven. Its heat flooded over her shivering body. "I'm calling Piper and Salm. Let loose of her, Ty," she said and waved her hands from Coral's head downward. She replaced the wet clothes with a warm, oversized towel. "You need one as well?" she asked Ty.

"Please, but I'll do my own clothes."

Piper came running in, had a brief word with Manta that Coral was too cold to follow and left. Then Manta pushed her to sit on a stool and handed her a hot chocolate. Warm, sweet sips were clearing her head when Salm entered, dressed in his wetsuit.

"Where?" he asked.

"Two coves south of Kittiwake Point," Coral told him, and he left.

Soon, Manta said, "He's found it." Then, "Oh bother. She's into the shallows too far already." She reached for the phone.

Spells. Poor baby Annie.

"Who's she talking to?" Ty asked. He'd dried himself and had a mug, too.

"Our father's brother, Uncle Ray, and his partner, Bert."

"I know this is going to sound like I don't care—and I do— but aren't whales usually dead or too far gone once they beach themselves?"

She shook her head. "Not always. Pop thinks sometimes it's confusion. He and the human researchers still don't know for sure. Annie isn't dead. They would have told me. We've known Annie her whole life, and Pop got to watch Taylor being born when he was a teenager. We have to save her." Not *try*. Save her.

"I get it. They're friends. Of course you must help." Ty waved his hands, and she realized she'd snapped.

By the Orb, this was awful. Coral pulled her towel tighter.

She'd never known one of their animals to die. "More than friends," she said quietly. "Like family. Taylor may not have another baby, and this one's a girl. We only have one other minke female in our waters." She grimaced. "That's not coming out right. We'd do everything we could to save *any* animal, no matter what. For us, it's more personal than being on an endangered list."

Salm burst through the doorway.

With a grim look, he took the phone from Manta and gave their uncle the precise coordinates for the cove.

Seeing her brother, Coral felt a sickening wave of guilt. Salm had complained—rightfully—that she hadn't helped to her fullest in their habitat. Now that she truly needed that power, she didn't have it. Because she was being punished for dueling.

Salm hung up and turned to them. "She's just over four meters, and Ray confirmed that's too big to move magically. Too risky to remove marine life that size from the water that buoys them. They've turned *The Grateful Seas* in this direction. We'll keep her from advancing onshore. Bad news is it'll be hours before they arrive."

"Who else can help?" Manta asked. "One of the local fishing boats?"

Salm shook his head. "They barely take direction from Pop. Do you think those old salts will listen to me, the scurvy dog generating the day's gossip?"

What did Salm do now?

Manta rolled her eyes. "If you'd only kept your mouth shut. Maybe Dar's son—"

Salm snapped his fingers. "Oyster! He's in town helping his uncle and an excellent swimmer. Our magic works well together. And that new chap Cor will surely lend his magic in some manner if Oy is involved."

"I'll get my suit," Coral said.

"Forget it," Salm said. "What can you do without magic?"

Plenty, with *borrowed* magic. She glanced at Ty. After all that kissing, his energy had filled her channels and could substitute for hers.

Manta elbowed Salm. "She understood the dolphins."

"Huh? How?" Then his gaze sprang to Ty, and a smile lit his face. His eyes flicked back to Coral. "How much this time?"

Warily, she edged toward Ty. "Don't ask. You need me —*Annie* needs me. Just leave me be and get back out there."

Ty had set his mug down and was reaching for her—then stopped, eyeing her.

Clearly, he'd side with her, even if he and Salm had been getting along. That was a relief. Gack, why had she stopped him from protecting her from Tiger? She'd love to see Salm try to get through Ty's shield...but this wasn't the time to tease Salm. They had work to do.

The look on Salm's face said he knew it as well. "Aye, will be easier with you." He eyed Ty with appreciation. "Good thing we all like you, mate. Very much," he added before leaving.

"Where's your suit, Coral?" Manta asked.

"The bathroom."

Manta left, and Ty pivoted, his brow cocked. "When Salm asked *how much*, did he mean what I think he meant?"

Ah, spells. Please don't let this turn ugly. She put her mug on the counter. "I've ended up with some of your energy. After we..." She puckered her lips in a mimicked kiss. "It works for me to talk to the dolphins. Do you mind if I continue to use your energy tonight, to coach them?"

"You won't get in trouble?"

"You heard them. Without Pop, the whale needs both Salm and me. It'd be nice if you'd come along and help, too."

"Me? Really?"

He still hadn't answered. "You're not mad I ended up with your energy?"

"No way." He laughed. "It's just as much my fault as yours.

Besides, it's, uh..." In a kind of mesmerized way, he pushed back her wet hair.

The normally innocent gesture was too intimate, considering she had nothing on beneath the towel. Ach. She'd done some serious cuddling before, but had always stopped things when she grew uncomfortable. Heat crawled over her face as she tugged the towel tighter and put on a smile that was half warning. "Touching?"

Ty blinked and dropped his hand. "Sorry. My energy's in you, but I don't have the right to go all possessive."

By the Orb, he didn't. But he'd acknowledged it and stopped, which was far better than Lemon, who would have tried to continue.

"You do the most amazing things," Ty said seriously. "*Fun* things. I'm honored you've asked me to help with your aquaculture work."

"Then you better fetch your wetsuit," Manta said.

They jerked apart.

Manta's violet eyes sparkled with laughter. She'd changed into her suit and held Coral's. "Sheesh, you two are like a pair of nervous rabbits. A word of advice: Don't act like that around Ma, or for sure she'll know what you're up to."

"I'll be back to take you out." He clutched his peregrinator and disappeared.

"Here." Manta offered Coral her wetsuit. "Dress quickly."

Coral grabbed it and stepped in.

"How does it feel? His energy?"

"Nice. Calm. Much easier than mine. It's incredible, Manta. I hardly have to work at all to control it."

"That's so strange, but perhaps another sign you do have this strong talent Pop wants you to train. Have you gone much further?"

Coral drew the zipper to her chin and cocked a brow at her sister. "Much further?"

"You know what I'm asking!"

"I do." She grinned wickedly. "I'm only trying to hold out like you always tried to do to me."

Manta flung an arm around her shoulders, laughing again. "I did not."

"I said you tried. We got to kissing."

"So how was it?"

"Wonderful." Their heads bumped together. "Strong lips, interesting movement and tasty. I could feel it all the way to my gut. 'Twas absolutely swoon-worthy!"

A throat cleared. They fell apart.

Ty stood on the other side of the prep table, wearing his wetsuit and a frown.

"Oh no," Manta squeaked. "I'll see you there." She dashed out the door, her wings unfurling.

Hotter than ever, Coral shifted in place. He shouldn't be upset. What she'd told Manta was true, a compliment, really. She wanted to smile at him, but hardly could.

"At least I know you liked my kissing." Ty grimaced. "Shall we go?"

She put out her hand.

They pereported to the beach they'd left and ran around the rocky cliff to the next cove. A dozen yards out, Salm stood next to Annie. The juvenile minke came to his armpits, the high tide washing around them. The incoming waves would work against their efforts to move the whale away from the shallows.

A pile of horseshoe-style life jackets lay on the beach, the kind that allowed them to still use their wings. Coral snatched up two, and they put them on. Manta arrived, put on a life jacket and flew out to join Salm.

Coral didn't trust flying with Ty's magic. She followed by walking, and the frigid water cut through her wetsuit. Beside her, Ty caught his breath. He wasn't as used to it as the locals, but then, neither was she used to the hours they'd likely be in it.

"Wait," shouted Manta, but Salm waved them forward, his words lost.

Still wading, Coral activated Ty's energy to hear what they were saying. *Spells*, Salm and Manta were fighting already, while, heartbreakingly, Annie was asking Salm for her ma, over and over. The dolphins zipping back and forth spotted her and chimed in: *Come, come, come… Danger, danger, little one…*

Coming, she called back to See-low, this pod's leader. *Wait there.*

"What's happening?" Ty asked.

"Ah, it's complex, the arguments and the calls…"

"How about you share it with me via…" A wave crashed over their thighs as he reached out with wiggling fingers. When she clasped his hand, his eyes grew wide.

Nothing I do is stopping Annie, Salm was saying. *We cannot wait for Piper.*

Coral will get too cold.

We'll find a way to warm her. Or Ty will. I need these dolphins organized to help, and I canna talk to them and Annie at the same time. I canna believe her mother lost her. She's too young, nursing still.

"Who else is speaking?" Ty asked, puzzled. "After the squeaks?" His hand tightened. "I can hear *them*."

"Oh, don't bother about their argument—*oh*. The dolphins!" She squeezed his hand as they jumped through the next wave together. "More than squeaks? Oh, that's so exciting for you."

Ach, a regular lighthouse those two are making, Salm snapped. *Perhaps the glow will turn Annie seaward. Coral's plenty warm now.*

Spells, the hurrying and excitement had raced Ty's energy and lit her like a giant bioluminescent jellyfish. Coral pulled it in and shoved forward into the next waist-high wave. It lifted her off her feet for a moment. The waves would be getting stronger as the tide came in.

Piper is here, Manta called. *Keeping a distance so as not to hit any dolphins. Coral?*

Coral!

Manta and Salm placed messages in her head—rather funny since she and Ty were at Annie's snout. But Manta was shoving at one flipper, and Salm must be doing the same on Annie's other side.

Piper paddled the kayak up behind the whale. Annie could tell. Beside herself now, the poor baby began to whimper in a high echoing. Two of the younger dolphins swam back and forth between her and the kayak, causing more confusion.

I'm here. Coral bobbed with the water and waved to Piper. "Ach, Salm has no control of them," she told Ty. "I'll be able to see and direct them once I'm in the kayak."

"I could pereport you," he offered. "I'll travel, wings out, and hover while I set you in the opening."

That sounded the fastest. She let Piper know they were coming. Ty unfurled his wings, rose and circled her waist. He pereported them, and in a second, she was slipping from his arms into the empty seat.

In the back of the kayak, Piper shook his head. "Manta said, 'Don't ask, don't tell.' But after I heard you thought-speak, I understood how you're doing this with a quash."

While Ty fluttered beside the craft, Coral leaned over the side and sent the young dolphins away with a shooing hand motion. See-low was the one she needed. She called him.

The big pod leader approached and put his head into her hand. *Job, job, job?*

Aye, she told See-low. *Gather the pod.*

They came. Using Ty's magic, she began greeting them, but See-low pushed into her hand again and sent her an image of two young dolphins. *Others.*

Aye, we'll all work together.

Lost. Others.

Pop isn't here, she told him. *We'll do the job.*

Lost. Others. Lost. He squeaked a summoning signal, and two young dolphins pushed excitedly among the others.

"No, settle. Settle!" She signaled with a dropping open palm—

The kayak pitched sideways, and Piper yelled, "Watch out!" too late. Coral saw the sea rush up—

Then she jerked to a halt. Something stretchy hauled her back… Ty's silver gel stuck like a tentacle to her shoulder.

Piper hooted. "Keep whatever that is handy."

Ty laughed. "Will do."

Coral swiped at her face. She should thank him—and chide See-low. However, the calls of these young'uns weren't right. They sounded like *Ni-lee.*

Ni-lee was what the other pod called their female leader.

She put a hand on each young dolphin head. *What do you call yourselves?* At their answering squeaks, she shot upright. *Salm? Two of these dolphins are from the other pod. The* missing *pod.*

Salm hovered up above the minke, searching out the dolphins and then her.

The rip!

NEW APPLICATIONS FOR TRAINING

Ty looked from Coral to her siblings as they snapped out complaints about their shield's rips and how difficult Tern Bay's council was being about the Isle of Giuthas' problems. Listening in brought home again how much of a stranger Ty was, not only to Tern Bay, but also to this island.

If only he weren't.

He knew the Seas better than when they'd nearly sailed into the rip, but he still hesitated to discuss his academy lessons on rips. Officially, the Windborne had no policy. Enclaves were self-governing and could make their own determinations, but he knew the current recommendation was to abandon the enclave. Shield rips presented a risk of exposure to the human world.

These animals traveling through a rip is the only explanation for this minke being without her mother, Coral grumbled. *Or dolphin yearlings being separated from their pod.* She pressed her hands against the yearlings' noses.

Later, we'll quiz the young'uns and find their family. First, we save her. Salm ducked down on his side of the whale.

I'll tell Granpop our suspicions, Manta sent. *He'll pass it on to Tern Bay and Giuthas. We just have to hope this rip isn't close by.*

Coral was already speaking to the young dolphins, assigning each lost yearling to an adult in this pod. Piper edged the kayak between the beach and the whale, paddling constantly to keep them from being cast beachward. It was the best spot for Coral, because she could see both sides of the animal. Salm was at one fin, Manta at the other, dolphins on either side.

Here's the process Uncle Ray told us to use, Salm said. *We have to get them to push the minke when the waves are coming in. Note that's in. The water will give her lift and raise her off the sand. Instead of letting her flow forward with the tide, we need to drag her out to sea. You understand the plan?* he asked Coral.

Got it. She explained the procedure to the dolphins in simple words and images she conjured. Then she gave each a station on the whale's body and sent them out.

The way she spoke with the animals looked easy, but Ty reminded himself that so did tossing out gel to catch someone, a technique he'd spent three years perfecting. Coral had gained the dolphins' trust over years of practice.

Give me a spot, Ty said.

Everyone startled at his question. *Mate! How long have you been on our frequency?* Salm asked.

The whole time. I figured everyone knew that when I shared magic with Coral it included everything.

Everything? Woo-hoo!

Salm, stow it.

Everything magical. Ty made sure his irritation came through the thought-speak.

Hoy! Piper's deep voice cut across the squabble.

Salm gave Ty a spot at the minke's tail, showing him how to hold the fluke by standing behind it with his arm slung over.

They're in position, Salm called from his side of the whale.

Coral called to the two at the whale's snout, *Batter her nose— not hard, mind you—but enough to show her who's boss. Then everyone else shove hard, shove her out to sea. Ready? Here comes a wave.*

Ty had just thought about the danger of the whale's bulk sliding over him and trapping him underwater if she popped loose when Coral shouted, *Push!*

Several futile pushes later, he knew he'd have plenty of warning if the minke began to budge. They tried through several waves—for three minutes, according to Ty's count of the lighthouse's roving double flash every fifteen seconds. The minke wasn't moving, and she began whining at the dolphins hitting her.

"Her distress is mounting, damn it," shouted Salm. "Where is Oyster? I could use that lad."

He's worked with us lots, Coral explained to Ty. *He can do magic with water that we can't.*

Ty might not have trained for saving whales or have the skills this Oyster fellow did, but watching had given him an idea. *Would it help if I magically hold the kayak?*

Aye, Piper called. *Everything will help at this point.*

Ty magicked out his wings and flew above the whale. *I can anchor two strands of energy, one at each end of the kayak, onto the whale's head, if it doesn't bother her.* She was big enough, but they might find it insulting to use the animal this way. *The kayak would rise and fall with the waves, but remain the same distance away from her.*

Huh. Salm? Piper asked.

Interesting idea. Go ahead. The rest of us will keep pushing.

Ty flung a strand of energy skyward and lengthened it by casting it out several times, like a fly fisherman, building a thick but flexible magical rope. He maneuvered the tip up to the whale and attached it with a suction-cup end. After doing the same at the prow of the kayak, he ran a spell through it to add rigidity. When he released it, his energy held the kayak at the prescribed distance.

"Impressive," Coral said between waves. "Where'd you learn that?"

"Academy. We learned to create a rope to tie up someone, or to secure ourselves for climbing. It can also be made solid to travel across if you damage your wings."

"Just where would you be getting into a situation like that, needing to tie up someone?"

"Oh, uh, around." He concentrated on casting and securing the second strand at the stern. Luckily, she was too busy to ask any more questions. Or too cold. She was shivering now.

"Hey, I remembered something else I learned from that class," he said. "It should stop your shivering. Wanna try?"

When she nodded, he lightly landed behind her and clasped her shoulder. He washed her skin with energy and heated it.

She sighed. "Oohh, nice. How'd you do that?"

"Combining the atoms. The energy released by the bonding is heat—a simple chemical reaction. You just need to pull the right two atoms."

"I'd like a lesson later?"

He wouldn't mind that at all.

With the kayak stable, Piper tucked away his paddle and took a position at the whale's tail with Ty.

"Hallo," someone hailed from overhead. "This is a sorry excuse for a party!" Two wizards descended from the dark, guys about Ty's age—oh. They were the guys Coral had greeted in the shop the day he met her.

"Oy! Cor!" Salm shouted. "Thank the Orb."

"Sorry it took us so long. Had to borrow Cor a wetsuit." The fair-haired guy, Oyster, gestured to his friend. "Hadn't planned on anything like this."

"Never do," Salm said. "Have you got much energy about you?"

Grinning, Oy spread his hands and briefly ignited a giant ball of pink-orange energy between them. "Arranged for more, too. I got a hold of Raven. He, Willow and a few others are pere-porting to the lighthouse. They'll be able to spot us from there."

"Oyster, I'll make you first mate," Salm said. "Let's you and I join Coral." He pointed toward the kayak. *Take my place, Piper?* he added, and Piper moved to the whale's fin.

Oy folded his wings and dropped neatly into the water next to Coral with only a small splash. Salm swam over. The other guy, Cor, hovered, looking from the circling dolphins to the length of the whale and meeting Ty's gaze.

"Hi," Ty called. "Ty Sterling. I'm clueless about this, if you have any instructions."

"Cor van Gruen," he said in his British accent. "I'm only here to lend magic and follow orders."

That's a welcome change, Coral sent to Ty. *Tell him he'll be with you.*

I heard that. Cor rolled his eyes and entered the water slower than Oyster had.

Coral said a quick, *Sorry,* and then, *Push!*

The nearest dolphin churned water over Cor. He surfaced and shook back his hair with a spray of water. "Trees don't bloody shove you around like this." But he was grinning. "My sister is going to be so jealous when I tell her she missed helping a whale. She's arriving tomorrow."

Ty showed him how to hold the fluke and explained the logistics of pulling with the incoming tide.

Cor reverently stroked the whale's tail, then hooked his arm over it. "Does it mind if we touch it?"

"I think she's so upset it doesn't matter at this point."

Be ready, Coral called. *And push!*

Ty just had time to dig in his heels and pull—

The whale moved.

"What?" Ty's feet slipped before he realized he had to keep walking—and that the water was now threaded with glowing pink wisps. "That guy is magicking *ocean waves?*"

Beside him, Cor laughed. "Oyster is amazing with water."

They managed another few steps on the next wave. More of

the water glowed luminescent pink, now with swirls of blue and gold mixed in.

"The blue energy has to be Salm's," Ty muttered when they couldn't move farther. He'd seen that over the last few days. "Where did the gold energy come from?"

"That would be me," Cor said quietly.

Yeah, he said he'd be lending energy…which meant that these wizards had merged. He nodded to Cor. "Thanks. This job wasn't going anywhere before you guys showed up."

Cor grinned back.

During the next wave, several more wizards arrived like a flock of nighttime birds—would those be night herons? Salm directed them into place, some in the waves at the kayak, others along the sides of the minke. The water now swirled with multiple energy colors—yellow, orangish, green and a variety of light blues. Wizards and dolphins worked through wave after wave, with Coral calling, *Push*, with every inward roll of water.

Minutes later, the whale's fluke shoved over Ty's shoulder, just as he'd feared. The dolphins swam furiously, splashing as they pushed the moving minke.

"Whoa," Ty shouted at the same time Cor shouted, "Bloody freakin'—" Their gazes met.

Coral's warning came into this head. "Out of the way!" he echoed and shoved himself upward with his energy. He popped free of the sea, wings unfurling.

Below him, Cor wasn't as fast. The tail rose—

Ty swooped, hand extended. "Here," he yelled.

Cor reached, their hands linked and Ty dragged him clear. Cor's dark wings unfurled, and he was airborne.

Ty searched the water. Manta clung to Annie's side, and Salm was at the whale's nose. Piper popped to the surface and swam for the kayak, which was still attached by Ty's gel to the whale's forehead, with Coral clinging to the sides. Other wizards surrounded or followed the whale, all lit with magic.

"Everyone accounted for?" Piper shouted, and when he got affirmative *ayes*, he added, "Stand by while Salm calms Annie and figures out if the dolphins can contain her under Coral's direction."

"Would she beach herself again if we let her go on her way?" Ty asked.

"Possibly," Piper answered. "It's best she's reunited with her mother and tracked for a bit."

Except for Salm, Coral, Manta and Piper, everyone landed on the beach to wait. Between the plaintive cries of the minke, Cor and Oyster introduced Ty to wizards from the Isle of Giuthas who'd come to help. Just two others were teens, Raven and Willow. Nebula, Luna's sister who'd helped with their regatta practice was there, but not Luna. Had she not been at home? If she wasn't there, why hadn't she been with Salm?

None of your business, dude.

Ty talked with the others around a small fire they'd started. After a half hour, Piper reported that the minke hadn't calmed much, but her efforts to break from the circling dolphins had been thwarted. "Likely because she's tired from her ordeal. Salm and Coral will keep talking her down. If Oy, Cor and Ty can stay as backup, we should be set."

Four hours later, with the tide turning, *The Grateful Seas* came into sight. It anchored, and the dolphins herded the minke out to where Ray and Bert magicked a net to keep her corralled while they wrestled a harness around her. Finally, Annie was secure, and Coral directed the dolphins to move off. Her uncles would keep Annie alongside their schooner until they could reunite her with her mother.

"Finding Taylor will be our chore," Coral said to Ty as they floated in the kayak alongside the ship.

Her uncle Ray flew down with a bucket of baitfish as rewards for the dolphins. "Coral? Brilliant work tonight. Dolph and Mer will be so proud." He hugged her before moving off to thank the others.

Along with everyone else, Ty grabbed handfuls of the fish to drop into the mouths of the waiting dolphins.

"They deserve it for sticking with the job," Salm said. "I wonder how hard it'll be to call on them in the morning to start our search."

"Bribe them!" Ty held up a smelly herring. "They can't seem to get enough of this." He fed another to the next dolphin.

Coral laughed as she shoved aside the nose at his side. "That one has you pegged. Because you cannot tell them apart, he is dropping underwater and coming up over and over."

"Who do I feed, then?"

"Coral," Manta said. "Take her home and feed *her*. We'll follow in a few minutes."

They pereported to the bakery kitchen. While Ty magically changed into dry clothes, Coral grabbed a muffin. She took only a few bites before rummaging in the refrigerator. "Ugh, this one contains only bakery ingredients, and we have no leftovers upstairs." She pushed back her hair with a hand that shook from cold.

"Do you want me to dry you before we fix—"

"I'll run upstairs to change. Instead, could you find us something to eat besides sweets and bread?"

"Eggs, bacon, that kind of thing?"

"Aye, thanks."

Ty pereported to Dar's kitchen, gathered what he needed and returned to Manta's. When Coral came down, he had Dar's microwave plugged into an outlet and humming as it cooked.

She picked up one of the dozen boxes he'd stacked on the kneading table and pointed to an image of an egg and bacon sandwich. "This looks good. What pans do we need?"

Bing!

He removed the hot sandwich. The waft of steam flooded his

nose with a familiar smell, and Coral looked as if she was about to faint, or fall upon him with a hundred kisses.

He grinned and handed it to her. "Tastes good, too."

Coral startled awake, her hand going automatically to silence her ringing alarm. The dream still enveloped her: She and Ty had been pressed together, energy merging.

A glow lit her bed in the predawn dark.

A silver glow.

No! She flung back the covers and stumbled to the bathroom mirror. A silver shimmer reflected back, her face surrounded by bright beads of magic. One slid the length of a strand of her hair, which she'd left loose after showering in the middle of the night.

Coral raised her hand and formed an energy ball. She stoppered the sink and dropped it in the basin, hardly glancing at its swirling mass before forming another. And another.

She groaned after the seventh. Still more of Ty's energy was present, an incredible amount considering the rate that she'd been using it to communicate with the dolphins. Had she unconsciously drawn on Ty's reserves because she'd been cold? Regardless, this went beyond accidental—possibly unforgivable. It was enough workable magic to conduct business as usual, to function as a wizard.

What if Ty believed she'd tricked him out of the energy, as she'd admitted she tricked her dueling opponents? Her face warmed at that thought and another: What could she, Tern Bay's top duelist, do with this much available power?

29

BACK TO THE [UN]USUAL

The rain slowed everything. Pausing on the sea cliff above Tern Bay, Ty peered from the hood of his yellow fisherman's slicker, unable to make out the misty beach in the dull morning light. He should take his usual left toward Fintail's, but instead, with a firm nudge, he forced Pepper to turn toward One Good Bun. "This way, old boy. You'll get an early treat." *And I'll get to see Coral sooner.*

The drizzle continued while they descended to the center of town. He and Pepper met fewer folks than normal, all disguised by similar rain gear. The visitors and vendors had vanished. Every indoor restaurant was no doubt full and using up their dairy supplies.

Ty steered Pepper and the cart under the bakery's overhang and waved a magical brushing over the pony's thick coat. The beads of water weren't sluicing off. Ty dug into his cores for more energy—and paused at what he found: Half his reserves were gone.

He'd expected lower energy levels after the whale rescue, but did talking to wildlife use that much energy?

It wasn't like he had anything magical to do today, but he

liked to keep complete power at his disposal. Ty chewed his lip and thought through the dairy chores he could do in this weather. To recharge his cores, he'd need more interactions with the natural world than tending cows would provide. Spreading manure? Turning the compost pile?

Heck, he'd skip recharging if Coral accepted his invitation to hang out together—maybe at the bookstore? He wanted to take advantage of a rainy day off from sailing lessons. He grabbed the first rack of bottles, rattling them so hard some could have broken.

"Calm yourself," he muttered under his breath. Coral might not be as excited to see him. He opened the door and called, "Hello."

Across the kitchen, Coral froze, wrapped in her too-big apron and carrying a tray of muffins. Belatedly, she smiled. "You're early."

He'd definitely surprised her. He felt a foolish grin coming on. "I couldn't wait to see you this morning."

Piper blocked Ty's way with another tray of muffins and tilted his head in a conspiratorial manner. "Spells, lad! You have it bad. You're supposed to keep them guessing a mite longer."

"I'm not into games. Had enough of them at academy."

"Set the milk yonder"—Piper nodded to the counter—"and take this to the pantry with her. Be quick, will you?"

"Thanks," he breathed. Tray in hand, he followed Coral.

Behind them, Piper burst out singing:

"When Irish eyes are smiling,

Sure, 'tis like the morn in Spring.

In the lilt of Irish laughter…"

Oh man. Did Piper have to do that? Ty's ears were flaming hot.

"And when Irish eyes are smiling,

Sure, they steal your heart away."

Ahead of him, Coral was laughing. She slid her tray onto a

rack, and he did the same.

He extended his arms. "May I?"

She was against his chest before answering, "Please."

He stroked her back. She smelled like the flour that dusted her, but also of cloves and maple. "What have you been eating this morning?"

"Everything! I'm still recovering from last night. The pumpkin spice are good, but I think the maple-frosted apple cinnamon are my favorite." She plucked a muffin from the tray she'd been carrying. "Want to try one?"

"I'd rather try you this morning."

Face freezing, she swayed back.

What was wrong? He dropped his arms. "I meant a kiss. What did you think I was saying?"

She hesitated. "Did you really not mind when I ended up with your energy yesterday?"

"No, I found the whole experience great." He squeezed her hand, hoping to reassure her. "Hearing dolphin speech was totally new. The training for that skill must have transferred with the magic, right?"

She chewed her lip, staring at him with her gorgeous eyes.

Had they gone too far? They'd ignored her enclave's rules, so maybe he wasn't supposed to talk about it. Or kiss her, and by the Orb, he wanted to kiss her.

"The training to actually talk to them is more complicated," she said distractedly. "Say, Ty—"

"There's more? I can't wait until you have your magic back so we can explore—"

"Ach. Not on my watch." Manta stood in the doorway.

Coral frowned at her. "Naught is happening on *your* watch. Shoo."

"Tomorrow." Manta picked up a tray. "Ma and Pop will be back tomorrow. Then you can explore anything you like." She left.

No wonder Piper had said to hurry. Ty took the muffin Coral still held and put it on the tray. "You never said about the kiss. May I?"

"Quick. I don't want her in here again. I'll be hearing about it all—"

He cut her off, *quick*. Sweet maple frosting, cinnamon and Coral. Just as his head started to muddle, he backed away. *Deliveries to make, and you have a job to do.* "Delicious, thank you."

Her gaze slowly rose to his. "I... Ty... you're welcome."

She seemed unsure, but he felt happy and confident in their being together. He pulled her into the hall. "You feel guilty about putting Manta in a spot?"

"She's not in a *spot*." Coral huffed. "You should have seen her *spots* a year ago. She and Piper in the sailboat, she and Piper in the storeroom, she and Piper in her bunk. I told you it was her fault I have these restrictions. After years of knowing Piper and not doing anything about bonding with him, she got into it. Really into it. She ruined her trust with Ma herself and does *not* need to blame me for any setbacks as she rebuilds it."

"Oh?"

They crossed the kitchen. Coral pressed her lips tight and propped open the door. He unloaded the rest of the delivery with her helping from the inside. They finished, and the rain began to fall in earnest. He caught the pocket of Coral's apron.

"Would you like to go to the bookstore with me this afternoon?" he asked. "Salm won't want to have lessons."

"Nay, don't worry. He's not missing his sleep. He'll be there."

"What about this terrible weather?"

She grinned. "You're showing your landlubber origins. We sail in all weather. Except dead calm, which isn't an issue today. See you at two thirty, sailor boy." She handed him raisins for Pepper and pushed him out the door.

He fed Pepper his treat, and they started down the alley. He was almost to the end when running footfalls sounded above the drum of the rain. Stretching a bright yellow rain slicker over her head, Coral dashed up, and his energy jumped.

"Whoa!" he called to both Pepper and himself. "Come for another kiss?"

"Oh, Ty." Wrinkling her nose, she dropped the slicker onto her shoulders. "Manta's right, you have changed your ways. She says the same thing happened to Luna when she and Salm first exchanged energy. I didn't believe her, because we have not *exchanged*. Manta said to tell you, or she'll ask Salm to. So..." She wrung her hands. "Do you feel jumpy? More inclined to do stuff you wouldn't before? Um, carelessly, I mean?"

He laughed. "Because I kissed you in the pantry, which, by the way, Piper orchestrated."

"*She* says it's a reaction to being with blue energy."

"No, I haven't changed. I clearly remember saying stuff to you without thinking before my magic ended up in your channels. I wondered then why I couldn't keep my mouth shut, but it was all me. Take my word for it, my energy wasn't in you long enough to be influenced by yours."

"Last night it was, for hours." She didn't meet his gaze.

Spells, Manta didn't have to make Coral feel bad—they'd done it to save a whale! "Cycling through, yeah," he said. "If any stayed with you, just keep it and use it."

"I have it locked away," she murmured. "You aren't missing...much, then?"

Should he tell her? *I'd rather tell Manta to butt out.* "I have enough. What happened to Salm and Luna that was so bad?"

"Manta says Luna was jumpier, more impulsive, until they became used to each other. I never noticed. Manta says because that's normal behavior for me."

"I don't think you're jumpy. Neither is Luna. Salm is another story. How long did Luna have the problem?"

She cast her gaze down again before meeting his. "Um, a

month. Look, sorry. Manta only told me last night and then started in about it again after you left just now. I figured I better… Ty, I have—"

"All because I couldn't wait to see you this morning? Coral, that's normal for a guy. Tell Manta to get over it. I really like kissing you. Don't you like it?"

From inside the tunnel of her hood, Coral blinked.

Her sister sure shook her confidence. He smiled and got a smile in return.

"Aye," she said slowly.

"There. We understand each other better than Manta does. Don't let her worry you, okay?"

She smiled in earnest now. "Goodbye kiss?"

Yes. Maybe he wouldn't chastise Manta after all.

Coral expected an argument from Salm, or at least a barrage of questions, when she proposed they search for the missing dolphin pod after Ty had headed back to do the milking. But Salm agreed. She hadn't mentioned she had magic to do it, and he didn't ask. Nor had Manta when Coral checked if her sister could finish the baking alone.

Neither questioned her, because Lemon had made the rounds of the businesses in midmorning, passing on for his mother that Tern Bay's council had closed their enclave boundaries in case there were other rips still to be found. Unless safe sailing routes could be identified into the harbor, they would stay closed and Fest participation would be restricted to those already present.

They took Dar's son's 420 that was now moored beside *The Peaceful Seas.* Once out of the harbor, they'd need the weight of the larger boat for stability in today's wind and waves. Hugging the coast—which search parties had determined was rip-free—

Salm steered the craft northward. In the distance to the west, the rip Salm and Luna had marked shimmered its magical warning.

From her place at the tiller, Coral asked Salm, "When was the last time you had contact with Ni-lee's pod?"

"While patrolling our western ocean boundary." Salm glanced at her. "I couldn't find her when we passed north of the isle, the day before we sailed into Tern Bay. Pop neither. He figured they'd catch up to *The Peaceful* once we put to port here."

Coral's heart felt heavy. She should have known this. She should have been paying attention. But, nay, she'd pushed off her duties, thinking only of the duels ahead.

Duels that got me into trouble. If it wasn't for Ty and his generosity, she'd have no way to help their animals last night and now.

She shivered. "I hope they didn't enter this rip."

Salm shook his head. "Granpop told me this morning that the elders believe as many as four ocean rips formed. That's how many of Giuthas' terrestrial rips have seawater in them. One is freshwater. They rechecked all and found no dolphins."

"Thank the Orb." Coral wiped the rain from her cheeks.

"If our elders—or we—can identify the connecting rip entrances and exits, that will relieve some of Tern Bay's worries. I hate to see them close Fest, not with all the work the enclave has put into preparing. All the work *I've* put into it," Salm muttered.

She should ask about his help to Luna's family, getting the lighthouse ready for tours, but they'd come upon the cove where Salm had asked See-low's pod to stay until they learned more.

Salm began calling to the dolphins through his energy. After a minute of no answer, she couldn't stand it and tried calling with Ty's magic, gaze scanning the rolling waves and the sea cliffs beyond.

Finally, a dolphin leaped. *Here,* See-low called back.

Coral blew out her breath. *Come!*

Three, then seven, then all of the dolphins cleared the waves in running leaps. They swam up and circled the sailboat.

"You talk to them," Salm called, "while I keep the craft as steady as possible." He took the tiller from her and held it and the mainsheet in a slow crawl along the troughs of the waves.

Salm never admitted that she was better at communications with sea mammals, but he always passed the delicate jobs to her.

She hooked a foot under the hiking strap and leaned over the hull. First a check—aye, every individual was present, including the two young'uns from the other pod. *See-low,* she called. *Where did you find others?*

See-low indicated they were with the whale when his pod arrived.

"You get that, Salm? They were already down past Kittiwake Point."

"I did. It'll be harder to question yearlings."

She questioned the first young dolphin. He sent her images of the cliffs up this way. She asked him again to describe his travels with the whale. Again, he sent images of the cliffs, fishing boats, the town, then the lighthouse, features the Seas had taught them that humans would recognize.

She confirmed the route by questioning the other young'un separately. "If Ni-lee's pod was never in this area, then these young'uns entered the rip somewhere else and came out here, not at a rip near the lighthouse."

Salm handed her the baitfish pail. "Give them a break, then ask about *before* the whale. With their pod."

That wasn't as easy to decipher. They sent random images. The pelting rain was finding its way under Coral's cinched slicker hood by the time she figured out to ask about getting lost.

That focused the images. The two young'uns had been alternately chasing each other. They came upon the young minke. It joined in...chasing, circling, following, chasing. *Land,* she thought to them. The male squeaked back, *Not me,* meaning he hadn't been paying attention to that.

A silhouette of a tall, narrow island popped into her mind from the female young'un.

Coral sucked a breath. *Lady Soila's? You were here?*

They squirmed in excitement under her hands.

"Coral." Salm's voice held a warning.

Oh no. Pop always cautioned them not to show enthusiasm for any particular answer. She brushed the wet from her brow, flexed her stiff fingers and put her hands back into the water again. She petted the dolphins for a minute before asking again, *Land?*

Only the female gave the image, but it was the same one.

Where? Coral wanted a confirmation of the name they used with the dolphins, one she wasn't sure so young of an animal could give.

Hat isle.

"That's it!" Salm hooted. "From the distance she's showing, they were a half mile out."

"Did you see the rise of its rock abutment on the right? That view is from the islet's western side." *The Peaceful* frequently circled the tiny islet west of Giuthas. The eccentric old witch who owned and occupied it wanted nothing to do with their enclave, despite her grandson being the head of its council and her great-granddaughter now working there.

Salm shoved the bait bucket toward Coral. "Still within our boundary waters. I bet the pod isn't answering because they're looking for these two."

"Maybe," Coral countered with a shake of her head. She dropped a fish into the waiting dolphin's mouth. "Or Lady Soila is up to her magical tricks again."

30

PROBLEMS WITH BEING HUMBLE

Back at the bakery, Coral tugged Manta from the sales counter. Several customers glared, so she called, "Whale situation!" by way of an apology.

"No," Manta cried. "Not another!"

"*Good* whale situation," Coral assured her once they were in the kitchen. "The young'uns told me where they'd been before—"

Manta put a finger to her lips. "They told *Salm*." She glared at their brother, who'd looked up from stuffing a dry bag with any food he could lay his hands on. "It must be *Salm* they spoke with, *because you're quashed*," she hissed.

Oh.

Coral's and Salm's gazes met, and he nodded. Of all the—

She crossed her arms. "Fine," she spat. The animals would get back to where they belonged, but—*blast it!*—Ma and Pop wouldn't learn that she was involved in any level of competency that would get them to leave her alone.

"The dolphins told *Salm* they'd played with the minke on the other side of the Isle of Giuthas. We can return them to their pod, search for the mother whale and"—she leaned toward Manta—"the entrance they used to travel this rip."

"We devised a plan," Salm said, "but we need Granpop to make the calls on the isle to get us through to Lady Soila's islet. I want Coral in the boat to encourage the pod to stay with us."

"And Ty," she put in. "It'll be good ocean experience."

Even as she said it, a look formed on Manta's face, one just like Ma would give her.

Coral clutched her sister's arm. "Then, Ty and I can handle the boat, while *Salm* monitors the pod, *because I'm quashed.*"

Manta smiled. "Aye, that's what Granpop and Granny should see when you arrive. And anyone—oh, you'll need Sir Humus with you to get into Lady Soila's waters."

Ugh. Did the head of Giuthas' council know she was quashed? Did her grandparents? She'd have thought Ma and Pop would keep news of her punishment within their immediate family, but now she wasn't sure.

While Salm got on the telephone to their grandparents, Coral paced the kitchen and considered if she'd need magic for this. She might. She could keep it locked down. Or she could give it back to Ty so she wouldn't accidentally use silver magic with Sir Humus there.

Not what I want to do.

Salm put a hand over the receiver. "Once we reach the isle, Granpop will lend us their motorboat. It'll be faster and more maneuverable if we happen upon another rip. Anything else?"

"Get permission for Ty to get into the enclave," Coral said.

After Salm hung up, she telephoned Ty. She might have been able to reach him magically, but it seemed prudent to start acting quashed.

When Ty joined them at their mooring, they had the sails up again and See-low's pod collected. He climbed in beside her and put on his life jacket while Salm eased out the mainsheet. The mainsail luffed. After passing off the lines, Salm loosed their tethering to North Dock and directed Ty to sail south of the marked rip. The fishermen had already checked that route's safety, and Manta had reported that they had one route confirmed into the enclave.

Rain still fell. It didn't seem any darker than it had been all afternoon, but the sun would be setting soon. The evening winds gusted, making the sailing rough. Thanks to their lessons, Ty now knew the predictable current and wind patterns and defaulted to them rather than making constant changes. Her chest swelled with pride to see him handle the craft so smoothly.

I should give him back his magic. Their gazes met. "I canna show any magic use on this trip," she said.

"You're leaving them to Salm?" He lifted his chin toward the dolphins swimming with the boat.

"Aye." Salm wasn't looking, so she palmed a ball of Ty's energy and pressed it into his hand. "Here."

"Whoa." He grinned. "I don't know whether to be honored that you trust my sailing or insulted that you don't want my magic. Why don't you just lock it away?"

She could. With Sir Humus there, she wouldn't be tempted to use it. She returned three more balls and hesitated. Did she really want to show Ty how much of his magic she had?

As they came into the lee of Giuthas' cliffs and the winds quieted, Salm crowed about his prowess at training landlubbers. Ty slid her a grin behind Salm's back.

She knocked Ty with her elbow. "It wasn't me either. No one gets this good in a week. What you said all along was true. You just needed to sort the ocean skills. You're a natural."

"Maybe it's the luck of having dolphins accompany us."

"You've proven yourself ready to race, mate," Salm called back. "This storm should blow through tonight, so the regatta might be scheduled for tomorrow, on the first day of Fest."

Ty headed into their cove, and she pointed toward the

floating dock extending from the mountainside in the protection of a rocky promontory. Though the Seas lived on the sea, this area of the Forest had been set aside for their family for generations. Staircases and boardwalks led to a deck and pavilion partway up, furnished with outdoor furniture, a table and chairs and a fire pit. Higher still, Granny and Granpop's cottage was sheltered in the pines with a beautiful view of the coast up the island.

Under a drizzle, three slicker-clad figures were making their way down to the dock. Coral recognized their grandparents, but the third wizard looked small for Sir Humus. If he hadn't come, then they'd have to hold the pod in the cove overnight. It wouldn't be the first time.

Granny and the unknown person climbed aboard their motorboat. They began wiping down the seats, but Coral had to crew for Ty, so it was another minute before she could look again. Granpop was waiting to tie up the 420, Granny joining him. In the motorboat, it wasn't Sir Humus. A girl pulled back her hood—she had brown bobbed hair, hoop earrings and a familiar grin on her cherry-red lips.

"Who's that?" Ty asked. "Not the head of your council?"

Coral grinned back and waved. "His niece, Duffy. She can enter her great-grandmother's boundary waters as well as Sir Humus can, and best of all, she gets in more trouble than I do. She won't give me away." She'd keep the rest of Ty's magic, and once they were out of sight of her grandparents, she could manage the dolphins.

They climbed out, and she introduced Ty to her grandparents.

Granpop shook his hand. "Watched you coming in, lad. Decent job of it, so I gather you aren't the beginner my grandson claims."

"I've been sailing for close to ten years, but not full time like the Seas do."

"You'll catch up soon enough." He gestured to Salm. "Caution the pod to stay to the bow of the motorboat. I'll ride along, if that's all right?" Without waiting for an answer, Granpop led the way down the dock.

She and Salm shared a knowing look. What could they say? Even though Granpop had turned the habitat management over to his sons, he kept a hand in it. Coral swung her leg over the hull. She wasn't going to ask what Granpop knew about her quash. Instead, she drained the rest of Ty's magic from her channels and packed it against her quashed core.

Granpop didn't act differently from usual in Pop's absence. He directed Duffy to drive the boat—she had plenty of experience—and Salm to monitor the starboard dolphins, while he watched the port-side animals. That left Coral and Ty sitting in the back like ballast—not even touching, because she couldn't risk anything happening. She always ended up being treated like a kid with Granpop, the problem with being the youngest.

They left and circled the southern end of the Isle of Giuthas. Lady Soila's islet came into view as a dark bump against the western horizon.

Coral perked up. Magic wasn't necessary to spot a rip. "Under these clouds, any sparkle will signal a rip's presence," she told Ty. "Stay alert."

Everyone sat forward, scanning the ocean for the pricks of light or strands of color on the waves they'd seen three days before. Nothing stood out as they approached the tall, hat-shaped islet. Duffy said her great-gran was expecting them and let them know when the boat passed through the magical border of the area Lady Soila had cordoned off as hers within the Isle of Giuthas enclave. Old wizards got away with stuff teenagers never did.

No one saw signs of a rip, but neither did they see the other pod.

"We'll head around to the dock side first," Duffy said.

"Great-Gran will meet us there, and she might have already spotted them today from the top."

The islet's dock was on its western side. "Salm? Wasn't it the western side that the young'un gave the image of?" Coral asked, trying not to give away that *she* had seen this image.

Salm straightened and glanced at her. "Righto. We should keep close to shore as we come around and focus our search farther out, I believe, based on the islet's size in their image."

Coral nodded.

They rounded the cliff, and the pier came into view—and so did the dolphins from Ni-lee's pod. Several were leaping and dancing for four figures at the end of the pier.

Everyone burst out laughing. "Who would have thought old Lady Soila would feed our animals?" Salm said.

Duffy grinned. "If it gets you out of her property faster, then she'll think it's worthwhile. The mother whale doesn't seem to be there, though."

Salm flashed a grin to Coral.

She suppressed a snicker. "A whale wouldn't be with the dolphins."

"Or attracted by herring. Does your gran keep krill on hand?" Salm joked.

"Oh." Duffy wrinkled her nose. "Didn't think about that—hey!" She yanked the wheel.

Coral slammed sideways into Ty. Granpop snapped at Duffy about her driving, then careened to the side where Salm hung over the hull. Coral surged to her feet to look, just as Duffy cut the engine *and* the back of the boat hit something.

She lurched. Ty caught her arm, and her—Ty's—magic lurched, too.

Spells. She fought it down, the opposite of what she wanted to do. "What happened?"

No one answered. Her body was roaring, the magic desperate to get out so she could speak with Salm. Coral spun to inspect the water off the stern, her stomach twisting. A hit at the back of a motorboat could be really bad—

"Is that blood in the water?" Ty asked at the same time that she saw the dark splotch.

"Curses," she yelled. "We hit a dolphin."

Handle it. Salm placed the message in her mind. "*We've* got an angry whale here."

31

WORKING 'WITHOUT' POWER

Coral scanned the bobbing dolphin bodies, but also activated Ty's energy and loosed it to her fingers—the more practical thing to do. A rush of Salm's pleading, the annoyed calls of the whale, the replies of the dolphins and Granpop's brusque directions flowed through her head.

She blocked them. *See-low. One hurt. Find hurt.*

Hurt? Hurt? See-low answered, and the other dolphins' squeaks resounded through her.

Ty squeezed her arm. "How long will it take him to find the bleeding one?"

She startled. She'd forgotten he'd also hear what she heard.

Found! The big male leaped so she could see him. He was halfway to the dock and chasing a dolphin swimming in a zigzag.

Aye, they'd hit him. Coral bit off a cry. She had to show no emotion. *Think.* The other pod was closer—and Salm might need See-low's help—so she called to Ni-lee to find and protect the young'un. Then she asked Ty, "Could your fancy gel be used as first aid to seal a dolphin's injury?"

He eyed her. "Yesss?"

"Good. We've got to stop the bleeding," she said, "or we'll have a worse problem—sharks."

Ty frowned. "Can't Lady Soila keep them out?"

"We aren't leaving our pod here."

See-low popped his head up at the side of the boat. *Found. Returned to mother. To Ni-lee.* He sent the image of the young'un at her side, the pod circling.

Thank the Orb. *We'll help, too. Fetch Roam and Tu-lee.* They were from Ni-lee's pod. She turned to Ty. "We're going for a swim." She stripped off her rain gear down to her wetsuit.

"I-I… Are you sure?" His eyes were wide, but he shed his slicker and boots.

The big adults she'd picked bumped the hull. *Good, See-low. You stay. Help Salm.*

Coral threw a leg over the side and clung to the hull. Granpop grumbled about the tipping, and Duffy darted to the stern to help, but Coral hovered as Tu-lee swam into place. She dropped into the cold water with an arm draped over the dolphin, her life vest buoying her.

Duffy was staring down at her. "Isn't your energy blue?" Her gaze shifted from Coral to Ty and back again. "Oh."

Orb take it. *I used magic to do that.* Coral shot a glance to Granpop in the bow. His back was still turned. "Please don't say anything. I'm, uh, also under a quash."

Duffy winked. "You owe me."

"Anything." Coral turned to Ty. "Do what I just did." *Roam. Catch him.*

"I assume this is your first dolphin ride," Duffy said to him. "Keep your mouth closed."

With Duffy holding to the straps of Ty's life vest, he climbed over the side of the boat and awkwardly landed in a bellyflop on Roam. He slid off and copied the way Coral had wrapped her arm around her dolphin. "Did you have to give me the one called Roam?" he muttered.

"Hold tight to his dorsal fin." She demonstrated by floating over Tu-lee's tail, and when Ty was in position, she crossed her fingers. *Roam, Tu-lee, carry us to Ni-lee.*

They took off, no leaps or play. The dolphins sensed the urgency of the blood in the water and the orders.

"What is going on here?" demanded Lady Soila as they passed the dock.

The dolphins didn't slow until they approached the circling pod. At Coral's request, Ni-lee's pod allowed them to enter. The young'un was at Ni-lee's side—oh. Ni-lee's pup?

Easy, easy. Help you. Coral ran her hands over the young'un's body and found the six-inch gash near his tail. He flinched away from her.

She caught him and tapped his forehead in a typical command. *Roll. Side.*

The wound faced up. Ni-lee understood what was happening and reassured him. Now to bring Ty closer. *Roam. Here.*

The big dolphin nosed Ty into place and then sidled behind him to keep him there.

Ty put his hands on either side of the bleeding cut, then glanced up. "It'll take a minute to set. Will he stay like this?"

"Wait," she said. *Hold up Ni-lee's pup.* Dolphins crowded them from all sides, and the young'un's tail rose higher above the surface. "You've got your minute."

Ty pushed the sides of the wound together. Silver gel oozed from his palms and plastered the area.

Hold still, everyone. I'm so sorry you got hurt, she cooed. *Good boy.*

Ty eyed her.

"You, too," she said.

Finally, Ty ran a finger over the magical bandage. He removed his hands. "Done." He grasped Roam's dorsal again. "Never imagined how long that minute would be with my thighs squeezed between dolphins. Can they let go now? My feet are tingling."

Coral sent the pod away from the bloodied area, then as she and Ty raced away, she tried to keep an eye on him. How numb were his legs? Dusk was quickly turning to night, and she couldn't see him that well. She was also distracted by Ni-lee's pod excitedly speaking to her. "Are you okay?" she yelled to Ty. He couldn't hear. She repeated it in thought-speak.

Show you, sent Tu-lee.

Yeah, Ty answered.

Good, she said, and Tu-lee split from the pod, with Roam and Ty beside them. *Hoy, what are—*

No, she had to be calm. Before she could ask what Tu-lee was doing, the water before them sparkled. And not because of the sun, which had just set.

Like a slow blink underwater, the view blurred then sharpened again. The silhouette of the coast lay before her.

Stop, she screamed, too late, because Tu-lee swam through a sheen of blue magic—Salm's energy that surrounded the rip north of Tern Bay.

Tu-lee obeyed, and she craned around in time to see Ty and Roam pop up from nowhere and dash past them. Ty caught her gaze, his expression frantic.

Roam, come back! Sorry, she called to Ty. *I lost track of Tu-lee talking to me. He said he wanted to show me something. And, spells, this is something!* She thanked Tu-lee and praised him for sharing this news, then reminded him he should *tell* her about new things before showing her.

Roam returned with Ty. "That was the weirdest thing to see you disappear and know you weren't pereporting."

She tightened her grip on Tu-lee. "Thank goodness Salm and Luna marked this one so we can see it. We need a way to identify the other end at the islet."

"I can do it."

They swam back through the rip to the islet.

Beri, another teen from Giuthas, flew up. "Thank the Orb,"

he shouted to them. "Lady Soila asks for you to come to the dock to explain what's happening, but I see you've found a rip."

Aye, she bet Lady Soila had *demanded* it. After working with many elders on the isle, Beri was very diplomatic about what he said.

Only the troughs between the waves had sparkles in them. Ty tossed a handful of magic toward one, and a silver balloon of energy materialized. It floated into a spot streaked with color— and disappeared. He tossed another far enough away not to float through, then she directed the dolphins to travel a wide circle while Ty flipped more balloons. Beri flew after them, anchoring them together to form a ring around the rip.

Coral called Ni-lee and explained that they weren't to go near the balloons, then Roam and Tu-lee took them to the dock's ladder.

Lady Soila and her companions rushed to help. Beri and Fern grabbed Ty's arms to assist him out, then lifted Coral up onto the wooden deck. Relief washed over her. Between that and the cold, she collapsed next to Ty.

"Warm them!" Lady Soila demanded, though Lady Lark, an elder from the isle, and Beri were already dousing them with magic that siphoned off the water and heated the air. Lady Soila wrapped gray wool blankets around their shoulders.

Fern handed out cookies from a bag in her backpack. "I can't do any of that, but I always have emergency snacks. Your rescue was amazing."

"Thanks," Coral mumbled. The heat was wonderful, but the cookies were really what she needed. She managed to introduce Ty to everyone, though she didn't know Lady Lark's grand-daughter that well yet, since the tall, flower-loving girl had just returned to the isle.

But she'd known Beri for years. Last year, she'd suggested he give the Seas a try...and her a try. The memory of the outcome of that brought extra heat to her face now as the robust redhead knelt on the dock facing them. She didn't have any delusions about his interest now—she knew he wanted to know about the animals, not her.

"Lady Soila told us of the dolphins' odd behavior before we went up to see her ratna collection," Beri said. "When Duffy's call came that you were entering her waters, we figured they found something for you."

Spells, if Lady Soila had known the pod was here, why hadn't she contacted them days ago? But Coral didn't need to ask why. Lady Soila kept to herself. Coral explained what they thought had happened with the missing pod and the rips.

Lady Soila cleared her throat. "My doing. I increased my perimeter wards two weeks ago. Too many peculiar things are happening in my waters. An increase in logs cast ashore, plastic debris floating on the sea's surface, and then an empty dinghy appeared." She harrumphed. "I am cleaning my waters every day and now have a collection of...of *things* I have no use for and nowhere to dispose of them."

"Plastic?" Ty got to his feet, and Coral joined him. "White and green pellet things?" Lady Soila nodded. "Oyster and Cor were tracking that on the mainland."

Lady Lark laid a hand on stern Lady Soila's shoulder. "Why haven't you reported these occurrences to the council?"

She pushed her glasses up her nose. "I am used to handling my own affairs, thank you."

But you could have saved everyone trouble, Coral wanted to scream. While Lady Lark told Lady Soila the same thing in a nicer way, Coral hugged the blanket tight around herself. "The rips brought that plastic here from miles away in Tern Bay."

Beri nodded. "Rips act like pereport shortcuts. Your dolphins were likely fighting with the whale because they blamed each other for their young disappearing."

"Right." She grimaced. "We told all our marine life not to

approach the rips. Tu-lee asked me for permission, but I didn't understand what he was asking."

"And neither would leave the place where their young'uns disappeared," Beri said. "We'll arrange with Oyster to add your debris to what they have to dispose of."

"The plastics could go back to the human cities for their reuse," Ty offered. "They recycle it into other things."

"If it is of value to them for that, why have they lost hold of their supply?" Lady Soila asked, exasperated.

"They have extra, ma'am," Fern said. "To lose some means nothing to them."

What has happened with the dolphins?

Salm's thought-spoken question startled Coral. She explained.

We'll send See-low with the other young'un, then we're ready to go. Uncle Ray is south of Giuthas on our border. He could be here in a few hours, but it'll be faster for us to accompany this mother down there—and far easier than pacifying her. Just need to get you into the boat.

Does Granpop suspect?

Granpop thinks Ty is amazing, and you better encourage that thinking. In other words, I didn't just tell you all that.

She groaned. "Spells, this is a lot to keep straight."

Ty gave her a sympathetic look. "Sorry. If it makes you feel any better, *I* think you're amazing."

However, he also thinks Ty is a bit touched for wasting time decorating the ocean. What was with that?

Salm, she ground out. *That's the rip—that I found.*

You. Have. Got. To. Be. Kidding. Me. He whooped, loud enough to carry to them. *We did it—well, you did! Lass, that will make up for everything else you, quote, didn't do on this trip, end quote.*

A QUESTION OF JUDGMENT

High-pitched wails of joy rang through Coral's head when they reunited the whales. It was rewarding to witness, but they still had to sail back to Tern Bay—in the dark. They dropped off Granpop to help Uncle Ray and Bert and said their goodbyes.

Coral managed a private moment on the motorboat to poke Salm in the ribs. "Ahoy! Am I doing my share well enough for you now?"

Her brother huffed. "Let's see you keep it up after Pop takes off the quash, and we've left port, and there's no Ty Sterling to show off for."

She narrowed her eyes. True. After this week, she wouldn't see Ty every day. "Aye, let's just see."

She and Salm were eating a late dinner in Manta's kitchen when Granpop called to let them know that he and Ray had gotten Lady Soila's approval to have a team on her waters to seal the rip next week when Ma and Pop returned to help. Salm began discussing what boat owners to ask to help, and Coral knew that the conversation would continue longer than her evening plans would allow.

She yawned and stood up. "I'm tired. See everyone in the morning."

At precisely nine o'clock that evening, Ty walked up the back alley to the bakery. Coral was waiting. She'd changed into her leather boots, canvas breeches and a work shirt, far from the skirts and girlie blouses she'd been wearing. But she looked just as pretty, a sentiment that reknotted his gut.

"You've chosen good clothes for riding a motor scooter, but you'll need a jacket." He gestured to the still-cloudy sky. "It'll be much colder riding."

"Aye, I get it's like flying, creating wind as you move." She patted a small rope bag slung across her chest. "I have something in here. And this. I finished it."

She held out his shark tooth, twists of black macramé extending from both sides. Accepting it, he examined the knotting and found fine, hidden wires crisscrossing the back of the stone tooth.

"Those make a tighter hold to ensure the tooth doesn't fall out," she said.

"It looks great. Help me put it on?" He handed her the necklace and turned.

She fastened it and stood back to admire him. "It fits your look, especially with this gray shirt and canvas—no, denim, correct?—jacket." She gestured down the alley. "Where's the scooter?"

He'd known when she asked for a *lift* on it, that she meant a trip to the duelists' welcome. His stomach twisted again, but he couldn't let her go without her magic. Plus, the promise of having her hugging him on the scooter sealed his decision. "I hid it at the edge of town. It's too late for its noise, although probably no one would notice with all the Fest activity." He made a last effort to redirect their plans by adding, "We could get some food."

Coral shook her head and led the way, looking up and down the alley.

What could she want to hide? A kiss. He was more than ready when she stopped.

Instead of moving toward him, she stepped into a small alcove between two sheds and took her bag off her shoulder. "Just a second, and I'll be ready."

"Another game of hide-and-seek?"

She set her rear to the wall and toed off her boots while flashing a grin. "Nay. Please keep watch while I change." She unfastened her breeches.

Oh Great Orb. She was gonna strip down. In front of him. They were getting friendly, but he didn't think it'd gone this far. He could see where she'd unbuttoned her pants that her underwear was black...and shiny. He gulped as she caught him looking.

"Your eyes are bugging out. Feeling jumpy?"

"No, I—why—"

"Turn around." She twirled her finger in the air. "I have on leather trousers under these breeches, but I need your discretion while I change shirts."

With a mix of reluctant relief, he turned. Propping his shoulder against one shed corner, he assumed a nonchalant slouch while collecting himself. Parts of him had to deal with the realization they were not going to see Coral in a bikini substitute. He'd have to settle for what he'd been anticipating—having her pressed against his back. Maybe letting her drive and having his hands at her waist.

The rustling of her changing her clothes behind him made him uncomfortable. Oh man, why had he imagined her in the blue bikini again? Wiping a hand over his face, he spent a minute in thanks to the Golden Orb that it was dark.

When she said, "Done," he turned.

Shiny black leather pants, topped by a matching high-collared shirt and a cobalt blue vest. She snapped the vest closed, an insulated vest, the type worn for—

"A dueling outfit?"

"You recognize it?" She stepped into a square of light falling from a second-story window. The soft leather followed her curves like paint. The blue vest clad her like armor, while both garments accented the delicate shapes usually hidden under her loose clothes.

His bulkier protective vest wasn't this form-hugging. "Yeah, after wearing one several times a week for the last few years, I do."

She smoothed both hands down her sides and then over her hips before cocking her head. "How do you like the way it looks on me?"

Unable to stop his eyes from running over her again, he groaned aloud. "Flights, Coral. You know exactly how it looks." *Terrific.*

"That, I do." A smile curved one side of her mouth before she gracefully knelt to collect her discarded clothes. They disappeared into her magical little bag, and she looped its strap over her head. "Several times a week you dueled?"

"In academy classes." Specifics about his defense training would lead to more talk than he wanted before checking out her energy. Ty took off walking, and she followed to the set of stairs up to the third level. They had four more levels to climb before they reached the top of the cliff.

"You did then, but don't think we should now," she persisted.

"I don't know how you're set up. Since it's on the moor, I assume there are no sides delineated, no boundaries, no padding if you fall." And his greatest concern: "And no rules."

"Ah, we have sides and rules. Trials determine appropriate

competitors, one-on-one matches, three pop-outs allowed for fifteen seconds each as breaks. Two wizards designated as backup to catch a duelist if they are disabled. No one is allowed to hit the ground, and the competition ceases if someone is disabled."

"No referee to stop the duel if someone goes too far?"

"Two for each match. Plus, peer pressure stops it." She frowned. "Until recently. Look, I'll be quitting, but I can't until after Fest."

"Why?"

They ascended another set of stairs before she answered. "I'm expected to duel the Misty Mews contender."

"Does that really matter if you plan to quit anyway? Tiger said Spike could duel in your place." They walked side by side up a ramp he used when making deliveries with Pepper. Coral chewed at her lip. "Just an option. I'm not telling you what to do."

"I know," she whispered. "I don't want to fight with you, Ty."

"Me neither."

"However, tonight…" She wasn't meeting his gaze.

He didn't want to go, but he also didn't want her going alone. "What do you have in mind?"

Pausing at the top of the cliff, she faced him. "Stopping by the Meet 'n Greet to welcome the visitors."

"Do you want me to back you up? I'm asking so there's no misunderstanding, like when Tiger ran up to us last night. Or…" Was this any less of a violation of his honor code? "Do you have enough of my energy to shield yourself?"

"Aye, there's enough." Her eyes flicked off as she said it.

Was she worried about what he thought, or the rules? *I know which I'm thinking about.* He raised his gaze skyward. *Blessed Orb, let me get through this unnoticed.* "I want you to have it to be safe. Show me your shielding."

A flash of silver erupted over her. The magical film solidified into a clear coat of dense energy within a second.

The quickness made him pause. She had good defenses.

"Your plays-well-with-others magic is very pleasant to work with," she said. "You don't need to protect me." She wrinkled up her nose. "Or look like you might, you ken?"

"Not my style."

"It's not, but I figured I better say so. Just be with me."

If he was discovered, that alone would be trouble enough.

At the top of the sea cliff, they walked a few yards down the cart road that led past Dar's. Ty reached toward a particular fence post. Instantly, the hum in his fingers connected to a cloak of his energy. He sucked the magic off the shiny red Vespa.

Coral ran a hand over it. "Since we made the 'ask before touching' rule, your energy response to me has settled. I was wondering if we could touch at the Meet 'n Greet?" Her gaze rose to his. "It'll be strange asking in front of the others."

Yeah, he wanted to be able to pereport them if needed. "We have to, if we're going to ride the scooter together."

"Can we start now?"

Ty grinned as he picked up two helmets. "Been thinking of it myself."

More businesslike than he was feeling, Coral directed him past Dar's and then north a couple of miles, the Vespa's single headlamp casting a lonely light over the packed dirt. The stars winked in and out between huge banks of clouds collecting over the moor. Would the wind stick around for a regatta tomorrow? Knowing Coral would crew for him calmed some of Ty's nervousness of having possible employers watching. He just hoped his energy wouldn't be roaring like the Vespa, as it was with her arms around him.

At what looked like a deer path leading off the road, she told him to stop and turn off the headlight.

Waiting for their eyes to adjust to the darkness, they both

shifted around—apparently with the same thought as their helmets bumped together. Ty dropped his and leaned in to kiss her. Her lips weren't as salty tonight. Coral shed her helmet and scooted closer so her legs rested over his, her deep kisses giving him a pleasant muddle.

She pushed back first. "I do appreciate you accompanying me. I like when favors come tit for tat."

"Huh?"

"You take me to the Meet 'n Greet, and I'll do a favor for you." A coy look settled on her face right before her fingers tickled a trail down his chest.

Great Orb, she couldn't mean—*no, no way*. Her fingers tapped dangerously low. Maybe she did. He scooped up her invading hand. She looked pleased. He wasn't. This was too close to the games Marissa had played. "You're teasing me."

"Having fun with you, flirting fun." She wove her captured fingers through his. "I thought since we'd established our liking for each other, I could. You don't like flirting?"

"I guess I do, and when you're dressed like... I don't know. You seem different tonight."

"It's still me. The clothes are part of my dueling persona. I can't go to the arena without wearing them."

"It's not just the clothes. Your confidence has grown. Is it knowing you'll be back as their leader and with magic?"

"No." Her forehead creased, then smoothed. "It's knowing you care for me despite all my issues and the involvement of my family. I like you a lot. Once I quit...I won't be able to claim being top duelist anymore to boost my confidence." She shrugged and shifted away. "I get in trouble a lot for my jumpy magic."

"But you're so good at working with the dolphins. Look at all you've done the last two nights. How much easier would it have been with your own magic?"

"Lots." She rolled her eyes, then nodded. "Thanks. That was

one of the best saves Salm and I have done without Pop. Honestly, nearly losing Annie makes me see how valuable my help is." She plucked at her vest, unsnapping and snapping the topmost fastener.

Please give up dueling, he wanted to say.

"Perhaps it's best I take care of business. Then we can spend more time talking, or whatever." She retrieved her helmet and settled into her seat with a questioning look.

Yeah, they had a lot to talk about. Later. Ty got his helmet and started the engine. He couldn't keep putting down the local dueling without actually seeing what it entailed.

Leaving the Vespa's headlamp off, he guided the scooter slowly along the dirt trail snaking through the heather bushes. Over one gentle hill, down, then up a second. She squeezed his ribs as they topped it.

On the horizon, lightning flashed below thick clouds. A storm out at sea. In the basin below, another kind of electricity flickered as the scooter descended the hillside and people turned to watch.

GETTING AWAY CLEAN

It wasn't Ty's first choice of how to make an entrance, but Coral didn't seem bothered. She signaled him to stop thirty-some feet from the dueling field on the flatter portion of this valley. Glowing lines outlined a huge circle bisected by a single line that was an extension of their approaching trail. Most everyone had a bit of energy lighting their fingers.

Ty cut the engine, and they removed their helmets. Coral remained seated, so he did as well. The wizards had shifted into about seven clusters and were looking toward them and talking. Five to twelve duelists were in each—far more people involved than he'd imagined.

"Tern Bay's duelists," she said, nodding to the dozen people in the center of the arena.

Right. Like Coral, they all wore black leather outfits topped by a colored vest in, he assumed, each wizard's energy color. Scanning the crowd, he noted identifying armbands, belts or shirt colors for the other enclaves. In the Tern Bay group, Lemon glared at them, arms crossed over a yellow vest and his hair looking wilder than ever. Beside him, Spike, with his long blond hair hanging in a curtain over a red vest, appeared to be arguing with Tiger and Octo.

Coral climbed off the scooter. "Here's Shrimp coming around from the side."

Her warning came just in time. Ty's magic vaulted to his fingers as the figure sneaked through the bushes. He clenched it before it showed—or he froze Shrimp. He shouldn't be so creeped out. He *could* take care of himself in a setting such as this.

"Sorry to surprise you," Shrimp muttered, only half paying attention as he peered back toward the dueling field. He had on the requisite black leather and a deep violet vest. Violet energy? Pretty powerful stuff.

"Hi, Shrimp. Where've you been the last few days?"

"Spike's been ruling us with an iron hand, fairly stepping into your place, with Lemon supporting him. It's such that Pearl thought we should avoid seeing you in public, but tonight she's changed her mind. The prat's taken it upon himself to direct the gathering, despite what anyone says to him. We're worried for you, Coral."

With a frown, she pivoted, putting her back to them. Ty felt her whole attitude change, from the rising of his energy to form an invisible shield, to her stance as she stepped a yard from the scooter and surveyed the field. "He has?"

Ty knew the younger guy felt her change as well. Shrimp shuffled into their shadows, now clearly hiding.

"We're hoping you can resolve this in a way that no one gets hurt," Shrimp said. "I'll back you. So will Pearl and Tiger."

Coral dipped her chin once. "Thanks, but it won't be tonight. Our guests don't need to see our housecleaning."

"Right, then. I'll see you over there?"

"Aye."

Shrimp sneaked back the way he'd come and within minutes was beside his sister at the edge of the field.

Ty jammed out the kickstand and climbed off the Vespa. Good thing Coral didn't plan to do anything about Spike tonight, when she had only a small portion of his power. Thank the Orb he'd verified her shielding earlier, because it looked like Spike was done talking.

He glared in their direction. Tiger caught his arm and said something more, but Spike shook him off and strode through the heather. The bushes slowed him some, but still his long, blond hair blew backward.

The guy was torqued, and the way Tiger paced, he'd borne the brunt of Spike's verbal attack. Perhaps Tiger was supposed to have talked Coral out of coming. But he hadn't. He wanted her here. But where was the promised support? Pearl and Shrimp had disappeared into the crowd, while Lemon led a few people after Spike. They spread out, picking their way through the bushes. Several cast around nervous glances.

Then Coral strode forward. The girl had some speed in her, but also the dirt trail to her advantage. Ty followed, trying not to appear to be dashing after her.

It didn't matter, for at twenty paces away, Spike shouted, "What are you doing here?" Everyone surged forward to hear.

Coral closed half the distance between them. Beneath the shuffling of the duelists jockeying for position, Ty barely heard her answer. "What do you think?"

"Leave this to me. It's more my port than it ever will be yours."

Coral thrust out a foot and crossed her arms, taking on a stance that snarled, *Don't mess with me.*

Spike halted ten feet before her.

"That's not what you had to say when you first challenged me three years ago," she said in a low voice. "I've earned my place, and I intend to keep it."

"Not if I have my say." His chest swelled in his red vest.

Red. Red energy wizards always had control issues. If Spike

so much as raised a hand, Ty would lock him down. Or shield Coral. Which plan wouldn't make her angry? He released energy to his fingers and held it subcutaneously. The shockball wouldn't restrict her.

The rush of bodies slowed and fanned out, surrounding the two. An expectant excitement hung in the air, just as if a duel was about to start. Ty left the path to stand to Coral's right, a good eight feet away, but less than half the distance he'd been able to throw out a flashshield the last time he'd done it. In the now-still crowd, he spotted Shrimp directly across from him, far to Spike's right. Pearl wedged through the ring of teens close to Coral. Ty flicked his gaze over the group led by the ever-scowling Lemon. No change in their positions. He found Tiger, who had his gaze on Pearl. The two nodded in mute communication.

"Fine, have your say, but not tonight, not this weekend," Coral said, her pleasant tone breaking the awkward silence. "Let's set a time for early in the week."

"A good plan," Tiger interjected. "Spike, Wednesday is soon enough to address this. We have guests who wish to get on to the fun of the evening."

A chorus of ayes followed his suggestion.

Spike narrowed his eyes, darting his gaze first to Coral, then to Tiger, but showing no emotion. Yet, behind him, Lemon looked ready to burst.

"Seems the majority agree," Spike finally snarled. He half turned, then whipped back around and hurled a shockball.

A ball of silver slammed Spike's red blast two feet from Coral, showering her with sparks. Through them shot two more balls of silver. Almost simultaneously, they hit, and Spike's body flashed a blinding white.

Seconds ticked by. The arena was dead silent.

Flights! She'd blasted as fast as Ty had, apparently ambidextrously. The townspeople's warnings came back to him—he *didn't* know who he was dealing with.

The glow on Spike dimmed, and a few red sparks fell from his clenched hand, but he didn't move. Paralyzed.

A low murmur commenced.

Without so much as a glance around, Coral walked up to Spike with a hip-rolling swagger.

Before anyone could notice, Ty absorbed the second shock-ball at his hand and checked the crowd. Shrimp met his gaze and smiled as he lowered his arm. He started forward, so Ty did likewise.

The two flanked Coral's diminutive frame as she looked up at Spike. Besides Lemon staring openmouthed several feet away, they were the only ones close enough to hear her say, "Do not dare pull that kind of stunt on me again." Stepping around him, she brushed his arm with hers and sucked off the silver energy as she walked past him.

Spike stumbled, but turned and followed her into a cluster of Tern Bay duelists, who all hastily cleared their faces of expression.

"Good evening, everyone," Coral said evenly.

Lemon and his little group sidled up, meeting no one's gaze, and listened while she made reminders of courtesy to be shown their guests—whose chatter had escalated across the arena.

Then Coral, with—*unbelievable*—Spike at her side, made the rounds of the groups, welcoming the visitors, introducing themselves to everyone and making small talk with the other leaders. By the time they reached the last group, a gaggle of young wizards trailed them. As soon as Coral and Spike finished their greeting, the tweens circled them.

No, circled *Coral*. They elbowed each other aside to shake her hand and have a word with her.

Spike slunk to the Tern Bay group, who were now at the sidelines, organizing a line.

I can't believe it. Was covert dueling this pervasive in the UK? Or just among these rural coastal enclaves? Never, anywhere else that Ty's family had lived, had he heard of such a setup. And with his parents' positions as defense instructors, he would have heard something. He and his siblings would have been told, in no uncertain terms, that they would be quashed for even thinking about participating. And now...

I'm a Master Wizard.

Ty crossed an arm over his middle, ill at the thought. He'd trained to regulate activities like this so the Windborne wouldn't expose themselves to the larger human populations. If the Department of Magical Regulation—the group who had administered the final exams that he passed—heard of this and turned up to shut it down...

I'll be arrested if I'm caught here.

HOW DEEP WAS HE IN?

Now eager to leave, Ty hung back.

So did Shrimp. "You've merged, I see," he said, his gruff voice pitched only for Ty to hear. "She used your energy as easily as her own."

Ty had to admire the younger wizard's direct, quiet manner, a contrast to Spike's, when clearly each was irritated that Ty had interfered with their plans.

"Everyone in Tern Bay knows she's a blue wizard," Ty replied, also in a low voice. "Will the use of my energy cause more trouble in your group?"

"Nay, use of another's energy is quite common among the prebonds and casual mergers. Those who can, do it. Not in competition, however. One would have to forfeit if found to be using the energy of others. But for something like this?" Shrimp snickered. "Entirely acceptable. In fact, it was more of a slap in the face that she used yours rather than her own to put Spike out."

Ty groaned inwardly. "Since everyone wears their energy colors, the visitors also know."

"It'll be the talk of the sidelines tonight and again tomorrow when she competes," Shrimp said, bitterness still edging his voice. "Embarrassing. Spike's best move would be to make himself scarce for the rest of the Fest tournaments. Typical of the Angler to play a clever trick."

A trick—ha! Not even Shrimp, one of her closer cohorts, guessed the real reason. Ty cleared his throat. "I'm only here tonight to make sure she stays safe."

Shrimp studied Ty for a moment, then said, "I've admired Coral for years, but I realize it's not gonna happen for me. From what I've seen of you, lad, you're much better suited for her than any of the others to whom she's been attracted. I wish you well." Shrimp nodded and melted into the crowd.

While they'd talked, the duelists had lined up along one of the glowing boundaries, and everyone else had cleared the central arena. Tern Bay wizards circulated among the crowd, and two worked the line, answering questions, encouraging the younger duelists and writing challengers' names on a clipboard for the beginners' tournaments. One of them, Pearl—in a violet vest like her brother's—reported back to Coral at the head of the line. Then the first two wizards flew upward into position, the whistle blew, and an aerial match commenced.

Ty only half watched from his spot on the perimeter. The other half of his attention kept a roving watch for any new arrivals. Overhead, dense clouds had moved in with the storm Salm had predicted. Surely they wouldn't continue if it began raining.

And when we do leave, what will I say to her once we're alone?

Yeah, he'd offered for her to use his magic, but he'd never expected her to throw it at someone.

She had no choice. He should just get over it, but curses, he didn't like it.

She didn't seem bothered. Her demeanor declared business as usual. Spike also circulated among the duelists. Lemon never left his side, his normally grumpy features blank. But his gaze met Ty's once, and a flash of anger erupted.

Ty pitied the competitor at the receiving end of that much emotion and spark—which he bet Lemon wished was him.

Octo, wearing a green vest, passed with a group of wizards Ty didn't recognize. The big duelist stopped. "Havin' a good evenin'?" He introduced his companions and added, "This is the bloke I'll be racin' to earn my duel with the Angler."

They laughed and wished Ty luck in the upcoming regatta.

"Dinnae worry, Yank. I aim to make double sure it's my place by beatin' Spike again."

Ty wanted to ask, *Why is that so important?* But he nodded and moved on.

So far, the rounds had run just as Coral had promised, the participants abiding by the rules more civilly than he had feared they would. Coral was talking with her Tern Bay friends and two visitors. Ty edged their way while the group watched the end of the current match and the start of another. One male wizard repeatedly leaned into Coral, too attentive to everything she said.

Good try, guy, but his girl had spent enough time without him by her side.

Ty didn't get there soon enough. The guy laid a hand on her arm. Coral patted his long fingers as she answered and removed them. Ty had to squelch the urge to dash over, wrap his hand around her and pull her away from the interloper.

Lemon shoved his way between the guy and Coral. "We've got some business," he told the out-of-towner. "Scram."

The guy and his friend did, and then Coral pulled Lemon down to whisper something.

"Polite or nay," Lemon said none too quietly, "you know you wanted him gone, and we do have business. Olive is keeping the list now and sent me to tell you the beginner matches are done, and she's starting the Level 2s. Octo goaded Spike into signing up for a Level 3 match. To renegotiate Spike's runner-up spot."

Coral glanced toward Pearl, who'd been in their group. "Who is refereeing?"

Lemon named two wizards and their out-of-town enclaves.

Pearl nodded, and Coral said, "If they want to compete, there's naught in the rules against it."

Lemon left, and as Ty joined Coral, Pearl and Tiger, the warlock said, "Their last match was close."

"Those refs are up to it," Pearl answered.

Coral smiled. "It'll be good to have other refs calling their penalties for a change."

That didn't sound good. But Coral noticed he was there and planted herself shoulder-to-shoulder with him, telling him who was up in the current match and cheering for a Tern Bay duelist. Pearl and Tiger stuck around—were they still watching out for her?—and discussed the duelist's chances. Soon, as Tiger and Pearl hung all over each other, Ty's hand naturally found its way to the small of Coral's back.

She leaned against him. "Perfect," she said between talking to those who came up to her. "Enough that people know we're together and not so much they hesitate to approach me."

"Are they speculating about me?"

"I rode up with you. There's no speculation. They think you're one lucky wizard." She grinned. "Smart, too, for not challenging me."

He couldn't resist asking, "What about the guy who had his hand on you earlier?"

"You always get one or two of those, like Lemon, who think they can convince you otherwise. Say, here's Shrimp—with a witch?"

Yeah, one Shrimp's age. He introduced Olive's cousin, a wide-eyed witch with brown skin and natural curls hanging to her shoulders. Briana stammered over her words and didn't take her worshiping gaze from Coral's face. After a few minutes, Shrimp made an excuse for them to leave, winking at Ty.

Coral saw. "What was that about?"

"I think I have Shrimp's approval to court you."

She laughed.

Pearl leaned in front of them. "They're up," she said. "Spike and Octo."

TOO CLOSE

The first blasts of the duel met midway, as Ty would have expected from closely matched competitors. Red and green sparks showered down—more than in prior matches. Additional shockballs sped across the arena, more green than red.

"That Octo was well named," Pearl said.

Tiger grinned. "Too bad his parents don't know it."

One hit Spike in the wing as he spun away. He faltered, dropping a few feet—the crowd gasped—before regaining his wings to rise. "Penalty," he shouted.

"No," Pearl snapped, just before both referees shouted the same.

"Ye moved into it," one added.

Octo let fly with another shockball.

Spike blocked with a shield.

Octo snickered. "Ya said anytime. Is this nae a good time?"

Coral's lips moved, and Pearl counted aloud, "One, one thousand, two..." Three seconds was the maximum allowed at academy training. "...one thousand, four—"

The red shield disappeared. Spike shot a...not-normal shockball. Sparks whirled off of it. Octo startled aside, but it hit his thigh.

He cursed. Spike darted forward and drove out another.

"Spells. He's as wrecked as I've ever seen him," Coral said to Pearl.

He was as wrecked as *anyone* Ty had ever seen dueling. Showing that level of furor would get you sidelined at academy. If it continued, you'd be out of the program. Fighting couldn't be personal.

This clearly was.

Octo shielded and dove. Red energy glanced off his protected shoulder—and ricocheted downward.

People screamed and scattered.

Ty stepped forward—and stopped. *I can't.*

"Halt!" Pearl shot skyward as the referee whistles blew.

Tiger launched after her. So did others. Coral's back flickered, but with a glance at Ty, she ran for the spot where the blast had landed. Ty followed, keeping watch above, around, everywhere.

In the time he'd hesitated, these duelists—*illegal* duelists—had assessed and acted. Overhead, eight airborne wizards demanded the match stop. It did. Everyone landed.

Along with Olive, Ty and Coral confirmed that except for a few burns, no one was hurt.

"That was close," Olive murmured as they watched Spike and Octo argue to continue. Lightning flashed off the coast, and a few raindrops fell.

"I have naught to lose if I go home burnt," Octo yelled. "I'll just say a jelly stung me pullin' up a trap in the morrow's predawn." He cockily lifted his chin. "What tale will ya spin to yer ma?"

"His mother will be too busy at the tavern to notice," Coral said. "This week, at any rate. It's Lemon's mother we all have to watch out for. She's head of the council."

The two out-of-town referees, who'd been talking on the sidelines, strode to the center of the arena. "This match is called for use of excessive magic. Win goes to Octo by default."

Spike flew at them, roaring. Several people threw out shielding, and others grabbed him, including Lemon. Spike let himself be guided away. His angry gaze roved, came to Coral and Ty and stopped.

Coral stiffened at Ty's side.

"I have to get up early tomorrow," Ty said. "Would you mind if we left?"

"Nay." She pulled her gaze from Spike. "The night will be called for rain soon enough. Let's go."

It was eleven once the Vespa climbed out of the basin beneath the rolling storm clouds. They were leaving in time— the wind was gusting fiercely, and more rain hit them. Ty magicked a shield over them, and Coral leaned into his back, her chin on his shoulder.

He wavered over the wisdom of saying anything about Spike, but finally had to. "That was some reaction Spike had to being told no."

"Tell me!" she said. "He's always been a bully, but this is beyond usual. Before you ask, aye, I've had enough. I'm quitting."

The question *When?* was on the tip of his tongue, but she continued, "I can't believe how strong your energy is. And you. One shockball that stopped Spike was yours." She tightened her hold around him in a quick hug. "Thank you for interfering this time. I'm happy your energy did the trick. For my defense only, of course."

"Yeah, defense." But the words sounded lame, so he added, "I'm glad you had my energy."

"Are you?" Her hands tucked under his jacket and smoothed his T-shirt. "Your energy makes me feel good, really good. But something tells me you'd have rather done it yourself."

"Uh, you're doing—did fine. You were so fast, Coral, and, uh…" It was hard to think with her fingers swirling right above his energy core. His energy followed like iron filings attracted to a magnet.

"Accurate. Very on target, with your aim, while, uh…" Ty licked his lips. "Staying so cool under attack. Spike's attack, I mean." Being close to her was great, but Blessed Orb, his energy was ramped. He'd better shut up. He could enjoy this a little, if he kept track of his magic. And the path.

They came to the road. He steered the scooter onto one of the wider tracks and sped up. His energy surged from his cores. He caught it—barely—and slowed. His innards careened wildly.

"Aw, speed up again," she whispered into his ear. "I love the feel of the wind rushing me. It's almost like it's inside and taking me away with it." Her hands smoothed down his belly.

His stomach plummeted, and his magic burst loose.

Coral sighed. "I'm sorry you didn't like me using your energy. Here, take it." A humming vibrated over his back.

All of his magic.

The newly freed energy from her mixed with his loose magic and sank into his skin. It raced through him, sparked at his fingertips, flamed his skin and, worse, clouded his mind like a dream.

"Ohh, a fog bank," she squealed. "'Tis making me feel all fuzzy inside."

It wasn't fog. Wisps of loose energy filled his head—their heads. All silver, all *his* magic, but definitely affected by its time with *her*. Ears roaring, Ty shook his head to clear it. He glimpsed the road and the heather shrubs rushing past.

He struggled to speak. "It's not fog. We're in—"

"Of course 'tis fog. Fluffy fog brought by the storm." She giggled, and the magic flashed. "See the lightning?"

No, they were in a merge. A deep merge. They shouldn't be merging without controlling it and definitely not on a motor scooter. But how was this even possible when she had no magic?

Fighting it revved the magic—and revved the Vespa. He was burning up, going too fast. *She* was going too fast. He released the gas. They hit a bump.

By some miracle, they kept their balance. He clamped the hand brake. The scooter bounced to a stop. His feet shot out and caught the Vespa before it could fall. Coral jolted into him and rammed him against the handlebars.

"Oof," Ty gasped, and he was falling—into the magical haze. He'd lost his anchor to the physical world.

Coral clutched his chest. "Ohhh," she cried. "How are you in the fog and not me?"

He couldn't answer. Was she right beside him or not? Despite her death grip on his ribs, she sounded far away. He gathered what control he could and tried thought-speaking. *Release me.*

Her hands flew off his torso.

Thank the Orb. He felt it in a far-off way, but nothing happened. His magic remained stuck, and in a flash, the horrible night of his last merge with Marissa played through his head.

She sat astride him, laughing and taunting as she'd held his energy exactly at the edge of merging. He realized what was up, and even though he begged her, Marissa had the upper hand when she trapped him in the most vulnerable situation for a wizard. She played with him for the longest time and then took exactly what she wanted—all of his powerful magic—and left.

"I can't see you in..." Coral's voice broke into his awful reverie. "What is that place?"

Some maneuver had to release him. Yet every magical effort showed it wouldn't work to pit his energy against what was still his energy.

"Talk to me. What's wrong?" Her words were earnest, completely innocent.

She didn't know. Unlike Marissa, Coral had no clue she'd taken him to a merge, or what she could do to him as his magical system lay completely open to her. If she left, he'd remain paralyzed by his own magic. She could lock down his magical system in a quash that only she could remove. Or she could drain him of every last bit of energy.

Sweat—or it might be rain—trickled down his temple. He forced strands together to communicate again. *Magically release me. Take the energy you've been controlling out of me so I can come back from the fog.*

"Oh." She rubbed his sides. "I can't get over to the fog."

Try, please.

Her stress escalated. The magic jumped in response. Strands zinged to him, and tendrils under her influence wound around him. They pierced his channels with painful pinpricks. His head screamed and eyes watered, but he had a precious bit to use. He just needed a few more—

"I made it to you. I'll...take back the part I had."

Strands separated, some going to her and others seeping into him. More hovered out of reach and drifted off, dissolving into the ether. *Not so fast, control your moves.*

It felt weird not to direct his own magic.

"I don't know what I'm doing." She started to cry, and all she'd gained flooded painfully into him, only to rebound off, gone before he thought to seize it.

Try again, please. If only a little more would move into him, he'd take partial control and...what? He thought quickly, going through every defensive technique he'd learned.

She pulled them from the fog. It was raining in the real world.

Good, that's it. Keep going.

"This?" Abruptly, the magic pushed them back into the merge.

Uh, no... Control slipped further away, carrying her with him.

He *had* to do something before they both were stuck. The next influx, the next chance.

His magic inundated him like a thousand needles pricking over his body. Steeling himself, Ty grabbed what power he could—

The blast threw them off the scooter. They landed, breaking bushes and tumbling hard to the ground. A furious rain pelted them. Within seconds, they were drenched.

Coral unfastened her helmet. "What did you do that for?" she gasped.

Breathing deeply, Ty rolled onto his back. He clenched his fists, closed his eyes and watched. His energy jammed his channels—but it was there. Half of it anyway. The pain and turmoil eased. His breathing returned to normal. *He* returned to normal. He checked... Yes, his magic was under his control.

Thank the Golden Orb. Ty let the raindrops cool his face before he rolled to face Coral.

She'd sat up, but curled into a shivering ball, head to her knees.

"You had my magic locked up in a merge," he said. "A blast was all I could think of to break it without another wizard to help us."

"I did *not* merge with you. I *returned* your magic."

She's a beginner. The patient reminders of Ty's numerous professors, including Mom and Dad, ran through his head. "What were you thinking about when you used your magic, well, my magic, but the part you controlled?"

She rocked her head. "About kissing you again and, um, maybe merging with you. I was excited. Being with you is like that for me." Her voice caught. "Like the excitement of dueling. The regular excitement, not what happened tonight. Sorry. I didn't think I needed to control magic that was yours, not like I would my own."

Excitement and no-boundaries control had gotten them into

the fastest, deepest merge he'd ever been in. And had nearly emptied his system of magic for the second time in a year. Unlike Marissa, Coral hadn't *tried* to do this to him. He had himself to blame, considering he was the better-trained wizard in their pairing.

Curses. Liking someone was no excuse to let down his guard.

"I'm sorry," Coral whispered. She reached her hand toward him.

Ty shrank back. "Please don't," he whispered back. "I can't handle any more." Spells, he didn't want to...but... Ty took a deep breath. *I barely escaped—we barely escaped.* "I...can't see you anymore."

Her face went blank. She didn't understand, or didn't want to. He felt terrible. "You—your power scares me," he admitted. "We have strong magic between us, and if we can't control it, the risks are...that," he finished lamely because she'd begun to cry in earnest.

PULLING IT TOGETHER

"Coral?"

Coral lifted her head. Manta knelt beside her, sunlight from the window lighting her baking smock.

"Why are you sleeping on the window seat?" Manta asked.

The memories of last night flooded back with more tears. "T-Ty broke off with m-me."

Skipping the part about the dueling, Coral told her sister everything else. "I had to agree we should call it quits," she mumbled. "I don't have control of my energy. Not like he has."

"But you didn't want to," Manta sympathized and held her tight. "I'm sorry, love." They talked about losing beaus for a few minutes, then Manta rose to return to the kitchen and the morning baking. "Perhaps it's for the best. You're going away to academy. It's not fair to either of you to be bound to the other while so far apart."

Nay, she wasn't going away—but Coral couldn't find the energy to argue. She went down to work, and over the next hour Manta left the kitchen often enough she had to have spilled the news to Piper and worked it over several times. He followed Coral out to open the shop.

"Did last night include a trip to the moor?"

Telling him the high points of the Meet 'n Greet was a relief. "Do you think I handled it badly?"

"Spike's attack was out of line, erratic even. I'd say you couldn't have done anything else. Lucky you had Ty's energy. Without it, you wouldn't be standing this morn'."

Coral nodded, blinking as she stocked the front counter.

"Still, it's a bit personal to see another use your power, especially for an activity of which you want no part."

She hung her head. "I know that now. I wish I hadn't taken him there. I-I'm ending my part in it."

"That bad, huh?" Piper asked, and she met his look with a grimace. "Aye, you've been updating me, and I just hate to think my boyhood pastime's gone down the loo."

At nine, Salm bounded through the front door, called, "Break time," to Coral's line of customers and steered her by the elbow to the hall pantry. "The regatta is today. Why does Ty think you aren't crewing for him?"

She shrugged and lifted a tray of bread to take to the front. "I never said I wouldn't."

"You had a falling-out, I gather." He picked up a tray of muffins and followed her. "Aw, lass, this isn't good. I was getting to love the idea of that lad in our family."

A lump formed in her throat, and her guts twisted. She blinked hard. *I will not cry.* "Sorry to disappoint you."

"I'm disappointed for you."

He was serious. "Thanks, Salm. Please tell Ty I'll be on the dock by noon."

Hurrying along North Dock with her lunch in her dry bag, Coral didn't see Lemon until he stepped in front of her. She jerked to a halt.

"Coral," he said in a clipped tone. "I wanted to bid you fair winds for today."

"Thanks." What else could she say? He was being civil, not trying to discuss a relationship or dueling. "Are you racing?"

"Not myself. I'm crewin' for Spike today. I shall see you out there." With a nod, he skirted her and walked off.

"Uh, good luck," she called after him. Odd. Lemon usually raced his own boat. But she forgot about him when she came upon a group of people gathered around Ty and their sailboat. These people weren't from Tern Bay, nor were they dressed like the wizards who usually came to the local festivals. Ty met her gaze, and the whole horrible ending to last night slammed into her. She clutched the dry bag, sucked a deep breath and continued forward as if nothing was wrong.

He stepped from the group to meet her. "My family arrived this morning for Fest. I had no idea. They talked to Dar and arranged the whole thing as a surprise."

"From Colorado? They came this distance the human way or magically?"

"Magically. After they got to talking to Dar, and he talked to people he knew, they learned there's a portal on Giuthas."

"Aye, I know about it. The lessons with Lady Heather that I told you about? The portal leads to her home."

"How come you never said anything?"

Spells, this made things more awkward between them. "I've had such a great time with you this week that I wanted to pretend no lessons waited for me on the other side of that passage. Leaving here isn't how I want to set my sails, despite my parents' insistence I learn these modern ways."

He glanced around to his family. "Hey, I want to introduce you, but would you mind not saying anything about us? I haven't quite worked out what…"

Right, he didn't tell his family every detail about his relationships, unlike her. Coral sighed. They were quite different. "Whatever you want."

"Thanks."

At the boat, she met his mom and dad, Isla and Dell Sterling; Juni, the older sister she'd heard about; his younger sister, Tana; and brother, Daval.

"Dave," the boy corrected as he shook Coral's hand. "Coral of the Seas? Why are you called that?" His direct gaze bore a strong resemblance to Ty's more modest confidence.

"Because our family manages the sea life in the waters surrounding our enclave."

He frowned. "You aren't old enough to be managing an ocean, or sailing alone, or teaching Ty."

"Dave." Grimacing, Ty pulled his brother back by the arm. "She's sixteen, and around here, teenagers that old do most everything. Coral talks to dolphins, tells them what to do and rescues whales. I helped her."

Dave shrugged off Ty's hand and continued to regard her through narrowed eyes. "Do you have your own sailboat?"

Coral smiled. "I'm saving up for my own. How did you get the name Sterling?"

"My parents' energy is silver. Mine, too. If it hadn't been, I could change my name to reflect my magic."

Oh. Windborne kept such different customs around the world.

"We'll explore the town and let the two of you square things away for the race," said their father.

"Thank you, Sir Sterling."

The man laughed. "You're welcome, young lady, but it's not 'sir' where we come from."

"Since my parents are professors," Ty said, "they go by master. Master Dell and Master Isla."

That's right, he'd said they worked at Terraqua Academy... oh. His mother looked familiar, and as the woman met her gaze, Coral knew why.

While Ty pointed out the bakery and suggested a few other

shops for them to check out, Master Isla took Coral's hand as if to say goodbye, but held it. "Have we met?"

"I visited Terraqua Academy earlier this summer."

"You interviewed? I was on your panel, then?" At Coral's nod, she asked, "Have you made a decision?"

Coral shook her head. Master Isla squeezed her hand, and the bit of Ty's energy left in Coral's channels lurched. She squelched it.

Master Isla released her and smiled. "We'll be here through the equinox if you have any questions I can answer."

"Thanks."

Coral watched Ty's family leave, knowing she was biting her lip but not able to stop herself.

"What's wrong?" Ty asked. "Did my mother ask you about us?"

"She didn't have to ask. She likes me much better than Marissa, the last witch you were with." Between them, she formed up the small amount of silver energy and palmed the mass over to a wide-eyed Ty. "I don't need any more accidental information from your family members."

"She never met Marissa." Ty avoided her gaze while he absorbed his energy.

She never would have met me if it hadn't been for the regatta. His mom was nice, and happy for them. It only made her feel worse. And this was probably the last time she'd see his silver energy. She blinked to hold back her tears, turning away before Ty might see.

"I think your parents are closer to you, or want to be, than you think," she said. "You better talk to her soon, since we're not together."

"Sorry," he muttered. "I don't know what to say. To you, I mean."

"Naught." She crouched at the side of the sailboat and put a hand on the bobbing hull to steady it as she stepped in. "Let's talk sailing."

Other contestants were doing the same prerace rigging checks, checking the wind and calming their nerves. Amid the dozens of boats scattered across the water, she pointed out the two anchored fishing boats flying orange pendants for the start and finish lines and the dock buoys with orange flags fluttering at their tops. Judges would hover at these turn locations to watch for violations.

After their review, they climbed onto the dock, and she offered some of her lunch to Ty, but he refused. Pacing a tight circle, he attracted the attention of Octo, who sauntered over from checking his boat.

"Rethinkin' yer decision to make this yer challenge?" Octo asked. "Ya've had to scramble to catch up to the local lads."

"Regardless of what happens, I've had a good run of sailing lessons this week." Ty's answer was uncharacteristically abrupt.

"Aye, I cannot deny that, Yank. Some of the best, and it shows." Octo's nod indicated his departure. "Best of luck. To ya, too, Coral."

"To you, too."

Coral waited until the other boy walked out of earshot before saying, "It's very out of character for you to be this agitated."

"Guess I'm not feeling myself." He attempted a halfhearted smile. "I'm nervous. I'll go for a walk to take the edge off."

Maybe it was only prerace jitters, but could the energy she'd had in her jumpy channels also be affecting him? "Fine, but you only have fifteen minutes until they expect us to head for the line."

Ty left, and Coral's gaze followed him. They never should have gone out last night. Then they'd feel more like a team, the regatta would be fun and meeting Ty's parents would have meant something special to both of them, rather than feeling like a shameful secret.

Ty didn't make it far before another racer stepped out to have a word, then the crowd of townsfolk and visitors swallowed him. When Salm turned up to wish them well, he was as excited as Ty. She sent her brother off to find his star student. Ty's family had joined the spectators and the first boats had headed to the start line before they returned.

"You have plenty of time," Salm assured Ty. "They have to wait for all the racers to arrive, and the first sailors will be fighting the wind longer to stay close to the starting line. Now go out there and snap a mast." He strode off.

"Is that the sailor's version of 'break a leg'?' Ty asked.

Coral rolled her eyes. "That's Salm's version of it."

She untied the mooring line from the dock, and Ty steered them out as the nonracing boats cleared the bay. They were one of the last to pass between the boats marking the start line a quarter mile out in the open ocean. Soon after they began circling around, wizards from the two starting-line boats threw out a shimmering orange energy barrier. It met halfway across the hundred-yard distance, creating a magical banner of light for the start.

"It flashes out when the starter calls for the three-minute start window," Coral said.

Ty nodded. "Salm told me. I want to be as close as possible when it does."

"Aye, as does everyone else in these rolling waters. I'm sure I don't need to remind you not to tap another boat."

"No. I didn't practice that hard only to get disqualified."

The wind blew as strong as it had the day they'd practiced the course with the others, and a few of the gusts promised to be stronger. The breeze made it difficult to stay behind the line, and like everyone else, Ty had the sails out and luffing, bringing the boat almost to a stop.

The starter called three minutes, and the orange energy disappeared in a flash. The regatta had begun!

THE REGATTA

In sync, Ty and Coral pulled in the main and jib sheets and trimmed their sails, finding the wind. The sails filled. Their boat eased forward and then shot ahead. Taking the lead position, they skimmed the waves on an even keel and picked up speed. Ty tried not to feel too confident.

It was hard. How was this possibly working when nothing else had gone right last night? It'd taken hours for him to fall asleep after he'd gotten home.

Attend to business.

Halfway to South Dock, several boats had advanced on them. Some of the sailors Ty didn't recognize, but Octo was one helmsman, and to the right, Spike raced with Lemon.

Spike had some vendetta against Coral, Ty was sure of it. And he'd just taken himself out of the running to protect her. And to continue to sail with her.

Focus.

He flicked his gaze forward as a good gust of wind came into the mouth of the bay. Ty reacted automatically to counter the sudden gust and hiked out. The boat tipped back, and his gaze met Coral's.

Yes! They could ride this gust—plane. "Sheet in," he called.

She slid aft—thank the Orb the crew never argued with the helmsman—and together they leaned out. The sailboat leveled and took off, skimming the water surface.

"Brilliant decision," she shouted, and his heart lifted with the wind. Coral was fully cheering him despite the breakup.

Focus.

Two closer boats copied their actions. How long would the gust last?

It strengthened before it died, allowing the lagging sailboats to catch up, but to his delight, he and Coral held the lead around the first buoy.

"Flights," Coral shouted. "We're ahead for the middle run. Let's hope you keep your lead, because as the others bunch behind, we'll lose the wind to them."

Ty only nodded and started his tacks across the mouth of the bay. When their being together had looked like a sure thing, he'd suspended his push to get a shipboard job. In the back of his mind, he'd figured he'd get to spend some time on the schooner with her, and a year of working at a dairy farm wouldn't be so boring. Now that was over. He had to resume his serious search for shipboard employment—winning this race would mean more than just a way to keep her from dueling.

Halfway to the buoy at North Dock, the leading boats joined them.

"Do not look to either side," Coral advised. "Just make your next tack to the left shorter and force them to turn before they have made their best use of the wind."

"I know, I know," he muttered, then regretted it. "Salm drummed it into me."

"Sorry. You're doing great, Ty."

"About five more tacks, then you check our competitors, and I'll decide on the turn position."

He cut that next tack shorter than he should have, but she

said nothing. He didn't look to check the closest boat's position, but could tell Coral had. Still, she kept quiet. Was it Octo or Spike?

Ty made the return tack short and the next even shorter, forcing the closely following boat to cross over on the far right. This might work to their advantage—putting their boat on the inside turn at the buoy.

But the two other boats had the benefit of long tacks that placed them ahead. Spike and Lemon sailed one, Octo the other. Ty had to stay in his next tack as long as possible to gain on them. He switched to the other side for only the briefest of runs before returning to take another long tack inland and force the others farther out from the buoy.

They were so close, he could have touched Lemon. Their hulls grated against each other, and Ty's nerves ground with the sound. In an instant, they pulled away.

"I can't look," he called to Coral. "Is anyone coming up between us and the buoy?"

She was already smiling. "It's clear if you move quick."

How had Spike fallen back? *Not my problem.* "Hold on, 'cause we're gonna take this sharp."

"Spells! Salm trained you in tight buoy turns as well?"

Heh, he'd been reluctant to try at the time, but now those daredevil techniques might pay off. At his command, she ducked under the boom and shifted all her weight to the outside edge of the hull. He shoved the tiller out, and their boat pivoted around the buoy.

She flashed a grin. "Watch your stern—ah, no, don't. Others have learned the trick from seeing Salm do it the last two years, and Octo is on our tail."

"Then let's give them a good run." Ty adjusted the mainsheet as the wind came across the beam, and she did the same with the jib line. The sails filled, and they shot forward.

So did a cluster of others, their sails in his peripheral vision.

If that was Octo gaining on them, then he'd take Coral's place in the duel. But they were going to win. They had the lead, and no one blocked the weak but steady wind blowing directly into their faces. They'd sailed more than halfway toward the shimmering finish line.

Then he felt it. A lull. He shifted the tiller, but there was nothing to catch. The wind had died, leaving every boat scrambling in the light breeze.

"Ach. That wind was too good to be true," Coral cried. "This is like the first day I took you out."

They had a bit of momentum, and Ty found the correct position, heading almost directly for the right-hand fishing boat. They drifted forward.

At the edges of his vision, he saw that others followed. It was all he could do to keep his gaze firmly on his target. He let off steam with a growled, "These others are too close."

"It's to unnerve you. Don't let it. We're leading."

The boats still gained, coming closer yet. Every boat had the same angle to the wind, the same tilt to the tiller and the same destination point in sight. Within meters of the finish line, a strong gust hit from slightly behind, from a completely different direction than the last wind that had carried them.

Their boat tipped. Ty threw out the tiller. "Hard-a-lee."

She let loose of the jib and scrambled to the far side, Ty throwing his weight after her.

They righted somehow and pulled in the sheets, but as they worked to regain their momentum, a boat overtook them and sailed by. Their sails filled, but too late. Octo's prow touched the magical finish line first. He might have finished first, but was he the winner?

Ty sailed across next, followed by Spike and then a cluster of others. Yards out, they released their sails, letting them go limp as the remaining boats skimmed over the line. Ty found his family, waving wildly. He waved back.

But who had won? Three minutes seemed like forever, then the cheers of the spectators wafted across the bay.

Coral grabbed his arm and pointed to the top of their mast. A glowing silver banner flew from it with a blue "2ⁿᵈ place" on it. Second. Who had—

Ty's gaze shot to Octo's boat. Draped in a gold glow of victory, a banner on his mast proclaimed "1ˢᵗ place."

As Ty and Coral circled around to return to North Dock, Salm flew out and hovered off the stern.

"What slip did you make there at the end?" he asked.

Coral frowned at him. "A northeastern gust hit us."

"Nearly took us over," Ty added.

"I could see that, but no one else tilted with it, so you must have overcompensated."

They were better sailors than that, he wanted to argue, but didn't. Right now, he'd rather share a hug with Coral. But that wasn't going to happen either. *Blast.* They should have won. What had happened? Coral stared at him, the same thoughts probably running through her head.

"Anyway, congratulations," Salm said. "Second is nothing to scoff at in this crowd, and you attracted a fair amount of attention since you handled the majority of the regatta so well. See that bloke in the red vest? He's anxious to meet you. Wants to expand his business come spring and is looking for a good hand. He's a fair fellow, so I told him I'd pass on the word."

Salm left. As they approached the dock, Ty said, "We both know an errant gust hit us. There was nothing else we could have done."

"I agree. We didn't go over and still came in second. We couldn't have asked for better."

"Well, yeah, we could have won, and then you wouldn't have to fight Octo."

"That's bothering you? I've fought Octo many times. It's not a thing to worry over."

How would she put the guy off until she had magic? And surely Spike would be there when she did duel. A dozen things could go wrong, and Ty didn't want to see her hurt. "You said you'd quit," he said quietly.

"That's hardly fair to Octo. Afterward."

"I feel responsible. Let me handle it some other way."

She shook her head. "You're only responsible for getting yourself into *this* challenge with him, and it may have worked to your advantage. You've taken well to the lessons, and now you have a job nibble."

She was brushing him off. Ty's heart sank. They'd broken up, so this wasn't his business *at all*. But again, his mouth didn't listen to his head, and he found himself saying, "Octo might be an honorable competitor, but why would you go out there when Spike will take any opportunity he can to hurt you?"

38

NO MORE BLUFFING

Instead of answering, Coral leaned out and scanned the dock. Manta waved when she saw her looking, and there was Ma waving, too. Her parents must have arrived back during the regatta. Ma called behind her, and Wind popped forward. They were waiting with Ty's family, and Pop was deep in conversation with Ty's dad. She groaned. That conversation could be only about academy.

As Piper caught the line she threw, Coral heard a hoot. Pearl, Shrimp, Olive and Briana came running along the dock.

"We watched from the shelter on South Dock," Pearl said.

Shrimp reached out to give her a hand up. "You made a really good show of outrunning Spike on the last leg. I had my binoculars on his snarling face while Pearl gave me a play-by-play of Tiger and his brother leading up the second group. I hope that lad appreciates her devotion. She didn't even realize you hadn't won."

"Spike was that close?" Coral asked. "With Lemon crewing, how did they not beat Octo and his brother?"

"Lass, you are a true sailor, not even tracking your competition. Aye, he ran behind Ty at the start, then Octo after the second turn. Then when you had your little blip, he—"

"Shrimp?" Manta jostled his shoulder and laughed. "Let the rest of us have a turn."

While Ma pulled her into a hug, Shrimp continued. "Aye, but wait. There's one more thing. A bloke on the dock was fair impressed and asked who Ty is. I gave them your location at Dar's, Ty, but he said he'd come to the dock to talk to you after the regatta."

"Ty, this is fantastic," Manta said. "You've several people interested." And she hugged him.

Manta *hugged* Ty. Ahhh, why was her sister—then the town descended on them. Ty hadn't won, but his earning second in the regatta pleased his many delivery clients and was far more surprising than Octo's win, since the town lad had consistently placed in the top three for several years.

Coral passed from person to person for several minutes, then the visiting fishermen and some of the locals arrived to talk to Ty, but also to her and Salm when they learned the siblings had taught him. Salm picked up a few contacts for part-time work when time allowed, but when the men saw how small Coral was, most turned aside—unless they needed lessons for their children. She made her contacts and watched the sailors loitering to have a word with Ty.

"I'm proud of you," Pop said. "From what I see, you kept productively busy during our time away."

"You mean Manta had no messages from anyone in town."

He laughed. "That, too. Except for Ray's. We nearly missed the regatta talking to him. Manta had to pull me off the phone to run down here."

"What did Uncle Ray have to say about the whale?"

"The minke has recovered completely now that you found her ma. He's been monitoring them, but thinks he'll head over for the Fest tonight. But the whale's health wasn't the main point of the call."

Pop smiled down at her. "He wanted to let your Ma and me know that you and Salm did a fine job keeping matters from becoming worse with both the whales and the rips you found and marked. I'm proud of you two. Of all of you. I'm not making light of Manta's and Piper's contributions, though they do not have the gift to do as much as you and your brother. And I understand you recruited this young man to help." He eyed Ty.

"Pop, Coral's tired, and she has to be hungry," Manta said.

Saved, thank the Orb. Coral hugged her sister. "I'm ready for some batter-fried fish and hush puppies from that stand at the end of the dock."

"Aye," Manta said. "Pop? Don't you think there's something else that'll perk her up?"

"Ice cream on a stick, covered in chocolate and toffee bits?" He started forward. "That vendor has set up adjacent to the fish man this year. Let's—"

"Pop!"

She and Manta grinned, and each grabbed an arm to stop him. He waved them off good-naturedly and grasped Coral's shoulder. His magic moved within her, split and unquashed each core simultaneously.

Blue energy spilled into her channels, not in its previous frenetic way, but in an easy roll that brought her body alive. It sparkled but didn't jump as it roved, searching for the silver that'd been teasing it for days. Her eyes filled, and Coral wiped them.

"Good?" Pop asked.

"Aye, better than I remember it."

"Righto. Shall we invite your friend and his family to join us?"

Coral glanced at Ty. His parents were listening in while

another fisherman described to Ty where he lived up the coast. "He's a little busy. I'll talk to him later."

But later never came. Coral, Ma and Wind helped Manta and Piper in the bakery. Coral took a turn running about town with Pearl and Shrimp. Among so many visitors, casually finding someone was difficult, but she saw Ty again. He and his family were with other people. He said, *See you later*, but did he mean it? Things were over between them. She didn't need to draw it out. Ty had offers of the onboard job he wanted and might even move away from Tern Bay. There would be no more chance encounters.

After two late nights, Coral wanted to crawl into bed. However, with the entire family there, she curled up on Manta's sofa instead, where she fell asleep amidst the talking. When the others woke her at nine to go to bed, Coral climbed the stairs as fast as she could without attracting attention.

She was running late for the duel, but no longer had to worry about how to get there. Bright spheres of magic swirled in her palms. With a gesture, she changed into her dueling outfit and stepped onto the window seat. Coral focused her magic. Blue energy hummed through her channels and over her shoulder blades. Seconds later, sparrow-brown wings unfurled through slits in her leather shirt and vest. She stretched her large feathered limbs.

They were stiff and achy. Spells, it'd been a week since she'd flown. Above the still-busy deckwalks at Fest was not the place to test things. Instead, she climbed out the bathroom window, glided down to the alley and sneaked to the edge of town, stopping at the place where Ty had hidden his Vespa.

Last night. No, no thinking of that. She magicked out her wings again and worked the stiffness out through a minute of flapping. Beating them, she jogged, got lift and hopped. She swept downward and rose into the air, flapping gently at first, then harder. Cool air rushed over her face and through her hair, but pumping her wings chased off the shivers. Below, the moor racing by darkened into a blur.

Flying again—ah, it felt great. Soon, she was speeding up the hillside to the hidden valley and crested the top. Below, dueling violet and red energy streaked above the glowing arena. Maybe Shrimp's or Pearl's, but it wouldn't be Spike against either, would it? She hadn't paid attention to the matchups, but in seconds, she'd be close enough to tell.

As Coral descended to their level, a flash that looked closer to orange surrounded the violet wizard...and froze them in midair. Another burst—stronger and definitely orange—flared, and the wizard fell.

Coral's stomach dropped. Where was the referee, the backup? *Flights, someone had to*—

She raced forward, throwing out an energy rope. Closer, a burst of violet energy wrapped the person, halting the dead drop.

Wings spread, Pearl drifted down, arms extended and trembling to hold her magic and Shrimp. "What do you think you're doing?" she shouted into the dark and quiet sky. "That's not your magic!" She landed, and others ran toward her.

An orange shockball raced downward. Tethered, Pearl twisted, but it hit her. Her violet magic cut off.

Shrimp fell.

Flicking a wrist, Coral flung an energy net. It caught Shrimp, and she lowered him with her.

Spike alighted meters away. "I see you've finally decided to grace us with your presence," he called.

She caught her breath. Her power churned with the sound of the footfalls of the crowd running up. Some slowed at Spike's words, but not the Tern Bay duelists. Olive, Tiger and Octo shoved their way through, all furious.

As Olive reached her side, Coral fought to keep her voice level. "Aye, and what have I arrived in time for?"

"A lesson in who's really in charge at Tern Bay," Spike snarled.

Tiger darted up to face Spike. "It's not you anymore." Standing straight, he lifted his chin and fixed Spike with an unwavering glare. "Turn Pearl loose. Then step down, and we'll deal with this later, when the visitors have gone."

"Aye." Octo joined him. "I canna believe yer pullin' this. Did ya think we'd stand aside?"

"It doesn't matter if you do or not." Spike jerked his head.

Lemon, accompanied by others from Tern Bay, crowded behind Spike. His face shone with a mix of malice and excitement.

The hair on the back of Coral's neck stood up, and her energy jammed to her fingertips. She held it hidden as she and Olive advanced to stand with Tiger and Octo. "I think it does."

Spike had his gaze on Octo still. "You're just the second runner-up. Shove off."

Speaking like this to a fellow duelist was out of line. Spike was all but blasting his way into another fight. Coral's fingers twitched, ready to break it up.

"Sorry?" Octo said, with nary a change in expression.

Thank the Orb, he and Tiger could keep their cool heads, but without Pearl and Shrimp, there were only four of them. Spike had four wizards behind him.

Mixed expressions crossed Spike's face as he stared at Octo. Finally, he shrugged. "You'll have your chance to duel her per that little deal you made with her keeper. Where is he tonight anyway?" Spike turned to her. "Ty disappointed he lost? You two figure out the gust hit only your sail? Just enough to *tip* you out of first place."

What? Why, that cheat—

"Are ya sayin' ya pulled that stunt so I could win?" Green energy balled in Octo's fists. "That's *not* my idea of a fair win."

"Don't flatter yourself," spat Spike. "I care nothing about

your win. Them taking another, more public, dunking was my goal."

Another? That's right, Spike had been on the dock during her first lesson with Ty, the day they'd toppled because of an errant gust of wind. Her energy flared, and Coral stiffened to contain it. Beside Spike, Lemon grinned. He'd been there as well, both times. Coral held her energy just under her skin, ready.

Ready for what? What was she doing? She didn't want to go four on five against Spike. Or even one on one. This was crazy. What had come over them, acting this way?

The whole deranged situation popped into sharp focus. *Ty is right, people could get hurt.*

People are getting hurt. Orb curse it, Shrimp had nearly hit the ground, and instead of checking him for injuries, here they were arguing.

She looked Spike in the eye. "It's time for everyone to go," she announced, loud enough for the uneasy crowd to hear. "Tonight's activities are canceled. Release Pearl so we can check on Shrimp and get him home."

One corner of Spike's mouth lifted. "My night isn't over until I duel you, Angler."

"I'm *not* dueling with you." She looked around. "Or anyone. I quit." Gripping her vest front in both hands, she popped the snaps open, shrugged it off and tossed the blue garment on the ground. "I'm done with dueling."

She pivoted to go help Shrimp and walked straight into Lemon.

He caught her by the arms. "Hold on, Angler," he said with a smirk. "Stay and fight." Energy entwined itself around her forearm.

"Nay," she snapped. "Get your magic off me."

Behind her, Tiger echoed the order, but at the fierce look in

Lemon's eye, Coral didn't wait. Her magic steamed through her skin, blowing off the yellow energy.

Yelling broke out. A green shockball flew past her ear and struck Lemon. He faltered, dragging her with him.

Coral stumbled. "Let go, or by the O—"

A blast of energy hit her between the shoulders, square in the upper core. A second hit her lower core at her hips, and she twisted in pain—and saw Spike's arm extended in its throw.

An orange glow lit her torso. It froze her cores, leaving her magic out in its channels with nowhere to retreat. Her magic buzzed angrily under and over her skin. She pushed harder to shake off the orange energy, but after using so much to save Shrimp, she didn't have enough to combat Spike's magic.

Hoy—Spike was a red wizard. This was orange—oh.

Red and yellow. Spike and Lemon. They had combined energies and merged, their magical alliance unregistered, no doubt, since they'd kept it quiet.

Inches from her, a wicked grin crossed Lemon's face. He slammed her with another shockball.

Pain screamed through her, and Coral blacked out.

39

NO LONGER ABLE TO HIDE

For something fun to do in rural Tern Bay, Ty took his brother and sisters up the coast for a nighttime flight. Weaving along the bluffs, they dropped down to the enclave's shielded beaches to play tag among the huge rocks. When that got old, they ended up wave skimming, the others daring to match Ty at the game he'd perfected over his weeks of solitary flights.

His brother braved it well until a higher-cresting wave caught Dave's feet. Ty had to whirl into the wind to hide his laughter while his brother tried to magically dry them without his siblings noticing. Coral would probably be pretty proficient at this. Ty blew out a breath. Now he wouldn't have the chance to find out. Her parents were back, and they'd be setting sail after Fest ended. He'd be interviewing with the sailors who had invited him to tour their vessels and test how they might work together.

He had to get over that he and Coral had broken up without him getting to see her energy.

Maybe it was a good thing it'd happened before her parents returned. Things might have been worse with her magic involved. He came around into a hover with a sigh. A merge might also have been damn exciting if they'd had a controlled one.

Juni and Tana got wet one too many times and went back to Dar's. Dave wanted to play longer, so Ty agreed to stay. Then, of course, after their sisters disappeared, Dave was ready to go.

"I sent them down the coast so they wouldn't get lost," Ty told him. "We can fly inland. It'll be shorter." And they'd pass the dueling basin. Not that they'd fly close enough to see any action. At least that was the excuse he gave himself.

As they neared the area, magic flashed brighter than usual for a wizard's duel.

"Let's go see what's happening!" Dave called.

Ty followed. "Er, might be an illegal duel." Would Coral be here?

"Really?"

Red flashes, then violet streaked above the low rise. Red could be anyone, but so few wizards were violet that the duelist might be Shrimp or Pearl.

Ty and Dave flew near enough to see the ground when an orange energy flared longer than the previous blasts. Why had the competitor's color changed?

Then all went dark. Doubly suspicious.

"Come on, it's our chance to fly closer since they're not looking up," Dave said.

The kid had no training, no basis for worry like Ty had. And the longer the basin stayed dark, the more concerned he became. Dave had gotten shielding lessons from Mom and Dad. All right, Dave had more training than some of these rural wizards.

"You be ready to shield and fly," Ty ordered.

Dave rolled his eyes. "Of course."

They flew closer. Most everyone was gathered around a small cluster of wizards who were gesturing and talking animatedly.

"Must be deciding who will fight next," Ty muttered to himself, but Dave said, "They're arguing?" and Ty knew it was true.

Flights! He had to get his little brother out of here. "Let's go!"

"Aw, I want to see them duel."

"No, something's happened." Something bad, because a figure stood awkwardly, arms up, and another was sprawled on the ground, both glowing orange.

Paralyzed.

"We need to leave." He'd get Dave home and return.

"You can protect me. Mom says you're the best."

"Part of being the best is knowing when to scram. Do it. Now." Ty took off. Mom would kill him if anything happened to Dave.

Curses, I've heard that before. Shrimp had said the same thing about Pearl that night on *The Peaceful.* Had that violet energy been Shrimp's? After the flash of orange, the violet duelist hadn't returned fire. Anything could happen in a loose situation like this, even if Shrimp was powerful. Damn. The red-changed-orange energy in the duel matched the paralyzing glow of the figures. Had the siblings been protecting each other?

Ty glanced around for his brother. Dave? Where was he? His worry doubling, Ty rounded to a midair hover and spotted him —still above the basin. "Dave!" Sheesh, this wasn't the place to yell—

Boom! Blazes of color silhouetted Dave's small figure.

Ty yelled, and Dave whirled. He bore down on Ty at top speed.

"Ty! Come back. A bunch of them went at each other, and your friend Coral caught it with her back turned."

Hell! "Stay here." He flapped hard—but flying wasn't fast enough. Ty found the peregrinator beneath his shirt, visualized the scene and materialized behind the paralyzed person. Shielded, he dropped to a crouch, energy in each hand.

A melee had erupted. Yelling, running and blasting surrounded him. Under the furiously zapping bolts of energy, it took him a minute to figure out that most people were clumping together to hold off others while their teammates collected. Then they shielded, beat a retreat to the field edge and took off into the dark.

These skirmishes diminished in seconds. The real danger burst from one turbulent clump. Six colors of energy flew, sparking, cracking and slamming bodies. Every wizard in the battle was dressed in black leather, topped by a colored vest—none of them blue. Where was she?

Ty reabsorbed his simple energy balls and conjured his gel. Running forward, he raised a hand, palm out, and flushed gel over the closest fighter. She froze under the magical isolator. He pivoted and thrust gel at a green warlock, a red witch and a golden warlock in quick succession.

That left only a violent battle of two against one, but that one blasted with a shimmering orange stronger than the others combined.

Ty zeroed in on the orange super-wizard. He turned—

Spike.

Ty shot silver gel. Spike stiffened, his arm extended in a throw. The gel coated his body, covering his arm last. It flashed orange. Yellow sparks erupted, turned to liquid and dribbled like pus from his fingers.

His opponents hesitated and then continued to attack him.

Spells, can't they see Spike is defenseless? Ty had no choice but to also gel them. One was Tiger, the other Octo.

He spun, prepared to blast again, but few people were still moving in the quiet arena, and none were blasting.

Where was Coral? Where was Dave? Ty scanned upward and

spotted his brother, who immediately pointed to the far side of the silver-coated fighters. Ty ran.

Coral lay sprawled on the ground. Someone bent over her. Who was—

"Stop that guy," Dave yelled. "He's draining her."

With a snarl, Lemon swiveled and threw a shockball straight at Dave. The boy fended it off with a flashshield and returned fire, but Ty's shockball slammed Lemon first. The blond wizard jerked under the jolting power and fell over.

Ty rushed forward. Sparks flew off Coral. Her still body flickered with loose energy—blue, red and yellow.

By the Orb, nothing like this had happened during his years of training. What could he do?

Dave squatted beside him. "Is she okay?"

With a sick feeling stabbing at his gut, Ty reshielded, coating his hand twice, and edged his fingers to the pulse at her neck. Coral's heartbeat pounded under his fingertips, and his own slowed slightly. "Alive. I don't know about okay. I'm afraid to send energy in to check. Dave, I have to take her home."

"Uh, Ty? Can we help?" a girl called from behind them.

Olive was accompanied by the young witch Shrimp had brought to meet Coral the night before.

"I had to duck out of the fight to protect my cousin." Olive nodded to the girl. "We know something of healing, like our aunt Anemone. Briana is more skilled than I am."

At Ty's nod, Briana knelt and placed both hands on Coral's leather-clad stomach. Sparks rose and swarmed around her fingers, but she paid no attention. Like those on the medic team at academy, she wasn't affected by the stray charges, which couldn't reach through her energy.

"She's bad off," Briana said. "Not like Shrimp." She inclined her head to where he lay, the orange glow gone. "I sneaked over and released him. He's in a recharge sleep now. I was about to do the witch, but Coral looks worse. Can you take her to town? We'll get Auntie Anemone to see her, won't we, Olive?"

She bit her lip. "We'll be in a heap of trouble with the council."

"I don't care. I don't want to come back to this circus, and you shouldn't either. The red fellow is a nutter. That one, too." She pointed to Lemon. "They were in it together."

Olive looked from him, to Pearl, to Coral, and shook her head.

Briana elbowed her. "I don't want you hurt either. What if I hadn't been visiting and you'd fought, too?"

Olive blew out her breath. "I never thought any of our own would attack…" She threw her arm around the younger witch. "Coral quit," she said to Ty, "and was walking away when they trapped her. That wasn't normal energy they used. They messed with it somehow."

She'd quit. Coral had—Ty huffed out a breath and focused on Olive's summary. "You're probably right," he said. "That liquid flowing from Spike's fingers was nothing I've seen before." He shifted his gaze to Briana. "Is it harming Pearl?"

"It's done what it was going to and is only paralyzing her now."

"Then don't touch what's on her. They'll want it as evidence. Olive, will you ask your aunt to go to the bakery? I'll pereport Coral back to Manta's and get help to sort this out."

And then, Orb curse it, his days as a Master Wizard would be over.

"Ty? What about me?" Dave asked.

He'd used most of his energy producing the gel to subdue the fighting. Transporting Dave elsewhere might empty him before he could reclaim his energy from his prisoners.

"Stay with me while Olive goes," said Briana. "We can watch out for each other."

Olive nodded, and Ty said, "Good plan. Shield yourselves.

Everyone's scattered, except these troublemakers, and they aren't going anywhere. I'll be back in five minutes."

After reinforcing his shield, Ty scooped Coral into his arms and pereported to the bakery kitchen. He pushed through the door to the base of the stairs. "Piper?" he shouted. "Manta? It's Ty and Coral. We have a problem."

"What in Neptune's world is going on?" Piper called as he pounded down the stairs. "Curses, she didn't quit soon enough. Manta! Come quick!"

"She tried to quit, but they attacked her. Piper, I need help back there."

"You'll have it. I'm alerting Salm."

Manta came down, wrapping a robe about herself. "Oh no! Coral! What happened to her?"

She reached out, but Piper snatched her hand away. "A dueling accident. Lead Ty upstairs to her room while I fetch your folks."

A minute later, Ty passed Coral's mother on the stairs and found the men of the family gathered in the kitchen.

"How bad is it?" Salm asked.

"I don't know. I stopped the fighting and left the duelists more or less tied up while I brought her home. A local witch is bringing Lady Anemone here to see Coral."

Coral's father exchanged glances with Salm and Piper. "Let's go check things out first," Sir Dolph said, "and then one of us can come back to call the town authorities. Ready?"

"I need to let Lady Anemone in," Piper answered. "Send me a message, and I'll make the call."

Ty held out his peregrinator, and he, Salm and Sir Dolph pereported together, returning to the spot next to Lemon's prone body, feet from the gelled wizards. This time, the dueling basin was eerily quiet.

"Ty!" The shrill call broke the silence, accompanied by Dave's and Briana's pounding feet.

"That's my brother and the witch who helped," Ty said quickly, but Salm and his father were staring at the silver figures posed in midfight.

"*Fireballs!*" Salm hissed. "What happened to them? They look like they've been overcome by a sea slug."

"Ty gelled 'em, boom, boom, boom," said Dave. "Anyone who was fighting got it."

"By himself?" Sir Dolph looked from Dave to Ty. "You stopped all of them?"

"Yep. He's a Master Wizard. He does what he wants."

"Dave. Not what I want, what *needs to be done*. And you aren't supposed to tell people, remember?"

"Duh, bro!" Dave waved his hand at the frozen wizards. "The writing's on the wall, and you're holding the marker."

Yeah. All that work to stay off everyone's radar was ruined. He'd never find work here, and after the report to the Department of Magical Regulation, he'd not be working there either. *Just let Coral be okay.* He'd find something else to do.

Sir Dolph wiped a hand down his face. "Ty, lad, from the positions in which I see these young'uns, there wouldn't have been many left standing if they'd been allowed to keep fighting. You've done a brave thing stopping them."

A grin broke over Salm's face as he clapped Ty on the shoulder. "Bloody hell, mate. We have to talk dueling lessons."

"No!" chorused Ty and Sir Dolph.

40

SORTING THE AFTERMATH

The elders were called. Ty stood alongside Dave, Briana, Salm and Sir Dolph—who was an elder on the Isle of Giuthas—while the witches and warlocks of Tern Bay's council walked among the gelled duelists.

Ty recognized all the elders from his milk-delivery route. But aside from Elder Bentha, the head of Tern Bay's council, being Lemon's mother, he hadn't known the others were elders or related to the duelists. Salm filled him in: The witch who owned Fintail's was Spike's mother. Sir Porbeagle, owner of the bookstore, was Pearl and Shrimp's grandfather. Ty'd had test sails with Octo's father and another boat captain who was a duelist's mother. Keenan from the diner—the youngest on the council— was the only one with no relatives here.

"If you think this is a tough group," Salm whispered, "wait until the last council elder gets here. Lady Anemone."

The elders finally collected around Pearl and Shrimp and, except for a few quiet comments, weren't speaking, even to each other. Elder Bentha came over to Ty's group. "We need an explanation. None of us can even tell who these youngsters are, except for Porbeagle's grandson."

Ty swallowed. This was going to turn ugly.

Before he could start explaining, several more wizards arrived. Piper joined them. Olive and a warlock, both carrying armloads of supplies, trailed Lady Anemone as she bustled straight to those on the ground. "I suppose I should be thankful no one has been moved. Briana? Who needs my attention first?"

Lady Anemone siphoned the orange energy off Pearl and produced a huge pickle jar to store it in. After Pearl was treated and wrapped in a blanket, she pointed to Lemon next. Rightly so, because Ty's gel was orbiting his body in slimy ribbons, rather than coating it. Even he didn't know why.

Lady Anemone couldn't get it off.

"Er, let me." Ty retrieved it and gladly placed it in a jar as requested. He didn't want that back.

She glanced at him. "Interesting stuff they're teaching in academy these days, Tydell."

When he straightened, Elder Bentha clasped his arm, her brows drawn together over narrowed eyes. "What did you do to my son?"

By the Orb, she was reacting worse than he'd feared. And she wasn't the only parent involved.

Keenan was right there, removing her hand from Ty's arm. "Ty said he stopped a battle. Let him go. This will be easier with his cooperation, which he's giving." Keenan pulled her away, and the council members and Sir Dolph began arguing about what they *thought* had happened.

Salm sidled up to him. "Dad says he hopes your tongue is as sharp as your magical wit. It'll take a fair bit of talk to work your way clear of this net."

Spells. He could easily get his parents to explain—and these elders were more likely to listen to other adults. But this was his training, his responsibility. He had a procedure he was to use.

A procedure he'd been dreading.

Ty extracted his wallet and thumbed out a card. He walked to the group, his gut churning.

"Excuse me. I think this will answer many questions." The elders fell silent, and he offered Elder Bentha his license. "I'm a certified Master Wizard, on probationary staff with the Department of Magical Regulation."

"Probationary?" Octo's father said. "Ya've gotten into trouble before this, then?"

Curses. It'd always sounded like that to him as well. Ty shook his head. "Probationary because of my age. I've passed all the requirements, but I'm not eighteen yet. My license explains it. I'm to call the DMR, the Department of Magical Regulation. Someone from the office will come to inspect the scene, and we'll answer any questions."

Elder Bentha's hand flew up. "We'll take care..." Her gaze shot to the witch from Fintail's, Spike's mother.

"Of course we will," she said.

They knew their sons were best friends and that Spike was probably here, too. It was too good to be true that he could avoid calling the DMR. But it was wrong to keep what he'd done a secret. He'd known about the illegal dueling. He was complicit because he hadn't reported it. Three people had been badly hurt —could have died—because he'd been thinking of himself.

"Ma'am, I'm required to call in. I'll lose my license if I don't. It'll be better for Tern Bay, too, considering the dueling wasn't limited to your enclave."

Elder Bentha's gaze darted to Briana and Dave. "Who are you two?"

Ty identified his brother and how they came to be there. By then, Olive had her arm around Briana.

"This is my cousin from Misty Mews."

"Were others from Misty Mews here as well?"

"Yes, ma'am," Briana answered.

"And...other enclaves?" At their reluctant nods, Elder Bentha pointed to Octo's father. "Secure the enclave. No one leaves. All the enclave councils of the visitors will be notified and their teens brought in for questioning." She turned back to Ty. "Give us a moment, please."

The elders talked together, including Sir Dolph. No one looked happy, and this was before they even knew if their kids were involved. But they'd probably figured out they were.

Lady Anemone hadn't said anything about Coral, and she was here, so Coral must be okay. Ty fingered the peregrinator, wishing this was all over so he could find out.

At one point, Keenan's voice rose. "I am the only one here with no current pushing my boat. As the only neutral person here, you darned well better listen to me." Soon after, Keenan came to ask him, "What is the effect of leaving these wizards covered in this gel until the department's inspection can be made?"

Ty still wasn't sure this meant they would let him call the DMR. "It's a viscous energy that increases internal friction and renders objects motionless. The wizards are aware that they're stuck, but their muscles aren't straining to stand indefinitely. Many people fall asleep. We use it to hold prisoners."

"Then why is my lad still out cold?" snapped Elder Bentha.

"Shockballs do that," Lady Anemone said dismissively. "Your lad's channels—"

"That was my doing," Ty admitted.

"Defending people!" Briana cried, and she and Olive vouched that he'd been defending Dave and Coral.

"As I was saying," Lady Anemone huffed, "besides his own, your lad's full of blue and red energy. There is more to the story than Tydell covering *defenseless wizards* in gel. Listen to this witch's story."

Pearl described how everything had started with Spike insisting on a match with Shrimp. "An exhibition *for show,* he said, to demonstrate to the visitors some of our upper-level maneuvers and skills. We didn't put any referees in the air. The first few exchanges were normal. Then Spike let fly with a shockball like I've never seen, huge and not his energy color."

She shuddered, and Olive patted her back. "Several of us called a halt to the duel," she continued in a shaky voice. "Which Shrimp abided by. He started to descend. Spike turned on him with a second blast of the weird energy. Shrimp fell. I caught him, but then Spike blasted me, and I blacked out. Sorry, but I don't know the rest of it."

Spike's mother covered her mouth.

Briana and Olive, with Dave helping, took over the story.

When they were done, Keenan pereported Ty to the town hall to make the call to the Department of Magical Regulation. Messages were relayed to the UK regional office, and two wizards from the closer Britain District arrived. Following the inspection and his report, Ty was asked to remove his gel. By this time, no one was thinking about what he did with his energy anymore, so he reabsorbed it. But having enough magic was now the least of his worries.

41

DECISION LIMBO

Magical cells were set up in the town hall, and everyone was taken there. Dave was put in one, and Ty overheard someone whisper that he should also be confined. Ty kept his face schooled. They didn't realize he could easily get out of it... but he wouldn't if it came to it. Since he and Dave were supposed to be home hours ago, Ty found Keenan and asked to use the phone.

Instead, Keenan made the call to Dar's, as was happening for the duelists. Those who were fifteen and younger were to be sent home under a parent's quash. Those sixteen and older would stay until their trial. Two dazed town clerks were carrying in cots.

After the call, Ty thanked Keenan. "I appreciate that you stood up for me."

He clapped Ty on the shoulder. "You're a good lad. I know you had good reason."

"Thanks, but I've also done some stuff I shouldn't. I turned over an illegal peregrinator to the department officials as part of my report."

Keenan's brows rose. "You're more talented than even Lady Anemone has guessed."

Ty crooked a wry smile. "Since its source energy is from Tern Bay, they'll return it once I've had my review. I'd like to wait with my brother."

They'd found Dave's cell when one of the DMR investigators intercepted them. Officer Lewis was a middle-aged witch in a tweed suit with a soft British accent.

She said, "We have some bits and bobs to go over," and led them to an office. Elder Bentha sat at the desk, and some of the elders had chairs, but many stood because five new wizards also attended, including a graying warlock, who was speaking with Sir Dolph. These had to be elders from other enclaves. Salm wasn't there, so Ty remained near the door.

Officer Lewis closed the door. "Thank you, everyone. We have identified all of the participating duelists from Tern Bay and the Isle of Giuthas and a portion of those from Misty Mews, The Moors, Loch Galloway, The Croft and…" She checked her notes. "Hidden Cove. We appreciate the cooperation of Tern Bay's council and the visiting elders."

"Additional officers are arriving to bring in all visiting youth for questioning. As soon as we have all parties identified and detained, Elder Bentha will lift the secure perimeter. Since this will take well into tomorrow, the trial will be held the following day. The charge for each wizard is participation in illegal dueling. An outside judge will be brought in to hear the testimonies and make a ruling. Any questions?" She looked around.

"What is the ruling likely to be?" Spike's mother asked.

"A determination of illegal dueling almost always results in a three- to five-year department quash, more—possibly permanent—if the accused is found to be acting maliciously. The enclaves involved also come under our monitoring for a minimum of five years."

The room was silent. Several people darted looks at Ty, and Octo's father pointed at him. "And this lad?"

Ty kept his gaze up. He wasn't guilty, not of this.

"Indeed," Officer Lewis said, an edge to her voice. "I've answered this individually several times, as has Master Wizard Sterling himself."

On the inside, Ty cringed as she restated his qualifications and probationary position within the DMR.

"We have spoken with all the witnesses. Everything Master Wizard Sterling did tonight to contain a volatile situation was by the book. He will not be held. He will not be on trial here. He will be giving testimony. Once that is complete, a department review will be made, as is customary when one of our staff is involved in an incident. Any further questions?"

Lady Anemone huffed. "I certainly hope not. I, too, will be giving testimony, *with evidence*. If any of you aren't blasted thankful that Tydell Sterling resides in this enclave, then you will be when I am done."

Regardless of what Lady Anemone said or did, Ty had the feeling he wouldn't be working in Tern Bay, at least not on a boat.

The meeting was dismissed, and Ty was the first out the door, Officer Lewis and Keenan accompanying him. Parents filled the waiting area, speaking to clerks and each other in all levels of distress and outrage. His parents were standing near the door with Dar.

They came forward to meet him, and Officer Lewis said, "Bring everyone back to your brother's cell." She and Keenan arranged Dave's release—no quash, since he hadn't been dueling—and Keenan ushered them to the front door.

"Thank you again," Ty murmured.

"Hold the door, please," Sir Porbeagle called, and he opened the other double door for a man pushing a wheelchair—with Shrimp in it. Pearl was in a second chair.

Ty waited until they were outside before he asked, "Are you guys all right?"

Pearl grimaced. "Quashed, but it's actually reduced the tremors my magic had after being coated in Spike's energy. It's bad enough that Lady Anemone made them let me go home under house restriction until the trial."

Shrimp nodded. "Better than I could have been," he said. "Rather than dead, I'm just dead tired. You?"

"The same," Ty said.

"Lady Anemone told me Coral is messed up pretty bad," Pearl said. "As soon as I'm out of house restriction, I hope I can see her." She glanced up at her mother. "Rumor is she and the other outside duelists won't be allowed back in the enclave."

Ty's stomach sank. Yep, the decision made sense, but...how would he see her?

Later, eating microwaved burritos at Dar's kitchen table with his mom and dad, Ty told them everything. First, the year-old story of Marissa and how she'd tricked him, then meeting Coral and how her energy attracted him, even quashed. He held nothing back—how their magic had interacted, the fast merge and how much it scared him. Finally, he brought up the little he knew about Coral's intent to attend an academy.

"I admit I've toyed with the idea of going with her to see what would happen." Ty slumped in his seat, his hand clenching and unclenching a crackling burrito wrapper. "But I can't. Interacting with her at her present level scares me. She needs to learn more about *her* power before attempting to combine it with anyone else's. Besides..." He met their gazes in turn. "I've waited so long to live the sailing life. I was finally fitting in here and getting interviews. If this hadn't happened, I would have gotten something. Even Salm says so. I-I might try at another coastal enclave if I'm blackballed."

His mom stood, wiped a few tears and hugged him while his

dad gripped his shoulder. "Letting go is hard. You've made a tough decision," Dell said.

"That's the problem, I don't know if it's the right one. I like her so much, and she likes me. I can't stop thinking about her and what it'd be like to see her more—if she trains. And after her sentence is served."

"I'm happy you're including the piece about training," Mom said. "She has a lot of work ahead of her. Terraqua would be a good choice for her. More blue Masters teach at our academy than any of the others for which we've worked." She shrugged. "We never took that into account in making our decision, since none of us need their help, but she should. I'll speak to her mother about it."

"You know we won't sway your decision," his dad said, "and you shouldn't try to influence hers either, but keep your options open. You're both young and facing big changes in your lives. Give this some time."

"Dad." Ty groaned. "You're sounding professorish, like this is a lecture about academic choices Right now, I can't believe I'm considering *anything*. I nearly lost her, and now I don't know if breaking up was right. I want to know how she is and see her again."

"Then do it," said Dar from the door. "Loosen up, lad. I told ye to put some fun in yer life, and ye have. I've not seen ye as alive as I did this last week with Coral. If yer parents won't tell ye, let an old widower do it. Catch the whale by the tail and hold on."

"Thanks, but that makes no sense."

Dar winked. "Love while ye can."

PAYING THE PRICE

"Breakfast!"

Coral groaned. Her mother's call pulled her from the drifting doze she preferred to the half-snarled mess her body was in the morning after the attack. "I hurt too much," she whimpered.

"Lady Anemone said to get your systems circulating. That's the fastest way to recovery."

Maybe so, but it wasn't fair, curses on Spike and Lem—

Youch! Searing pain zinged through Coral's channels. Panting, she curled into a ball and thought of ocean waves, stretches of sand, petting Skipper—things that were *not* magic. Any thought that made her magic rise—in particular, what magical revenge she'd exact from those boys—hurt her scorched magical system. The combined blasts from Spike's and Lemon's energy had left her channels with holes, twists and pitted walls. Spells, she'd almost rather be in jail with the others than in this much pain. *Almost.*

Ma and Pop came up the stairs. Pop set a tray at her side, and Ma helped her to sit up and handed her a mug. "Sir Porbeagle sent this herb concoction. He swears it will calm your energy."

Coral took a sip. Nasty. But she drank it while Pop told her what he'd learned last night and this morning.

"The officials indicated everyone will be quashed," he said.

Coral nodded. She'd expected it.

"For at least three years Possibly more, depending on individual involvement—"

She choked on the drink, sending it spraying over Manta's lovely comforter.

Ma took the mug, patted her back and handed her a napkin. Otherwise, Ma didn't fuss—an indication of how upset they were. Coral had already admitted the extent of her involvement to the officer who'd come last night.

Ma stepped back again, and her parents looked at each other.

There was more?

"Manta has heard that a number of the duelists' parents will be approaching the assigned judge with plea bargains," Ma said. "You've been accepted at three academies. A monitored program of training that would separate you from your cohorts is a reasonable bargaining offer."

Coral leaned back and closed her eyes.

Her father cleared his throat. "Tern Bay's council told the officers that they cannot afford to lose two-thirds of their youth's magic. It would affect their ability to maintain the shielding. With the boundary rip you discovered, Elder Bentha's campaign for leniency has some bite."

Of course she'd fight to free Lemon. It was so unfair.

"None of the duelists from other enclaves will be allowed to return to Tern Bay for a period," Pop continued. "The other enclaves are considering the same. For most of our trips to other ports, you must stay with your grandparents."

Orb take it. She was going to kill those—

"Ouch," she spat.

"Think about it," Ma said, and they got up to leave.

Her grandparents' isolated home on the isle, with no magic,

or academy in a city, with her magic monitored? She sighed. When put that way, going away to academy sounded like a treat. "There's naught to think about," she said. "I'll go. If they let me."

All morning, Coral shifted and rolled between her pillows, searching for relief from the sparks shooting through her body and the sunlight filtering through the gauzy material draped over the canopy frame. Drinking Sir Porbeagle's nasty herb hadn't helped a smidgen, nor had Lady Anemone's after-break-fast efforts to sort her raw and tangled energy strands.

Just as she found a comfortable position, a knock came. "Coral?" Ma called.

Must be time for Lady Anemone to return. "Aye."

Ma came up the stairs. "Ty is here. Are you up to seeing him?"

Her heart leaped, but she held her face in what she hoped was a calm look. "I'd like to. I need to thank him before I go."

Ma held out her blue robe so Coral could slip her arms into it. "You're thinking proper."

"Aye." She sighed and folded the material over her pajamas. What choice did she have?

Ma gave her a wan smile and left. A minute later, another set of footsteps sounded in the hall, and Ty's brown hair appeared.

Her energy rose, popping off little sparks throughout her body. "*Aahh!*"

"Hello?"

"Wait," she squeaked, and he stopped. She calmed her breathing and put her energy away as much as possible.

"I'm sorry." His voice came through the blur of her efforts. "Your mother said you'd agreed—I'll go."

"No. That's not it. I, oh, just come on up." He did, but hung back from the bed. She tried smiling, but could tell she hadn't managed much more than a grimace. "I do want to see you, but you make my energy jump, and it's not in any condition to be jumping. I'm a mess."

He grinned. "Can't tell from here."

Flights, his smile made it worse. She averted her gaze. "Thanks, but I am. Lady Anemone can't even sort it out. Talk to me while I make it behave."

He magicked a chair to the side of her bed and slouched in it with his hands stuffed into his jeans pockets. He told her the little he knew about the testimonies being gathered.

"Are you in trouble for using your magic against duelists?" she asked.

"Not that, but the DMR will review what I did. And two of the Tern Bay boat owners have withdrawn their job consideration. I expect others to do the same. No one wants to admit this happened under their noses."

"I'm sorry," she said. "You were right about the danger. All those years, we were lucky no one took advantage of anyone else. You couldn't send anyone home so bad off their parents would question it."

"That saved everyone until certain people's hormones took over."

"Did they ever. I had no idea Lemon felt so strongly—*ouch*."

He flinched sympathetically.

She dampened the shooting sparks. "It's horrible to think of the attack right now, but it's all that's on my mind. Salm said you came for a peek just when it broke out. I know you hate dueling, but I'm glad you looked in. Thank you for helping me."

His gaze flicked around before settling on her again. "My being there wasn't *completely* by chance. I was wondering if you were there and how you were. It could have been worse."

"I don't know. This is pretty bad."

"Nah, you have your energy. It'll be right in—um..."

He'd likely heard she'd be quashed.

"Worse is when it's gone," Ty finally said. "Sounds like Lemon was so over the top he'd do anything to reach your energy, even paying off Spike, who was the better duelist." Ty took a deep breath. "There will always be wizards out there you don't want to be involved with because they're power hungry. I know, it happened to me."

Her eyes narrowed. Was this the root of the story about silver wizards being thieves? "You took energy from someone?"

"No. Someone took it from me."

"Oh. In a merge?"

A bright red crept over Ty's face. "Many merges," he whispered. "Merges that had me so hooked on her energy that I agreed to…other stuff."

By *other stuff*, did he mean…

He leaped to his feet and strode to the window.

Aye, he'd gone all the way. Her hands tightened on the covers, and she squirmed down into her robe. Though he said he'd agreed to do *it*, something was off about the way he'd said it.

"I don't understand," she said in a low voice. "Fellows always go on about how much they want to do it."

Ty rounded on her with a hurt look. "I agreed, but not to what I thought. She seduced me, tricked me into merging with her and then magically held me and drained me. It knocked me out cold. It was a day before I came to and a week before the first wisp of energy reappeared."

Spells! His experience, probably his first, had been terrible. She bit her lip.

He dropped his arms and shook out his hands, and she could imagine him doing this typical wizard move for weeks, trying to force low levels of energy to his fingertips.

"Sorry," he muttered. "She still… It's incredibly humiliating to be duped by someone you've given your heart to." He stuffed his hands into his pockets again and leaned on the wall.

He sounded utterly defeated. Nothing in her experience matched this. He'd completely trusted a liar. The thought made her sick. "How long before—"

"Three months before I built back to full power. When you have nothing, the channels have to grow again. At least it didn't hurt, because there wasn't anything snarled up, or even there."

"Did your parents help you with the recovery?"

He shook his head. "I withdrew from classes and kept myself out of everyone's way. As you know, it's not so hard when the community limits magic use in public."

Right. Her worries about the quashing had been for naught. Only Lemon had been seeking her magic, and he'd not dared to do anything in the open. "You didn't tell anyone?"

"Not then." Ty shook his head slowly. "Last night, I finally told my parents. You're the only other person I plan to tell."

"Why?"

He shoved off the wall and shuffled to the side of the bed. "I like you, Coral. There's a real attraction in our energy I'd like to explore. But…" He drifted toward the window again.

She knew he liked her. She liked him. She wanted to prebond, but he—*oh, now she got it.* Knowing this story now, his reaction the night her magic carried them to an uncontrolled merge made sense. "You're scared I'd drain you and leave?"

"Yes, maybe…I don't *think* you would, but your control is terrible. I never want to relive that experience. I'd like to be casual about a relationship and merging, but I guess I'm not ready."

She couldn't help it. Her lips tugged into a smile. "That's real ironic considering I imagined with you being a silver wizard, I'd have to be defending myself from your savage theft of my magic."

Ty turned enough to roll his eyes at her.

"Hoy, come sit down." She patted the bed.

He perched on the end, not looking at her while she trailed her gaze over him.

Oh flights! He was so handsome, so muscular, so magically strong and yet so timid about this. He'd been taken advantage of and hurt, and that made a difference between them. Or did it? She bit her lip. Actually…she'd never let any of her beaus get too close, always finding reasons to back them off. Oh, fine—she *had* gotten really good at bluffing, even to herself.

Coral tightened her fingers on the edge of the comforter and made sure her magic stayed locked away. "I've done some kissing and messing around, which doesn't break the rules here, but, as you know, does break the Giuthas ones. They're so much stricter, I—" She shrugged. "I haven't had sex. Breaking that rule is over the top, even for me."

"Even for you?" He halfway smiled.

"Aye." She reached out. "If you thought I was going there without bonding, then I'm sorry to disappoint you."

"Well, I wondered." He slowly moved his hand to hers. "I've never met such an honest girl before. I should have just asked. I could have saved myself a lot of wigging out."

She squirmed. "Probably. Before I met you, I may have said I wanted to, even though I wouldn't have. I did promise to be totally honest with you, and I will. Not that I'll have much chance to be."

He raised his brows, and his questioning look of concern sent an ache through her. She sucked in a breath. *Oh spells.* Why did such a fine boy have to turn up in her life now?

"My father is putting in a plea bargain for me to go to academy," she whispered. "After what happened, I want to be properly trained to use my energy for the Seas in the best way I can. The animals need me, and the Orb has gifted me a power to help them." She hurt, but she wasn't lost anymore. That made her smile. "I'm finally ready to listen to my family. And you.

Salm told me how you stopped everyone without hurting any of them. It sounds incredible to have those skills."

"Really? You'll go for training?"

"Aye, I leave—" Her hand in his warmed, something spreading through her arm. It coated and soothed her tender, frayed energy channels. "Oooohhh!"

"Sorry." Ty dropped her hand and scooted back. "It slipped out. I got too excited for you. If I stay back, my magic won't irritate yours."

"It felt good, like your magic was smoothing my frayed ends. Could you do it again?"

"Well…"

She scrambled aside to put some space between them and extended her hand. "Hand touching only. I can't even bring up my energy, let alone merge. You have naught to worry about." She giggled. "Even though this is my bedroom and we're here alone."

"What will your mother say?"

"We'll hear them coming up the stairs before they see us."

He slid his hand into hers and washed out his energy. "Whoa, nothing in your system is right. I thought you said Lady Anemone was repairing it."

She sighed. "It's better than it was, but she can't do much before my energy strays. The more she pushes, the more it jerks and jumps."

He shook his head. "My mother would have a fit to see a wizard in this state—so much power and so little control. She'd take you in hand so fast your energy wouldn't know what to do. How are you going to get academy interviews now? Classes are already in session for the fall. They'll hardly accept you in the middle of a term."

"I interviewed over the summer and *was* accepted at three of them."

"They may let you in late with tutoring, if your interviews went well. Did they?"

She grinned at him. "Aye."

"Which academies accepted—"

Tap, tap, tap.

Ty withdrew his magic, dropped her hand and slipped off the bed as footsteps sounded on the stairs. By the time the witches appeared, Ty was headed to the stairs. He greeted Lady Anemone and Coral's mother, then added, "See you later, Coral."

She started to wave, but Lady Anemone caught her hand. "Good morning, miss. How are we feeling this sunny day?" As always, the healer flowed in her pumpkin-colored energy and felt her way through Coral's channels. Her eyes widened. "It's smoother and looser, your bitin' blue. What have you been doing, lass?"

Coral's stomach sank. Her gaze darted to where Ty's head was just visible above the floor where he'd frozen on the steps.

"Coral?" Ma said firmly.

"It's better, right?" she asked. "It should be easier to unsnarl the strands. Let's start."

"Aye, lassie." Eyes closed, Lady Anemone stroked Coral's hand in her warm brown ones. "'Tis humming along, like..." Her eyes flew open. "Like you've been merging. Or the attempt of it."

"N-nay," Coral stuttered. "Not with this mess."

The healer's sharp orange-yellow eyes bore into her. "Is Tydell your prebond? Why did neither of you say? 'Twould be much easier if—"

"Coral." Ma's frown carried the promise of another quash.

She groaned. Trapped. If only she could fly out the window and disappear into the beautiful day. "Ma, naught *happened.* Attempting a merge is allowed. How else would I know if he..." Spells, she was just getting in more trouble.

The sound of a tern calling outside the window filled the silence, followed by the creaking of the stairs. Her mother's stern gaze shifted to Ty walking around the railing.

"Ma'am, Manta told me your rules, and I've stuck to them."

"Aye, he has," Coral said, "Despite what I—"

"You are *not* helping your case," Ma snapped.

"Ach. Get over it, all of ye," Lady Anemone bellowed. "'Tis obviously the right thing for these two. Come here, Tydell."

But Ty didn't move.

Ma's stare shifted between them again, before she threw up her hands. "Go ahead. Help Lady Anemone, if you can. We'll talk later." She left.

Coral sank into her pillow. Ma would go to the ship and talk to Pop. Neither did anything without the other.

Lady Anemone waved Ty over. "Do what you were doing."

He sat on the far side of the bed and took Coral's hand. "I flushed in a wash, like this."

Holding her other hand, Lady Anemone nodded. "Ah, a silver wizard. I should have guessed with calming her magic. Did you know of this trait?"

He nodded. "My mom is silver. She can always bring my dad back to ground, as she calls it. He's a pretty wild wizard, and if they aren't careful..." Ty glanced at Coral and turned red. "They, uh, can..."

Lady Anemone grinned. "Can spin it up pretty high?"

"Get carried away and lose power," Ty said carefully. "She's always cautioned me to be careful, so, um, I... This is all we've done."

Lady Anemone chuckled.

Coral frowned at her. "I don't need this spread—" *Oh spells, Lady Anemone is an elder.* She took a breath. "I'm simply ready for my magic to be straightened out so I can make it through the trial tomorrow. If Ty agrees to calm my energy, I'd like for you to repair it."

Lady Anemone shook her head and muttered about today's youth not knowing when they were right for each other, but Coral was sneaking a glance at Ty. The crease in his forehead had disappeared, and the smile he gave her before Lady Anemone claimed his attention was enough for her.

The healer got down to the business of directing Ty's silver wash through Coral's channels, intoning a rhythmic chant to urge it along. Like the waves creeping up the beach at high tide, it was hypnotic. Coral closed her eyes to focus. The tension in her magic eased, then her muscles, and she slid into sleep.

PLEA BARGAINS

During Coral's evening and the next morning's sessions with Lady Anemone and Ty, the sparking in her channels reduced to dull pricks. She couldn't call up her magic without pain, but she'd gotten several hours of uninterrupted sleep and could walk with no burning jabs if she didn't make sudden moves. Still, Lady Anemone sent over a wheelchair for her to use to attend the trial.

"Sit," Ma insisted. "It will be faster in the rain."

"You're just trying to make it look like I'm an injured party so they accept my plea bargain," Coral grumbled as Ma tucked her cape around her. Though secretly, she hoped they would. Being quashed under Granpop's watch would mean lots of chores. By hand.

"You *are* an injured party," Manta said in exasperation. "You, Pearl and Shrimp are the worst off."

And Manta, with her gossip chain, would know.

When Coral and her family entered the packed audience room of the town hall, people made way for them to wheel her to the reserved rows in the front. Pearl and Shrimp were also in wheelchairs. Octo had one arm in a sling, Spike was limping, and Tiger and others were marked with burns. Ty sat with the inspection officers at one end of the front row. She met his gaze. He nodded, and she nodded back. That was it.

Within minutes, everyone had assembled. The Department of Magical Regulation judge and officers were introduced, then they read a list of duelists by enclave. Each duelist had to answer that they were present. They hadn't missed anyone.

The officer who had come to Manta's yesterday to interview Coral stood up and read a report that included everyone's accounts. Coral's part was exactly what she'd told the witch. Then Ty was asked to read his account of his part. Pop read his account, and Keenan read the council's. Lady Anemone put two jars of magic—one orange and one silver—on a small table up front and gave her medical report.

Then the judge called up Spike and Lemon. "I have your statements here." He read them. To Coral's surprise, Lemon had admitted that he was mad at her for breaking up with him. Spike had said he was jealous of her magic. Their plan had been to steal her magic—as a prank, they'd claimed. The judge asked a few questions, then said, "Explain why you attacked your competitor during a supposed demonstration and then his sister when she tried to save him."

"It was a stupid prank," Spike muttered.

"I don't believe it," the judge said. "You attacked multiple people with intent to harm. I sentence Marlin and Barney each to two years of confinement in the Bonterra juvenile prison and five years of a Department of Magical Regulation quash. Officer, take them away."

Whispers broke out around the room.

The judge picked up one of the stacks of papers from the table before him. "These verify that none of the councils involved had any knowledge of illegal dueling taking place within their enclaves." He picked up a bigger stack. "These are statements from each of the thirty-two duelists, verifying that they participated in illegal dueling within each of those enclaves. Multiple times."

He leaned over the podium. "We don't need to review exact numbers and details. You are all guilty." The room was dead quiet, and Coral didn't dare look anywhere but at her folded hands.

"Now for what to do about it. Every one of you should be quashed for a minimum of three years. However"—he picked up a third stack of papers—"plea bargains have been entered. Thirty-two of them. Thirty-two of you have suddenly decided that you need to seek magical training that requires you to keep your magic. You will be assigned a time to discuss your plea with these officers this afternoon. I suggest you keep that appointment. Before you leave here today, each of you will be quashed by a DMR officer, and when you leave this enclave, you are restricted to your home enclave unless written permission is otherwise given. Remain in your seat until you are called."

Coral was called first. She and her parents went directly into their appointment. Apparently, she was one of only two duelists who actually had acceptances from academies and stood a chance of going away. Their travel arrangements to visit the possible academies were approved. If the academies didn't withdraw her acceptances, given her new circumstances, the DMR would make probation arrangements for her.

It would be better than staying home.

After the trial, Officer Lewis was assigned to escort Ty to Bonterra. There, the DMR had arranged for a hearing about his actions. A panel reviewed the reports, the judge's decisions and spoke with him. As he'd known, he should have reported the illegal dueling the moment he learned of it. Like Lemon, he had to admit that personal involvement had influenced his decision-making. They commended him for his quick and correct actions to halt a dangerous situation, but they suspended his Master Wizard license for three years. Since he wasn't a full staff member, just certified to become one, he could attend continuing-education classes in department policy and procedure to regain his license.

He wasn't sure he wanted to.

He could still use the gel and special techniques he'd learned —he couldn't unlearn them, after all. But if he used them defensively against someone, he had to report it, and he'd better have a life-or-death reason for having done so.

Back in Tern Bay, Ty walked home to Dar's. There, he had another message of a canceled offer for an interview with a fisherman.

44

THE EQUINOX...BRINGING BALANCE

After the storms of the days before, the morning of the culmination of the Autumnal Equinox Festival was clear and crisp when Ty gathered the cows. Lady Anemone had scheduled an early session with Coral so everyone could get to the beach. He left Manta's bakery with an invitation for the Sterling family, as well as Dar and Ms. Scallop, to join the Seas at their picnic blankets. Manta also pressed picnic gear into his hands.

Already, large areas of the beach were filling up. He found Salm and Luna right below the shop, laying out two beach blankets and chairs.

"You have plans for tomorrow?" Salm asked.

Not anymore, he didn't. Another two boat captains had canceled their interviews with him. "What's up?"

"Come spend the day on *The Peaceful Seas*. I told Pop of your interest, and he said to invite you to help while we seal the rip. We'll be shorthanded with Coral and Ma taking off for Bonterra, so this isn't a sightseeing trip. You'll be put to work." Salm shot Luna a smile.

Ty wasn't sure what secret they were sharing, but with Coral leaving, he needed a distraction such as sailing on a schooner.

He left for the farm and soon returned with his sisters, Dave and their family's gear. His parents and Dar, on break from his work in Ms. Scallop's booth, arrived while he and Salm retrieved Manta's hampers. The adults set up the picnic, and the rest of them went to rig the sailboats and sail.

Dave, Tana and Juni had rides before Ty begged off around noon. That's when he spotted Coral finally walking down the staircase to the beach, her mother holding her arm and Skipper's leash.

Ty wove through the blankets. By the time he caught up with them, they'd stopped to talk to a short witch, who was about his mother's age and was with some of the teens he'd met from the Isle of Giuthas.

Coral smiled at him, so he joined them in time to hear her mother saying, "Two academies agreed to a late admission."

"One is Terraqua?" asked the witch.

"Aye, Lady Heather, it is," Coral's mother said. "May we use your portal, and would you be our guide again for the North America trip? We're visiting each again before Coral makes her decision."

His heart leaped. If Coral chose that academy, then she'd be in the same city as his family. When he visited home, he could see her.

"...go to Bonterra Academy first," Lady Mer was saying, "then we'll head to Colorado."

His heart fell. He'd have no excuse to go to England.

Lady Heather nodded. "Friday for Terraqua, then? That sounds fine. In fact—" She rubbed Fern's arm, the only one of the group dressed in jeans and a T-shirt. "This would be the perfect opportunity for you to visit Terraqua Academy. And you, Beri." Her scrutiny fixed on the guy with messy red hair.

Even Ty felt the weight of this witch's look. *Don't refuse,* he wanted to say.

Beri looked her in the eye and softly said, "Aye, 'twould be interesting to see a modern Windborne educational facility."

"It's top-notch," Ty said. "I attended there."

"Thank you..." Lady Heather looked at him.

"Ty," Coral quickly said. "Lady Heather, this is Tydell Sterling. You've met his family, and I think Ty has met everyone else here. Ty, this is Lady Heather of the Meadows."

She shook his hand, then Raven leaned in. "Good to see you again, especially since we heard you'd all been involved in a dueling incident—"

"You *would* know the gossip," Coral snapped as Willow elbowed him. "Not your business."

Lady Heather scanned the group. "I believe we all may join you."

As soon as the travel arrangements were made, the Giuthas wizards left. Ty accompanied Coral and her mother to their blankets, and they were soon passing around the picnic food. Surrounded by family, Ty and Coral didn't say much to each other, but his spot next to her low beach chair was comfortable, especially after his magic had spent so much time with hers in the healing.

When the time came to gather for the equinox ceremony, Coral reluctantly rose with the others. She had her magic still, simply because Lady Anemone was seeing her twice a day and had said, "I see no reason to set back our progress when you canna produce more than a spark."

Even with permission, it was hard to act normal when everyone thought you were quashed, and your system was...tender.

She looked over at Ty for what seemed like the hundredth time. No one from Tern Bay had dared approach her with him at their blankets. That made her all kinds of happy…and sad. She'd gotten used to being with him. Tomorrow, she'd be leaving early for Bonterra.

He met her gaze. "Would you stand next to me?" she asked. "I can't risk anyone's energy bumping me. My family will be on watch, but I'll feel more secure if you're watching out, too."

"You bet," he said. As her sisters and parents collected around them, facing every which way as everyone in town clustered onto the beachfront, he moved close enough for her to feel the heat of his body. The smile he flashed her melted her heart.

Oh, why hadn't things been different?

Ty looked around and confided, "When my family's gone to parks—open lawns—we've usually formed a circle. Being in a clump of family members and friends feels more intimate and friendly."

An older warlock walked to the center of the first-level boardwalk above them.

"I don't know who that is," Coral whispered. "Usually the local council runs things. I haven't seen any of Tern Bay's elders today."

"Busy, I guess," Ty whispered back.

The warlock gave the invocation, thanking the Golden Orb for bearing energy to them in the continuous source that supported their gifted lives. The formal words were similar to what was said in every port that held the equinox ceremonies, a tradition in the Windborne culture.

Then, just before two twenty—the exact time of the Autumnal Equinox—the warlock and those around him raised their arms, palms to the sky. "We petition you," he started, and everyone in the crowd raised their hands. Coral didn't, but she joined in the prayer:

"Golden Orb, the source of our most highly regarded gifts, continue to deliver your blessings to your grateful people, the Windborne."

With that, every wizard with raised hands let loose a burst of energy. The flares united, and the combined colors shimmered white over the upturned faces. The crowd cheered.

Ty cheered, too, but kept his gaze on her, which was nice of him. Her mother was doing the same, and Coral noticed that Ma smiled past her, at Ty.

Ma was being strangely friendly, considering Ty had reported her to the authorities and had been next to merging with her behind their backs. But then, because of Ty, Ma and Pop had gotten her agreement to go to academy.

Afterward, everyone went back to their picnics and the Fest activities. Coral retook her chair and stretched her legs in a lazy way. She was tired in that odd way that came with being ill, and even though she'd been in bed for two days, she wanted a nap. Ty lay back on the sun-warmed blanket and closed his eyes. Coral let Ma and the others talk around her as she snoozed.

She woke up before Ty, the scent of frying dough teasing her. Ma and Wind were talking about sewing, so she stood, her stomach ready for a treat.

"Sit down, love," Ma said quietly. "You shouldn't tire yourself."

"Ma, I'm not physically an invalid. I haven't been out in days and want to take Skipper for a walk."

"The dog has just come back from a run and is exhausted."

True, Skipper was crashed out in the shade of the next chair. But Coral crouched to collect his leash. "I want to go for a walk."

Her mother pursed her lips and glanced toward Ty. Ma smiled that smile again. "Take Ty with you."

"He's asleep—oh." His eyes were open. She made a helpless gesture. "Will you?"

He got to his feet. "Let's go."

They wove between the beach blankets, then along the lower

boardwalk and its vendor stands with snaking lines. She stepped into the line for the booth selling funnel cakes.

"This is what I really wanted. Ma wouldn't approve." She ducked her head to his and whispered, "It's handy having a Master Wizard about. She didn't even want me out in public today. Pop insisted naught would happen."

Ty just nodded.

"They were sketchy describing your qualifications, like it's assumed everyone should accept that your training is all above question. Is there anything I can know?"

He grimaced. "I'm good at it?"

"*It* is a little murky. I know lots of *its* you are good at. Blushing, kissing, merging—"

"Ssshh! Okay, I'll tell you the little I can."

She bought her funnel cake and shared it with him as they walked past North Dock and the fishing businesses. Once they were on the deserted beach, her body told her it was done walking. They climbed onto a section of cliff rock, a flat-topped, black basalt that was warm from the sun. Perfect. Coral pulled up her knees and hugged them tight, her blue energy crackling under her skin.

"Get on with the telling, then," she said.

"Magic is easy to work for me. I graduated top of my class. I passed every magical level test I took, emphasis on the 'I took' phrase. It's true, they don't share what the final levels of training are, and after acceptance into the DMR, my parents suggested I stop testing because of my age. Too much attention focused on me, and word got around to Mom and Dad through their academic connections, word that was supposed to be confidential."

"Oooohh, can I touch you?" At his confused look, she laughed. "It's that joke, you know, about maybe your skill will rub off on me? What kind of work does all this testing lead to?"

Ty hesitated before he met her gaze again. "I'm not sure

anymore. Training-wise, I still have those skills, but they suspended my license yesterday."

"Oh no!" She clasped his arm—and her fingers sparked. She snatched her hand away. "But you helped us."

"A little too much." He told her what the department had decided.

"Can you do the required coursework during whichever sailing apprenticeship you decide to do?"

"Probably." He flicked some sand off the rock. "Do you feel well enough to be visiting academies?"

She recognized a change of subject when she heard one. "I have to. Any later and they might not let me in."

"Are you scared?"

She eyed him. "Aye. Everything is happening so quickly. Even Lady Heather has been surprised that the Windborne cities are so different in the states."

"She's right. It's nothing like here."

Coral sank her head onto her knees. Spells, this would be so bad.

"Bluffing works in academy, also."

She peeked up, confused. "Does it?"

"Yeah, lots of people do it. It's hard to tell who's not until you know them."

"With a merge, you mean?"

His energy flared at that. "No, not a merge. You don't have to go that far when meeting people," he said firmly.

Why would he… "Jealous?"

Ty caught his breath, his silver eyes fixed on her. "Please, if you find yourself getting that close to someone, will you let me know and give me a chance?"

Blessed Orb, really? This was as hard for him as it was for her. "Aye, if you do the same for me?"

He nodded, and her energy seemed to untwist and settle with this agreement.

Or was that his energy she was feeling?

This couldn't be it. She had to see him again. "I return for only a day before classes start somewhere. I'd like to hear what job you've picked. Can you come to see me on Sunday, over on Giuthas?"

He squinted toward the horizon, and Coral felt a sense of longing in her energy—from him.

"I'd like that," he said. "I'll ask your dad if I can get permission to sail over with your family."

"Thanks, Ty. Let's go back." She looked anywhere but at him as she climbed down and walked with her arms crossed, holding her energy tight. Because now she knew that Ty was working just as hard as she was to hold everything together.

45

REPAIRING BOUNDARIES

The next day, Ty was busy from the moment he arrived on *The Peaceful Seas*—good, because he'd spent too much time already thinking about how this was the first day in over a week that he wouldn't see Coral.

Get used to it.

"Hoist the mainsail!" Salm called to him, and this time it wasn't a joke. They did every task Salm had reviewed, and more, to get the ship ready. Everything except *Kiss the gunner's daughter*, though Salm tried the line on Luna, who ordered him back to work.

"Gotta love a witch who knows her mind," Salm muttered, but he was grinning. Something had happened between them this week, but Salm hadn't shared what it was yet. Manta and Piper, who had come along to help, were eyeing them, and Ty suspected they knew.

The schooner left the harbor waters and headed northward, along with a fleet of fishing boats and another schooner, *The Bountiful Seas*, Coral's sister Wind's boat. *The Grateful Seas* waited outside the shimmering blue and silver barrier. The three schooners anchored in a rough triangle well back from the rip.

After they dropped the sails, Sir Dolph flew to a gathering of numerous wizards on Ray and Bert's schooner, while Salm was left captaining *The Peaceful*.

"This might take a while," Salm said. "Want to hold the helm?"

"We aren't going anywhere."

"You can pretend."

Ty rolled his eyes. "Will this take long because your island is short on magic?"

"Now there's an interesting thing. Surprised no one has thanked you, mate. Tern Bay has come into a wealth of extra magic handed over—albeit grumpily—by eleven quashed duelists."

Ty's jaw dropped. "Spells, no! I'll never hear the end of this."

"You and Elder Bentha. She's resigned her position. Keenan suggested Tern Bay help their Isle of Giuthas neighbors and approached Pop to offer the magic. Since this rip is on our enclave boundary, it should work perfectly. The time is in the coordination of all the wizards—who will be where and what magic they will use."

None of them knew who was taking Elder Bentha's place, but Luna was grinning widely about the news. Only one of Ty's remaining interviews was in Tern Bay, so likely he wouldn't be around to find out. Manta had heard Shrimp was applying to Bonterra, and Tiger would be apprenticing to a boat-building craftsman. Pearl was deciding which to do. Ty knew Lady Anemone had given Olive and Briana references for a magical medical program. Octo was entering a fish-rearing program in Scotland.

"Everyone will be restricted to campus and monitored," Manta said. "Both magically and academically."

"No floating!" Salm grinned. "Spike and Lemon have already been transferred to their juvie program on a Windborne farm. They work the land, and since they're quashed, the generated energy is also harvested. A portion returns to Tern Bay."

Salm locked the helm in place and pointed out a few of the Giuthas people to Ty and Luna. Ty couldn't keep them straight at this distance, and soon the wizards dispersed to the boats, many carrying orbs of varying colors of magic. He cringed when several alighted on the schooner's railings with yellow and red.

Well, at least the source of Coral's trouble would help her enclave.

Sir Dolph returned and issued instructions. Manta took the helm. She might not sail now, but she'd grown up sailing this ship, and Piper had enough experience to back her up.

Salm and Luna dropped their barrier. Sir Dolph and Salm shimmered blue energy over the waves and pulled back the waters from one side of the rip, while Oyster—the guy who worked water magic so well—swept waves into a high crest with pink and gold energy that he held with his prebond, Cor. A black seam of waterlessness appeared. Flying wizards dove to either side, tossing magic and weaving it with others across from them.

As the rip edges drew together, a familiar orange appeared. Ty had to look away.

Luna had returned to the ship and came to stand next to him. "Awkward reminder, huh?"

"Awful," he admitted.

Then someone shouted, "That's working far better than any of the others," and Ty had to look. Spike's and Lemon's energies had formed a solid orange coating.

"More of that at the other end," Keenan called from high overhead. "If it's that secure, we have a chance to do this quickly."

Several wizards flew to do that, and orange energy polished each end, with violet, greens, yellows and assorted blues and browns in between.

If these had been different circumstances, Ty knew he and Coral could have contributed their easy-to-merge energy.

At his side, Luna sighed.

He followed her gaze, which was on Salm, hovering over his rolled wave and joking with Oyster. "Something wrong?" Ty asked.

Her lips twisted into a wry smile. "Have you ever been afraid to take the opportunity to do something you aren't sure you'd like?"

He stared at her. "Are you reading my thoughts?"

She laughed. "No, sorting mine."

In another minute, the rip closed. The elders from Tern Bay and Giuthas swooped low, checking it. The colorful strip rippled with magic, mixing and sealing. It gradually disappeared. Still, the wizards watched.

"That was too easy," Sir Dolph called. "I don't trust it. Luna? Can you reform a barrier so we may check the spot?"

Luna startled, but she launched into the air, spreading her silver around the perimeter of the trough.

"Thank you, everyone," Keenan shouted. The wizards released the waves of water, and a cheer went up.

People landed on the nearest boats to congratulate each other and rest for a few minutes before heading home.

Keenan came down, shook a few hands and strode over to Ty.

"Well done." Ty extended his hand. "It's a nice change to see you outside of the diner."

"Heh, I might have to hire a cook with the time council duties are taking up these days. May I speak with you a moment?"

"I can't cook," Ty said, but he followed Keenan out of view around the side of the deckhouse.

Keenan held out a cord with a glass globe glinting at the end. Ty's peregrinator. "It's yours," he said.

Ty peered at him. "It's illegal."

"Not if you sign this." Keenan unfolded a paper from his pocket. It was a peregrinator permit, filled out with his name. He handed Ty a pen and pointed.

Ty signed it. "Thanks, but it still needs council approval."

Keenan took the pen and signed it. "Done." He winked. "I'm the new head of Tern Bay's council. Lady Anemone and I convinced the others that it was better for Tern Bay to have you available at a moment's notice."

"I—thank you."

Giving a two-finger salute, Keenan left.

Ty stared at the magic swirling in his glass bobber. A few people still trusted him. With this back, and the ties Tern Bay had to the Isle of Giuthas, the lone interview on the local fishing boat might be his best chance at getting into the isle to see Coral.

Salm and Piper had already begun raising the sails. Ty pitched in to help while Sir Dolph said goodbye to the last few wizards. They had the ship ready, the anchor winched up.

"Manta?" Sir Dolph said. "Could you sail *The Peaceful* toward the northern cove? I'd like a word with Ty."

"Hoy," Salm said. "What about me?"

"She needs the practice. Ty?"

With a bad feeling churning in his gut, Ty followed Sir Dolph below deck. This would not be as good as getting his peregrinator back. In fact, it was looking like it'd be a don't-you-dare-touch-my-daughter lecture.

46

A "WORD"

Coral's father motioned Ty to the chair opposite his in the salon. "You handle yourself well, lad, on the sea, in the attack and with the townsfolk, and from my children's reports, with our sea life. Salm tells me you are looking for work aboard a ship."

Ty nodded, and Sir Dolph leaned forward.

"Salm put forth a high recommendation for you, something my son does not do lightly. I'd like to offer you an apprenticeship with me aboard *The Peaceful Seas*."

Stunned, Ty flattened back against the chair. Sailing aboard this schooner was his dream—hold it. A surge of doubt clouded this momentary thrill. It was painful, but he had to speak up. "If this is because of Coral and me—" He cleared his throat.

"Not at all," Sir Dolph said. "This offer stands free and clear of any relationship you choose to have or not have with my daughter. I understand things could be awkward if she were to be aboard, but she won't be."

"Yes, sir." Was this a dream? He couldn't have imagined this a week ago—*whoa. Pull it together, dude. This is a job offer.*

Sir Dolph nodded. "A fair plan. Tell me, will it bother you

that our part in the local fishing industry doesn't involve fishing, but management of the wild-based aquaculture?"

"Not at all. Your research fascinates me, and I've never been much on fishing."

Sir Dolph laughed. "It's a rare person in these parts who wants to discuss fish for reasons other than catching and eating them. Your magical training would be a nice bonus. Salm described a rather creative adaptation you made when working to save the whale." Coral's father tapped his finger over his lips, like he was trying to stop a smile. "In addition, rumor has it you've already shown an affinity for our magical wildlife communications."

Oh no, what had Salm said? Probably everything. Ty took a deep breath. "If you mean understanding the dolphins, yes, I heard them when Coral and I shared energy." Sir Dolph was smiling, but maybe he wouldn't be after hearing the next part. "Coral and I are at a break in our relationship, and of course she's leaving, so I don't know how I'd get trained, or whatever it involves."

The seaman waved a hand. "Any of us can train energy that's trainable if you have the aptitude and interest. Although, I'm sure you would rather have my daughter doing it."

Oh man, had Coral's father *really said that?*

Ty's surprise must have shown, for Dolph laughed more heartily than before. "Manta warned me not to tease you, so I'll just say you have plenty of time to train. Talking to the animals isn't the first thing I expect an apprentice to learn. Coral will be coming home for semester breaks, and home is a very confined place. If the two of you decide to engage in the training, fine. If not, fine. I give you the option to take off when she's home on break."

Ty released a breath he hadn't realized he'd been holding. No expectations.

But just as he relaxed, Dolph said, "There's an even trickier point I want aboveboard."

Ty clenched his hands. Here it came, some repercussion from the trial.

"I canna promise an apprenticeship with me will lead to a full-time job or a place on the Isle of Giuthas." The wizard rubbed his bearded chin. "Our sustainable resources hang in a balance. This rip repair was simple compared to others the enclave is struggling to mend, and our council, frankly, has their attention on that."

Now he was outright confused. This had nothing to do with him reporting the dueling? Why had Sir Dolph offered—

"Lad, if they say no, you can still work with me on the treaty waters that we share with Tern Bay. You're a resident there, and our Giuthas elders have no say over who lives on my schooner. I'm sorry I can't tell you acceptance into the isle enclave will be automatic, but the elders are willing to meet you, and we can petition for a formal trial to apply for residency. My father presented his testimony of your assistance with our wildlife, as did Salm. My lad is also considering new courses in life, so I'll need a good hand."

This was more complicated than Ty had realized, and *more* than he'd realized. The Isle of Giuthas wanted someone permanently. Ty wasn't sure he wanted permanent. He was only getting used to the idea he couldn't call himself a Master Wizard. Then there was the upheaval of his feelings for Coral. He shouldn't jump into a decision since the position involved her family. But then, after his interview cancellations this week, he had no guarantees of other offers, or if those enclaves would view him as an outsider also.

"I didn't realize you're looking for someone for forever." Ty told him about the DMR suspending his license and admitted he wasn't sure what he wanted to do.

"A real shame," Sir Dolph said. "But perhaps this turn of the tide suits us both to test the waters?"

It'd been only a month, but he liked living here. He liked the Seas and their earth-friendly lifestyle. This would be a more fulfilling experience than a fishing boat apprenticeship. Ty smiled. "When can I meet with your council?"

WANTING MORE

Five days later on Sunday morning, the first frost of fall coated the grass when Ty greeted the cows. Dar joined him to hurry along the chores, and as Ty loaded the cart, the old dairyman brought out Salt, Pepper's grumpier companion, to hitch up.

"Ye take off now, lad. I may as well get used to doing deliveries again," Dar grumbled good-naturedly. "Give the lass a kiss for me as well."

"I don't know if—okay." Ty grinned and shook Dar's hand. It wasn't goodbye—they'd arranged a schedule. "Thanks for giving me the day."

"The day? I dinnae want to see ye back here until she's gone. Ye are to make the most of yer time with her, ye ken?"

"Yes, sir." In the dairy yard's predawn semidarkness, he unfurled his wings. His brown feathers lifted in the breeze as he stretched wide, then flapped and hopped. He rose above the yard, tilted a wing to circle and waved to Dar before whirling seaward. Across the moor, the wind picked up at the edge of the cliffs. Once over them, he spotted the silhouette of the schooner flying all canvas out on the Irish Sea. If he hurried, he'd be watching the sun rise over Scotland with Dolph, Salm, Luna, Manta and Piper. The bakers had taken a rare day off to spend with Coral on her last day home.

Ty beat hard, not so much to fly faster, but to burn off his excitement. Finally, finally, Sunday had come. He'd weathered three other interviews here and up the coast. Those boat captains—both men and women—had been curious about the attack but not hesitant about him. He'd been offered a choice of different boats, various training, expectations, hours, pay and living arrangements.

The more he'd learned, the easier it'd been to choose. All the while, his heart knew that the Seas and the Isle of Giuthas offered something special, something he wouldn't find anywhere else. No, their council hadn't promised more than Sir Dolph had said, but until Ty spent more time with Coral, that was okay. He couldn't wait to see her, to tell her his news and in turn hear about her academy visits. And her decision.

The Peaceful Seas arrived and anchored in the Seas' protected cove. After days of talking to different folks, Ty begged off going up with the others to wait with Coral's grandparents. He unpacked the things he'd stowed on board the night before and moved into Wind's former cabin. He played with Skipper, who'd come back to find him, and sat on the sunny aft deck to practice his seaman's knots.

A piercing whistle cut the quiet, making him jump.

Coral—*flying*! She came over the stern, her wings flapping a slow beat.

Blinking, he caught his breath. He'd never seen her fly—and she looked great. She wore her long hair loose, and the strands whipped around her mouse-brown wings. They seemed large for her petite size, and her legs looking long in a pair of white pants that ended at leather ankle boots—fancier clothes that must have been bought new for the trip.

His stomach dropped. He'd missed her. Lots. What if he

never saw her again after she went to academy? Ty got unsteadily to his feet.

Coral fluttered closer, studying him with a grin. "Woo-hoo, sailor boy, been chummin' the fish again today?"

Trust her to quickly size up the flips his stomach was performing. "Hold yer tongue, wench, or ye'll see the broad side of me sword."

"My, my, ye've been hanging with the rough boys, have ye? They'll make a sea dog out of ye yet."

"Aye, that they will. Ye better prepare yerself."

"Ah-ah, watch your tongue," she said, switching from her affected brogue to a perfect imitation of his mother. "Juni told me of your bet that you won't pick up an accent, and it wasn't a bet for fun. A week's maid service is at stake over the solstice break. I've seen her apartment, so ye better prepare *yerself*." She wagged a finger at him as she sank to sit on the stern railing, balancing with neatly folded wings and ignoring the drop to the water.

He hadn't seen this acrobatic side of her, but the witch blended with the girl he knew—and he liked it. So did his energy now that she'd closed the distance between them. Ty leaned on the rail, careful not to touch her. But he couldn't help staring. A few things hadn't changed—her smile, the blue of her eyes and her shell macramé necklace. He fingered the shark tooth he wore at his neck and smiled.

She opened her magical knotted bag and held out a paper to him. "My schedule. I've chosen Terraqua Academy."

"Yes!" He'd have excuses to see her. At a glance, her classes looked familiar from three years ago. He'd be able to picture her on the campus and in the classrooms. He handed it back, and she folded it into her little bag. "My mom didn't twist your arm too badly, did she?"

Coral frowned, "Twist my—"

"Put a lot of pressure on you to pick Terraqua."

Her expression cleared. "Oh, no, she was most helpful, taking me to meet a blue energy master and lining up tutors so I can catch up. Your family's help has made all the difference in relieving my mind, and Ma's, too, about the distance. Especially for housing."

"No! You're not going to room with Juni?"

She laughed. "Juni wouldn't offer. You know how proud she is to be on her own. I'm living at your house for this semester, in your sister Carlese's old room."

"Hey, that's an excellent idea. No wonder you look so happy. Everything's settled, right?"

She shrugged, "Well, almost. Which academy, classes, where to live. There's just..."

Ty held his breath. Would she say...*us*?

"It's not so much leaving and being on my own that bothers me. I've prepared and knew eventually I'd go. Then I met you." She sighed. "I've never met anyone like you, Ty."

This got his hopes soaring.

She crossed her arms over her belly and stared across the sea. "But a real relationship with you is more than I'm ready to handle, not being able to manage my own magic. If I want to know you better, then I must know myself, and be able to control myself at all times. I guess what I'm saying is, and though I don't want to leave *you*, going is for the best."

So what did she think about *them*? His gaze fell on her nearest hand. "Hold your hand? No exchange."

Her fingers twitched, and he sensed the withdrawal of magic. "Aye."

"Thanks." He interlaced their fingers. "You're moving to where I've finished, and I'm in the place you're leaving, right?"

"Aye, we're headed in two different directions."

"Well, yes, but that gives us more in common. I know what you're facing, and you know what I'll be doing. My family lives in Terraqua, and yours lives here. Did you know on the other side of the portal, Lady Heather's house can't be more than fifty miles south of Terraqua?"

She groaned. "I do, but it's a two-hour flight."

"Yeah, a two-hour *flight*." He paused to let that sink in. "What's your Tuesday morning class?"

"Defense something."

"Defensive Movement." He nudged her with his shoulder. "By midterm, Master Girard expects mastery of awareness of yourself." His voice shifted to mimic the professor's high-pitched voice. "Always locate yourself before objects, because knowing yourself in the dimensions of space is far more useful in defense than any weapon you may think to acquire and use."

Coral laughed.

"That's a tidbit from the first day's lecture you missed, but I'm sure you'll hear it again. You likely have the spatial thing down because of your dueling skills. About now, Master Girard starts teaching his students to visualize precise locations and move with a peregrinator. He takes his classes on field trips into a human wilderness area where you memorize various location points. You train until you can pereport feet, dozens of feet, hundreds, then a mile, then several miles."

"Several *miles*?"

"Some wizards"—Ty winked—"challenged the instructor to greater distances, and the top student managed 20.2 miles."

Coral giggled and sagged against him. "I suppose we shouldn't mention this talented lad's name in case the competition dares to try to steal him away."

"The poor bloke must remain nameless." Ty squeezed her hand. "When yer master gives ye the pass, a trip of fifty miles can be pereported in a matter of minutes, ye ken?"

"I ken." Her gaze held his for a long moment, then dropped to their clasped hands. "Oh, Ty, do you really think I can?"

"I know you can. I've seen it in you. You're gonna be a whiz of a wizard. A couple of years at academy and there won't be anything you can't do."

Her eyes met his, and he'd swear they sparkled. "Anything?"

"Just what did you have in mind, girl?"

The rising hum of her energy overcame her, and she had to pull her hand loose. A few sparks fell.

He licked his lips. "I have some news. I have an offer of apprenticeship and wanted to run it by you to see if you approve."

She squealed and half hugged him before sliding away. "I canna believe you didn't already say. Who?"

"Sir Dolph."

"Sir—*Pop!* Work aboard *The Peaceful?*" Her face scrunched into a frown. "Because I'm leaving. He waited to offer it to you until I agreed to go, so there was no"—she waffled her hand to and fro—"hanky-panky."

Ty laughed. "Fooling around, we call it. He did, but I think he waited to see how things would fall out in Tern Bay." He told her about the council changes and Keenan returning his peregrinator.

Coral whistled. "Peregrinator approval is a seal of approval from that enclave. You've won over the important wizards. And Pop maneuvered you in so Ma wouldn't worry about what you and I were up to."

"Exactly what I was thinking. I wondered if this was only about keeping an eye on me, and not…me."

"Oh, no, Ty. Pop wouldn't give you the job if you had no skills or interest. You nearly won the regatta. And surely Salm has told him of your keenness to learn."

"Salm more than spoke on my behalf, particularly about my ability to hear dolphins."

Her eyes widened. "Salm didn't!"

Ty shrugged. "It helped. Salm has pummeled me with questions about my academy training, and in turn, I've learned about your isle and its different families. When I went to your elders' interview—"

Coral groaned. "Oh no, they can be horribly stiff."

"Yeah, it was intense, but after Salm's inquisition, I knew exactly what skills and ideas to talk up for assisting marine animals, as well as wildlife in your other habitats—Forest, Meadows, Ponds, Streams, all of them. Yesterday, the elders agreed I could have a year's trial."

"Only a year?" Coral sounded outraged. "I'm quashed if I leave my academy-monitored program in less than three years. You canna—"

He put a finger over her lips. "The apprenticeship agreement Sir Dolph and I drew up is renewable every year, whether the enclave accepts me or not. I-I haven't decided what I'll do about my suspended license."

She frowned.

"I verified with the DMR that I can use the Master Wizard techniques to work with wildlife. They asked for examples and then assigned me to an officer liaison with HIT. I hope it'll all work." Ty dropped his gaze to help suppress a grin. "After all, I'll be living in very tight quarters with people who've lived together for years. Some of them might turn out to be bloody scoundrels."

Coral swatted at his head, and he ducked and laughed. "You know very well you fit our family perfectly. And there's extra space since I'm away."

"Maybe." The rest of the family news wasn't his to share. "Anyway, I still have a room at Dar's and a job. Because I can pereport, your dad has agreed to let me continue the morning milking and deliveries, the ones most difficult for Dar."

"A dairyman who's not an early riser?"

"Not the last few years, given his arrangement with Ms. Scallop." Ty quirked an eyebrow. "The best part is, I can keep saving to buy a sailboat."

"Wait a second. You're saving to buy a sailboat?"

"Of course. How else is a guy supposed to fulfill a dream of life on the sea unless he's captain of his own craft? I can't rely on bonding into a family with a boat. Like Salm, I might want to woo some unsuspecting landlubber who has no idea of what she's getting into. I'll dazzle her with my ship."

Coral rolled her eyes and laughed.

Thank the Orb. Their joking would make it easier to get out the thing he dreaded asking.

"Ach. You are so full of it."

No, not by half. "Yeah." He steeled himself. This was it. He'd been thinking about this moment for days. "Coral? Can I touch you?"

She grimaced. "I cannot keep holding in my energy."

"I don't want you to. I want to check it out. Can I?"

She swung her legs to the inner side of the railing, drew in her wings and slid to the deck. She clenched and unclenched her hands. "What if…"

When did she become such a talker in these situations? Blowing out a breath, Ty wrapped his arms around her. She felt so good, though his energy wiggled frantically. He held it and her, waiting.

With a sigh, Coral released her energy—a sparkling, Colorado-sky blue—and washed it over him, skin-deep only.

Flights. He'd seen its color, but as worn snarls her body was working to repair at the time. This was dazzlingly fresh and running smoothly through a fine network of channels. "Can we try a merge, please?" he asked.

She nodded, and her energy sank, slowly…steadily.

He laughed at how determined she was to remain in control. "That's not going to be much fun." He ran his hands down her back and, briefly, lower. "Where's the witch from the beach and the hot duelist in leather? She had more flame than you, with no magic."

"I'm concentrating on being good, but if you touch my bum once more, all bets are off."

He froze his hands at her shoulders. "Oh yeah?"

"*Yeah*, and I will not take the blame this time."

"Deal." Ty inched his hands down teasingly, getting as far as her middle back when magic flashed off her shoulders. He flinched. "Better not bait the shark."

"Too late, sailor boy." Her brilliant energy swam over him like scores of tiny fishes, glinting in the sunlight and wiggling out an invitation to join their migration.

He let loose a few strands to weave among them and pressed his lips to hers. No tang of salt spray today, just a soft sweetness that felt so right to get reacquainted with.

Her fingers slid around his neck, then combed into his hair. "C'mere," she murmured.

This time, it felt okay. Still controlled, Ty released his magic and mentally stepped back to watch. Her energy was lively—as she'd said it would be—teasing his to play. When his kept within the bounds of a light merge, a we're-just-testing-this-merge, the energies settled surprisingly rapidly. They seemed evenly matched for power and respectful of each other. At that thought, they mixed to a tinted metallic color, the sea under bright sunlight.

Coral's lips broke from his. "I actually did it," she murmured. "Thank you."

The magic continued to ebb and flow across their torsos while they slipped down to sit on a coil of rope. Skipper appeared on deck and, discovering Coral, pressed his way between them, yipping in delight. She petted him and crooned as the dog rolled around on Ty's lap as much as hers.

Well, so much for them. "Is this one of Manta and Piper's spots?"

She smiled wickedly and sent the dog off. "It is," she said, pulling him closer. "You want to see the others?"

He cleared his throat. "Uh, no. This one will do."

Her soft mouth molded to his, and she snuggled against him again. "I ken that this will do also." Her lips moved as sweetly as her energy lulling in time to the schooner's rocking, the sun warm on their bodies, the breeze bringing just the right amount of cooling as they pressed tight and kissed, and kissed, and… kissed. Oh man, he had missed kissing. Kissing *her*.

After a while, she raised her head. "You like this?"

"Don't you?"

"Aye, but it's my first real merge. It's wonderfully calm, not at all what I expected of you showing me your stuff. Don't misunderstand, I'm happy to wait for…I mean, it's all we should really do for a first check."

"Well, merging with you is nothing like I've ever done before either. I think somehow our energy practiced together a lot, even with yours quashed."

"We need more practice at kissing, don't you think?"

Ty stroked a finger over her lips. Even though the Giuthas rules specified handholding only, he wouldn't argue. "We do." This time when his lips touched hers, he heard voices in the distance.

Ye should see, 'tis so cute.

Cute or serious?

Ach, how do ye tell?

When he started to focus on the voices, Ty found he could hear them better.

Perhaps an afternoon visit to Magemoor is in order.

It's Sunday, the office will be closed.

Tomorrow?

She has class tomorrow.

'Tis a seven-hour time difference to Colorado. Be in the line before the office opens, and ye have plenty of time.

"Uh, Coral?"

"Hmm?" Her tongue explored his open lips.

We could go over tonight and stay at that lovely bed-and-breakfast.

All of us? I remember 'tis a three-bedroom place.

The kids could bed down on the floor.

Mother, they're hardly kids anymore.

Aye, and bedding down together is hardly appropriate.

Ty patted her lips with an insistent finger. "That's not dolphins, or Salm and Manta, so who is it?"

Her eyes flew open, and she snatched all her energy back from him, cutting off the conversation. "Ye heard that?"

"Uh-huh. One sounded like your dad, but…"

She squeezed her eyes shut and bent her head to his shoulder. "Aye, my parents and Granny. Someone—probably Granpop—came to check on us and started a thought-speak conversation with everyone included. Pretend you didn't hear. No one will say anything."

Whoa. He cuddled her close and rubbed her back while racking his brain. "Do you suppose your parents would take us to Magemoor today?"

Her head jerked up. "Huh?"

"Oh, it's Sunday. They'd be closed, but we could get in line first thing tomorrow. Then I could go to Colorado with you and pereport you up to Terraqua in time for your first class—what time did the schedule list?"

Her eyes narrowed. "Why are ye repeating what they said? I dinnae ken what ye mean by it."

"Will you prebond with me?"

Now wide-eyed, she pushed back, her fingers pinching his shoulders. "Are-are ye sure?"

He washed her with his energy, inviting another merge. "I'm sure."

Her eyes sparkled, and she grinned crazily. "I'd like to, very much." Their lips met, and their energies snapped together.

Ach, those two are at it again!

Better hold back their fillets from the grill.

Ye can delay their lunch, but I think the trip is on.

Now, Mother, you cannot push today's young people. Look at Salm.

What about me?

Coral sighed, separated a strand of blue and directed it to block the conversation. "There, that's better."

"Yep. I finally get to kiss the gunner's daughter in peace."

ACKNOWLEDGMENTS

Delving this deeply into a story about sailing wouldn't have been possible without Janet, sailing instructor extraordinaire! Thank you so much for your tireless checks on my sailing.

Thank you to Karen Corkran, Michelle Davis and Eileen Lloyd for critiques of my early version, *Seaside Sorcery*. Thanks to its judges in the Put Your Heart in a Book, On the Far Side and Finally a Bride contests for encouragement, finals and wins. Many thanks to Corissa for pushing me to publish Coral's story. Thank you to Andy, Chuck, Joey and many CritiqueCircle critiquers for helping me hone this final version. As always, I so appreciate my copy editor, Joyce, and cover designers for their finishing touches! Love to my family who continue to stand by me.

And a hearty shout out to PirateVoyages.com for their vast pirate lingo listing. Salm wouldn't be nearly as funny—or annoying—without their website!

ABOUT THE AUTHOR

Before kids, Laurel Wanrow studied and worked as a naturalist —someone who leads wildflower walks and answers calls about the snake that wandered into your garage. During a stint of homeschooling, she turned her writing skills to fiction to share her love of the land, magical characters and fantastical settings.

She's the author of *The Luminated Threads* series, a Victorian historical fantasy mixing witches, shapeshifters and a sweet romance in a secret corner of England, and *The Windborne*, a nature-focused YA fantasy series set in our world.

When not living in her fantasy worlds, Laurel camps, hunts fossils, and argues with her husband and two new adult kids over whose turn it is to clean house. Though they live on the East Coast, a cherished family cabin in the Colorado Rockies holds Laurel's heart.

Visit her website at www.laurelwanrow.com.

facebook.com/laurelwanrowauthor

twitter.com/laurelwanrow

instagram.com/laurelwanrowauthor

bookbub.com/authors/laurel-wanrow

pinterest.com/laurelwanrow